Aria

Aria

{a novel}

Studio City '01

SUSAN SEGAL

To Mary –
I hope you enjoy the book!
Thanks.
Susan Segal

BRIDGE WORKS PUBLISHING COMPANY
Bridgehampton, New York

Published in the United States by Bridge Works Publishing Company, Bridgehampton, New York, a member of the Rowman & Littlefield Publishing Group.

Distributed in the United States by National Book Network, Lanham, Maryland. For descriptions of this and other Bridge Works books, visit the National Book Network website at www.nbnbooks.com

FIRST EDITION

The characters and events in this book are fictitious. Any similarity to actual persons, living or dead, is coincidental and not intended by the author.

Library of Congress Cataloging-in-Publication Data

Segal, Susan, 1956-
Aria : a novel / Susan Segal—1st ed.
p. cm.
ISBN 1-882593-45-6 (alk. paper)
1. Female friendship—Fiction. 2. Women singers—Fiction.
3. Composers—Fiction. 4. Widows—Fiction. 5. Opera—Fiction. I. Title.

PS3619.E43 A88 2001
813'.6—dc21 2001020218

10 9 8 7 6 5 4 3 2 1

♾ The paper used in this publication meets the minimum requirements of American National Standard for Information Sciences—Permanence of Paper for Printed Library Materials, ANSI/NISO Z39.48–1992.
Manufactured in the United States of America.

In memory of Ava Greenwald and Sally Segal

And for Benjamin

Acknowledgments

This book was written with a lot of help. I am deeply indebted to Mike Leneman for his sailing expertise and for putting up with my countless phone calls to ask "just one more question." Also to Michael Daniels for the invaluable opera-world background and for similar patience. I am grateful to Whitney Otto for her endless support and valued friendship, as well as for the *Aria* box. Maria Caruso, Margaret Ritchie, Laurie Foos and Celine Keating were invaluable readers of early versions of the manuscript. Alexandra Shelley has expertly guided this book to its final harbor. More thanks than I can ever express to Susan Ramer, who wrote the book on never losing faith. The Macdowell Colony, writer-heaven, afforded me time and space to complete an early draft of this novel. Finally, I am ever grateful to Pamela McCrory, who made this and all my work possible.

Aria

Niente, niente!
Ho creduto morir
Ma passa presto come passan le nuvole su mare.

It's nothing, it's nothing!
I thought I was dying
but it passes as quickly as the clouds pass over the sea.

—Giuseppe Giacosa and Luigi Illica, *Madame Butterfly*

1

Once I saw a man throw himself on a coffin. I was only twelve years old then but I still remember thinking that there was something over the top about his behavior, melodramatic—though I doubt that particular word was yet in my vocabulary. Which is not to say that the man was insincere or in any way aware of the impression he was making on the other mourners; indeed, I hadn't then, nor do I now have any way of knowing whether the other mourners shared my discomfort. Chances are they were all somewhat discomposed by this extreme display of emotion, but did anyone else bristle at all from the theatricality, the movie-of-the-week-ish-ness of the gesture? In fact, I knew the man who threw himself on the coffin—he was a boy, really, just eighteen—which seemed grown up to me then of course; now when I remember the boy I realize that he was just a few years older than Nick would be today—and confronted with the first real tragedy of his life. He was distraught, there's no question of that. He stretched himself over the top of the coffin as if trying to make every inch of his body contact its surface, and he called out the dead girl's name, "Maria, Maria," over and over again in a broken, newly deep voice. No one did anything about him for a very long time. I remember thinking that if he wasn't pried off soon he'd go down into the earth with the coffin—and gladly too; he'd stay with her always, his Maria. At that moment I found the boy romantically thrilling even as I felt vaguely embarrassed for him. And even though I, too, was sad, I was not as sad as the boy, nor as sad as my older sister, whose best friend Maria had been, nor as sad as my parents, who had looked upon Maria as a third daughter; I secretly reveled in the romance, the hyper-tragedy, even as I grieved. These opposite emotions coursed through me like twin rivers. I was twelve. I knew that Maria had been unfortunate. I knew that the rest of us would live forever. It felt good to cry.

*

Today when she calls, I ask my sister about Maria's funeral. "What was the story with that boy?" I ask her. "He was Maria's boyfriend, right?"

Molly sounds shocked. "How could you forget," she says in a hushed voice. "That was Rod, her boyfriend, the one who was driving when they went over the embankment."

"Oh, yes," I say, "I forgot." I'm sitting in the lounge area of the hospital, next to a wall of windows. "A little sunshine," the nurse with the rosebud mouth whispers to me. She is a very pretty nurse, but I usually shrink away when she comes near me—she always looks like she's about to kiss me. There isn't a ray of sunshine to be seen. The sky is the color of faded black jeans and now and then a distant roar of thunder rattles the solarium windowpanes.

Three round tables fill a tiny concrete courtyard. No one is eating out there. The small shrubs surrounding the courtyard look pathetic, though valiantly green. Australia, what little I've seen of it, is very green. I'm talking to Molly on a cordless telephone the rosebud nurse has given me. "Call me Kate," the nurse says, looking sympathetically at me. She looks like she is going to cry so I grab the phone rather roughly from her, hoping she'll be a little offended. But I am quickly discovering that someone in my circumstances is permitted and forgiven every form of bad behavior. In fact, it seems expected of me.

"It's amazing how well I hear you," I say into the phone. Molly coughs and I figure that I must have interrupted her while she was talking, though I never heard a word. "You could be down the street," I say.

"Do you want me to come?" Molly says.

"No."

"You don't have to yell." Molly sounds hurt. She is probably the only person in the universe to whom there are no circumstances under which it would be excusable for me to be rude.

"I wasn't yelling."

"Yes you were, you still are." Molly begins to cry. I can hear each little hiccough in her soft white throat and that little choking sound she makes when she's trying to control her emotions. I pull the phone away from my ear and stare at it. It looks like the cordless phones at home—the only thing different is that there are no letters under the numbers on the push buttons. I shake my head. The wonders of the world.

From a long way away I hear Molly saying my name. Reluctantly, I return the phone to my ear. " . . . let her come," Molly's saying.

"What," I say politely.

"Mom. Didn't you hear me? She's beside herself. I actually had to block the door yesterday, though I don't know where she thought she was going to rush to. The airport, and just hop a plane? Anyway, she doesn't understand why you don't want anyone there, and frankly, neither do I." Molly's voice softens. "Eve," she says as if talking to her ten-year-old daughter, "you shouldn't be going through this alone."

I say nothing to that.

Molly goes on as if I've given her some encouraging response. "Ma keeps talking about what Dad would do. That he wouldn't take no for an answer, that he'd be on a plane already, whether you like it or not. She kept giving me that look—you know the one—as if she expected me to do it, or to make reservations for her or send George, or do something. That is, not respect your boundaries. Which I do, even though I don't understand them and I wish you'd reconsider."

"Boundaries?"

"Ma also wants like an hourly report on what the doctors are saying. Last night she calmed down from her hysteria long enough to go on about what if you never walk again. You know she's called the hospital directly." Molly sounds expectant now, as if waiting for me to denounce our meddling, anxious mother. Just as she did when we were kids, Molly is still waiting for someone to get in trouble.

"Poor Ma," I say.

"Eve," Molly snaps. "Are you on something? What are they giving you there?" Then, more concerned, "Are you in pain, honey?"

I think about that question.

The first day I go, the physical therapist berates me for not helping her undress me—"You don't want to stop taking responsibility for your body, luv; before you know it you're thinking like an invalid. Always remember, luv, in your mind you want to think like Hercules." She has stopped undressing me and steps back, waiting for me to help, or maybe do the whole thing from that point on. It's no skin off my nose one way or the other. I'll sit half naked on the tissue paper-covered table all day if it comes to that. It is bit cold, but cold like comfort to someone who's been bone chilled as I have. If she thinks she can wear me down with cold she has another think coming. I've been to the bottom of the sea and nothing will be cold like that cold. Put me back there, I think, if you want to make me beg, if you want to see a woman disgrace herself by clinging to her life, by doing whatever it takes to stay alive, because now I'm no longer interested.

At this point, the nurse who wheeled me in intervenes. I like this nurse, though she too has a thing about getting too close, bringing her face up to mine. She is older than the rosebud nurse, with turkey jowls and heavily powdered cheeks, and milky, kind eyes. She has a slightly worried air about her, as if afraid of hurting someone. Once she mentioned that she had seven grown children, and then put her hand over her mouth and blinked at me, as if she'd just confessed to child molesting. Her name is Ellen, though I think of her as Turkey, because of the jowls. She's been standing by the door to the physical therapy room but she comes rushing over when the therapist steps back from the table and puts her hands on her hips.

The physical therapist has the reddest hair I've ever seen—really copper, like the bottoms of my pans; my ex-pans, I should say, now perhaps a rusting haven for a school of fish—a color I figure has to be natural because it's too fake-looking for anyone to actually dye her hair that shade. She has narrow eyes that make her look as if she is perpetually sneering, even when she is cooing and billing and congratulating you on your progress and declaiming "Hercules!"

Anyway, Turkey comes rushing over and smiles. "Mrs. Miller may not be quite up to snuff as yet; let's just lend her a hand for a wee while longer, shall we?" and as she is saying this her hands are flying over my body, magically pulling the stiff cotton gown from my arms and wrapping me in a scratchy but ample white towel. She turns me over on my stomach on the table and brings her mouth to my ear. "Now you just relax here, Mrs. Miller," she whispers. "Don't you worry about a thing. We'll have you in full feather in no time." She's wearing a familiar perfume—something fruity that you smell in Beverly Hills restaurants all the time. I register the scent with a kind of wonder—as I did the cellular telephone—like I am taking inventory of all the sights and sounds and smells of land—this land familiar and yet strangely foreign.

Turkey turns and whispers furiously to the physical therapist. There is a quick intake of breath and something like, "Oh, *that's* her?" I hear the rustle of starched uniforms—curiously blue striped rather than the crisp white I am used to from U.S. hospitals. The physical therapist approaches, and I have to give her credit for not leaning down and slobbering conspiratorially in my ear. She speaks to me like an adult. "I'm sorry," she says. "We'll take things a bit slower."

Her hands knead the permanently chilled muscles of my back, gently skating the area with the damaged vertebrae. It is evident that she is straining not to ask when . . . how . . . why . . . but mostly, mostly what they all burn to ask, including the reporters that I've been told are lurking around the hospital driveway as if I am the president or a movie star: "What in the world does it feel like?"

"Here's a taste of today's pile then, Mrs. M." Turkey places a stack of envelopes on the table next to my bed. "There's a lot more where that came from," she adds, patting my pillow. I am lying under one sheet and sweating. They have the heat turned up something awful—it's pouring rain outside, but the drops hang on the window panes, fat and languid. I have been concentrating on breathing—it feels like taking cotton into my lungs every time I draw a breath—cotton with razor blades stuck in it because there is a stabbing pain too, with each inspiration. I am okay with the pain though, welcome it, in fact—it's so close to where my heart used to be that it feels like heartache; it feels like what I am supposed to be feeling.

"Don't you want the sound then, dear?" Turkey is looking up where the television is mounted near the ceiling. I blink. I didn't realize the television was on, but sure enough, there are images flickering in colors so vivid the edges of people and objects are blurred. A sapphire swimming pool. A woman rising out of the water like a glittering nymph, dark hair slicked against her perfect skull, breasts heaving in fire-red spandex. A man stands by the side of the pool in a ten-gallon hat and a three-piece suit. Even from a distance you can see that he is smirking at the woman, that he's bested her in something and she doesn't know about it yet. I watch them while Turkey rifles through the cups and tissue on the bedside table till she finds the remote control for the set.

"Don't," I say, when she finds it.

"Dear?"

"I don't need the sound," I say. "I've seen this one before—it's years old. That's J.R. and that's his sister-in-law in the water—I've seen every episode. This is right before J.R. gets shot."

"J.R. gets shot?" Turkey sounds angry and inconsolable at the same time.

"Don't worry, I won't tell you who did it. We had to wait a whole summer to find out."

"Oh you shouldn't fret yourself," Turkey says. "I reckon I don't watch it that much." She lifts her head. "A bit on the warm side in here, innit?" she says, her brow furrowed. "I'll see to it. You should have said something."

Maybe I have become so used to extremes of weather, to uncomfortable conditions I couldn't influence, that it would never occur to me to request that the climate be changed. Heaven knows what expression I wear on my face but Turkey suddenly pats my sheeted leg and says "no worries, no worries," while busying herself straightening out the blanket and checking the chart that hangs from the end of the bed, just like in old movies. I am in a semiprivate room but the other bed is empty. No one said anything to me, but I know that they deliberately left me alone—I'm not sure whether for my sake or the sake of someone trying to recover from something and being faced with the woman of the "AMERICAN DREAM GONE WRONG."

They kept newspapers from me but I saw that headline a couple of days earlier. They were wheeling me into the physical therapy room—I was still on the gurney then, flat on my stomach, my face turned toward the pale-pink hospital wall. It wasn't Turkey who pushed me, but a chattering younger woman. She left me in the hall for a while and I lay on the gurney, hearing the chimes of telephones, the anxious drone of conversation, the squeak of rubber-soled shoes on linoleum. A man of indeterminate function dressed in hospital greens was sitting in a chair against the wall with the paper spread open in front of his face. The headline was there. Maybe a picture; yes, I confess I saw the picture before I had the presence of mind to close my eyes. It was a family photo from before—of course, the ones from the voyage have swum away—probably the one we had done at Sears for my parents' fortieth anniversary. But I didn't want to think of it beyond that, didn't want to let into my mind what we were wearing in the photograph—whether Jessica, who would have been an infant, was squirming in my lap or Charlie's, whether Charlie's tie was straight, whether Nick was smiling or doing that cross-eyed grimace that he loved to pull out at the last minute, causing my mother to berate me for not making my child behave enough to send his grandparents a decent photograph.

But I did get a good look at myself. My picture looked like no one I recognized. I stared at it, at first thinking there was some mistake, trying to find myself in the solid and grinning woman who looked so boldly into the camera, honey-colored hair falling in attractive waves around her shoulders, gray eyes wide, sharp chin tilted down in that Princess Diana way that de-emphasizes an overly long nose, newly muscled arms tight around my daughter. Compact and confident, the woman in this picture knew that her eyes were arresting; that her daughter's curls made strangers comment; that her son had her open gaze; that her family was inviolate. She looked nothing like the shrunken self I now catch painful glimpses of in the shiny surfaces I can't avoid. Unaccountably, while I'm now skinny and bent and weathered like someone twenty years older, my hair is still thick, framing my face like a wig on a skeleton, as if it hasn't heard the news.

Only a day later did it occur to me to wonder where they got that picture for their newspaper 7,500 miles away from home. That someone had to have given it to them. Someone who had possession of one, someone from my family. At the moment that I realized this, I let the plastic water pitcher I was holding slip out of my hand, then drew satisfaction from the mutterings of the disgruntled orderly who mopped up the mess. I would have felt even better had the pitcher been glass, had I been able to hear it shatter, see it draw blood.

I wanted to tell them to be sure there were no newspapers in my path anymore. But I didn't want to get anyone in trouble. Besides, while I knew I was their special project, a bit of a celebrity even, there might be some lengths to which they would not go for me.

I generally wake up before the sunrise. There's a small leaded window in my room through which filters a gray, blurred glow that throws shadows into the corners—and I stare at them until the growing brightness makes them disappear. Someone comes in soon after that—not Turkey, she's the afternoon shift. Sometimes Kate, the nurse with the rosebud mouth, sometimes a man named Walter who is tall and beefy and has such a deep bass voice that I expect him to break into a chorus of "Old Man River" at any moment. Like many men of his size and bulk, he is amazingly gentle. When he walks in I sit up slowly, painfully, fighting a terrible urge to pee. He insists on helping me out of bed although I try to protest. He reaches behind my broken back and grasps my left arm and places his right hand on my limp right arm. His hands are cool and smooth—the skin like fine leather gloves—they remind me, inexplicably, of my mother's hands. He lifts me as if I were just this fraying nightdress they've given me to wear—nothing inside—no bone or muscle, no organs or coursing blood. He says little, perhaps a soothing phrase now and then ("There now, Mrs. Miller, let me help you there"), his voice thick as chocolate pudding, his starched uniform smelling of some detergent or scented dryer sheet—a piney scent I can't quite identify. It's been, what, two years since I used a dryer sheet—an expendable item, like cottage cheese and mascara, that would have simply taken up precious cargo space on the boat.

I pee and then brush my teeth standing straight up since my back won't bend right now, not the way it used to. Inevitably I drool a noodle of white, bubbly toothpaste down my chin. I focus on the noodle, rather than on my face as a whole, watching it glide down my leathery skin, and I stare so hard at it that it ceases to be what it is, my skin ceases to be skin and the toothpaste and spit form a white stream running down an inverted creek bed of smooth, slightly pitted stones. Well, not really, but that's what I tell myself—I tell myself that if I am going to write (it was to be a book or a series of articles of our experiences, a collection for Nick and Jessie to pore over when they grew older; to show their children, their grandchildren; to say, in my youth I did this marvelous, this unheard of thing; in my youth my parents took me on an adventure from which we never wanted to return) I'd better start thinking like this. In metaphors. Metaphors are perhaps the only viable, bearable means of survival. I symbolize, therefore I am.

Walter helps me back into bed, his red skin warm, his breath damp on my cheek, murmuring, soothing; I fight the urge—stronger that I would have predicted—to relax into his arms, let him envelop me in his hugeness, to press my face against his chest and listen to his breath moving in his lungs, swirling about his heart. Since the accident I have not really wanted anyone to touch me, if for no other reason that there isn't an inch of me—skin, bone, muscle—that doesn't hurt. Except when Walter presses his stalwart self against me I want to curl up in his embrace and close my eyes. I can't explain it, but he reminds me of my mother at her nurturing best.

After Walter is gone, one of the aides dressed in purple who call themselves Lavender Ladies brings the breakfast tray. I try very hard to eat the breakfast to please everyone who has been so kind to me.

Actually, that's a lie. It's not hard to eat at all. I am quite hungry for breakfast every morning. It does seem to me that I *shouldn't* eat, that I should have completely lost my appetite and be willing—no, anxious—to wither away. But on the boat I used to get up before everyone and make a huge breakfast—the sun would just be splitting the ocean and I'd step out onto the deck first, to breathe the smell of kelp and salt and virgin air before I'd go back down to the galley and make coffee, cook a huge pot of oatmeal and toast half a loaf of bread and cut up melon and pour out orange juice into the yellow plastic pitcher, or scramble eggs or make pancakes and bacon. We ate like, well, like sailors, all of us—even Nick and Jessie, who had been fussy eaters at home. We were hungry all the time at sea and we all lost weight. We worked hard, we stocked up. Two years of eating like that and you get used to it—a piece of toast and a small glass of juice just don't cut it anymore.

Breakfast in the hospital is often less than recognizable. A mess of scarlet, a pockmarked circle of white-and-beige triangles which I believe translate to fried tomatoes, eggs and bread. It tastes like a cross between french fries and potato chips. I eat, I drink the weak coffee; I draw the line at the supposed orange juice which has some kind of fizz to it. The Lavender Ladies always seem surprised that I eat so much—as if they expect me to wither away too, as if we all agree that I have no right to go on.

My room is far from the nurses' station at the other end of the ward and yet someone is there almost before I ring. Turkey told me they put me as far away from reception as possible to make it easier to keep visitors away: "So many of them," she said, shaking her jowly head. "Reporters by the dozen and a few who won't say who they are so I reckon they're solicitors. You're very popular, you know," she said, with an encouraging smile.

Every day she brings in a selection of the mail I've received. "There's more where this came from," she's fond of saying. "We have mailbags full up at the station," she says. There's a sort of hopefulness in her voice when she says this, as if she's anticipating the time when I'll ask to see it all, when I'll show an interest in how interested people are in me.

The letters are written on all kinds of paper—fancy embossed stationery, lined notepaper, and lots of tissue-thin blue airmail. The sympathy cards often have praying hands on their covers or crosses or pictures of an impossibly rainbowed sunset with the word Jesus somewhere in the sticky prayer printed across it. They are all from strangers. Perhaps Turkey weeds out the ones from friends and family; who do I know who would talk about Jesus in any way that didn't involve an expletive? Despite the fact that I handled a lot of the arrangements when my father died, I don't remember the etiquette for sympathy cards. Chances are my mother knows. It's the sort of thing Myra knows. She would know whether you are supposed to send a sympathy card that expresses your regrets in your own religion or in that of the bereaved. Not that we were or I am now religious. And it certainly wouldn't make any difference to me whether the cards had Jesus prayers or the *Kaddish* on them. They could have Buddha on them for all I care. I guess in normal circumstances sympathy cards are like Christmas cards—a balm to the ego—the more you get, the more people must love you or need you.

There's money coming in too. Of the few letters I have opened, more than half contain checks or cash in a variety of currency, mostly American or Australian dollars. Turkey's been keeping the money in a strong box for me and she's marking down the names of strangers—who's sent what and their addresses, "for when you start your thank-you notes," she says, and I'm thinking, thank-you notes? *Thank-you notes?*

I open the letters Turkey brings me because I don't have the heart to tell her I don't want to see any of them. But I don't have the heart to look closely at what she does show me. I sift through the pile she lays out (only a sampling, she reiterates) on the high Formica table that rolls across my bed. I see handwriting cramped and expansive, pens of various colors and thicknesses, margins uneven and rigid. Words leap out: *tragedy*, *loss*, *terrible*, *children*.

Every other day the psychiatrist comes. Felice sits unmoving near my bed, her hands draped over the arms of the chair. Her hands are quite beautiful—long, elegant fingers and subtle pink nail polish, as if designated to soothe the potentially psychotic observer.

She usually starts by asking me something innocuous, like how did you sleep or did you have breakfast yet. Then she says, "How's everything else." Not, how are *you*, or how are you bearing up, but more like the inquiries of a concierge: how's everything; as if she were asking if the mushy fried tomatoes and institutionally scratchy sheets were to my satisfaction. I say, fine. I say, hanging in there. She sometimes suggests that I sit outside more, take in the air. Do you good, she says. As with everything else, I go if they insist, but I try not to. Outside in the concrete garden I swear I can smell the sea. But it's chilly out there—July, the heart of winter in Australia.

Sometimes I'll make a remark about one of the nurses—tell her an anecdote about how distressed Turkey was, say, to find out that she's years behind on *Dallas* episodes, or how another nurse who seems quite young and a little unsure of herself brought me a newspaper one morning, and then burst into tears when I asked her to take it away and she realized what she'd done. I tell Felice these little stories because if I don't, she'll say something like, "Eve, you need to talk about it."

Felice first came to see me the third day I was in the hospital, two days after I was fully conscious of my surroundings. That first visit I was still too—what—too disoriented? Stunned? No, too dreamy to hear much of what she was saying.

The second visit Felice was all business. She wrote furiously on a yellow legal pad. History of depression in family? History of alcohol or drug abuse? I told her that both sides of my family were the types to drive others to drink and suicide while they nursed their one cocktail a week and hesitated to take aspirin. Felice didn't crack a smile. She kept her head over her pad and said, "How about you? Alcohol or drug use?" "Well," I said, "I'm forty-four years old. I was in college in the early seventies. What do you think?" "How about now," she went on, scribbling. "We brought a case of wine on the boat with us, if that's what you're asking," I said, glaring.

It went on like that. Anyone in my family seen a psychiatrist? How about me? "I thought about it once or twice," I said.

Felice looked eager. "Why is that?"

I shrugged. "I forget," I said. She opened her mouth but then shut it again, cleared her throat, and moved on to the next question.

Eventually she got around to the real question, the one lurking under all the other ones. She'd prodded the past enough, and now she put down her pen, patted her yellow pad and looked me square in the eye for the first time. "How have you been feeling about things since the accident? Do you ever think about doing harm to yourself?" She was unblinking, staring me down. I thought of a dozen answers, but her gaze was so steady and unflinching that I wasn't sure I could get away with any of them. I said, "Who wouldn't."

Then I said, "I wouldn't." Said it forcefully. "I couldn't."

I expected her not to believe me, but she nodded slowly, as if this confirmed something she already knew about me. Her next few visits were mini wrestling matches. Questions questions questions. If I wouldn't talk about the accident, then how about telling her about the voyage. What was it like for the children? How did they feel about leaving the only life they knew to sail around the world? How did Charlie and I get along on the trip? How did we get along, period? I spoke one word sentences. Yes. Fine. No. Okay. She always maintained an air of utter calm and serenity. I must have been frustrating the hell out of her but she would sit almost unmoving for the full hour and push, ever so gently, at my resistance. I felt so powerful it was almost exciting, waiting to see if she would snap.

After a while she changed her tactics. She prescribed medication that I was doing my best to avoid taking. On her visits she now spends the first half hour up to her usual tricks, telling me how I am sure to have a future meltdown if I don't address things soon, threatening to up the meds. The second half hour she tends to spend in silence, leaving me to fill in the gaps. Like she can wait me out.

Finally one day I ask her if there isn't something more she wants to say to me.

"What would that be?" Felice says.

"I don't know, isn't there something more therapeutic you're supposed to be doing?"

"Like what?"

"Ah," I say, "now you're beginning to sound like a psychiatrist."

Felice grips the arms of the chair tighter and pulls herself forward. Her face is as smooth as the skin of Jessica's stomach, which had still retained it baby velvety-ness although the rest of her skin had weathered in the sun and was covered by its share of seven-year-old scrapes and bruises. Felice wears a thin gold wedding band which she takes no pains to hide, though I'm not sure why I think she should.

"Eve," Felice says, leaning toward the bed, "There's no kind of therapy, no kind of medicine that can undo what's happened to you. All I can say is that talking about what happened, as fully and as soon as possible, is therapeutic in and of itself, and can actually prevent future problems. But you are a strong woman. You're not going to talk because I ask you to. I am going to keep trying to convince you that talking will help, but I'm willing to wait a while. So I'll sit here with you every other day, at the ready." And then she does sit back and resume her usual position, which now that I really look at it, holds a kind of readiness in it, the kind of vigilance you notice in new mothers sitting by their sleeping children: not expecting to be called to action, but more than prepared to be.

Although Felice's speech is clearly designed to put me at my ease, I actually prefer her pushing at me, analyzing my silences while I ignore her. But her calm scrutiny becomes so intense that I can't bear it. I even turn on the television in the middle of the session just to see if it will faze her. It doesn't. She watches along with me. A voice is straining through the speaker on the set, forcefully singing the notes of some opera. The picture shows a smallish woman, wrapped in a pale fur coat, standing in front of a building, her long scarf billowing behind her in a fierce wind. Her face is partially obscured by a profusion of flowers from the bouquet she's holding and her eyes are hidden behind enormous sunglasses. Her head moves just enough for you to tell that she is speaking, but she holds herself with a kind of regal stillness that is riveting, even through the television screen. The soprano voice blares on and then a male voice speaks while the camera remains trained on the woman who has cocked her head to one side as if listening to a compliment. She lowers the flowers then and smiles; her mouth is impossibly wide but seems just right for a head that is too large for her body—long and chiseled like the face of an Egyptian statue. Then the camera pulls back and the building rises behind her like filling sails. "Hey," I say to Felice, "that's that building. The one they always show." Felice perks up. "The opera house?" she says.

"Yeah. That's what you always see when you see pictures of Sydney."

"It's the performing arts center, didn't you know that?" Felice says. She seems a bit peeved at my ignorance.

"I've never liked classical music much."

"That's Isabel Stein. She's American, do you know her?"

I say no.

"She's here doing a recital. I'm going tomorrow night, in fact. We're big fans. She's quite popular in the states, I believe."

"The only opera singer I know is Luciano Pavarotti," I say, noting the "we" in Felice's last words and wondering what he's like, this husband who loves opera and presumably Felice and who even now might be thinking of her or waiting for her at home.

"Oh, that's a shame. She's wonderful."

I turn back to the diminuitive figure on the TV screen, now shown head to toe. She is flanked by what seem like hundreds of photographers and others and yet she stands so still she might be alone. Her fur coat is open and underneath she is wearing something long and red with lots of fabric. It swirls about her in the wind as if someone has planned the effect it would make. She looks celestial.

And then the image is gone and replaced by a balding man with sweat on his upper lip reading from a sheaf of papers in his hand. I am still thinking about the impressive figure of the singer and so don't immediately register that the man is saying there are no leads yet in determining what hit the American boat last week, containing a family of four who . . . I close my eyes immediately and feel Felice pry the remote control from my hand. The room falls silent.

I take that opportunity to tell her the story of how Myra took Molly and me to see a matinee of *Madame Butterfly* when I was five and Molly was seven, thinking we would love the music and costumes, and how I fell asleep and Molly threw up in the theater bathroom and so essentially opera carried a rather unfortunate set of memories for me. Felice doesn't even crack a smile.

The physical therapist leans over and grabs a handful of my back muscles. I clutch the tissue paper covering the table I'm lying on. Ever since she learned who I am this woman has taken to gracing me with hackneyed advice regarding the importance of prayer and time in the healing process. But her new-found sympathy hasn't done a thing for her massage technique.

Pressing into my shoulder blade with the weight of an elephant, she suddenly puts her mouth to my ear and whispers, "They're in a better place, your little ones. You have to believe that." I am so busy marveling at the temerity, the idiocy and the crass sentimentalism of such a statement that I don't immediately react.

Later, back in my bed, I turn on the television. Some kind of surfing competition is on. A long-haired man rides a surfboard into the pounding ocean and disappears under mountainous, crayon-colored waves. I don't recoil or turn it off because I am only registering it with my eye—my brain is replaying the physical therapist's words. Then I hear a sound coming from the TV set, underscoring the voice of the narrator saying something about the surfer, who is now toeing the end of his surfboard, his arms flung out Christ-like as he skis the waves, a sound like water pipes protesting, a resonant moaning that is a little like music. It grows in volume until I turn and ring for the nurse because the remote control doesn't seem to have any effect on the TV set. My finger presses the button and I see that it is trembling and the sound is getting louder and there are little choking sounds accompanying the moaning, like coughs and by the time the nurse comes running in I know it is me, I am making the noises and I try to tell her that she can leave, that I've figured out the problem but instead I throw the remote control at her and thrust myself forward on the bed with a strength my back doesn't actually have and indeed, from far away I feel the pain but stand up anyway, shove her out of the way and head for the door, my eyes fixed on the glittering green exit sign at the far end of the hall, out of the hall, the building, the country, back to the *Orlando*, to the gleaming galley with the copper-bottomed pans, to the mainsail and the pitted steering wheel, and my children sleeping in their hard comfortable beds, sleeping dreaming dreaming till the last possible minute the way Nicholas did, his final image of a dog, I like to think, a dog bigger than life, a shaggy coat the color of honey, a slick pink tongue loving him from the bottom of his feet to his night-black, badly cut hair, tasting him, coating him, loving him to death.

I ask for more drugs after that. I complain about not sleeping, about Felice's green-and-white capsules not working. She ups my dosage without so much as a protest and adds something to help me sleep. It was a mistake to try to stay awake; I was wrong to think that sleep would drive me crazy with unbearable images. I see them everywhere in my waking hours, in the television programs I turn off and the newspapers whose residual evidence is everywhere on the blackened fingers of recent readers, in the crowd I imagine I hear milling in the waiting room—still there two weeks later, waiting for a glimpse of me, a word, as if I were that diva who I'm told is coming to the hospital herself today, for some vocal-cord problem. Turkey told me this, after explaining to me that Isabel Stein is an aging icon of opera aficionados. Not including Turkey herself though, whose idol is Garth Brooks, but she's still excited by the prospect that a genuine "identity" is coming to the hospital.

I tell the doctor that I've changed my mind about the muscle relaxants. I imagine eventually he'll coordinate things with Felice but for the moment he's happy to prescribe. The drugs leave me listless and unfocused, which is what I thought they'd do, but until now

I wouldn't allow myself the luxury of retreating; I thought I should force myself to experience every waking moment of the rest of my life. But I'm weak. I'm weak in ways I'm still learning about.

Not that I haven't always been good in a crisis. I grew up in a family whose attitude toward life was embodied in the concept that a candle allowed to burn to the bottom is a conflagration waiting to happen, a new mole spells cancer, a stomachache requires hospitalization. In the face of that kind of perpetual anxiety you can become a raving lunatic or a confirmed and stolid pragmatist. Working in advertising, where a new flavor of ice cream is cause for two-day international conferences, confirmed my attitude that he who stays calmest, triumphs.

I watched my father die a slow painful death, and managed to keep composed enough to let my mother collapse under the weight of her grief. I had the strength to endure difficult pregnancies, the vicissitudes of family life and the complications of leaving everything we knew and had behind—selling our house and most of our possessions, saying good-bye to family and friends—of setting sail around the world, of the two years we were at sea. I endured the weather and the illness and the food scarcity when we didn't plan right and the close quarters and the fear and the realization, somewhere in the middle of the second year, that it was Charlie's dream we were living, that for all the saving and planning and expectancy, I would rather (it struck me one day when I was alone on deck at dusk and the sky in the distance appeared to be sinking in a flaming mass into the sea) be at home in front of my computer facing the dull paneling of the den wall and agonizing over a short story idea rather than sitting out here in this magnificent emptiness trying to come up with a title for a cute article about life with my family at sea.

I even had the strength to endure the first few hours in the merciless water when Charlie and Jessie were still with me. I was the one saying we would get through it. I was the one exuding shivering calm, encouraging words, aphorisms. And I believed them. I felt an absolute serene certainty that we would make it because I simply could not imagine any other outcome.

I only got weak when Charlie and Jessie were gone. I didn't recognize it as weakness right away because I told myself I was waiting for them, that their heads, his black and flesh-colored from where he was balding and hers black as the sea was that night, bobbing a bit away from me, his over hers as he clutched her and swam toward me, I told myself that these images would appear before me momentarily, and then the moment after that and the moment after that, each moment new and fresh, full of possibility, each moment erasing the growing number of moments that had come before. I didn't know my own weakness until the middle of the next day when the sea had gone silent and gentle, after I righted the dinghy for the last time and climbed into it from the warming waters, when the sun seared my back as I lay like drying clothes across the bottom of the dinghy, when I emerged from a kind of salty fog with only a vague idea of what had happened so far. I only recognized the full extent of my own weakness when I realized that my fingers, which had lost feeling the night before as the three of us clung to the dinghy and rode the ferocious waves, had refused to do what they should have done by instinct as soon as Charlie and Jess were gone. Red and split, cramped into claws, frozen and useless, they had absolutely refused to let go.

Turkey brings in my lunch tray with a particular sort of suppressed energy. The corners of her mouth twitch and everything about her suggests a secret she cannot contain.

"This is one you have to read right away," Turkey chirps. She's holding out a piece of eggwhite paper; it's wavering in her excited hand. "It's from *her*," Turkey adds, almost in a whisper. I'm feeling a little seasick, watching the paper bob in the air, so I take it without a question and open it up. A few lines of huge handwriting—great looping I's and S's. It's the largest hand I've ever seen. I force myself to read because it seems to mean so much to Turkey, but I do so out of the corner of my eye, so that I can stop at any moment.

Dear Ms. Miller, I have heard news of your terrible situation. Please accept my warmest condolences. You may have heard that I am here at Sydney Hospital myself for a minor throat condition. If you at all feel up to it and it is convenient, I would like nothing so much as to visit briefly with you this afternoon, a fellow American far from home. Sincerely, Isabel Stein.

The S in "Stein" loops up so high that it overlaps much of the text in her note.

"You will see her, won't you dear," Turkey says, leaning close.

I smile at her. "You just want to meet her yourself, admit it, Ellen."

She smiles back. "Go on," she says, waving a hand at me. "It might do you good. You haven't had any visitors. It's not healthy, you know, luv, lying here day after day with no one to talk to."

"She's a celebrity," I say. "She'd probably do most of the talking, don't you think?"

Turkey frowns.

She's been so kind to me, so protective, so willing to keep me cushioned from newspapers and mail and people. She's avoided all the platitudes, never tried to get me to talk or do anything I didn't express a desire to, except eat. But the thought of talking to strangers about myself is insupportable, and talking about anything else seems impossible. "I'm sorry," I say, and turn away from her crestfallen face.

Some hours later, a Lavender Lady ushers in two familiar-looking men in dark suits. Before I have a chance to ask what she thinks she's doing, one of the men, the one with a broad flat nose and prominent forehead and an air of authority, introduces himself and the other man as investigators from the Maritime Safety Board. "We interviewed you the day after your accident, in case you don't remember us," he says dryly.

They are both standing a rather deferential distance from the bed with their arms straight at their sides. My heart goes all jumpy.

"We thought you'd want to know the progress of the investigation, for one thing," the authoritative man goes on, still not moving. "We thought you'd like to know that we now have a definitive list of every ship that was in the area of the collision that night and we have investigators out to each and every one of them, across the globe."

I think about "across the globe." It's a romantic way to word something, like the way Charlie worded it to me when he first told me what he wanted to do. He said something about seeing the planet, its every depth and surface. He said something about how different the stars look from different points on the globe, what the sea is like in the dead of night and how he couldn't imagine what life was for if not to get out to that place, that spot in the middle of the lapping ocean where you could finally feel your soul unwind, your presence on earth. "Ironic," he said, "how I never feel fully on the ground except when I'm at sea."

That was, what, fifteen years ago in a frozen yogurt shop—our third or fourth date and he had preceded the speech about taking to sea with the statement that blurred everything he said afterward: he'd watched me licking my plastic spoon with an expression more fitting to witnessing a miracle and he'd said, "I know I'm not supposed to say this yet, but I think I'm falling in love with you."

I had waited years to hear someone say that, someone who still had his clothes on. I felt, not thrilled so much as becalmed—finally at a place of rest and comfort, a place to stop. I had never stepped foot on a boat in my life other than the motor boats that chugged along a track on the Disneyland ride. I already knew Charlie well enough to know that he wouldn't go flying off to sea without all the preparation and money he needed and that therefore it would be years until I actually had to consider the prospect of giving up everything on land. In the meantime we would live together in a bliss of authenticity—both of us more ourselves for being with each other—no emotion too strong, no problem too complex that it couldn't be unraveled by love and commitment and creativity. The idea of quitting work, selling everything and sailing your family around the world for four years was thrilling and romantic and I imagined myself gathering material for more than one book; I imagined us side by side with the sea wind blowing in our hair, Katharine Hepburn and Spencer Tracy. At the same time, I believed it highly possible that we never would go at all. In the meantime, to prove my gameness, I took sailing lessons; I crewed on a 40-footer one summer to Hawaii; I helped Charlie pick out our practice boat, the *Mariana*, a 30-foot fiberglass coastal cruiser that we took out every weekend and holiday and each of our vacations for shakedown cruises to Ensenada and the Channel Islands, where Charlie said the winds would more accurately simulate the open sea.

We were so well prepared.

The investigator, the one with the flat nose, is still speaking, his companion staring sad-eyed at a point across my right shoulder. Something about Russians and Japanese, about freighters and cruise ships. The investigator reads back to me the words I'd spoken to him the first night he questioned me.

"You were remarkably lucid, Ma'am, and you've no idea how helpful that is. You described the ship as possibly a fishing vessel, you told us what had been happening moments before the accident—how you were on watch and the others were asleep, how the seas and the winds were high . . ."

I close my eyes, but keep hearing him, hear "five-foot hole and winds at thirty-five knots." Hear how there was nothing to be found of the *Orlando* nor any of her contents and I forgive him even as he says it, says "contents," because he obviously isn't thinking, isn't remembering the only contents of the *Orlando* that could possibly matter and, because despite his officiousness, he has a kind face and gentle manner; he would feel terrible about having said the word, having referred to Nick as contents.

"A few more questions," he says. With his accent it sounds like "Christians."

"Please," I say. I open my eyes but the nurse has left the room. I start to reach for the buzzer but my neck seizes up and I can't move. The flat-nosed man promises it will go quickly and wouldn't I please bear with them.

"What color was the *Orlando?*" he asks.

I almost laugh. "Aesthetic questions?" I say. They both stare at me blankly. "Green," I say finally, looking hard into the quiet one's sad slivered eyes. "Kelly green," I say. Jessica's favorite color I don't say. She picked the color, Nick picked the name, that was the deal and though Charlie and I managed to dissuade her from a bright pink that perfectly matched an outfit worn by Brenda Bride, the doll she was bringing on the trip, that was as far as our success went—she would not transfer her affections to a darker khaki or olive. We fared better with Nick, who was a year older and wanted to please us as well as himself. We all agreed that *Orlando* was a good compromise, since it covered both a Teenage Mutant Ninja Turtle and a novel by Virginia Woolf, which pleased me and I promised Jess would someday please her. Charlie was least represented by the name but he came up with the notion that Orlando was his parents' favorite vacation spot and everyone was happy in the end.

". . . we'd find the color on the hull of the ship that hit you," the man is saying. "So that's very helpful. Now, just a couple more questions. You told us that you were under sail that night. Going at about what speed would you say?"

I close my eyes again. I try to remember, not the details of that night, but why they are important since they are so not important to me. I try to focus only on the moment that man is asking me about. The waves and the dark and the hard whistling of the wind and the intermittent crackle of the radio. The children safe in their bunks, Charlie snoring so loudly I could hear him from the deck when the wind died down and the ocean was momentarily, deceptively calm. I tried to think no farther than that moment, and what the instruments said, gleaming darkly in the flickering moonlight of the stormy night.

"Five or six knots," I say, not breathing.

"Did you have a lookout?" the sad-faced man says quietly.

"No official lookout," I say. "The weather. It was raining. The sea was heavy. My watch was enough." I open my eyes. "We thought it was enough," I say.

Were the lights on on the mast and hull?

What frequency was the radio turned to?

What time again would you say it was?

Were you steering?

Yes, three, red green and white; Channel 16, the all-purpose Marine frequency; I started the watch at about 11 P.M. the children had been asleep for about two hours and Charlie was nodding off but I could hear him snoring later and that doesn't usually happen till he's been asleep about an hour and I have a vague recollection of checking the time at midnight so I'm guessing now, I could not be accurate seems to me that's your job anyway but I would say 12:30 or thereabouts the water was so angry I was thinking about that and how I wasn't sure if I had done the right thing to come out here whether or not I was really happy and could really stick it out but how even if I left tomorrow I could never forget the night sky and the water I could never entirely give them up so who would pay attention to the time with thoughts like that thoughts that were to do with fourteen years of marriage and two children and whether I loved all of them enough to stay or whether loving them all meant to go and what was the other question? Oh yes and the automatic steering was on.

"We have some leads," they say.

"We're on top of it," they say.

I say thank you and hear footsteps and then they go away. I lie there thinking about what I would do if and when they found the ship that hit us. I look up at the cottage-cheese ceiling (just like an American ceiling) and have a clear image of my hands closing around the neck of some faceless ship's captain, some pig-faced coward who would beg for his life and scream about acts of God and accidents as I slowly squeezed the life out of his sniveling face. At the same time I feel indifferent—not so much because I realize that my becoming a murderer would change nothing but because it seems silly somehow—puny—as if the snuffing out of one life or of the whole ship's crew, for that matter, would even begin to touch the enormity of the loss of one day of Jessie's life, one strand of Nick's hair.

2

I have a plan to hoard the pills. I spent most of the day considering various alternatives that would outwit the staff. Molly's best friend in high school, the Maria who later died in a car crash, used to hide cigarettes in her impossibly teased, enormous hair—she had seen it in some prison movie—but my hair is hardly up to the task. I could always fall back on the store-them-in-your-cheek device—something I think *I* saw in a movie about a mental hospital—but I wanted to come up with something more creative, something they wouldn't anticipate.

I am practicing coughing and then shooting my hand under the mattress when the door to my room flies open and a small woman in a wheelchair rolls up to my bed. It is the singer. She is wrapped in a gold-and-green brocade robe that shimmers in the fluorescent light and her auburn hair is in attractive disarray around her head and shoulders. We peer at each other for a long time. She could be anywhere from thirty to sixty years old. Her flesh is olive toned and stretched taut against knife-sharp cheekbones. She isn't wearing an ounce of makeup and except for sleep circles under her eyes she looks perfect.

I open my mouth to speak but she gets there first. "The wheelchair's silly, isn't it. I'm perfectly capable of walking but I find that if I ride around in the wheelchair people actually pay less attention to me—they just assume I'm a patient and they don't really *look* at me." She leans forward with her silkclad elbows resting on the armrests of the chair, her hands clasped under her large breasts. "I know you didn't necessarily want to see me. But I *couldn't* bring myself to leave you alone when I know you're thousands of miles away from home with none of your family around you and those vultures perched right outside your door practically, with their notebooks and cameras and questions and you with no way to avoid them and I won't be able to speak in an hour and I just had to say something to you before that." It is the longest speech anyone has made to me since I arrived and it exhausts me. Her voice cracks on every other word; nonetheless, each is enunciated perfectly. She seems to have the slightest of accents—it could be New York or English or it could just be the way her voice lilts. She doesn't so much look *at* me as *through* me, as if there were a higher purpose to her speech than I could ever hope to conceive of.

She thrusts out a small, manicured hand. "Forgive me. I'm always doing that, just barging in expecting you to know. I'm Isabel Stein. I sent you a note." The hand, much whiter than her complexion and sporting a silver ring thick as a cigar band, hangs in front of my face. I have a compulsion to kiss it. As soon as she sees me try to move, she withdraws.

"My god, I'm an *idiot*. I heard you had a back injury, of course it would be difficult . . . maybe *impossible* for you to shake hands. I'm always blundering my way into things. My husband calls me Yenta—do you know what a Yenta is?—he says a hundred years ago I'd have been arranging marriages and telling housewives how to get pregnant. He's always analyzing my need to barge into people's lives, but I just think I'm . . . well, I'm *interested*. Anyway, I hope it's not too terrible of me to come here to see you."

She takes another deep breath and smiles at me. Her mouth looks huge, her teeth impossibly white. I blink at her.

"Listen," she says. "You don't have to say a word. I completely understand. How *could* you speak, what is there to say? I'll talk, shall I? I don't pretend to know what you're going through. I can't imagine such a tragedy. I'm certain I wouldn't have your courage, which I can tell you have just by looking at you."

She leans forward in her chair. There is something avid about her, something hungry. "Of course the papers are sketchy on details at this point and I wouldn't presume to ask you about what happened, but if it would help to talk about anything, you know, I'd be happy to listen. All these Brits are well-meaning and everything, but it's not the same, is it, as talking to someone from home, someone close to your own background?"

"They're Australian," I say.

"Excuse me?"

"They're not British, they're Australian."

"Well of course they are. Anyway, they're all very kind, aren't they. Actually they are treating me better here than the doctors in the states ever do. I have this *ridiculous* throat condition you know—well, if you must know, it's tonsillitis." She waves her hand in front of her face as if to erase the offending organs. "I have to be the only person of my age not to have gotten them yanked when I was five, right? So now they give me no end of grief. Here I am in the middle of a tour and they flare up—I mean, I practically have to carry one whole suitcase just full of all the antibiotics they give me at home and none of them work so now I have to come here and have them shoot me full of something more powerful. It's too much. I absolutely *refuse* to miss any more recitals. I go back on in two nights and I simply have to be ready."

"Sounds difficult," I say.

"Please. You don't know the half of it. The minute I'm back home I'm getting them yanked." She stops and brings her hand to her mouth. "Oh god, I'm doing it again. Please forgive me. How could you let me go on like this."

"Well, I am a little tired," I begin.

"I just wanted to say that if there was anything I could do. If you want to get word to your family or need help getting them here or something. I mean, I have someone whose job is pretty much only to book me on airplanes so we could whisk your family here in a minute if you want, and if it's a question of money . . ."

"That's very nice of you, but I'm fine."

Isabel Stein smiles again, but this time the smile is slow and pained, conveying an almost transcendental sadness. "You're wondering what I'm up to," she says. Her voice cracks. "What ghoulish interest I have in you. Maybe you're even thinking I'm going to tell the papers something." She shakes her head twice slowly, letting her wild hair swing across her face. "*Believe* me, the last thing I want is those vultures descending on either one of us. I can't tell you why your story has affected me so much. Leo says I'm always picking up strays but this is different. I suppose it's partly because of . . . it's the children, you see."

I hold my breath. Close my eyes.

"I can imagine losing Leo—I mean it would kill me, but not forever, not in a way that I couldn't go on. But I have no children, you see, and I have imagined them all my life. I've imagined them so hard that they're practically real to me—they're this sort of gleaming, nonpresence. But in all my imaginings, I never thought about what it would mean to lose them and I just want to *do* something, to *say* something, that gives you even a moment's ease."

I open my eyes and see that hers, which a moment ago were clear and shining, look as if they were melting, so quickly have they filled, as if responding to a silent cue. "I'll leave you now," she says, her prominent chin trembling. "I'm sure you'd much rather be in the company of your family. Just do tell the nurses if there's anything I can do for you, will you? They'll get a message to me."

"Thank you," I say, for what seems like the hundredth time. Is this what it's going to be like from now on? Will I be saying "thank you" a thousand times a day to a thousand different well-meaning, insufferably kind and careful people, each wanting to do something, to make what happened not have happened, or else to make me act like it hadn't happened? It's a form of gloating, really. To be the one that it *didn't* happen to must be something like being the star of one of Isabel Stein's operas: you imagine yourself in my situation and feel all the pain of it, all the guilt about what you have that I don't have. There is applause and appreciation for your sympathetic connection to so much heartache. Then you go home and get a good night's sleep. In the morning you awaken refreshed and with a new appreciation for the little things, the loved ones in your life.

Isabel Stein is backing her wheelchair away from my bed. She is still giving me that suffering Madonna-like look and I find myself saying, "Try not to worry. Everything will be all right."

She smiles sadly. "Oh, don't you worry about *me*. *You* are the one with the incredible courage," she says. Then, in an abrupt shift of tone, she asks, "When do you expect your family?" as if she were a secretary updating my social calendar.

I take a couple of very deep breaths, hoping she'll think I've fallen asleep.

"They are coming, aren't they? There's no problem, is there?"

I open my eyes. "No problem," I say.

She looks at me expectantly.

"I've asked them not to come," I finally say, defeated.

As I knew they would, the eyes grow wide, the large mouth curves itself into an O. "But," she begins, "but surely you want them to be here. You must have people with you. You must want them to . . ."

"It was very nice of you to come visit me," I say. "Good luck with your treatment." I close my eyes again and begin the tortuous journey of turning over onto my side, away from Isabel Stein and her gigantic sympathy.

She sends me an enormous bouquet of the most amazing flowers. I have never had an eye for them—I barely know a daisy from a tulip—but the colors and unusual projections and curves of the leaves and petals are truly impressive. Along with the bouquet she sent two boxes of Mallomar cookies and two notes. One was attached to one of the Mallomar boxes. It read: "You can't find these anywhere in Australia or Europe so I carry a case with me on tour. Thought you'd like a taste of home." The other note was attached to a plastic stick in the flowers. It read: *Dearest Eve, Please forgive me if I disturbed you yesterday. I was very glad to meet you. I hope we meet again soon, Isabel Stein.*

Once again, the nurses are thrilled.

In another life I might have been curious to hear Isabel Stein sing. It seems as if that would tell me something important about her—like what so interests her in me and how sincere she is. When Walter comes the next day, I ask him what he thinks, since I'm fairly certain he's completely uninterested in opera and therefore likely not to be bowled over by her. "What do you think makes her so interested in me," I say. "I don't know about here, but where I come from, when someone you don't know at all is this kind and attentive, they're usually after something."

Walter has been folding fresh towels at the foot of the my bed. He stops for a moment and clears his throat.

"Go on," I say, "you can tell me what you think."

"It's a bit . . . I mean, I don't know how much you want to know about what's going on," he says. He appears to be blushing.

"Go on."

"Well, I . . ." He clears his throat again. "I don't know if you realize how much publicity . . . how much you are in the news. Almost every day since you've . . . been here . . . there's been a story in the paper about you. The lounges are still filled with reporters. Did you know that there's a hospital spokesman giving out updates on your condition? So, I guess I can rather understand her curiosity."

Walter goes. Another nurse comes in, this one with meds. I swallow them because I can't be bothered to try to figure out a clever way to hide them right now. After the nurse leaves I open the bedside drawer to find a Bible whose condition is so pristine that the black fake leather cover glows. I might be able to wrap the pills in toilet paper or something and then stick them between these obviously unread pages. I assume the Bible was left here by some hopeful and terrified patient whose faith ran out after Book One. Or maybe some well-meaning nuisance strategically places them there, like the Gideons back in the states, to discourage just such a thing as I am doing, this hoarding of escape methods.

I'm sitting upright on the side of the bed, which is the only way I can open the bedside drawer. Even from this position the slight twisting to my right is pleasantly excruciating. They tell me not to do this, not to do anything that causes me pain, which is probably the most pointless advice I've ever received. I've just closed the drawer when yet another person barges into my room. I wish this were a hotel, Gideon Bibles and all, so that I could order up a bottle of scotch and put up a "Do Not Disturb" sign.

This person is a tall man with thick white hair and fashionable wire-rim glasses. He's wearing an expensive-looking wool sweater and dark corduroy pants. When he identifies himself as Leo Stein, Isabel Stein's husband, I'm surprised. I'd imagined him as mousy and withdrawn, dwarfed by her presence, rather than dapper and imposing in his own right. He fills most of the doorway and when he speaks his voice floats—deep and pleasant—over my bed.

"I won't disturb you, I just wanted to let you know—Isabel can't use her voice for a few days and she wanted to be sure you got this message before we leave Sydney. Oh good, you got the flowers. I don't think they'll need much care. You can ask the nurses. I imagine they're very knowledgeable about this sort of thing—flowers, chocolates."

He clips off the ends of his sentences as if they were pesky hangnails. His speech, his stiff stance in my doorway, his roving gaze, bespeak a man who hates waste—of time, words, emotions. It makes me wonder how he handles his relationship with his wife, who seems pretty emotionally improvident.

"Anyway, what Isabel wanted me to propose was this." Now Leo Stein takes a step toward the bed, his thin lips pursed as if unwilling to have taken this verbal pause. I begin to sweat.

"She gathered from your last conversation—of course it was your only conversation but Isabel does exaggerate—that you were not anxious to return home immediately."

I want to say, My home is at the bottom of the sea. But looking at his tight face, his broad torso half turned as if for imminent departure, it seems an overwrought, melodramatic thing to say.

"Isabel has this whole notion that . . ." He stops, shifts his weight and crosses his woolly arms across his chest. "Well, she had the impression from your conversation that you don't necessarily wish to immediately rejoin your family when you're discharged from here." He clears his throat and frowns. His eyes behind his glasses are that thin blue that's close to the color of nonfat milk when you hold it to the light. People with very light eyes like that look ever so slightly inhuman to me. "I told her I'm sure you'd be making your own arrangements and that this is none of our business, but she kept on about it and since she's not well and can be quite . . . insistent when she has a . . . project . . . I thought it was best to promise that I'd come see you. I'm sure you are anxious to get home. I'm sure you don't welcome this intrusion."

For some perverse reason I am enjoying his discomfort. Maybe it's just that his wife, despite her pushiness, at least seemed to have genuinely kind impulses and he seems just as clearly not to.

"Actually," I say, "we sold our house in L.A. Most of our things too."

"I see." He uncrosses his arms and assumes a straighter, more businesslike stance. "Well, then maybe you will be interested. Isabel thought you might like the use of a little guest house we have—a cottage, really, outside New York. I told her I hardly thought you'd be interested in staying three thousand miles away from your home in a place where you know no one, but she thought that might be just what you wanted. I'm afraid you'd be quite on your own there; it's close to the main house but we won't be there much and the fellow who's staying there is hardly likely . . ."

He's older than he looks. Late fifties probably. Despite the gray hair he has round cheeks and a youthful mouth. His dismissive sociability reminds me of Charlie's father, Ed, a retired corporate lawyer who still has the ability to carry on a pleasant conversation with you, all the while making you feel simultaneously intrusive and irrelevant. You only develop this quality with age or tragedy.

"It's an old place, quite nice really; parts of it date back to the Revolution. We refurbished the carriage house into a guest house. Isabel tends to install her . . . protégés there. It turned out quite nicely—there's a small bedroom and living room and an adequate kitchen." Here he allows himself a twitchy smile, as if he's done the renovations himself. "Anyway, as I said, you'd be left on your own and if you needed regular attention I'm afraid you'd have to hire someone. And it's over an hour from the city, so I don't really see it suiting you. But Isabel wanted to be sure you considered the offer." He takes a small step backwards as if to indicate that he's finished what he came to say and has no interest in spending another minute in my company.

I'm suddenly very tired and no longer interested in torturing this man into thinking I might come to disturb his obviously carefully ordered life. I thank him and tell him to thank his wife. I tell him I'll probably make my own arrangements but I appreciate the offer. He smiles tightly and turns to go. At the doorway he stops, as if he's just thought of something. He turns back to me. "You know," he says, "there is one advantage to taking us up on this offer." (Now it's "our" offer.) "The media don't know about the country house and if we're careful when you leave they'd never make the connection between you and Isabel. So if you want to avoid them, at our place you'd probably be completely undisturbed."

"I doubt the press will stay interested in me much longer," I say.

Leo gives me a knowing, pitying look. "Don't be so sure," he says. Clearly as an afterthought, he reaches behind him and pulls out a white piece of paper from his hip pocket and places it on the nightstand. "Our itinerary in Australia," he says. "One more week in Sydney, two in Melbourne, one off to relax, then back to Sydney to make up the two recitals Isabel's missing, then home." There are hotels and dates and phone numbers listed, he tells me, and I can call anytime, up to the last minute before they leave for home. I close my eyes and thank him again. Having dispatched all his duties he reaches out a thick, tanned hand and touches my shoulder in a gesture that is surprisingly gentle. "Of course," he says softly, "you might *want* the press to find you. I mean, if you're short of cash, they'll be willing to pay. And lots. You could stay at the cottage as long as you like."

He turns and walks firmly out the door.

The Steins' is not the only, nor the strangest offer of shelter I've received. For the past two days Turkey has been coming in when her shift is over and opening some of the mail for me. She reads aloud the ones she thinks will interest or amuse me. I've been offered guest rooms, guest houses, whole estates unused for the winter, basements—even a room in the back of a store. Houses in Sydney, in Melbourne, in places that sound like exotic confections in Turkey's mouth: Mawson, Weipa, Canberra. Denver (too close to California). Helena (where is Helena?). Palm Beach (air like wet cotton). There are job offers and therapy offers and offers to read my aura, my palm, my chart. There are three letters from publishers offering me large sums of money for my story. All three of these letters open with a paragraph of heartfelt condolence before the paragraphs about fame and fortune. They make me laugh. This seems to worry Turkey.

I tell Felice that I have two goals for my future. Avoiding physical therapy and sleeping. She says she guesses that that's perfectly normal. I like the way she qualifies her reaction. She fixes that penetrating gentle therapist stare on me. "Just remember, Eve, that you must take it slowly, but you do have to think of what comes next. They're going to release you soon."

She has come over to the bed and is helping me sit up, gently pressing on my wrist and one shoulder. I breathe deeply, trying to focus my swimming gaze—there's a black edge around my vision, as if everything is lined in crepe. Felice doesn't seem to notice anything odd. She promises to see me day after tomorrow, then adds her usual closing line. "If you need to see me sooner you have only to ask."

"Felice," I say.

She turns back from the door.

"What will I do about the pain?"

She steps back into the room. Her face looks sorrowful and hopeful at the same time. "Oh Eve," she says, and reaches out a hand to me.

"I mean when I leave here," I say. "What will I do for the pain medication? And the sleep? And the antidepressants?"

She drops her hand and her face recovers itself, the eyebrows drawing together into a frown. "Of course we'll give you enough to get you to your next location and then we'll talk to your doctors there—in the states or . . . wherever you'll be."

"Thank you," I say.

"I thought you didn't want the medication that much," Felice says.

"Rainy day," I say.

Felice looks at me speculatively. "Talking is better than meds, Eve."

"Cheaper too, I hear," I say.

In the morning Molly calls my hospital room. "Ma's on her way," she says, no preliminaries or niceties, as if she is still harboring hurt feelings from something I said. I am in my bed this time, recovering from a round of new X rays and blood tests; something to do with releasing me soon. I can tell by the tense looks on everyone's faces, the doctors, nurses, physical therapists, even the ones who seem most attached to me like Walter and Turkey, that my presence here is a strain on their resources and patience. I have the feeling that they're beginning to hold me responsible for the regular crowd of reporters, photographers and other assorted hangers-on taking up their lobbies and waiting rooms. I can't blame them. Although it's not hard to imagine being on the other side, hearing of a headline-grabbing tragedy and lusting for its details out of the collective ghoulish curiosity. As someone whose job entailed spending weeks agonizing over the exact way to word a superlative description of an antibacterial soap, I can hardly blame the journalists for doing their uncomfortable, unsavory job.

"Are you there?" Molly says.

"Yes."

"You don't sound that upset."

"There's nothing I can do about it now. You said Ma's already on her way."

Molly begins to cry. I hold the phone receiver away from my ear so she sounds distant and tinny, like the volume on the television. "Last time she called the doctor said they're going to release you soon. She was so upset I thought she was going to have a breakdown. You've been in the hospital two months and you didn't tell us they were going to release you. She said she's going over there to see what's what whether you like it or not. She'd booked the plane and began packing before I even got over to the house."

Molly is saying all this in between sobs. I know there's some response I'm supposed to have, something full of feeling that I should say that would release some pain in us both. For the life of me I can't think of what it is. I am trying to figure out if I've hoarded enough pills to use them before my mother arrives. Then I think about swallowing what I have, and at least getting sick, maybe going into a coma. That might have been a solution before I knew my mother was coming. But now, doing it would not give me escape. It would simply put me at her mercy.

"I have to go now, Molly," I say.

"Eve? Honey, please don't hang up yet. I wish you'd let us . . . Eve? I talked to Charlie's parents a few days ago. I've been keeping them from calling too, from going out there. I've been trying, Eve."

"Thank you. I really do have to go now, Molly."

I hang up. If I believed in hell, I would go straight there for how I was treating my sister, my family, Charlie's poor parents, Ed and Lucy. But the part of me that knew how to behave in the world that exists now, the world after the accident, has been shorn off by whatever sliced open the *Orlando*. I have lost the capacity, not to see someone else's distress, but to feel as if I had any participation in it. This is the one gift of my injuries—this utter lack of feelings that is not numbness so much as a sort of sublime indifference.

"How long does it take to fly here from Los Angeles?" I ask Walter, realizing I should have asked Molly exactly when the flight left. Knowing Myra, she would get here as fast as possible.

"About fourteen hours, I should think," he says. He is changing my sheets while I sit in the chair Felice usually occupies. I walk to the bathroom on my own these days.

Myra wants to take me home. She wants to care for me and look after me and help me "recover." She wants to share my grief and believes that the only way for me to heal is to be in the bosom of my family. I know this woman; I know what she's thinking.

"Walter," I say. "I need to send a fax."

The reply comes two hours after the fax was sent. "Thrilled to hear from you. Arrangements are being made already. I'll come to see you when we arrive back in Sydney on the 25th. Best, Isabel Stein."

Felice comes in the afternoon. "What will you tell your mother?" she asks me.

"The truth," I say.

"How do you think that will make her feel?"

I used to care deeply about that sort of thing. Even after I was married, had kids of my own—I would go to great lengths to avoid hurting my mother. Charlie used to call it the curse of the Jewish princess, but I saw him being just as solicitous and careful of his mother.

"I'm sure she'll be very upset," I say evenly. "But I can't do anything about that."

Felice says nothing.

"You know, I always wanted to be able to say that," I add. "Do you usually find that people like me become more honest? Or cruel?"

"I've never known anyone like you," Felice says. It is stated as a fact, not a compliment.

So of course when she actually shows up, Myra almost catches me in the act. Story of my whole life. It's early morning and I have barely gotten the bedstand drawer closed when she blows into the room in a gust of humid air, dishevelled and breathing heavily, as if she's run all the way from the airport. I still have my arm outstretched, ready to grasp the Bible and stash my supply of pills, and if it weren't for the unusual circumstances, Myra would know in a nanosecond from the look on my face that I am guilty as hell of something. As it is, she simply says my name in a kind of half-moan. At the sight of her standing there, puffy-faced and clutching a bulging totebag, her eyes wild and fixed on me, all the arguments I've been planning to present her with disappear. I say the first thing that comes into my head.

"What's in the bag?"

She starts, stares down at the totebag with blank eyes, then raises them to me again. "I honestly don't know," she replies, and then it seems the most natural thing in the world to hold out my arms to her and bury my face in her spongy chest, breathing in the smell of lavender sachets and Chanel No. 19 and simply Myra's skin, fragrant as my warmest safest childhood nights, safe as locked doors and immortality.

3

The airplane engine thrums comfortably under the First Class seat. I am rigged up with special pillows for my back. The plane gives the illusion of not moving at all. Its noise is nothing like the noise of a boat engine, the slapping of the sea. Ahead and to the right Isabel Stein is sleeping, her head fallen against her husband's broad shoulder. Next to me, Myra is doing the crossword puzzle in the in-flight magazine and pretending not to be checking on my condition every few minutes. I am enjoying a coma-like state, courtesy of champagne and muscle relaxants. For the moment Myra is in charge of my medications but before we got on the plane back in Sydney I retrieved the pills I'd hidden in the Bible. I stowed them in the pocket of the jeans Myra had bought me before she left L.A.—two sizes too big. Typically Myra, at once farsighted and mistaken in anticipating my needs.

Myra was magnificent, silently holding onto me for as long as I clung to her those first moments in my hospital room, then rousing herself to take charge, getting copies of my charts to take back to the American doctors, talking to Felice about medication and treatment, crying a little in Felice's comforting serene company—I am impressed.

Myra was magnificent, because even though she predictably put up a fuss about my going to New York rather than Los Angeles with her, she eventually gave in and hasn't mentioned my defection. Maybe she's even a bit relieved.

But that's not fair. Myra's eyes still look as if the surrounding skin has been packed with cotton, from so many puffy days of crying. She clutches her bag to her chest so often that I know it contains photographs of Jessie and Nick. And she says, mercifully, nothing. My eyelids flutter a little as the plane jerks and a word swims into my head that I haven't thought in thirty-five years: *Mommy*.

Myra says my name and I open my eyes, squinting a little in the light that pours through Myra's window. "I said, when we get to New York you're going to need so many things. Do you think you'll be up to shopping?"

I blink. "I'll be fine, Ma."

"You don't have anything but the clothes on your back."

I don't show her any reaction to that.

"I'll just do some shopping for you. A few things. A few pairs of underwear, for heaven's sake."

"Okay," I say, because Myra looks like she's about to cry. "Just remember, I wear a 10, Ma, okay?"

Myra sniffs. She turns back to her puzzle, but not before reaching up with her right hand and patting my arm. She pretends to focus on her puzzle and I feel that little wave of shock I felt when I first saw her the day she arrived in Sydney. I hadn't seen my mother in two years. And while we were separated, every time I thought of her face I saw the face from my childhood—my mother at young middle age—the age I am now. I have to remind myself that she has not aged overnight, that she doesn't look that different from the way she did when I last saw her. It is my memory that is snagged on a glitch in time. So many more fine, almost delicate wrinkles radiate from the corners of her mouth than I could have possibly imagined. Myra is almost seventy and it's there in her face. Yet she is still beautiful, in that careful artistic way she always was—curling strands of hair cunningly escaping from a brown bun, powder and rouge coating her face like peach fuzz, a hint of pearlized lipstick staining her mouth. *Mommy*. If my damaged neck would only permit it, I would rest my head on Myra's willing shoulder.

The flight attendant approaches with offers of drinks, magazines. Myra speaks for me, rushing in to say no newspapers, no magazines. At the Los Angeles airport the newsstand was awash in tabloids with headlines about my story. The investigators have narrowed down the possible suspects to a Russian fishing vessel and a Chinese freighter. The Russians are cooperating; the Chinese are being cagey. One paper had a companion story that reported rumors that the American survivor of the tragic accident was being released from the hospital soon. Myra is obviously hoping I saw none of this but I saw it all. Saw it and had uncharitable thoughts for Turkey and Walter and whoever else might have leaked my departure to the press. Myra has already figured out that her cousin Birdie in Boca Raton is the one who must have sent the press the photograph of my family that I saw in the hospital. Myra is still torn between calling Birdie to "give her a few pieces of my mind," and never speaking to her again.

"I vote for firing squad," I said.

"The one year I send a holiday card," Myra moaned. "Though how it made its way to the Australian papers I'll never know." So I explained how wire services worked and Myra looked at me as if I'd just revealed a knowledge of how to smash the atom.

"You always forget my advertising days," I said, noting that I felt none of the old fury at how my mother could dismiss or forget seventeen years out of my life, as easily as Charlie had expected me to.

Nothing makes me furious now. I can stare at the offensive publications with detached interest, as if the story belonged to someone else, someone romantically melancholy, posed beautiful and mute on a deserted plain, like Meryl Streep, windblown and tragic, in that movie a few years ago.

"The important thing is that the vultures weren't *there* when you left the hospital," Isabel said when I saw the magazine containing the story of my departure. "Leo handled that beautifully." Isabel ran her palm down the sleeve of Leo's jacket as if petting him. Indeed, Leo had notified some local reporters that Isabel was back at the hospital after her return from Melbourne. They descended, to me more like a group of excited schoolchildren at a museum—eager and a bit embarrassed—than the vultures Isabel thought them, and seemed only mildly disappointed to find that she'd come back to the hospital only to thank the doctors who had treated her for their excellent care. The reporters and camera people still surrounded her in her fur coat and ubiquitous bouquet of red roses and asked her pointed questions about whether her voice was really up to par and about believability in opera roles, a not-so-sly dig, according to Leo, at the fact that at fifty-six she is about to do *Madame Butterfly* at the Met.

I am still wondering what Isabel's real motives might be behind all her kindness, but nonetheless, at the airport terminal I thanked her in a druggily effusive manner that I think embarrassed her a little. "I still can't quite believe that anyone other than Myra could have such an interest in my life," I told her and she smiled conspiratorially at me. "Oh yes," she said, rolling her eyes, "mothers."

My last interview with Felice: We sat face-to-face this time; no longer allowed to keep to the bed, I was forced to walk three times a day now, loaded down with all kinds of instructions about exercise and stretching when I reached my new destination. I sat across from Felice, a small table between us with two cups of tea and a plate of cookies that looked like ginger snaps and tasted like very dry graham crackers.

"It's important that you continue therapy in the states," Felice said. "You should be prepared for anything, any emotion that might come up."

"Better late than never, huh?" I said.

Felice looked perplexed.

"I was making a little joke," I said.

Felice smiled wanly. "Anyway," she continued, "I was speaking of what you might expect in the next few months. It would be useful for you to know that there are some fairly standard responses to delayed grief, some or all of which you may experience."

"Delayed by what?"

Felice ignored me. "For instance, I would describe what you are feeling now as a form of shock. I think you're probably already aware that that's what's happening to you—you're a smart woman, Eve, and that can save or ruin you, depending on what you do with those smarts."

She'd never talked to me like this before. There was a hard edge in her voice, urgency in her manner, as if she was done with the prologue and was now getting to the meat of her material. "So far you've been fairly numb, right? You've been compliant and polite and occasionally cracked wise and the nurses have tended to put things in your chart like 'doing as well as can be expected.' From what you've said to me you feel very little—like you're in a dream, like you'll be all right if you just don't have to think about anything. You must know that you will not remain in this condition."

Ah, yes, I thought, but you don't know about my cocktails. I had my little hoard and all kinds of plans about what to say to the doctors to increase my supply. So far the doctors had been surprisingly compliant about my medication requests. I suspected it was because they too didn't know how to cope with what had happened. I thought, I most certainly can remain in this condition indefinitely—I absolutely plan on it. I sipped my tea. It was strong and bitter and I had a momentary memory flash to someone handing me a big mug of the stuff soon after they pulled me off the rocks—some large man in a dark sweater and knit cap who smelled like seaweed and carried me like a baby to the shore and no further because he was afraid of doing me damage. I had this image of him holding a huge mug of tea under my nose and urging me to drink. But how could this have happened? Was the man wandering the beach carrying a cup? Did he go back to his house and come back? Did he take me somewhere and feed and warm me before calling an ambulance? How could this memory be real? How then, could it be a memory? I felt flooded with hope at the thought that I couldn't trust my own memory.

"Eve, I'm telling you all this so that you take seriously the need to continue therapy and to continue the meds for a good time to come. You're listening to me, aren't you Eve?"

"Oh, yes." I was still buoyant from the idea that the whole thing might be some enormous mental illness I was suffering from—some aberration of brain chemistry and synapses so severe that I could actually imagine myself to be the victim of the most unspeakable tragedy when in fact I was merely a raving lunatic. In which case, in which case Jessica and Nicholas could come to visit me in the bin.

For a few minutes I was joyous.

Turkey cried a little when I left. Myra rolled me down the hospital corridor, noting the phalanx of Lavender Ladies grouped in front of the nurses' station. I walked out the automatic doors of the hospital for the first and last time, Myra and Walter trailing behind me with the four canvas bags of mail that had accumulated. This was partly how Myra had convinced me she should stay in New York for a while. To help me "get settled" and to go through all the mail and sort it out. She'd already pored over the letters from publishers and was urging me to respond to one of them.

"You always used to talk about wanting to write," she said one morning a few days before we were to leave. She was accompanying me down the hospital corridor—a task the nurses had entirely given over to Myra, or perhaps she had wrested it from them. I no longer needed to lean on someone to walk—it wasn't exactly a pleasant sensation, but the pain of moving on my own had considerably diminished. Still, Myra had offered her sturdy arm the first day we walked together and I now took it automatically every time we ventured out of my room—the way I had done when I was small and sure that if I let go of her hand, Myra would lose me forever.

"I did write, Ma. I wrote for a profession," I said.

"Oh yes," Myra said dismissively, "that commercial stuff, well, I wasn't counting that. Do you count that?" She waved at a nurse at the station whom I didn't recognize. In three days Myra had learned more names than I had in the whole time I'd been here.

I told Myra that I guessed my seventeen years as an advertising copywriter didn't count as serious writing. Who, after all, would want their obituary to list as artistic accomplishments their being the author of "it won't let you down" in regard to a brand of cheap coffee or "the one for the rest of us" describing a particularly user-friendly type of computer? The stories that I used to write at night and almost never had the courage to send out wouldn't count to Myra because she'd never seen them. Only Charlie saw them, and a few editors of literary quarterlies whom he urged me to send them to and who sent back complimentary rejection letters whose nuances of phrasing I was learning to decode for the true level of the editors' future interest in my work. How is it, I wondered, as I moved slowly down the corridor on my mother's arm, that Charlie is the one who first gave me courage to think seriously about my writing and also the one I came to think of as responsible for my stopping altogether? Because everything became subsumed in the boat, the Voyage. Charlie's fault, I had concluded by the time we were actually at sea and I was writing little more than to-do lists.

"So," Myra said, steering me gently back to the room when she saw me falter for a moment. "You used to say you wanted to write a book. You were always a wonderful writer, Eve." We were at the door of the room and I turned to look at her. I am almost a head taller than my mother and yet in my mind she has always loomed large—another reason it's a shock to see the real Myra.

"What makes you say that," I said.

"All the things you wrote when you were a child. The A's you used to get on writing assignments! The letters you wrote home from college. I used to read them to Aunt Jean on the phone and she'd have to put the phone down she'd be laughing so hard. The poems you showed me in junior high." Myra was trying to move me into the room but I was too stunned to move. Myra sighed. "And especially, the letters from the boat. I felt as if I was there with you, that's how vivid, how wonderful they were."

I let Myra maneuver me to the chair. She laughed at the expression on my face. "You're surprised that your old mother remembers all those papers and letters and poems, aren't you?" She smoothed a light blanket over my legs and turned back to the table where the publishers' letters lay. "But I remember everything," she said, in a weak voice. She didn't turn around again for a while.

"Anyway!" she finally said. "About these offers. You do need to think about your finances. These hospital bills . . . I still have some people to talk to, but it looks like your insurance won't cover all your medical costs. I know you and Charlie had your reasons, but I told you, remember, I said that it wasn't a good idea to stint on insurance. . . ." She stopped, saw my face. "Well, never mind that now. The point is you are going to need serious amounts of money. You've been in the hospital two months. You have months more of physical therapy and medication and all the rest of it to go. Eventually you'll want to settle someplace permanently." She raised her eyebrows in an expectant expression.

"I can't think about all that right now, Myra," I said.

"I just don't see . . ." she began, then she pursed her lips—Myra's universal sign for "there's so much I could say but look at how well I'm biting my tongue." Usually this would elicit enough guilt in me to make me let her have her say. This time, though, I simply watched her struggle with her impulses. "I just don't see, Eve, why you prefer to stay with strangers rather than your own family. Do you really think that these people can help you more than I can?"

"I'm not looking for help," I said.

She caught her breath. "Well I just don't understand. What can these people offer you that your own family can't. God knows we're all suffering too. . . ."

I let her go on for a while. In all the fights I've had with her through the years, her ingenious blend of guilt-inducing arguments and anger have defeated me time and again. If I'd only known how powerful indifference was.

She gave in, though, sooner than I would have thought. She was even able to be gracious to Leo and Isabel.

Now, watching her surreptitiously watch me from the next seat, I wonder what has engendered this change in my mother. Has she simply mellowed with age? Did I exaggerate her pushiness and criticism, or has what's happened shocked her into some new, more reticent personality? If I could still feel anything good, I'd feel revivified love for my mother. What I do feel though, when I feel anything at all, is something ugly and malignant, a kind of furious jealousy. If I'm not vigilant, I find myself looking at Myra's ravaged face and wanting to grab her, to shake her until her teeth rattle. I want to make her suffer for what she has not lost. Yes, she has also suffered terrible losses, but she has something still that neither I nor Charlie's parents have and so she cannot be suffering as we do. After all, Myra's child survived.

I drift in and out of consciousness and so am startled when my stomach flutters from the sensation of going down. I grip the cushioned handrests of my seat and try to control my breathing. Myra's hand covers mine. "It's just the plane descending, darling, you remember how that feels."

"Uh huh," I manage.

Myra strokes the back of my taut hand. "You're white as a sheet," she says.

"Ma," I say, "could you get me one of those little triangle-shaped pills please?"

A limousine, long and sleek, is waiting for us in front of baggage claim. The young driver loads Isabel's many bags with deferential good cheer. Leo enters the car first, heading for the couch-like backseat.

"Leo!" Isabel says harshly. "You don't expect Eve to sit in one of those back-facing seats, do you? Or Myra, for that matter."

Leo backs out of the car and holds out his arm to help me into the backseat. "I wasn't thinking," he says, smiling at Myra, whose face goes quite red. I notice how Leo's eyes crinkle when he smiles, in a way I know charms the hell out of Myra.

The car has that leatherette new-car smell that marks my presence back on land as surely as the crowds and airplanes and stoplights and artificially lit night skies. My nose twitches for the sea. As we glide down the highway, Isabel chatters, nonstop it seems, describing her relief to be through with her recitals, her excitement at starting a new opera, her hopes that I'll be comfortable in my new digs.

"The big house is usually unoccupied," she says, "except when Leo and I can get away for a few days."

"Or when you house strays," Leo says.

Isabel throws him an exasperated glance. She is wedged in the backseat between Myra and me and Leo has settled across from us in the jump seat behind the driver.

"You have someone staying at your house now?" Myra asks.

"I was getting to that," Isabel says in her lilting voice. "He is not one of my 'strays.' He's a composer. Noah Stewart. He's writing an opera for me."

"Oh, how exciting," Myra says.

Leo snorts.

"What?" Isabel says, snapping her head in his direction.

Leo crosses his legs—a movement he makes look graceful even in the cramped position of the jump seat. "Well, we haven't seen much of this so-called opera yet, have we."

"Well, now, Leo, that's not really true. Noah's played us some of the first act and Robbie is working on the libretto in the city."

"The first act has taken almost a year."

"It takes as long as it takes, Leo." Her voice quavers and I turn, getting a mouthful of the long hairs on Isabel's white fur coat. Isabel is glaring at Leo, as if trying to get him to say something, or not say something. "This *will* happen, Leo," she says icily. He blinks and coughs at the same time. It's strange to see his smooth exterior suddenly ruffled.

Myra clears her throat. "Where would this opera be performed?"

Isabel laughs. I like her laugh. It trills up and down in a broad, pleasing arc. Perhaps her singing voice sounds like that. "Oh that's the next step. I have a few venues, a few directors in mind. We might go to a regional company first, though if the opera turns out as wonderful as I expect it to, we might go straight to the majors. But Leo's right, first Noah has to finish the opera. It's taking a bit longer than we'd hoped, which is why I have him ensconced at the house. If he'd stayed in that loft in the city I doubt he'd be much beyond the first scene right now. Honestly, Myra, you should have *seen* this place he was living in." She touches Myra's hand with her own. Myra nods in sympathy, imagining, I'm sure, some artistically rat-infested hovel.

"It wasn't the place he was living in that was distracting him, as Isabel well knows," Leo says pointedly.

"Oh Leo, you're impossible." Isabel laughs again but she gives Leo a sharp look. "I'm sure Angelique is a perfectly nice girl. She may be a bit . . . well, forceful, perhaps, and maybe you're right, maybe that was distracting Noah." She turns back to Myra. "Noah's lady love. She's a painter. Very ambitious. According to Noah she has a very . . . strong personality. Treats him like he's a fragile genius. . . ."

". . . Which I'm sure he loves," Leo says.

"Well, maybe so. Anyway, Eve, I just wanted you to know that Noah would be up at the house for the next few months but he won't disturb you in any way. He likes his solitude as much as you do."

"Sounds ideal," I say, and if she notes any sarcasm in my voice she ignores it. After that I turn to look out the window at the unrolling countryside, letting their chatter wash over me.

The countryside is nothing like California's. There are large expanses of green land interspersed with thick glades of trees. We go for miles without seeing a building, then one lone white or stone building appears, looking as if it dated back to the Revolutionary War. Evening is falling but it's light enough to see that the trees are half bare, and much of the land is covered with a profusion of leaves in varying burnt shades of orange and brown and olive. I put my palm up against the window and feel the cold. I keep my hand there, watching a thin fog form on the glass in the shape of my hand. An eerie feeling comes over me and I turn to look ahead. Through the thick glass that separates the passengers from the driver, I can see the driver's eyes fixed on me in the rearview mirror. He has no expression, is just gazing at me with neutral interest—another of the idle rich—no cares that can't be paid away, he might be thinking, but not unkindly. I meet his eyes briefly, then close mine.

It's getting dark when we arrive. We pull into the circular drive and stop in front of the two-story house that looks smaller than I guess it really is.

"We should just check with Noah," Isabel says as the chauffeur comes around to open the passenger doors. "I gave him detailed instructions about getting the guest house ready, but I just want to be sure he did it all before I send you down there." There is an almost frantic efficiency about her, as if the twenty-some hours we've been traveling have not affected her at all. I, on the other hand, feel a familiar, profound exhaustion. I make no move to get out of the car. I lay my head back on the plush leather seat and close my eyes. As I begin to drift a jolt of panic hits me and I sit up abruptly, heart throbbing. I was seeing myself spread-eagled at the bottom of the dinghy, my face mashed into the rough damp wood, immobilized. If I could just sleep, I remember thinking; if I could just close my eyes. And was jolted awake just like this, over and over again for hours.

"Are you coming, Eve?" Leo leans into the car, holding out his hand to me. His craggy, handsome face looks concerned rather than peeved, but he can probably be a good actor when he wants to.

"Could I just wait here for a bit do you think?"

"Absolutely," Leo says. "You just stay right there. We'll drive down to the guest house in a minute. Your mother is just using the bathroom."

"I can be left alone you know."

"Of course you can," Leo says briskly and is gone.

The night is black but low lamps light the circular drive, sending a ghostly glow over the gravel. I smell cigarette smoke. I open the car door and ease myself out. The chauffeur is leaning against the limousine, his cap pulled over his eyes, smoke trailing out of his nose. He seems to be contemplating his shoes, which glow in the reflection from the misty lights. When he hears my step on the gravel he turns and nods to me and silently holds out his cigarette pack.

It's Marlboro Lights. My brand, when I smoked. The familiar gold-and-white box looks delicious. I take a cigarette and put it between my lips. He holds out a lighter.

"I'm sorry," I say softly. "I can't lean over." So he walks up to me, very close. He lights my cigarette, cupping his cold hands around my colder ones. I choke a little on the smoke. He hesitates, giving me a quizzical look, ready to help, but not insisting on helping. I smile and he resumes his position leaning against the car, one ankle crossed over the other, his hat low. I inhale the cigarette lightly this time, and savor the way it rasps in my lungs.

The chauffeur stares into the black void beyond the drive. It's the first time I've been with someone other than Felice who doesn't feel the need to fill up silence. It strikes me then that this is the longest I've been outdoors in two months and by instinct I lift my head to look at the stars, a habit from the boat. The sky is clear and the stars waver in the blackness, like the stars in all the waters and countries I've been. But these stars are spread out in a completely unfamiliar pattern, as if tossed like children's playing jacks into the night sky. A curl of smoke escapes my mouth and sails upward.

I have smoked two cigarettes by the time they come back. Myra has freshened her makeup and Isabel carries a pile of linens in her arms. Isabel and Myra come around to the side of the car where I'm standing, both of them clucking disapproval at me out in the cold air. "Why didn't you come in?" Isabel demands.

"It was nice out here," I say. I have to smile, noting that Myra makes no comment on the obvious smell of cigarette smoke that clings to me. Myra, who used to lecture both me and Charlie mercilessly, cataloging the relatives and friends who died horrible deaths, pointing out that Molly had never so much as taken a drag in her whole life (Myra was never above exploiting one sister to make a point to the other). In the end it was wanting to get pregnant that made Charlie and me quit, but we let Myra think that the years of haranguing had finally paid off.

We continue down the driveway, beyond the main house, and arrive in few minutes at the guest cottage. When I emerge from the car this time the ground gives way under me like water and then I am being swept up by a wave except it feels so secure and constricted and no of course it isn't a wave, it's someone's arms it must be that boy's arms—stronger and more functional than they look, sweeping me up and carrying me away to someplace where I can sleep.

4

I awaken to sun, hard and bright in my eyes, and my first thought once again is that I am back in the dinghy. My second thought is Oh, I see, there's a window next to this bed the chauffer put me in; is he the one who took off my clothes, did he glimpse my ravaged body and, as he did last night, make no comment, offer no comfort? No one has drawn the drapes, which are cream-colored with a blue rose-bud pattern. I can simply draw them tonight and I won't wake up thinking I'm at sea.

It is morning. Or afternoon. I am sitting in the living room of the guest house. The kitchen is behind the wall that I am looking at, in front of which sit a television set, a VCR and a stereo. The kitchen is barely large enough for one person to walk around in, according to Myra, who has already cased the whole house thoroughly. Still, Myra has admitted, the kitchen, indeed the whole house, contains everything you could need—microwave, blender, oven, coffeemaker. The fireplace works. All the amenities, Myra declared triumphantly, reminding me eerily of myself the day I showed her around the *Orlando* after she'd been all fitted out—the television, the VCR, the tiny washer and dryer in the forepeak.

I watch the television in an overstuffed chair covered with the same cheery fabric as the drapes on the bedroom window. My chair is next to the couch where Myra slept, refusing, no matter what I said, to trade places—"You need a good mattress until your back is completely healed. I'm fine darling," like a parody of a self-sacrificing Jewish mother. I am watching *The Price Is Right*, surprised to find that the show is still on the air. Bob Barker looks like he's dyed his hair silver. I put a hand to my own hair, unaccountably still honey colored. If I didn't have Myra's good genes, I'd be stark white by now.

"My goodness they've thought of everything," Myra calls from the kitchen. "There's eggs, bread, cheese—even fresh milk."

I rouse myself. "They probably sent the composer to the store."

"Well, it's awfully nice of them, don't you think? Who would take in a perfect stranger and house her rent free indefinitely and then be sure to stock the refrigerator?"

Who indeed. I take note of Myra's change of heart regarding the Steins. They've completely charmed her. I, on the other hand, am still wondering what Isabel Stein's angle could be. I am actually beginning to consider the possibility that Isabel is exactly what Leo called her—a collector of strays—just because she has a big heart and a big purse. And certainly, I'm like something the cat dragged in. On the other hand, I am just as sure that Leo is less than a Good Samaritan. Before I met him I guessed that he simply acquiesced to all his wife's whims because she was the stronger personality. But now I suspect it's Leo I should be wary of, though once again I can't figure out what I have that anyone would covet.

"Scrambled or fried?" Myra is leaning against the kitchen door frame pointing a white plastic spatula at me. I mute the television and look up.

"And don't give me that look and tell me that you're not hungry because every time you say that that's another day I'm staying, to be sure you eat." The spatula bobs up and down.

"In that case, scrambled," I say.

Myra is relentless. "We're going to have a routine, darling," she says. "That's the only way we'll get through this."

And so we do: At eight Myra pads into the bedroom in her new fuzzy slippers and shakes me until I open my eyes. "You're taking too many of those pills," she'll say every once in a while and if she weren't in charge of them I'd ignore her, but instead I try to perk up, assure her that I'm fine. She tends to look at me skeptically. She waddles me off to the shower where I stand under the hottest water I can tolerate, scalding some sensation into my skin. Then she trots me over for breakfast, then our first walk of the day through the woods behind the Steins' country house. A graveled path snakes behind the main house and past the guest cottage. Soon after, the gravel runs out and the terrain gets hillier. We take the inclines slowly as they make my vertebrae feel like saw blades. The trees that line our walk are the kind I've only ever seen amassed in L.A. parking lots at Christmas time. I asked Myra once if she thought the Steins chopped one down every Christmas and she looked at me like I was crazy. "I'm *sure* they don't celebrate Christmas," she hissed, as if to think anything different was to preclude her friendship with them. Part of how she's worked out their generosity to me—to us—is that they're acting on shared ethnicity, a thousand-year history of victimhood to be rectified in small acts of charity.

The walks are beautiful. I recognize this in the sturdy reaching of the barren tree trunks, in the profusion of colors that paint the leaves, carpeting the tree bases and crunching under our feet—the pumpkins and siennas that I imagine look like the light that hits an Italian piazza at dusk. I couldn't wait to see Italy, couldn't wait to drink Chianti with Charlie and see Michelangelos and indulge Jessie's obsession with Roman ruins that emerged mysteriously one day, as sudden and intense as some boys' obsession with dinosaurs. Needless to say, we never got there.

I breathe in the sharpness of the chilled air that is so different from the stinging smog of an L.A. afternoon or the salty thickness that coats your lungs in the middle of the sea. This air tastes as if it's been purified—thin and piercing, it crackles in the lungs. Occasionally I shiver in the navy blue wool coat Isabel lent me, which is supposed to reach my knees but barely covers my thighs, with sleeves that end well above my wrists. But I welcome the sensation.

After walking is stretching and weight lifting, now that Myra got into Kent, the small town a few miles away, to buy up a storm. Weights to strengthen my arms, my neck, to build muscle and bone. I am suddenly weak as a child, uncertain on my feet as an old lady—I who had become so strong over the years, the muscles in my arms bulging like a man's from tailing the line when we hoisted the sails and rowing the dinghy and swabbing the deck and the countless other tasks that left me aching and oddly satisfied at the end of a long day. I could lift Jessie in one arm and Nick in the other and did so just to hear Nick's goofy laugh and see Jessica's tentative smile that indicated her confusion as to whether or not this game threatened her dignity.

Myra spends most of the rest of the day going through the mountains of mail—hundreds of cards and letters. "If people knew where you were now the stuff 'd still be coming in daily," she says, which I interpret to mean that on her trip to town she couldn't resist stopping at the magazine stands. The most gossip Myra has ever allowed herself to descend to is of the sort found in *People* magazine. Molly bought her a subscription to it soon after our father died, and though Myra made a show of disdaining the gift, on every subsequent visit to her house I came across dog-eared issues scattered around. As far as I know Myra still turns up her nose at the sight of frazzled housewives thumbing through the pages of the *National Enquirer*, the *Gazette*, the *Star*, but at a time like this, it seems, even Myra has difficulty resisting the lure of her daughter's name or face in garish, smudged colors calling from the pages of publications she'd never be caught dead reading in ordinary circumstances. It's impossible, it seems, to hold out against the irresistible lure of tragedy with its conferment of instant celebrity, even when the tragedy is yours.

For instance, one day a couple of weeks ago when Myra was up at the Big House (as we've both fallen into referring to it, like *Upstairs Downstairs*, said Myra) I fell asleep in front of a game show and woke up to the image of a woman with hair the color of lemon peel screaming into a microphone that clearly Tawanda was a terrible mother and there ought to be a law about who could have babies and who couldn't. Cut to Tawanda whose face was hidden by hundreds of dangling beaded braids, weeping silently. Cut to the white-haired host approaching Tawanda, kneeling in front of her. Do you *want* to change, he kept asking her. Because I can't help if you don't *want* to change. I had to find out what Tawanda had done to earn the disfavor of the audience and the smarmy concern of the talk show host, not to mention her own shame.

It turned out that Tawanda had not had a chance to do damage to her children—her offense was that she kept having them and giving them up for adoption. Chump change, I thought.

"At least watch Oprah," Myra says. "If you have to watch that stuff let it be Oprah, who at least has a brain and something like a conscience." But Myra doesn't understand that the whole point is to watch the most revolting and exploitive shows. I want to hear the worst stories. Each one I then secretly measure against my own story—testing it like a new product against its competitors—"not nearly as horrible," "as horrible," "much much much more horrible." It has become justification for getting up in the morning, this little contest I run with the woebegone of the world. I keep winning, but I am looking to lose.

A couple of nights a week Myra eats up at the Big House. She tries to get me to accompany her but I tell her I'm not ready. Myra usually comes back with her cheeks flushed from wine and her eyes glowing from conversation.

"I'm going to the city with Isabel and Leo when they go back on Tuesday," Myra informs me one night about a month into our stay. "I want to get you a few things and arrange about doctors."

I have just taken a pill so I simply nod my heavy head.

"Both Isabel and I would love for you to come shopping with us."

She is standing in the door of the bedroom, wearing the same dress she's worn twice this week already. It strikes me that she packed very little when she came racing across the ocean and that in the shopping trips she's made already she obviously hasn't bought a thing for herself.

"She'd really like to see you, Eve. But you know she won't come down here without an express invitation."

"What about Leo," I say.

"He's less inclined to come down here but he always asks after you."

"I think Leo wishes I were gone. I think he wishes that guy were gone too. I think he wants Isabel all to himself."

"I don't know what gave you this sour attitude about him, Eve. This man has been nothing but kind to both of us since the beginning. I saw that man lift you in his arms and carry you like a scared puppy into this very bed."

"When?"

"When? the night we got here, of course, that's when."

"Leo carried me?"

"Yes, of course. Who else?"

"I somehow thought it was the chauffeur."

"Who?" Myra says.

"Forget it," I say. "Listen, Ma, I will see them, I promise. Soon."

"Come into New York with us?" Myra says with a hopeful smile.

"Another time," I say.

She frowns. "You know, you have to come sometime soon. You've got to see the doctors."

"Uh huh," I say.

"You've only got a couple of weeks worth of medication left," she says cannily.

I am momentarily nervous, but then it occurs to me that I have no idea if I will make it to a couple of weeks from now so I don't let it bother me.

"Why don't you bring Isabel back here after you come back if you like."

"I told you, they're staying in the city for a while. Isabel has to start working on *Butterfly* beginning next week. They'll only be coming out the occasional weekend."

"Well as soon as they come back then," I say. Myra gives me an exasperated look and turns away to make up her bed.

She stacks the flowered cushions in a neat pile to the side of the couch and pulls out the hidden bed. She moves so slowly now. In my memories she's always racing around like a wind-up toy, never idle, hands never empty. Bending over tables and ironing boards and stoves and my bed late at night, a cool kiss on my forehead, a silky hand smoothing back my hair. I watch her spread the sheet over the bed and smooth its corners to perfection. It occurs to me that if I asked her to, she'd be happy to sit beside me as she used to, stroking my forehead and planting kisses on my cheek. I don't ask. I close my eyes and wait for her to go away. But not too far.

In the days until she leaves for New York City, Myra makes a lot of phone calls, writing down various appointments in a new leather-covered pocket calendar I am somehow sure Leo has given her. Myra keeps insisting that the Steins are two of the most charming people she has ever met. As for the young man, Noah, well he could stand to learn a few manners, but Isabel seems very fond of him.

The night before she goes to the city, Myra informs me that she is leaving me some of the letters she's read through so far. "Only the really meaningful ones, I swear it. I've weeded out all the nonsense. These are people with heartfelt things to say. Please look them over while I'm gone, Eve," she says. "I can't handle it all alone—writing to all these people—at some point you're going to have to take it over."

"Burn them," I say under my breath.

I don't look at the letters she left. I don't walk and I don't stretch and I don't lift weights. I watch television and sleep. At around four I am pouring myself a glass of chardonnay when the phone rings. It's Molly with her every-other-day call. I try to sound competent and healthy. I pick my words carefully so that they won't slur from the muscle relaxants and antidepressants on top of the chardonnay. Molly is her usual efficient, concerned self. Am I eating, is my back healing, how is Myra holding up. When am I coming home. Yes yes fine and I don't know. "Can I come see you then, Eve?" Molly says and her voice pains me.

"Yes of course, Molly," I say impulsively. "I miss you."

She begins to cry. "That's the first time you've said that," she sobs. "It means so much to me."

More than once recently Myra has gently chastised me for my treatment of Molly. "She's your sister and she loves you so much. You've always been so cold to her." This surprises me. I never felt as if I was particularly cold to Molly. I just thought that she and I had so little in common that our relationship was based almost entirely on shared genes. We had the occasional barbecue or trip to the zoo or Disneyland with Molly's family, but I thought it was more that our kids liked Molly's three a lot—Kevin and Sarah, the two oldest, were very good with Nick and Jessie—neither of them was far enough into adolescence yet to ignore and disdain them, and Alice, the youngest, was only a year older than Nick, so they played together well. I never thought that George and Molly particularly enjoyed our company—we tended to get along best just watching our children enjoy each other. George is a civil engineer and thinks of advertising as glamorous, so Charlie and I could always find things to talk about to him. But Molly and I really had to stretch to keep the conversational ball rolling. We couldn't be more different if we were completely unrelated. Molly did everything my parents wanted—she became a teacher, got married in her early twenties, bought increasingly bigger and newer houses with George. I, on the other hand, took a corporate job and had artistic pretensions—I married a man whose foremost goal was to desert his in-laws for four years and take their daughter and grandchildren with him.

I tell Molly that whenever she wants she can visit. Her voice lightens and after we hang up I imagine her wiping her eyes and smiling a little to herself, some of her pain alleviated, and I am reminded again of how far-reaching the fingers of loss are.

At about five the doorbell rings. I had dozed off in the flowered chair; my empty wineglass fallen. The news is on the television. Usually Myra is here to turn it off and I fumble for the remote control. The bell rings again. I've never heard it before. Surprisingly, it is a typical suburban ding dong. Somehow I expected Isabel to have chimes—something vaguely operatic—to announce visitors. I ease myself out of the chair, and, holding on to the wall, go to answer it. I can't imagine who it could be other than someone to tell me that something happened to Myra.

It's raining and getting dark. I flip on the outside light. A man in a night watchman's cap stands dripping at the door. His right hand is shoved into a dark leather jacket and his left holds a plate of food covered with plastic wrap. As soon as I open the door he thrusts the plate out, as if anxious to dispense with his errand as quickly as possible. I wonder if the pills and drink have made me hallucinate a pizza delivery man.

"I'm Noah," the apparition says, his voice impatient. "Myra asked me to bring this down to you since she's not going to be back till after supper." When I don't respond right away he pushes the plate further toward me. "It's a little wet out here," he says, snappishly. I rouse myself and take the plate and thank him. I suppose I should invite him inside but I'm having a little difficulty focusing. I'm wearing a sweatshirt with sweatpants that don't match. My hair is plastered to my head and I can just catch a whiff of my own, housebound odor. As soon as I take the plate he turns to go. He turns back, though, to say that he is going to pick up Myra from the train station at 8:20. I can't tell if he's informing me or inviting me. He doesn't seem at all happy with the task. In the dim light I can make out a profusion of dark curls brushing his neck, eyes glowering under the hat cuff. "I *have* to get back to work now," he says, as if I'd demanded that he stay.

5

Myra lets me sleep in in the morning and it's after ten when I hobble heavy-headed into the living room. She sits at the small desk next to the fireplace looking at yet more mail. She wears a deep purple sweater that flatters her pale coloring. "New sweater?" I ask.

"I picked it up in New York when I bought you a few things. They're by the couch over there in that shopping bag. Anything you don't like you can return when you get to the city. The shopping there!" She says all this while sorting envelopes and cards, without once looking at me.

"Thanks, I'll look at them later. Is there coffee?"

"In the kitchen, as always."

She is hunched over her task but I hear the impatience in her voice. I pour myself a cup of coffee in the kitchen and come back in, settling into my chair. As I am reaching for the remote control I hear Myra's chair scrape on the hardwood floor. Then she is next to me, dropping something in my lap. At first I think it's mail and I start to protest until I see that it's a legal pad and pen.

"What's this," I say.

"This," she says in her best mother voice, "is the beginning of your writing career."

She makes me get up so she can move my chair around to face the couch, where she perches herself, her hands primly in her lap. I brace myself against my chair, feeling a bit panicky without the remote control in my hand. Myra begins quietly, almost tentatively—not her usual lecture voice.

"I've spent most of the morning trying to think of the best order to say things I need to say to you and how to word things. I want to start by saying that I love you more than I can bear, and I am doing only things I believe will help you, even if you don't."

Omigod, I think, it's going to be as bad as that.

Myra resettles in her seat, smoothing nonexistent wrinkles in her black wool slacks with her plump hand. "First of all, I ran a number of errands yesterday besides shopping. I did see the doctor who has your X rays—his name is Dr. Wallace and he's very nice, I think you'll like him. I made you an appointment for October 20th. It's a Monday and Isabel and Leo will be able to give you a ride to the city. Dr. Wallace is very positive about your prognosis. And you should also know," here Myra hesitates, reaches her hand out as if to smooth her pants again but instead reaches over to touch my knee. "You should know that I found him a very sensitive person—he knows all about your situation and he won't push you any faster than he thinks you can handle. For now he wants to take more X rays to determine if you need more physical therapy. He wants to be sure you don't suffer permanent damage."

I don't point out the obvious. I say, "Did you get a new prescription for muscle relaxants?"

Myra clucks her teeth. "I didn't. I asked, but he wouldn't give it to me. Said he had to examine you first."

I start to speak but she interrupts me.

"You have enough to last you through to your appointment. And maybe by that time you won't need them." Her voice becomes animated. "You must think I'm the same fool you thought I was when you were a kid if you think I'm not aware that you're taking too many of those pills and that you're sometimes drinking along with them. I told the doctor I can't distinguish when you're really in pain from when you just want to go away. He said that he could understand that. Actually, Dr. Shepard said something similar."

"Who's Dr. Shepard?" I say, dispiritedly.

"She's the psychiatrist I went to see."

I snap to. "You didn't tell me you were going to see a shrink."

"Didn't I?" Myra says, her eyes wide. "I guess I assumed you'd assume."

"That's bullshit, Myra."

"I hardly think you have to use that kind of language to express yourself," Myra says reflexively. I can tell that her heart wasn't in it. "Anyway, I went to Dr. Shepard as much for myself as for you, if you want to know the truth. I've been so distraught—so unsure of how to handle things."

This throws me. To me Myra has been the picture of confidence and efficiency. I have, in fact, been obsessively questioning whether this change has occurred in the two years since I've seen her. But perhaps it began in the years my father got sick and she had to take over a deskful of financial obligations, car repairs, phone calls to plumbers and lawyers and bankers that he had always seen to, playing nurse as he became increasingly debilitated and, after all these years of quiet acquiescence, telling *him* what to do. Now I realize that over the three years of her widowhood, this new air of certainty has solidified.

"So did this psychiatrist help you," I say gently.

Myra gives me a penetrating look. "She did, in fact. I talked for over an hour about . . . well, about you, about the accident . . . about . . . well, you know, Charlieandthekids." That last said in a torrent as if she were holding a hand over her mouth to shield me from her words. "She helped me think about how I can cope with it all . . . actions . . . you know, that I can take."

"What kinds of actions," I say.

"Well, for one thing . . ." Myra pauses and reaches into her pants pocket, pulls out a Kleenex and wipes her eyes before they've even gotten wet. "You know it's a very hard thing for people of my generation . . . well, it's not like we raised you kids religiously at all or anything, but there are certain rituals . . ." Her voice breaks and she pauses. When she starts to speak again she is really crying, but she pushes on anyway.

"The fact that there were no funerals. This is very hard for me. And for Lucy and Ed too. In our religion you must bury the bodies twenty-four hours after . . . It's been almost three months. At least with your father there was . . . Dr. Shepard called it something—'emotional closure,' or something, but whatever." She waves her tissue in the air as if pushing away the remnants of psychobabble. "The point is, I saw them put your father in the ground." She hesitates before the word "ground," hunches her shoulders. "I sat *shiva* for a week. I couldn't deny the fact that Nathan was dead, that I was really alone and going to have to look out for myself. But with . . . in this situation, especially because I hadn't seen you in so long and—" She sneaks a sly look at me before returning her gaze to her mangled tissue. "—I didn't see you all that much before that."

"Myra," I say in mock horror, "Mother guilt, at a time like this?"

She ignores me. "You know, to this day I wake up almost every morning and reach across to touch your father's sleeping face. And every morning I get a jolt that he's not there. I have to *re*-remember every day. I've even gotten myself a single bed since you've been gone." She looks up at me, her face striped by tears. "Did you know that? But it didn't work. I may not feel as empty as I did three years ago, but every single day, from the moment I wake up to the instant coffee I make because there's no one there to share a pot with, to the one car in the garage, I re-remember. Nathan is dead. I am alone. I am a widow. Sometimes I say it out loud to myself over my coffee, like I'm saying *Kaddish*." She squeezes her hands together. "But you know what? Sometimes I'm grateful for those reminders. It keeps my life feeling . . . well, real, I guess. We're supposed to say the *Kaddish* every week for the first year, you know. I think this may be why—we say it until we don't have to be reminded to remember the dead."

She clears her throat. "But there's nothing like that with the kids and Charlie. I'm so used to their not being around anyway that there's nothing to force me to remember. So then when I do remember, it's so much worse than anything I feel about your father. It's like falling in space to think of them—nothing to grab onto like an empty bed or dinner for one. Nothing to give me . . . oh what the hell was it . . ."

"Emotional closure," I say.

"Yes, right. I need to say good-bye to those babies, Eve." She is trying to unfold her tissue but it is flaking off in snowy particles onto her lap. I push myself out of my chair and go into the bedroom to get her the box of Kleenex there. When I come back in, her face is in her hands. I touch her shoulder and hand her the box. "Myra," I force myself to say, "There were no bodies."

She pulls a fresh Kleenex to her face and sobs. We stay like that a while—Myra crying into successions of thin tissues, me standing straight because I can't lean over, my hand clumsily perched on her shoulder like a dead weight, watching her cry with a kind of scientific sympathy, thinking, This is what it looks like, this is what unbearable pain acts like.

Finally she composes herself, brings her right hand up to her shoulder to pat mine, tries to smile. "I'm all right, darling, go sit back down."

My palm is wet from its heavy purchase on her shoulder.

"Of course I know there couldn't actually be funerals," Myra begins again, "and with you injured there was no question of memorial services right away. Of course Lucy and Ed are aware of that too. It's just that we're hungry for something, for some marking of what's happened. I'm just telling you how we feel, darling, not that it can be any different."

I picture Charlie's parents in their tract house in the desert where they retired five years ago. Where they are only just getting to know their neighbors; Charlie's two sisters far-flung in L.A. and Oregon; many of their own friends dead or back in L.A. Charlie tried to talk them out of moving and isolating themselves so completely from their past. What, I wonder, do these new neighbors—whom I imagine to be resolutely tanned and Protestant—make of covered mirrors and candles burning twenty-four hours a day and platters of food arriving in the arms of those few friends they do have left?

"I'm sorry," I say.

"Don't be sorry, darling. It wasn't for you to think about. You have your own trials. I just needed someone to talk to about it and Dr. Shepard was very helpful. She also wouldn't renew your medications without seeing you, but she said she'd evaluate you on the 20th. She said to be sure that you especially did not mix the antianxiety pills with alcohol."

"Don't you think you're treating me like a child?" I say. But all I really care about is that I have enough medication for now. Come the 20th I can devise some reason to postpone my appointments and get refills for the interim.

"No one's treating you like a child. In fact, there's one more thing I wanted to tell you about my talk with Dr. Shepard. When I was talking about how difficult it is without any ceremony, she came up with the suggestion that we do hold a memorial service for . . ."

"Oh no oh no." I start to push myself out of the chair, closing my eyes to shut out her voice, and Myra is at my side, easing me back in the chair, soothing voice assuring me it's not what I think, it's something she wants to do when she gets back home—with Lucy and Ed and Molly and Charlie's sisters—nothing to do with you Eve if you don't want it to be, not yet, this is about me, about us, this is not for you.

I gulp down some breaths and try to slow my heart. I finally say, "Okay, okay Ma, that's fine with me just as long as you don't expect me to do anything and now could we please change the subject."

"I only wanted to tell you this because it spurred me into another area which I took up with her, about when I should leave. And we both agreed that it should be soon. That's really why I wanted to tell you this now. I went from Dr. Wallace's office to the American Airlines office and I booked my return ticket for three weeks from now. October 19th, right before your appointments. So maybe we'll all go to the city together and spend my last day there. I'm going home, Eve."

At any other time in my life, if you had told me that I would be anything less than relieved to see my mother leave me after a long visit, I would have said you were thinking about another Eve, a more charitable, patient Eve. But I do not feel relief. I feel panic. Betrayal. How could she—how dare she—Myra, whose stifling love has been the subject of more than a few years of angst; Myra, who claimed to love her children so much that she gave up teaching, the job she adored, for the first thirteen years of my life to stay home and be the perfect mother; Myra, who, when Jessie and Nick were born, moved in and drove me crazy a hundred different ways and yet without whom I think I would have given the new child back or else killed Charlie, or both.

"Darling," she says in the nourishing voice she used to use when I was sick, "you didn't even want me to come in the first place, if you remember."

"No, I . . ."

"I wouldn't be doing this if I didn't think it was best for you. Dr. Shepard said it's too easy to become accustomed to having other people take care of you and that it can lead to a kind of permanent invalidism. And I know what she means. If I don't wake you, you don't get out of bed. If I don't feed you, you don't eat. At some point, Eve, *you* have to make the decision that you want to go on with your life. And there are things I need to do at home. Things for Charlie's parents." She is crying again, quietly.

"Ma," I say, "I'll wake up on my own from now on. I swear."

"Oh baby." She moves so quickly from the couch to the side of my chair that I don't really see the action, just feel her arms around me, her hands pressing my face into her chest, my cheek meeting the center of her right breast, pliant and ample as I remember it, and I know then that I have to let her go, that keeping her with me is too easy.

"I'll change the ticket," Myra says, "I won't leave till you tell me to."

"No." With some effort I pull my head away from her chest. "You're right. You need to go. You should do a memorial service if you want. Something that will give you some comfort—and Ed and Lucy. I haven't thought enough about them, I haven't . . ."

"Shh," Myra says, "shh." She pulls my head back to her chest, strokes my hair, murmuring childhood endearments.

Later we eat a brunch of the fresh bagels and whitefish salad she brought back from New York. While I am gnawing at half a bagel she drops her last bombshell.

"There was one other place I went when I was in the city," she says, overly matter-of-fact.

"Where was that," I say, putting down my bagel.

"I went to see a literary agent."

"What?"

"You know, an agent who represents authors; makes deals for them with publishers."

"I know what agents are, Myra, I want to know why you went to one. How did you even know to find one?"

"Well, actually, it was Leo who made the appointment for me. I figured I'd tell you about it afterwards, in case it came to nothing." Myra takes a nonchalant bite of her bagel, then meets my gaze defiantly.

"I had told Leo and Isabel about the letters from the publishers and how you were thinking about writing about your experiences. Well, both Leo and Isabel pointed out that it would be crazy for you to negotiate directly with any publishers. They said it's like any artistic endeavor—you need a professional negotiating for you or you'll get screwed on the money."

I push my chair back. "Do you hear yourself, Myra, do you hear yourself?"

"Listen to me," Myra says. "I'm just being practical. Nothing I've done obliges you to do anything. Eve, how do you think you can support yourself in the near future?" She reaches toward me.

I recoil. "There's the money we had left in the bank," I say, my voice low with the effort to keep from shouting.

"Minus your medical costs. I'm sorry to be harsh, darling, but you barely have the clothes on your back." She takes a deliberate bite of her bagel and chews it carefully, letting the silence build. "You'll be wanting to get your own place and start replacing the things you've lost."

She stops abruptly. I glare at her until she meets my eyes. "You know what I meant," she says gently. Then, more defiantly, "Do you think you're in any condition to go back to work?"

"If I have to," I snap.

"Well, you have a lot of healing, physical and mental, that you have to do before any doctor is going to certify you well enough to go back."

I take a deep breath. As quickly as it flared, my fury abates. What does all this matter?

"There's the boat insurance money," I say wearily.

"Which you don't know when you'll see. Now supposing you did decide to write a book," she persists. "According to this agent, you could get half your money up front. And he seems to think it would be . . . a lot of money. If you invest it wisely, you could never have to worry about money again. Add to that the fact that Dr. Shepard thinks that writing it all down—regardless of what you do with it—could be healing. Supposing your story was worth a million dollars—don't look like that, darling, this guy was bouncing around numbers like that—"

She goes on in that vein for some time. She barely takes a breath between sentences, anticipating my objections, but I say nothing—it all sounds surreal. "Investments," "income," "future." Words that used to mean something. Words that kept me up nights—me and Charlie—words for the living. Now the idea of where or how I would get money just can't adjust itself into a serious concern in my head. My thinking comes to an abrupt halt no more than a few days into the future. It's not so much that I think I'm about to die, as that I'm certain that any day now there will simply be no existence for me. "Ma," I say at last, "I'll think about it, okay?" And she smiles and pulls out a business card from her pants pocket, handing it to me shyly.

The pad mostly sits on the coffee table for the three weeks that are left to Myra, who, to her credit, does not harp on it. We keep to our routine, though I pick up the pad while watching television, for her sake, and make meaningless doodles.

One Saturday afternoon I am hunched over in the living room, swinging three-pound hand weights. Each movement makes a small crunching noise in my shoulder but contains no real pain. The doorbell rings. All aflutter, Myra ushers Isabel in. I said that Isabel should come anytime she wanted but I'm not prepared right at this moment, sweaty and foul-tempered as I am. On the other hand, her arrival is an excuse to stop exercising so I push back my damp hair and take Isabel's soft, extended hand, surprised at the firmness of her handshake. She exudes an air of studied casualness—crisp white shirt and faded jeans hugging her plump hips.

"I hope I'm not disturbing you," she says. She smiles, showing many of her teeth. Myra settles her on the couch and goes into the kitchen to make tea. "You look so much better," Isabel says. "You have a bit of color and you're . . ." She pauses, laughs girlishly. "I was going to say 'taller,' you look tall, which of course you are, aren't you, although everyone looks tall to someone like me, but what I *meant* was, you're not as stooped over as you were before. You really are *quite* lovely, you know, with that height, and your lovely hair."

I am standing in front of her, glistening with sweat, my hair plastered to my head, and yet she almost has me convinced that she means what she says. The rather caustic reply I was planning dies on my lips. Isabel holds out to me the shopping bag I hadn't noticed she was carrying. "I brought you these on Myra's suggestion," she says. "I hope you know I'm not in the habit of thrusting my work on people who aren't interested."

I take the bag. There must be thirty CDs inside. I lift one out. *Don Giovanni* it says above a drawing of an Elizabethan cavalier. Underneath the drawing are the names of several people—I only recognize Isabel's.

"They're a few of my albums," Isabel says, lowering her eyes. Her auburn hair glints in the recessed lighting. Her small hands flutter. "There's some recital albums and a few complete operas. I'm afraid I've never liked the sound of an operatic voice singing standards—that's what Myra asked me for since she knows you don't like opera. But I never made any of those. I did include a couple of Dawn Upshaw albums—she's one of the few sopranos who can alter her voice to sound more . . . well . . . pop, and I think she's quite successful at it. Anyway." Isabel laughs and shakes her head, as if shrugging off her own discomfort. "I brought these all because Myra seems to think that if you listen now, you might . . . you know . . . appreciate opera in a way you didn't when you were a kid."

"She told you the *Madame Butterfly* story," I say.

Isabel looks at me from under her lids. All of her gestures and expressions, her lack of self-consciousness about displaying her curvaceous body, make her seem much younger than fifty-six. "My mother had this terrible tendency to tell stories about when I was six and danced naked into one of her dinner parties or said something that embarrassed the hell out of her at the time but which somehow turns cute at my expense later."

"I know exactly what you mean," I say. "Myra has those too." We smile at each other. There are lovely crinkles around her eyes.

"Anyway, feel free to just put these on a shelf and never listen to them. It's really okay. But it makes Myra feel good to think that . . ."

"I know," I say. "She wants me to show an interest in the world. It's like when I was ten and she wanted me to join the Brownies because she thought I spent too much time in my room reading. She thinks I'm constantly on the brink of being pathologically antisocial." Isabel smiles again and then I see my chance.

"Why am I here?" I ask her.

"What do you mean?"

"Here, in your house. Why do you want me? I only present a difficulty for you."

She takes a moment. "You present a lesson to me. In survival. It seems to me it's everyone's obligation to be there for our survivors. Look at all the mail you've gotten—more than all the fan mail *I* get. I'm not the only one who feels responsible for you."

Her expression is completely guileless and I can't think of a single reason not to take her at her word.

Myra comes in with tea.

Isabel turns out to be more modest than I took her for. During tea Myra keeps trying to get her to tell me about all her musical triumphs but she demurs, saying things like "I doubt Eve is very interested in that kind of thing." So it is left to Myra to impress upon me what an accomplishment it was for Isabel to be a finalist in the Metropolitan Opera competition at twenty and how impressive it is that she is still going strong all these years later, doing *Butterfly* at the Met, no less.

"In some ways opera is a very forgiving medium," Isabel says, sipping her tea. "Other than a few obnoxious critics, no one blinks an eye when a middle-aged woman plays a fifteen-year-old geisha. In that way we're much more fortunate than actors. Old hags like me can still get good work."

"Oh now," Myra said, waving her hand at Isabel, "you're in your prime. Me, I'm an old lady, but you're still young—both of you." A nod to me.

Isabel gives me a sidelong, knowing smile, then turns to Myra. "You know the best part about being a successful opera singer?" she says. She presses down her left index finger with her right one. "For one thing, you get to feel like you've never worked a day in your life because you are doing the thing that gives you the most pleasure in the world. For another," she ticks off the next finger, "you have the most loyal adoring fans who are always there, even on the days you feel ugly and like your voice is made of sandpaper. Men write you letters telling you how beautiful you are and what joy you've brought to their lives—they pledge eternal faithfulness; they propose marriage."

"Really!"

"Third, you get to play out your most intense feelings and you're applauded for it instead of considered crazy. And best of all. You get all that, and on top of it, nobody cares if you're fat."

Myra laughs heartily. Something shakes itself out of me that might be a chuckle.

"Anyway, there aren't a lot of operatic parts for middle-aged women. That's why I'm excited about Noah's opera."

"Oh yes, tell Eve about the opera," Myra says eagerly.

"Maybe Eve's tired." Isabel looks at me.

"No," I say. "Really, between you and the barbells, it's no contest."

Isabel chatters on but her smile begins to shimmer like heat waves before my eyes. Blood rushing through my head. Isabel going on about Noah's genius, the opera about the English queen, Henry VIII, money notes, riding the waves, Jessie's laughter, the aria of the winches, the chant of the creaking hull.

"Are you all right Eve?" Myra's voice above everything else, sharp, insistent.

"Just tired." I force myself to lift my head.

"I should go," Isabel says, getting up.

"Oh, no," Myra says. They both look at me.

"Excuse me," I say, "I think I'll just go lie down for a while."

Although I suppose that I actually like Isabel, I didn't agree to go to dinner at the house because of that. The idea of sitting politely at a table with real linens and salad forks, the idea of having to make any kind of conversation at all feels not so much impossible as ludicrous. I agreed to go to this farewell dinner for Myra partly because the Steins have been letting me stay in this little house for weeks now without a demand or uninvited intrusion, and partly to prove to Myra—and, I suppose, to the Steins themselves, who are perhaps a little worried about their liability should anything happen to me—that I am functioning and competent. Able to access my own medications. Can be counted on not to off myself.

Myra bought me mostly lounging clothes: sweatpants; a loose caftan; three high-necked, flannel nightgowns. Old-lady clothes. For the dinner at the Big House, however, she bought me a pretty, pale violet dress that swirls down to my calves. She tried to get me to put galoshes over the violet flats she got me to match, but I refused—the shoes were half a size too big anyway and with galoshes to weight them down they'd come right off at the first hint of wet ground, I told her. But I was also conscious of the impression I would make. I had visions of Leo taking one look at me, declaring me too unfashionable for them to risk anything more on, and throwing me out into the street.

The rain has abated to a fine mist but I still cling to Myra's arm as we trudge up the road. Halfway up the gravel drive Leo comes out with an umbrella. He takes Myra's arm and holds the umbrella over both of us, ushering us up the walk like the valet parking guy at the overpriced restaurants favored by my clients when I was in advertising. "So good to see you, Eve!" he exclaims, and I manage a tight smile.

The inside of the house is far less baronial than I expected. Instead of soaring ceilings and sweeping staircases, it has low, wood-beamed ceilings. The dark wood walls make the house dim in the dusky light. Leo takes our coats and leads us down the two steps to the living room, which registers in my brain like a painting, in one dusky impression. Everything from the salmon, camel-backed couch to the mahogany secretary table with the stained-glass lamp looks as if it came with the original house. Molly would be able to identify it all—whether the table under the leaded window was, in fact, mahogany and the lamp Tiffany, what period the couch dated from, the name of the manufacturer of the porcelain shepherd and shepherdess on the mantle above the crackling fire. The ceiling in this room is so low that every time that Leo stands up I'm afraid he's going to hit his head. Certainly, if he lifted his hands up he could palm the ancient wood—so inky and smooth that it looks wet.

On the coffee table sits a platter of alternating slices of orange and white cheese glistening with droplets of oil, a basket of crackers and a bowl of black olives. "What will you have to drink?" Leo asks brightly. Myra says a vodka tonic. I have recently taken two muscle relaxants and ask for a glass of red wine. Leo gestures for us to sit down as he pours. Myra takes the chair whose poofy cushions match the fabric on the couch where I sit gingerly. It gives softly under my weight and I lean against its surprisingly plush back. I was assuming that living in this house would be like living in a museum, but like so many of my assumptions about the Steins' life, that is proving to be incorrect. Everything is beautiful, yes, but the house has been decorated with at least an equal eye to comfort as to aesthetics.

Leo brings our drinks and turns to stoke the fire. "Isabel and Noah will be in in a minute. They're fussing over the ravioli."

I drink my wine. It slips down my throat like warm silk and almost instantly my fingers loosen around my glass, which I realize I'd been grasping to within an inch of its life.

"Isabel said Noah was a terrific cook," Myra says as Leo fixes his own drink.

"Yes, so she says," Leo says, a sneer coating his voice. "I guess the couple of times she's been up here without me he's cooked for her. So," he walks back to us, clinking the ice in a large highball and smiling smoothly, "tonight we're in for a treat. I'm told pasta is his specialty." He unfolds himself onto the chair opposite Myra's, next to the fire, crossing his black courduory-clad legs with the grace of a dancer. His arms rest proprietarily on the arms of his chair. Despite its grandeur, the chair is no match for Leo's insouciant elegance. Wherever Leo sits, I think he will always look enthroned.

Leo samples his drink and makes no immediate attempt at further conversation. For the first time I hear singing—a female voice, plaintive and echoing, seeming to come from so far away that I might be imagining it. Leo cocks his head. "That's Iz," he says. "*Un bel di*, you know it?"

I shake my head.

"From *Butterfly*, the most famous aria." He pauses and we all listen to the faint but pure notes floating down the hall. I close my eyes and drift away on the music—with some help from the pills and wine. "She's singing it for Noah," Leo says abruptly. Myra coughs. "She has a problem with phrasing sometimes," Leo hurries on. "He's probably helping her. I hope they don't overcook the ravioli." We listen again, but the singing has stopped. Leo turns all his attention to me. "So, how are you feeling these days, Eve?"

"Uh," I scramble, "My back improves every day."

"She still needs to see the orthopedist. You will see that she keeps her appointments after I'm gone, won't you Leo?" Myra interjects.

Leo lifts his shapely eyebrows.

"Ma, you don't have to be asking people to look after me. Especially not Leo and Isabel, who've done enough already."

Leo rises, his slim frame moving in front of me. He lifts the platter and holds it out to me, the tangy smell of good cheese stinging my nostrils. "Well," he says, "we just might have to consider a relocation for you, if you're going to be in the city that much."

It's something I haven't thought about, spending a lot of time in the city. There might be a kind of anonymity in its distracted crowds that the empty countryside doesn't afford me. The open stretches make me feel exposed—as if anyone looking could find me too easily.

I reach for a piece of cheese without answering Leo. What, after all, can I say? I am, in a sense, at his mercy. I am living on his property—on his charity. If he announced that he was going to relocate me there wouldn't be much I could do about it. Except break away and find my own place. The thought makes me dizzy. I can no more imagine taking off on my own than I can think of returning with Myra to California and all the care and cloying sympathy waiting for me there.

Myra is clearly disappointed that Leo isn't proposing a plan, promising to look out for me. Typically, Myra expects everyone she knows to have the same concerns and priorities as she. She expected it of her children, but, more embarrassingly, she's always expected that my friends, my friends' parents, my teachers, should all agree that my well-being, my health, my good behavior was paramount. I feel the same flood of embarrassment for her that I used to as a child when she'd corner one of my teachers, not content to just get a progress report, but insisting on telling the teacher the minutiae of my life. I remember tired young women's eyes rolling as Myra droned on about my propensity to spend too much time alone in my room, my shallow sleep, and yes, even my occasional constipation.

Just as the silence is becoming uncomfortable, Isabel appears at the door. She is breathless and laughing, an elaborately embroidered blue dress falling loosely around her to the floor. Streaks of white cross her forehead and chin and her hair is falling out of a bun on the top of her head. She embraces Myra, then approaches me with her hand outstretched, quickly pulling back again and wiping it on a checkered towel she carries and laughing again. "I've got flour all over me! Noah has made a right mess in there—you should see his hair!" After wiping her hand she gives it again to me to shake. "Pour me a Lillet, will you Leo," she says, still looking at me. "I can't tell you how glad we are that you've come. I hope this will be the first of many meals we share."

"Speaking of which," Leo says, rising, "when do you suppose this famous dinner will grace our table?"

"Ha! Sooner than you think, my dears. Noah is not the neatest of chefs but he knows his stuff. You should see what he does with his hands. How that boy can knead!" She is still chuckling when Leo hands her a drink. Taking it, she drops her smile. "No, really, it should just be a few minutes longer. You've all gotten drinks and you're having some of this wonderful cheese? We have this *fabulous* shop in the Village, did you tell them Leo? They just sell cheese—acres of it—from all over the world. I found Abondance there, which is made in just the Savoie region of France. *Not* easy to find. Delicious. This is Edam and Wisconsin cheddar, actually. I didn't know your taste so I didn't want to get anything too exotic. Did you have some olives?"

Myra assures her that we are well taken care of and that she can go back to the kitchen if she needs to. "Oh no, I'm not going back in there, Noah will drill me through another aria! Did you hear me squeaking in there, Eve, didn't I sound like something the cat dragged in?" She gives me the sort of look that Jessica had perfected, wide blinking eyes and twitching mouth, the expression of someone whom anything but praise will clearly destroy. It got me every time.

"It was lovely," I say with more feeling than I intended. Isabel smiles delightedly.

Dinner: we are seated around a large table whose dark wood matches that of the walls and floors. The walls are bare save for a giant oil painting behind Leo's chair, of Isabel in the breeches and brocade coat and feathered hat of a 17th-century gentleman. More candles burn on the table; the brass chandelier overhead is dimmed. The tablecloth feels like silk. The crystal wine glasses are tall and paper thin.

I am alone on my side of the table. Leo opens two bottles of wine—one red, one white. I'd take one of each if it wouldn't raise eyebrows. I'm feeling comfortably dreamy, the wine a perfect accompaniment to the painkillers and antidepressants. I'm wondering when this will wear off. "Isn't this all so beautiful," Myra says, admiring the cut-glass butter dish, the small bowl of white flowers in the middle of the table.

Isabel comes in carrying four salad plates—three of them lined precariously up her arm. "My waitressing days," she smiles. "They've come in so handy since!" Leo narrows his eyes. "It's Noah's wrists, remember?" she says, moving about the table and placing salad plates in front of each of us. Just as she is taking her seat, Noah walks in, dressed completely in black—corduroy pants and a turtleneck sweater framing his prominent chin, a painful grimace distorting his features. I stifle a giggle by sticking my face in my oversized red wine goblet. All he needs is a missing ear to complete the picture of the tortured artist. Noah carries the fifth salad plate before him in two hands as if the weight were too much to bear. Emerging from the long sleeves of his sweater, both of his hands appear to be wrapped in beige material, laced up like some instrument of torture.

He places the last salad in front of Isabel and takes his seat next to Myra, nodding gravely to everyone at the table. "Dinner will be just a few minutes," he says, sounding as if he were announcing the death of a loved one. He bows his head over his salad and his heavy curls fall over his face. His hair is cut in that fashionable way that Nick wanted and that I resisted—very short underneath, but the top layers left long, which has the effect of making your hair fall perpetually into your eyes. I wouldn't give in to Nick's demands and pleas. He had hair like Noah's—curly and thick and utterly unruly. I pointed out how his friends who had the cut he wanted all had straight thin hair that fell into place without even being combed. As compensation I let him grow his hair long but it wasn't what he wanted—he *wanted* it falling in his eyes. I wouldn't let him have that, and for the voyage I made both him and Jess cut their hair to within an inch of its life.

The diamond carving in the stem of the wineglass cuts into my palm and I gently lower it to the table. The hundreds, maybe thousands of trivial things that I denied them, thinking that each of my victories mattered, that I was seeing to it that my children didn't become selfish or spoiled; I parceled out their freedom to them in the delusion that when they were grown they would be responsible, frugal adults, thinking first about the welfare and responsibility of their own children and on down the generations.

Noah lifts his face and peers at me, curling one corner of his mouth. I was right about the brooding, long-lashed eyes. His nose rises sharply at his brow then descends in a straight, Roman statue plane that ends just above his upper lip. If it weren't for the sneery, slightly sour expression which seems to go with his face in repose, he would be beautiful.

"Have you two ever officially met?" Isabel says brightly. She shifts in her chair a little and looks at Noah as if she were trying to communicate something silently to him.

"Officially, no," he says sullenly. "How do you do."

I smile weakly and spear some salad.

"Noah will be here much more than Leo or me," Isabel says, glancing across the table at Leo. "For the next few months Leo will only make the weekends." Noah looks up sharply. Isabel keeps looking at Leo. "I might be able to make it a bit more often, Eve, depending on my schedule. Noah has kindly offered to be at your service—drive you anywhere you might need to go, get your groceries or whatever. But we don't want to interrupt his work too much so I'll try to do some of that for you too."

"You don't have to—" I begin, but Isabel goes on.

"No, well, I wouldn't disturb you," she says, turning to me. "I really do so much prefer to be here than the city, lately. If I can possibly get away, I will."

"I'd say it's unlikely, Isabel," Leo says.

Noah shoots him a look. "I'm going to need to run the revisions on the first scenes by you," he says to Isabel.

It's the longest sentence I've heard him speak so far. He has a deep, resonant voice that he uses almost without any inflection.

"Well, you may have to come to the city for that," Leo says, lifting his red wineglass. He sips, then adds, "I'm sure you want to see your girlfriend—Angelique, isn't it? The painter? If she's anything like I am, she must miss you a lot when you are off with the muses." He smiles sardonically. Immediately, I visualize a thin delicate creature with fluttering hands and darting eyes, pacing the floor of her apartment waiting for Noah's return.

Noah looks like he's about to say something but Isabel gets there first. "I'm sure Noah can arrange some trips to the city but we don't want to interrupt him too often. It'll work out, Leo, rehearsals don't start for another month and I'm keeping the coaching schedule light. I mean, how many times have I done *Butterfly?* And the recitals will be a piece of cake."

"So you keep saying." Leo rises with his salad plate and moves around the room collecting everyone else's. "But I still say you should see Doctor Hershberg a few times."

Isabel hands Leo her plate and pats his hand. "You worry about me too much, darling." She turns to me. "Leo is concerned that I'm not fully recovered from the tonsillitis."

"It's not that, and you know it," Leo says coolly. He reaches out his hand to Noah who murmurs, "I'm not finished," and goes back to contemplating his half-eaten salad.

"I simply think you need to acknowledge that the last bout might have weakened your voice and you need some work and attention to strengthen it. Does that sound crazy?" He directs this at Myra, who looks uncomfortable and shakes her head. Leo leaves with the salad plates. Noah focuses his brooding gaze on Isabel, who looks quickly at Myra and me and then says, "We'll work it out. My voice is fine, Noah, don't worry, I will do justice to Catherine."

"That's not what I'm worried about," Noah says. He pushes back his chair and fairly stomps out of the dining room with his salad plate.

Isabel laughs in a forced-sounding way. "I'm afraid they're a little jealous of each other," she says, pushing a few fallen tendrils back up toward her bun. "Jealous of my time."

Dinner is pasta, veal in lemon and butter, fresh green beans, roasted potatoes, then lemon tart, coffee, after-dinner drinks. To my surprise, each flavor is more intense and delicious than the last. How can I still take so much pleasure in food?

Compliments all round to the taciturn Noah, who is clearly in competition with me for the grimmest guest.

We sip cognac, which I've never liked much but is so useful in perpetuating the lovely buzz I've been cultivating all evening. Leo chats about his business, which seems primarily to be made up of managing the commodity that is Isabel. Not just her performances, but sales of her CDs, pictures, the fanciful autobiography ghostwritten two years ago, television rights to her performances, tee shirts even. Myra expresses surprise that there's so much—well, *business* in opera. "I thought that sort of thing was reserved for movie stars and athletes."

Isabel laughs. "You think opera is above all that crass commercialism, huh?"

"It should be," Noah interjects. Both Leo and Isabel give him similar looks of tolerant amusement.

"Why?" Leo says simply.

Noah stares at his cognac but speaks emphatically. "The work should speak for itself, shouldn't it? Great singers, composers, musicians, they should be celebrated for their talents and gifts—not for their pretty faces or overdeveloped biceps. Opera is becoming Hollywood, corrupted by turning artists into commodities."

Isabel laughs again. "But Noah, darling, you have to admit: name identification, recognition, fame, if you will, these are essential to an artist's real success. Like it or not, if you don't achieve some level of recognition by the public, you don't get to practice your art, or else you do so in a vacuum." She gives him the kind of look you'd give a puppy who'd done some small mischief that you can't quite be angry about.

"If you're good, you should be able to carve out your living because of your talent for your art, not your talent for self-promotion. *You* don't do it, Isabel. You don't act outrageously or throw tantrums or do whatever it takes to get your name in the paper."

"Maybe I should," Isabel says dryly.

Noah starts to reply but Leo interrupts him. "At any rate," Leo says, uncorking the cognac decanter and making the rounds of the room. "If you think about it, Noah, you need the very fame you deplore if you ever expect your operas to have more than one-night debuts before they fade into obscurity."

As Leo approaches, Noah puts his hand over his glass. Myra takes the opportunity of this brief silence to ask Leo if his being a lawyer helps him in his work and he says certainly, in contract negotiations, rights sales, and all that, and I swear Myra throws me a look that says there's how you get a country villa and an apartment on the Upper East Side and a limousine to ride around in, there's a worthwhile thing to be doing with your life, not sailing away on doomed adventures. Luckily, I'm too buzzed to take up the gauntlet. I turn away to see Noah staring at Isabel, who appears to be listening intently to Leo and Myra's discussion but who, I am sure, is nonetheless aware of his steadfast gaze. Her cheeks are flushed and she is blinking a lot, as if her fluttering lashes speak some secret language.

"What are those things on your hands," I say to Noah. All night I have been staring at the things that look like clip-on, full-length, fingerless gloves.

He looks at his hands as if to see for himself. Then he gives me the blankest of expressions, which somehow manages to convey the utter ignorance that my question betrays. "For my wrists," he says. He lifts his glass of cognac, indicating that this will be the sum total of his explanation.

"Noah has a repetitive stress injury," Isabel says. "From playing the piano. He has to be very careful of his wrists. Those are braces for them. He's supposed to wear them as much as possible, right Noah?" Noah sips his cognac. "I say he got it from the horrible chair he uses at that loft he shares with Angelique. It was too low, not a proper piano bench at all."

"It was all I had, Isabel," Noah says.

"I know that, I'm just saying that it was another reason to bring you back here where the music studio is beautifully outfitted, where the piano bench is state of the art."

"Sounds ideal," I say heartily, and every eye turns to me in collective surprise, as if I've just awakened from a coma. "I do speak," I say, and everyone, except Noah, laughs.

6

Leo drives us into the city in his Jaguar. Isabel, Myra and I sit in silence for most of the journey. Isabel's head is partly diminished by the high collar of her white lynx coat, and Myra is pressing against my arm in the back seat, occasionally sniffling and dabbing at her eyes with well-worn Kleenex. *You should be coming home with me*, these sounds and gestures say, *You can't really mean to deprive me of your presence when I've already lost so much*. We are crossing the bridge, Leo weaving through honking, howling traffic, and the city rises before us like in a Woody Allen movie, the high-rises graduated and sparkling like jeweled staircases. Myra exclaims at the perfect views and Isabel says dramatically, "I never get tired of this moment. Seeing it all as if for the first time."

I came to New York a few times for business—before the kids were born and I asked to be removed from the accounts that require a lot of travel. I can still recall the way my stomach dropped away at the sight of the island as the plane lowered itself onto the landscape. I remember thinking that I had fallen in love with something I could never have—the teeming, rising city, whose energy matched something in me. The car speeds down the drive along the river, and it occurs to me suddenly that I could live here now, if I wanted to, I could live anywhere I chose. I realize this with a jolt of something like fright—the concept of having this kind of choice having disappeared from my life when I married someone who already had his future so mapped out.

I dreamed about this, fantasized about being on my own and moving where I wanted, taking into consideration no one's preferences or needs but my own. Thought I was like every other mother who tires and becomes resentful of the constant need to be unselfish. But now I wonder if I was wishing too hard, wanting too powerfully. If I crossed some line.

"What, dear," Myra says. I look down and see that I am gripping her hand until her fingers are overlapping each other.

"We'll be there soon," Leo says, as if he's seen this exchange. "Another few blocks."

Isabel turns back toward us. "You know, if you're up to it, I'd like to take you around a bit, show you some of the museums maybe."

"And if *you're* not otherwise engaged," Leo says. "You have coaching, appointments with Hershberg, publicity gigs, don't forget, Iz."

"I'm sure I can find a little time to spend with Eve if she's so inclined," Isabel says coolly. "Leo would have me working twenty-four hours a day," she tells us in a pseudo-whisper.

We pull up to a glass-fronted skyscraper whose entrance, with its potted shrubs and sliding glass doors and gold trim-uniformed doorman, looks more like a hotel than an apartment house. The doorman glides to the car and opens Isabel's and Myra's doors at the same time. He takes Isabel's hand with all the delicacy with which he might handle a baby chick and she rises out of the car as if there were cameras on her, all grace and humility and self-conscious beauty. Leo opens my door and I take his perfunctorily offered hand to rise with as much clumsiness as Isabel has shown grace. The doorman is old, with lines like crevices running down the sides of his mouth, but his reverent gaze is that of a boy's. Isabel continues to hold her hand out like royalty, her wrist cocked at a 45-degree angle, the tips of her fingers resting in his white-gloved palm.

"*So* nice to see you again, Eric," she intones, and again I have the feeling that somewhere there are cameras and microphones, that she is speaking for more than just this one besotted man. Indeed, two women heading to the door have stopped and are staring at us, the taller one leaning down toward the shorter one, who is clutching her Gristede's plastic bag to her chest as she rivets her gaze to Isabel. I'm not sure if they recognize her exactly, or if they simply are aware that this is a personage, someone they think they should know, someone who almost certainly has been on television. A newspaper of some kind sticks out of the Gristede's bag. I shrink back as this moment prolongs itself, Eric placing his other hand over Isabel's and seeming to be overcome with emotion, saying, "It's wonderful to see you, Miss Stein, you look lovely as always," his voice hushed, worshipful, the one woman rustling her shopping bag and the other grappling with her purse, looking for something; Leo watches Isabel court this almost nonexistent audience, something catlike and self-satisfied in his immobile attention; Myra is off to one side like a handmaiden, with her overstuffed pocketbook and bulging totebag. All I can think about is the newspaper in the shopping bag, the likelihood that it's a tabloid, that it might contain my face, grainy and blotched and stretched like a comic-strip panel on a piece of Silly Putty. The thousands of people now who know me without knowing me. How can Isabel stand it? How can she *court* it?

"We just have a few things, Eric," Isabel says to the doorman, her voice smooth and rich as pudding. "We'll only be a few days. We have some guests." She dislodges her hand from Eric's and waves it in a regal arc, turning to Myra. "Shall we?" She touches Myra's shoulder and guides her toward the entrance, looking back at me and inclining her head to indicate that I should follow and if a camera were recording the moment it would not miss the solicitude she shows to an older woman, the humble bend of her impressive head. At the entrance to the building we are met by the two shoppers, the shorter of whom has found a pen and a used envelope which she now thrusts at Isabel with a kind of aggressive shyness. Isabel raises a hand to her mouth, the gesture that of a child who has received an unexpected and delightful gift. "How sweet," she says, smiling at the woman, who bats her eyes as if flirting. The woman nudges her companion, who laughs nervously and says, "We don't mean to disturb you."

"Of *course* not," Isabel says, the pen flying over the envelope. "How could you? It's *lovely* to see fans." She hands the envelope and pen back to the shorter woman.

"We live on the 12th floor," the woman babbles. "I'm 12 C and she's 12 F."

"*How* lovely," Isabel smiles. As she speaks she manages to maneuver her way around the two women so she's well inside the lobby. "*So* nice to meet you," Isabel says to the two women as she deliberately turns her back. The women look confused for a moment, then seem to understand that they have been dismissed. I notice the one holding the envelope peering down at it, as if uncertain of the signature.

I sleep restlessly in the Steins' twenty-first-floor apartment and awaken to that terrifying jolt of disorientation I've had periodically since the accident. I lie on the huge bed, waiting for my heart to slow, and stare up at the molding. I have a room to myself—Myra is next door and the faint rumbling of her snoring is audible through the wall. The bed is hard, the sheets soft and my aching back is grateful. Today Myra leaves and I have agreed to go to the airport but I consider reneging. I consider lying here all day staring at the ceiling till I see a crack, a chip, some flaw in Leo and Isabel's perfect home. Lying here for days or months, for the rest of my life, or until everything changes back to the way it was, whichever comes first.

At the last minute it turns out that Leo and Isabel arranged to upgrade Myra's ticket to First Class, which seals Myra's already undying devotion to them. Isabel has a doctor's appointment, so only Leo is at the airport to receive the full force of Myra's gratitude. At the ticket counter she clings to him, weeping prodigiously, until the right shoulder of his navy cashmere coat is black. Leo endures it. He pats Myra's head and lets her return to his arms three times. "Everything will be all right," he tells her, and I feel a rush of gratitude toward him that surprises me.

Myra extracts multiple promises that Leo will look after me, make sure I see all the right doctors, the book agent, the error of my ways. Leo waits at the ticket counter while I walk with Myra to the security checkpoint. "What the hell is this!" she demands when she sees the signs that only ticket holders can go beyond this point. "This town!" she says, grabbing my arm and pulling me toward the cafeteria. "They don't trust anybody. I can't imagine what you see in this city, Eve."

We buy coffees we have no intention of drinking and find a table in a relatively unpopulated corner. Above Myra's head a television blares. This morning I took a muscle relaxant along with my antidepressant and one antianxiety pill and everything has a bit of an echo. Myra makes small talk and I focus on the television, where the camera peers down unsteadily from a helicopter as a blue pickup speeds down the highway, followed closely by a squadron of police cars.

"So is there anything you want me to tell Molly?"

"Like what," I say.

Myra sighs. "I don't know. That you love her, I guess. That you hope to see her soon?"

"I love her," I say. "Tell her that, if you think it will help."

"When do you think you'll come back?"

I have a vision of Molly's backyard—the patio with the gas barbecue, the sparkling pool, the plastic slide and Kevin sliding down it to splash into the deep end with Sarah and Alice, who, in reality, last time I saw her, had not yet learned to swim. But in this vision they are all there, splashing and screaming with laughter while George, clad in long red barbecue mitts, waves and smiles at them as Molly sits at the umbrella-ed patio table, sipping raspberry iced tea and looking as if nothing in her life is missing.

"Don't know, Ma," I say. I pat her hand and stand up. We walk back to the security check. There's a long line now, people looking impatient at the delay. Myra smiles shyly at me. "I love you so much," she says simply.

"I know."

"I want you to come with me more than anything."

"I know." I wait for her to cry, but her eyes remain clear, her voice steady.

"Okay. You have to do what's best for you right now. The only thing I ask you, darling, is that you consider the fact that you may not be thinking entirely clearly right now. Maybe you have to . . . you know . . . trust other people's judgment. I'm not saying me," she hastens to add, "but I'm just saying. You must be sure you see the doctors—the psychiatrist—you must pay attention to what they say." She grips my arm. "But be careful Eve. It's hard to tell who really has your best interests at heart—outside of family. Don't assume that everyone does." She seems about to say something more, then changes her mind.

"Don't worry," I say. I think of Cousin Birdie who sent the pictures to the press and consider Myra's comments about trusting family. We stand together awkwardly for a moment, both looking at the floor. Finally I say, "Almost there," since we are nearly at the front of the line.

She looks up at me; now her eyes are teary. "I don't understand this God," she says. She blinks and tears run down her face. Something lurches inside me. I'm an agnostic at best, but I forgot that Myra isn't and that along with everything else, she has to reconcile how her God could do this horrible thing to her family.

"Neither do I, Myra." I hug her hard and start to turn away. She touches my arm. I turn around again and she's weeping openly, but also smiling. "You're a strong girl. I know you will be all right. Do you?"

Rather than lie, I don't say anything. Myra reaches her hand up and places it on my right cheek. Her hand is smooth and smells of the almond in her lotion. She used to do this whenever I was upset about anything that didn't have to do with her. She was a great comforter when someone else had hurt you, one hand on your cheek and the other on your forehead, like a faith healer. That's how it used to be. Myra reluctantly removes her hand and gathers her things; she walks through the metal detector that does not sound an alarm as she goes through. It seems a fitting symbol that Myra passes back to the other side, the world I can no longer imagine being part of. Her head bobs in between the crush of bodies that have converged on the long corridor to the terminal gates. Her small hand lifts up, the fingers wiggling in a blind wave. I watch until she is swallowed up completely and then I stay there a while longer.

People brush past me and I am rooted, feeling like nothing so much as my twelve-year-old self waiting in front of the school for Myra, who was always late to pick me up, me always standing in front of the empty building, toeing the concrete and hanging my head like Little Orphan Annie, plotting revenge—I wouldn't speak to her on the whole ride home, I'd eat an entire bag of Oreos and get chocolate on the furniture, I'd reveal the location of Molly's stash of cigarettes. I was so furious that I was crying, so bereft that I felt exactly as I do now.

Not furious that she's going—I want her to go—but that she's going with such confidence in me. She would arrive at school at last, careening up to the curb in her wood-paneled station wagon, blithely unaware of my state of mind. If I said a word about her being late she'd hiss at me the list of the million and one things she had to do before picking me up, implying my gross ingratitude in asking that I be moved up on that list, and anyway, it wasn't nearly as late as I was making out and why did I always have to complain, there were some kids who had to walk home, I was welcome to do that. I'd shrivel, not because of her anger—which I somehow knew even then was a veneer for her guilt—but because of her lack of concern for what might have happened to me. Her certainty that at twelve years old I was perfectly capable of taking care of myself felt like the worst kind of abandonment. Just now Myra walked away with that same set of assumptions that seem so erroneous to me—assumptions about a different daughter altogether.

The echo of the airport rises—conversations and computers and unintelligible announcements over a loudspeaker. People of every imaginable configuration stream around me with grim or joyful purpose, with somewhere to go, someone to welcome, someone to let slip away. They surge against and around me like a raging river parting for a rock embedded in its midst.

When I finally turn to go, a skinny man in a Hawaiian shirt and a woman who is apparently his wife are blocking my way. They both rock on their feet a little, smiling eagerly.

"Excuse me," the man says. "I'm sorry to bother you, but Carol and me couldn't help but notice."

"Couldn't help it," Carol says, nodding. "We saw your picture just a minute ago on the TV," the man says, bobbing more forcefully. "And I say to Carol, isn't that the lady you saw in the *Profile*—"

"And it sure was," Carol beams. She pulls a magazine out of a bag hanging from her shoulder, which says "I ♥ NY" in red letters. Carol thumbs quickly through the magazine and I wait politely because I have the idea that they've somehow mistaken me for Isabel, that I have only to hear them out and then I can set them straight. Carol finds what she's looking for and holds the magazine open to me with a lunatic smile.

There we are again, the same family picture I saw in the hospital in Australia, plus some grainy ones from the hospital itself. And another, new picture of me, actually a very old one, from when I was in college and sported the Farrah Fawcett haircut and heavy eyeliner. Here is the result of Myra's compulsively sending the family pictures to the relatives for every little event. Is it some newly enterprising second cousin who betrayed me? Or the mercenary Cousin Birdie again?

"It is you, isn't it?" the man says.

"We don't mean to intrude," Carol says. She's dropped her smile, as has her husband. "We just wanted to tell you. How we feel for you."

"You're in our prayers." The man puts his hand on my arm. He wears a thick gold ring with a dark stone. He bites his fingernails.

"We pray for you," Carol says. "Bobbie and me have three children of our own. I can't imagine . . ." She shakes her head, tears in her eyes.

The man squeezes my arm. "Can't imagine how you cope," he says, his voice cracking.

"Who'd have thought we'd see you here, in the New York airport? We heard that no one knows where you are. We assumed you'd be in . . . California is it? Isn't that where you come from?" This is Carol, the smile coming back to her face.

"We're from Tucson, ourselves, not that far from you," the man says. "This is our first time in New York."

"I don't think the lady wants to hear that right now, do you, honey? I'm sure you want to get back to . . . well, wherever it is you're going. You're not on our flight, by any chance, are you?"

I shake my head and go back to staring at Bobbie's hand on my arm.

"Was that your mother you were saying good-bye to? How's she holding up?" Carol asks.

"Fine," I say because Bobbie won't let go of my arm.

"And how about . . . was it Charlie? How are his parents? And your all's siblings? We pray for them all."

I have never bitten anyone down to the bone. I consider what Bobbie's flesh would taste like—a little metallic from the dirt he can never quite wash off from whatever work it is he does with his hands. I wonder what his face would look like when he began screaming and begging me to let him go.

"I go to the San Fernando Valley a lot on business, you know," Bobbie says, interrupting my thoughts. "Our office is maybe five miles from your house. Your ex-house, I guess I should say."

"My house?" I say, surprised that I can speak through the clot of panic that's risen in my throat. "You know where I live?"

"Well, uh, yes." Bobbie lets go of my arm and takes a step back, as if he's finally divined my thoughts. "Yes, I mean, it's all been on the news so much."

"We saw your house on the news, it looked lovely," Carol says happily.

"I have to go," I say.

"Of course. We're keeping you," Bobbie says. He throws Carol a knowing look. She responds as if they've rehearsed this.

"Just if you would, before you go . . ." She thrusts the magazine at me along with a black felt-tip pen. "Would you mind just signing the *Profile?* Just to share with all the people at home who are praying for you. It would make them feel their prayers were . . . worthwhile. We'd so appreciate it."

"They won't believe we've met you, otherwise." Bobbie takes a step toward me. Carol follows suit. They're blocking my way. A small group of people is now looking at us, seeing Carol with her pen thrust out to me. "You've made a mistake," I say. "You have the wrong person."

I knock the magazine out of Carol's hand and she steps back in alarm. I plow through the opening she's left me. Behind me I can hear her startled exclamation and Bobbie's anger and the excited buzz of the people who were watching. It seems entirely possible that they would chase me so I race toward the terminal lobby. Leo is waiting in front of the American Airlines counter. I've rarely been so glad to see anyone. He catches me before I fall over completely.

On the drive back Leo asks me no questions about my breathlessness and what I imagine to be my panicked look. He plays the radio and at some point as we race down the highway I ask him to turn to a news station, which seems to surprise him. Still, he complies. I watch the gorgeous earth tones of the dying trees whoosh by us like streaks of paint and listen to a drone-voiced cop describe the details of a crime scene that he and two other officers came upon.

"You really want to listen to this?" Leo says.

"Shh," I say.

The cop is saying that the dead man had apparently just told his wife he was leaving her. The wife allegedly had a handgun, he says.

"Someone recognized you in the airport?" Leo says.

"How did you know?"

"There was a television set over by the chairs where I sat down. I saw the promo for the news. An 'in-depth update,' they said. What? Why are you laughing?"

"'In depth.' Get it? It's a pun."

"Huh," he says. "Like it or not, Eve, you're a kind of celebrity," he continues. "You might as well figure out a way to turn it to your advantage."

"Why do you suppose that is, Leo?" I say.

"What?"

"That people become celebrities because something terrible has happened to them. Why do you think they become public property after that?"

Leo gives me a sardonic smile before returning his gaze to the road. "Oh come on, Eve," he says. "This is the age of confession, isn't it? The people we vote for sure as hell better let us know whom they've slept with and what drugs they've taken. And as long as we're going there, I want to be sure that my favorite actor's stint in the loony bin is open to my inspection as well. Because I want to forgive him; I want to forgive them all. That way, maybe I get a little forgiveness too." He shrugs.

"This is different."

"Yes and no. There are certainly people like Isabel, people who want to be in the public eye, who covet any kind of attention and they get what they deserve, right? For someone like Isabel, even bad press is good press, because—well—it's press, right? And then there are people like you who really are being invaded by the public's hunger for confession and tragedy. But the point is, you, every bit as much as Isabel, are being *empowered* by this."

"That's insane."

"On the contrary," he says coolly. "You are now a celebrity. That confers favors upon you, whether you believe it or not. Six-figure book deals or appearances on talk shows that would be yours for the asking. I'm talking about people offering you obscene sums of money just to tell your story over and over and over again. No need for talent, just have something unspeakable happen to you."

The fingernails of my right hand are sunk so deep in my left arm that the skin begins to ease open. When I speak my voice comes out almost in a whisper. "I don't understand how your mind works, Leo," I say.

He smiles. "It works like America."

7

The next day Isabel and I go to the orthopedist. She insisted on coming with me. I said I'd be fine, but her presence in the cab was vaguely comforting. "I can use the ride," she said, "I've been cooped up all day with Hershberg and then I have the afternoon with the Met coach—I need some air, to see the city in the fall." I believed her, but I also knew she was fulfilling some promise to Myra to look after me.

The doctor races through my examination. "Hmm," he says a lot, probing my back and asking me where and if it hurts, checking the X rays, his fingers moving like he's speed-reading Braille.

He asks the nurse who's been hovering by the door to get Isabel. "I'd like to go over things with both of you," he says, peering at me over the top of his reading glasses. He busies himself with my file while I shiver in my paper gown, but when Isabel comes in he drops what he's doing and rushes to take her hand, looking for a moment as if he is going to kiss it. He is suddenly short of breath and blushing, unable to let go of her hand. "I'm a huge fan," he says. "I saw you in *Tosca* at the Met in '77. One of the great nights of opera."

Isabel bows her head. "It was a fine evening, wasn't it? Those magical nights don't come along too often." She looks almost shy herself, shy and beautiful with her magisterial head cocked and her eyes lowered, her skin glowing from the praise. I can see why she said that men tend to fall in love with her at the drop of a hat. She said it without a trace of ego—she referred to it as a kind of phenomenon, having almost nothing to do with herself as she really was, but rather with all the attributes and gifts that are projected onto her.

There's something to that, I think. Fame is about projection, about people imagining that what you do or what's happened to you could happen to them, imagining then that since they can so readily put themselves in your place—in front of spotlights or paparazzi or surviving a shipwreck—they know how it feels to *be* you, and that, given the opportunity, they have a right to check their imagination out with the reality that *is* you. Like Leo said, there's not much difference in how people behave toward you if your celebrity comes from actual accomplishment, or just plain disaster.

"I was just saying to Eve, her—" the doctor says, and I lose the train of what he's saying because he wasn't talking to me before, he was silent as he poked and prodded, as he frowned over the X rays. He goes on about good progress, the importance of more physical therapy, I even think I hear Myra's name, since indeed she did come to see him. He's very interested in my case, he tells Isabel, and feels he should supervise my care on an ongoing basis. He's making no pretense of talking to me.

"Star Fucker," Isabel says flatly the minute we leave the office. "Did you see? He was dying to ask for my autograph but he thought it would affect his dignity. Did you see how he never looked at you? He talked to me like I was your mother and you were twelve years old." She speaks with contempt, but I didn't notice her trying to dissuade the doctor from ignoring me. As if reading my thoughts, she adds, "On the other hand, I think you got better service from this guy than you would have if I hadn't been there. He's supposed to be one of the best in the city, but he seems a little, well . . . abrupt." She smiles that self-deprecating smile again. "Next time I'll have to tell him—you're in more magazines than I've been in my whole career."

Next stop: Dr. Shepard, the shrink. Asks the usual questions, mumbles the usual platitudes. It's clear that for all her bland ease and friendly smile, she is clueless as to what to do about me and relieved to send me off with prescription renewals and an appointment in a distant month's time.

"Now," Isabel says, "I'm supposed to drop you off at the agent's office. But I don't think I will unless you want me to. Maybe you'd like to come to my coaching session instead."

We are sitting in a cafe drinking cappuccinos. Mine is getting cold. I only agreed to sit down if we could take one of the corner tables indoors—Isabel looked longingly at the wrought-iron chairs set up on the busy sidewalk, but acquiesced.

"Who is this agent?" I ask.

"He's the literary agent Leo knows. Nigel Baker's a terrific guy—did my autobiography a couple of years ago, did you see it?" This last said a shade or two louder than her normal voice. In her usual disarming way she quickly catches herself. "Of course you didn't—you were probably at sea by then, and even if you weren't, you would have hardly been interested in anything about an aging opera diva." She laughs demurely and sips her coffee.

I don't say anything.

"Listen to me. I sound like I'm fishing for compliments, don't I? Well, I suppose I am. You do that a lot at my age. At my stage in my career. I'm *too* heartless to expect it from you, Eve, please forgive me. The book was junk, anyway. I had a ghostwriter who used to get drunk every morning before coming to the apartment. She knew as much about opera as . . . well, as you do, actually. But she'd ghostwritten best-selling biographies of that terribly saintly nun and some football player so the publisher thought she'd put the right spin on the book. It was mostly fiction, believe me—exaggerating my youth, for instance; but it did moderately well. Apparently Nigel's done a little fishing expedition already, and there's enormous interest in your story on the part of a number of publishers."

She suddenly stretches her hand across the table toward mine. It doesn't quite reach. "I told Leo I'd do it but I'm not going to, Eve. I can tell . . . I'm beginning to know you a bit, I think, and I don't think you're interested right now in trying to write a book. Leo only has your best interests at heart but I think he's off base here, am I right?"

"Yes," I say, tempted by her outstretched hand.

"I know. I tried to tell him. He said just take you to meet Nigel and Nigel would do the rest." She sits back in her chair and fluffs the fur collar of her coat. "But I won't. I won't subject you to it. If and when you're interested, you let us know. I'm sorry it even came up."

Only at this last sentence does she meet my gaze. She has all the appearance of a woman taking a substantial risk in defying her husband. I'm struck again by the way she seems to shrivel in the face of Leo's expectations. Just like Myra with my father. Was I this way with

Charlie? Her fragility surprises me into revelation: "I can't see making a profit over my dead children," I say. Isabel's eyes fill with tears. I take her hand then. We hold on tight.

The opera house rises in three grand arches at the top end of the horseshoe that is Lincoln Center. My feet seem to float over the thick red carpet as I follow Isabel through the lobby. We take the elevator to the second floor where the rehearsal spaces are and find ourselves in a tiny frigid room that reminds me of the gym in my elementary school: gray and linoleumed and smelling faintly metallic. A grand piano dominates and a middle-aged man with shoepolish-black hair rises from behind it and rushes to take Isabel's hand.

"An honor," he says with a strong accent.

"Signor . . . Bosco?" Isabel says. He bows his head. "So nice to meet you."

"Ah, but you don't remember? We worked together in 1978. *Così*. My first year with the Met."

"Forgive me," Isabel says, breezing by him and approaching the piano. "I have a memory like a sieve. That was many *Così*s ago." She laughs lightly and splays her fingers across the keyboard. "Oh, by the way," she says, "my friend here will be watching the session. You have no objections, I hope?" The look she gives him indicates her complete lack of concern whether or not Signor Bosco has any objections to anything whatsoever.

"Whatever you wish." Bosco is unfazed. "It is my honor that you have decided to work with me."

Isabel bestows one of her charming smiles on him. "Nonsense; it's my pleasure. I'm told you are the best coach the Met has to offer. My usual coach, Leona Auguste? Do you know her?"

"Yes, I—"

"She's out of the country for a couple of months, and since the part is only Cio-Cio-San after all, I didn't think I needed her expertise. All I really want to do here Signor is to sing the part into my voice. I mean, how many times have I played Cio-Cio-San!" She looks at me, as if I'm keeping her calendar. "Yes, all we have to do here is to sing it back into my voice, rather than any real coaching *per se*."

Their eyes lock, smiles frozen on both their faces. Bosco's melts first. He glides to the piano and they stand at the keys together for a moment, as if squaring off for the piano bench. Eventually Isabel moves from behind the piano to the music stand.

"So, Signora! We begin with the *Che tua madre*, yes?"

Isabel inclines her head. The coach plays some notes on the piano and Isabel begins to sing, never once looking at the sheet music in front of her. The music is doleful and Isabel sings softly, barely above a whisper, her voice hoarse and plaintive.

"Excuse me, Signora?" Bosco stops playing.

Isabel eyes him.

"You are quite comfortable?"

"Quite. Why do you ask?"

"It is only that . . . you are marking, Signora, and I wondered if the room was too cold, or perhaps you are not feeling well today."

"I'm just fine, thank you," Isabel snaps. "Do you have some objection to marking? It is, last I heard, fairly standard practice."

"Of course not, I simply—"

"Do *you* have an objection to marking, Eve?" Isabel says, this time not even bothering to look at me. They are both silent, seemingly awaiting my answer.

"I don't know what marking is," I mutter.

"The way I'm singing," Isabel says impatiently. "Softly. Sparing my voice. A time-honored practice, as one would think Signor Bosco would know. Shall we continue?"

Bosco resumes playing and Isabel sings on, her voice no louder or stronger than before. Suddenly she brings her hand out low in a caressing gesture, as if stroking an imaginary child. Her face is contorted in an expression of both adoration and anguish. I have no idea what she's singing since I don't speak Italian, and her voice keeps catching, but tears spring to my eyes. I can see this child she's singing to, smaller than my children, Japanese, I guess, aching to relieve his mother's distress. Just when I'm afraid I'll make some awful sound, her volume increases as she reaches for a high note. Her voice cracks like a skipped record. She immediately lowers her volume but Bosco stops playing.

"Signora," he says. "Perhaps we could go back over that last phrase?"

Isabel stares at him a moment before answering. "I beg your pardon?"

"*Maestra,* forgive me, but this passage—you are singing it beautifully, of course, but the B flat appears to be giving you a bit of trouble, and that might be . . . made better . . . perhaps you are singing a bit too *animato* right now? If it were not so light you might get more power into the note, and be truer to the interpretation? This is a very hard moment, *tanto male,* as Butterfly says. She is talking about what will happen if her husband forsakes her. This is a terrible thing, she says; she will end up on the streets, yes?"

"Yesss," Isabel says.

The coach coughs and begins again. "I know you wanted just to sing into your voice but it is my job . . . your interpretation here; you are speaking to the child as if this is not a very terrible thing—the singing is not very . . . dark here, as much as it should be. *Tanto male*. If you see what I mean."

"Signor Bosco," Isabel says.

"*Maestra.*"

"I first played Cio-Cio-San when I was twenty-four years old. Back then, I did exactly as you say. I sang the *Che tua madre* with little sobs thrown in every few lines. I wept all over the place. I was plenty dark."

"Yes, well, *Maestro* Puccini himself tells us in the score that—"

"I know the score notations and the score itself backwards and forwards. And I can tell you this. Neither *Maestro* Puccini nor yourself is a woman. Yes, of course Butterfly is speaking of horrible things, of a terrible fate awaiting her and her child. But her words are meant for another adult, are they not?"

"She is speaking to her child but for the benefit of the Consul, yes but . . ."

Isabel nods and smiles. "Now, how old is this child?" He starts to speak but she interrupts. "Three years old. Would she want to terrify him any more than necessary? I think not. She may be trying to get the Consul to understand how desperate her circumstances are, but her child is right there in front of her. *Maestro* Puccini—and you, Signor Bosco—are masters of the music, but for the emotions . . ." she looks to the ceiling, "for the emotions, I'm afraid you must both defer to the expertise of a woman."

She remains frozen in her Madonna-like pose. I can't take my eyes off her, nor can Bosco, though he is holding himself so tightly that he appears on the verge of exploding.

The session ends soon after that. Isabel walks briskly to the street to hail a cab, doing furious imitations of Bosco with an exaggerated Italian accent. I know I should offer some sympathy for her distress, but I can think of only one thing. "Isabel," I say excitedly as she waves her impatient hand at every cab that passes, whether off-duty or not, "you said you didn't have children."

"What? Of course I don't. *Blast,*" she says, as another cab passes us by.

"It's amazing," I say.

"What is. That I'm doing this part? Pay no attention to what that pea-brain said. He obviously thinks anyone over thirty is washed up. I wouldn't be surprised if he ran out and fed this whole thing to the press. . . ." She sees someone getting out of a cab up the street and runs after it as I lumber after her.

"No, it's not that," I persist. "It's what you said about mothers and children. You got it exactly right. How did you know?" My words come out in little gasps.

She lowers her taxi hand and turns to me, eyeing me appraisingly. "Darling, that's my job," she says, but I'm sure there's more to it, some deeper feeling she has than she is willing to admit.

8

I take the train back since Isabel has rehearsals and Leo has business in the city. They see me to the majestic train station, repeat the instructions about when and where I should get off, where Noah will be waiting—Myra-speak I find oddly comforting. I resist the urge to suggest that they pin a note to my coat. It is evening, rush hour, and the station's straining with people; every single one of them, even the children clutching their parents' or nannies' hands, seems in an enormous hurry.

Just as we are saying good-bye a middle-aged man in an expensive-looking coat comes up to Isabel and pants out a request for her autograph. Isabel hesitates for a minute, glancing at me, but Leo says, "Of course" to the man as if it were his own signature that was being solicited. Isabel gives me an apologetic look and turns to the man, who hands her a pen. Then she dazzles him with her smile.

The train is crowded. Most of the people are reading or sleeping; many wear discreet Walkman earplugs, tailored suits and highly polished shoes. They all appear to be in various stages of exhaustion. But if you really look, you can tell from their serious expressions and slight tension in their shoulders or hands—even the sleeping ones—that they are intent upon their destinations, so eager to arrive that it's hard not to run up to the conductor and urge him along. I remember being that exhaustedly eager to get home—sitting on the L.A. freeways in a five-mile traffic jam, the air-conditioning doing nothing to dispel the gas fumes that wafted through the sealed windows of the car, thinking about Nick and Jess at home checking the clock and asking their sitter for the hundredth time, "Is she almost here?" I burst into tears when the sitter told me they did this.

"Are you all right?" The woman next to me is looking concernedly into my face. She is young and pretty and holds a cellular phone in her lap.

I realize that I've been holding my breath. "Cramps," I say when she won't stop looking at me. I turn my face to the window.

That night Molly calls and asks about the doctors' visits. Because I can remember times when the banal details of life were what made up that life, I answer patiently and Molly is satisfied. When I'm ready to hang up, though, she insists on putting Sarah, her oldest, on the phone.

"I'm really tired now, Molly," I say.

"Just a quick word, please, Eve, she's been really bad off. She's taking it worse than the other kids. Just so she'll hear your voice, know you're all right."

This is the first time anyone has asked me to do them a favor since the accident. It's amazing that I have any favors left to bestow.

"Auntie Eve?" Sarah's voice is tiny and childish. I do a quick mental calculation and realize she must be around fourteen.

"Hi honey," I say, trying to keep my voice normal.

A pause, just this side of uncomfortable. "How are you?"

"I'm all right, Sarah, how are you?"

"Fine."

Another silence. "I miss you." Her voice even smaller now, and a little choked and I think, Don't you cry, goddamn you, don't you start bawling on me. Children's voices all sound so similar on the phone. I force myself to speak over her breathing, which has that suctiony wheeze of allergic children who breathe through their mouths. Sarah has always been the designated "delicate" child in the family. She gets monthly allergy shots and has prescription nasal spray and 40 SPF sunscreen and can't wear nonnatural fibers and can't eat wheat or lactose. Her blonde hair hangs limply against her pale face, and her arms are white and thin. She was never my favorite of Molly's children—I often had the urge to stand her next to Jessica, seven years her junior and as vibrant as Sarah is pallid, and make subtle comparisons about muscle tone, energy and hair luster. Sarah on a sailboat for four years? Never happen, I used to think smugly, watching Sarah falteringly toeing the waters of Molly's pool where the other children had already jumped in. I could never stand to have such a child, I used to tell myself.

"I miss you too, Sarah," I say, my breathing shallow, my fingers numb against the telephone receiver. "I have to hang up now," I say.

"But Mommy wants to—"

I cut her off. Her voice is so insubstantial it would be blown away in the slightest gust of wind.

Myra gone. The bedroom closet, which had few things to begin with, has even less. The breakfast dishes from three days ago, when we went to the city, crusting in the kitchen sink. The TV guide on the couch, opened to the crossword puzzle, three-quarters filled in with Myra's blue ink. The guest house muted, thick with silence.

Yet the bedroom seems almost welcoming. It's been my bedroom for a little over a month, but it's the only one I've had on land in two and a half years. Charlie and I gave our bed to Good Will. We slept in my parents' house, the single beds of my childhood, the night before we left. Our berth on the boat was always too small, Charlie butting up against me, me flinging out my arms and hitting him in the nose. This bed, here in Isabel's guest house, is large and firm and comfortable. It's not mine.

Oddly, I miss Charlie's snoring, sonorous and rhythmic, keeping time with the rocking of the boat. But I don't miss his tossing and turning that woke me up ten, twenty times a night, every night for over fourteen years. On land sometimes I would go downstairs and sleep on the couch, just to get the occasional uninterrupted sleep. On the boat there was nowhere to go, so I used to take the watch as often as I could and stay up late, deep into the night, staring into the stars.

I cannot remember the last time I was completely alone at night. Even at the hospital, someone always lurked, sidling in with meds or to tap an IV or adjust a monitor. I don't think there's been one night in the last fourteen years where there's been no one to hear me if I cry out.

At 3:00 A.M. I spring up for the third time, despite an extra sleeping pill and a muscle relaxant. When you wake up in the middle of the night it's not always noise that has roused you. It's whatever you don't expect that pulls you up out of deepest sleep. Silence, for instance. I used to wake up suddenly, my heart throbbing, if Charlie went too long without snoring or I couldn't hear one of the babies breathing in the monitor, say. There is never complete silence on the ocean and you'd wake up suddenly if there were. Now I wake up wondering where the slapping of the waves has gone, waiting for the resonant drone of Charlie's snore. It's just as Myra said—the absences are louder than screams.

In the blue-black darkness I have the wildest feeling—a suspicion, really, a crazy idea certainly born of too many pills and too little rest and the hollowness of my bones. I want to search the house. I want to find what has woken me, or what hasn't woken me.

I open the bedroom closet. The clothes Myra bought me hang in multicolored array, like circus costumes, next to so many empty wire hangers. I push them all—clothes and hangers—first to the left, then to the right. Get a chair and search the top shelf where we never put anything anyway. I tell myself I'm seeing if Myra left anything by accident. I look in the dresser where her nylon underwear had lain. Open the cabinet under the sink in the kitchen. The drawers of the desk in the living room. The long pantry cabinet, the doors above the counter where the dishes are kept. The medicine cabinet in the bathroom. Nothing. Then I get a knife.

Back to the bedroom closet; work the knife under the matted beige carpet there. Just a corner. I have this idea there's a door under there. A secret passage.

Work the front right corner of the carpet up. It makes a tearing sound. No door. I put the carpet back.

In the kitchen I try to twist the nut around the trap under the sink to disconnect the pipes. I look for a wrench but there isn't one. Work at it with my hands until they bleed.

There could be a passage there. I mean, I know there couldn't be. I know it's too narrow, but I have to make sure. The only way to get a wrench is to find Noah. He'll think I'm crazy. Then I eye the kitchen linoleum. Hiding what? Back to the bedroom for the knife. Pass by the bathroom and the pills. Go in and take one extra of everything—antidepressant, antianxiety, sleeping. I get back into bed and sleep a long, dreamless time.

I knew they weren't there. I wasn't really crazy. I knew they weren't there but I couldn't stop myself from trying to dig them out.

That was Tuesday morning. I awaken Wednesday afternoon, hands aflame and crusty with blood. Head weighing too much for my neck. Clothes everywhere—thrown over the bed, the floor. Lurch my way to the bathroom to wash my hands, throw water on my face, drink glass after glass of cold clear water.

My hands feel almost exactly as they did right after the accident. I struggle with the cap on the bottle of sleeping pills, rub my torn index finger across the raised lettering on the top: "child-resistant cap." Pour the whole bottle of sleeping pills into my left palm. It isn't bleeding now, just abraded and fiery. I add the bottle of tiny, triangle-shaped antianxiety pills, throw in the green capsules of antidepressants for good measure. They just fill my cupped palm, a tricolor mound looking like some new and exotic candy. I fill the cup by the sink with water and bring the candy pile to my mouth. I feel the slick texture of the green capsules against my lips. Close my eyes and try to envision Jessie and Nick in Charlie's arms, waving to me.

Cowardice.

Couldn't see them clearly enough. Couldn't even be sure it was them.

Punishment, too.

I already had my chance. I had almost two days in the dinghy to let go and slip under and I didn't. I gave up something then—a privilege I can't claim now. I return each pill to its designated bottle.

The house is in complete disarray. The contents of the drawers of the desk are all over the living room floor and the kitchen is covered with spilled Ajax and cereal which Myra stocked up for me.

There doesn't seem much left to do but write. To avoid tearing up the house again or having the Steins or Noah show up and find me drooling and babbling on the bathroom floor. To avoid the temptations of those three amber-colored bottles. Maybe once I finish the story I can send it off to this agent they all keep going on about. Certainly I'll have repaid everyone's concern. And then I will be able to swallow all the pills I want.

I've been wearing the same clothes for three days. The aromas of sleep and sweat and blood have become familiar, almost comforting.

I sit at the desk with the unused legal pad. Piled in front of me are the letters and cards Myra was still waiting for me to read. I write: "It all started when." Stop. Stare at the pile of correspondence. The silence grows more absolute. I lift a cream-colored envelope from the top of the pile. The letter inside is in cramped handwriting. *Dear Eve,* it says, *I have just read about your ordeal and I felt I had to write and tell you that you are not alone.* A woman, I know it immediately. I skim the platitudes till I get to the second paragraph. *It's been two years now since we lost our Jill. She was the light of our life . . .* blah blah blah till I get to the meat: *. . . crossing the street with her best friend Luanne . . . never saw it coming. Eleven years old, our only child.*

Eleven years old. *Dear Cream-Colored Paper,* I write on the pad. *Eleven years old? And you want me to sympathize with you? That's three more years than I got with Nick, four more than with Jessica. Who the fuck is this Jill, anyway? Maybe if you'd taught her to look both ways before she crosses the street, this never would have happened.*

I find some paper clips, pin my reply to Jill's mother's letter. I will answer one letter a day. In the meantime, I begin a fresh page and write:

I met Charlie when he became an account executive at the advertising agency where I'd been writing copy for three years. I saw him cry three times in my life. The first time was after my miscarriage before Nick. He was at work. I called him there when I started to have contractions. When Charlie arrived, I was already back in my hospital room and my mother was dozing in a chair beside the bed. Charlie took my hand, held it to his face and sobbed into it. If I hadn't been so weak I would have stroked his head the way I stroked Nick's years later when he was hurt and baffled by the random cruelties of life.

The second time I saw Charlie cry was when a British corporation bought out the ad agency and Charlie was laid off in the subsequent restructuring. He wept in my arms that night after we'd finished off a bottle and a half of red wine. I had much less sympa-

thy for him that time. I knew he would get another job quickly enough—he was still young and successful and respected in the business. I knew he was mostly upset because he envisioned a major delay in our departure, which was about three years away. I was even a little exasperated with him.

The last time I saw him cry was on the dinghy before it capsized the first time but after we knew that we had lost Nick.

I never saw him cry like that before.

Up. Out of the chair. It's too quiet. In desperation I turn to the pile of CDs on top of the cabinet and pull out the one that I've heard of: *La Bohème*. I put the CD in the player; if it's too awful I'll find the one of the woman singing Christmas tunes.

The music begins, rather festive and innocuous—certainly not unpleasant, so I let it play. But it doesn't drown out the sound now planted in my head: Charlie. First screaming Nick's name over and over, long after it was obvious that that was fruitless. His voice rising above the thunder of the storming waves like the cry of gulls, screeching, soul-piercing, calling Nick's full name when he didn't answer Nicholas Alan Miller as if otherwise Nick might think we were calling for some other child, some other boy whom we'd chosen to save over him. Nick who slept like a rock. I said, in that controlled, authoritative voice I'd been granted for those hours, I said, *Charlie, he sleeps like a rock, our baby, he never woke up, I promise he was gone when we were hit; Charlie*, I said, *he died dreaming*. But Charlie called on.

Now the music has grown slower, more romantic. A woman is singing, her voice high and pure, like prolonged cathedral bells. It must be Isabel, though I don't recognize her voice in this beautiful sound, so much clearer and lovelier than the near-whisper in the rehearsal room. It's not what I think of as opera singing at all. She does not sound like an angry schoolteacher; she sounds like an angel.

I close my eyes and see Charlie's face—the sharp angle of his jaw, his close-cropped thinning black hair, the way his nose bends to the left, which, under certain circumstances, such as the influence of alcohol, he will say he broke in a street fight when he was a kid, when in fact he was born that way. When I try to envision him in full I see a face that is unfamiliar to me because he only had it for two years—the full beard he began as soon as we boarded the ship, the way his scant hair hung over his ears and down the nape of his neck, the rough ruddiness of his skin.

Now the man is singing something alone and his voice, too, is more beautiful than I might have imagined. The music draws me—I try to envision what could be happening in the story thus far. Now Isabel sings her reply, also slightly melancholy. There is this one moment—I put my pen down—she holds a high note and then lets her voice fall down a few notes. That's the only way to put it, as if it has naturally tumbled in this perfect melody and it actually makes me shiver.

This is when the doorbell rings. I answer it in a kind of trance. Noah is standing there, his face half hidden by a densely woven black-and-gray scarf, his hands in his jacket pockets.

"Your mother just called," he says crisply. "She's apparently been calling for a few days. She said she hasn't been able to reach you. I just tried your phone and there's no answer and the machine doesn't come on."

"Oh," I say.

He peers at me, his green eyes narrowing. "Are you okay?" he says grudgingly. He wrinkles his fine nose and I remember my stench. I blink and make no move.

"Should I call someone for you?"

"No. No. I'm fine. Do you want to come in," I ask him because I have a vague memory of not asking him last time.

"No, I want you to call your mother and tell her you're all right so I can go back to work."

"Of course. Good-bye." I try to close the door and he thrusts out a hand enswathed in its brace to block me. "Are you sure you're okay?"

"I've been a little unwell but I'm better now. I'll call Myra."

He cocks his head as the music wafts over to us. His eyes soften. "That's Isabel."

"Uh huh." I push gently on the door so that he moves his hand and then I close it. I imagine him on the other side, standing awkwardly for a moment, wondering if Isabel will be upset with him if he goes back to his piano, which is where he really wants to be.

I go back to the living room and lie down on the couch and listen to the rest of the opera. It is clear to me now that if you listen closely enough to the music you know all you need to about the story. Mimi was miserable for the whole third act and dying in the fourth. Rodolfo could not bear it. I listen to the fourth act in the slowly descending shadows of the afternoon.

I can't turn the music off then any more than I could have asked Myra to stay in New York. The same act of self-castigation keeps me riveted to the couch, listening as Mimi's voice grows weaker and weaker, Isabel panting, her voice no less exquisite, but sounding as if she hasn't the strength to sing one more clear, ringing note. Rodolfo is crying and she sings to him, easing his pain. He tells her not to speak—I've had enough rudimentary Spanish to understand the Italian "non parlar"—to save her breath. I hear false hope in the gentle, broken way he sings to her. Isabel breathes out the last bright notes of Mimi's life and I think of a line I last heard on the boat when we were off the coast of Mexico. They were showing *The Wizard of Oz* on some channel and I watched it with Nick and Jessie while Charlie was on deck watching the night fall. Spanish words ran across the bottom of the screen in wavering subtitles and Jess kept reading parts of it aloud, proud of her pronunciation, if uncertain of her comprehension. Nick kept telling her to shut up and I threatened to turn off the television if they didn't just watch the damn show. It is the moment that Dorothy is finally going home: the Good Witch is there to take her back at last and she goes to each of her friends and says good-bye and when she gets to the Tin Man he looks away from her and says, "Now I know I have a heart because it's breaking."

I don't want her to die please don't let Mimi die I'm thinking as the tears run I'm sitting up now soaking my filthy sweatshirt and she's still pushing out the last few notes, and then there are funeral horns and I know it's over but I think somehow Rodolfo doesn't because he is speaking now, not seeing, saying something about *tranquilla*, which I think means he thinks she's sleeping and then and then someone says *Coraggio* and then he's calling her name over and over and I've seen this before, I saw this before at the funeral of Molly's friend, Maria, I saw the boy call out his love's name too late. I heard Charlie calling for our son.

For the first time, I sleep without pills. Beyond exhausted. Never moving from the couch.

I shower the next morning, the days of grime and sweat and dried blood and tears sucked down the drain like the tide. I wash myself clean and raw, aggravating my abraded palms, stick my head under the hot water and keep it there, the ache in my back increasing the longer I stand there, pushing at the pain, daring it. I make coffee and breakfast and dress in jeans and one of the sweaters Myra bought.

Still thinking about Isabel's dying song, I pick up the CD and pull out the liner notes. There is a synopsis of the story. I have to write a story, maybe I should read one.

What a letdown: This woman is sick, she meets this guy, they fall in love, they separate, she comes back to die in his arms. Big deal. It's only the music. The music is the only thing that makes it epic.

But then, maybe all loss is banal to those who haven't suffered it.

I sit down at the desk and reach for the top letter in the pile in front of me. *Michael was ten when he fell . . .* it says in shaky, crabbed handwriting, *such a precious loss.*

Dear Michael's Mother, I write, *Fell off a ladder, did he, your precious Michael? What the hell was he doing on a ladder! Who was supervising? My children were always a few feet from me, do you understand that? I watched them like a hawk.*

9

There was a series of books about a boy detective that Nicholas was addicted to. If I'd let him, he'd have read those books twenty-four hours a day. I would watch him sometimes from the door of his bedroom, his green eyes locked onto the page, mouth slightly open, tongue poking out intermittently from between his lips. I often had to take the book out of his hand to get him to hear me when I spoke. Though I was gratified and excited to know that he loved to read, that the video games his friends amassed only mildly interested him, I knew this series, the *P. Worthington Oppenheimer Agency*, was pulp fiction that might have little better effect on his mind than mind-numbing hours of television. When I'd take Nick to the library and try to get him to read *The Wind in the Willows* or *A Wrinkle in Time* he'd make his way to the section with the two shelves' worth of the green-backed series, so identical in content that they had to be numbered so you could tell one from the other. On the boat Nick took fifteen or so of the newest *P. Worthington Oppenheimers*, as well as the address where he could write for more when he ran out. Charlie said I should leave Nick alone—that what was important was that he loved to read and that he'd soon outgrow these books and then, since we had a captive audience, we could urge on him our own more edifying selection of material.

I have a similar unsettling feeling about my listening to *La Bohème* obsessively for a whole week. I have the feeling that what I'm doing is bad for me, though the operas are so wiping me out that I've cut back on the sleeping pills. I always cry at the same parts—the third act where Mimi and Rodolfo part, the fourth where Mimi dies. I'm sure these are the parts where most people cry, but the thing is, I know I'm not crying for the people in the opera. That's what makes me wonder if there's something seriously wrong with me. That I can only cry for my family by pretending to cry for someone else.

There is nothing left in the house. No coffee or eggs or milk or the frozen dinners I eat if I don't have cheese and crackers, of which there are none now either. I don't see how I can get out of going to town and facing strangers who might ask after my family, as if they know me, know I'm supposed to have one, have perhaps somehow misplaced them.

The walk up to the house feels like scaling a mountain. My legs are heavy and uncoordinated, as if I'm drunk. I stop and take a few deep breaths. A cold breeze ripples through my hair. The gravel on the walk is strewn with dry leaves. The back of the house rises before me, identical small windows climbing its two stories, its overhanging roof throwing shadows onto the walls in the dying light. I rub my feet against the ground. This is land, I tell myself, this is hard ground.

Noah answers the door with a martini glass in his mummified hand and stares at me for a moment before he lets me in. The living room is lit with only one electric lamp and many candles and a roaring fire. Isabel half reclines on the couch, another exotic, flowing gown spread around her. She, too, holds a martini glass. She looks like a Sargent painting—her large, chiseled head swaying sphinx-like above her picturesquely positioned body. She doesn't rise when I enter but her welcome is effusive. At the sound of her voice—so familiar now from the CDs—my heart flutters. I gulp down the martini Noah hands me. I'm getting a taste for these. They work fast and they taste bitter but they go down easily. The red eye of the olive winks at me while Isabel talks about the end of the opera's first act with Noah. "It's going so well," she confides to me before asking if I mind if they talk shop for a minute or two.

They talk about trills and high C and coloratura and the words sound like beautiful paintings to me and I drink another martini and their voices swirl around me like mist. Then there is silence. I lean my head back and close my eyes. But then I think I feel the martini glass slipping from my hand. I look up and Isabel and Noah are standing next to the fireplace now though I never heard her get up. They are standing three-quarters facing out and her large head is bowed and she's looking up at him from under her eyelids so that he appears to be towering over her although he's only a few inches taller. Isabel turns and smiles at me. "Noah has made a lovely salmon."

At dinner Isabel trains her full attention on me and I feel a woozy affection for her. "So, you've listened to some of the operas?" Her eyes search my face as if she is avid to hear everything I have to say.

"I haven't listened much. Or rather, I haven't listened to many. I've been listening to *La Bohème* mostly."

"Oh yes of course." Isabel claps her hands together. "It is the most beautiful, isn't it? And that's a very nice recording, the one with Borg as Rodolfo. Such a nice man—not always there on his top notes, but he knew when to defer. I'm *quite* happy with that recording."

"How can you bear it," I burst out and then clamp my lips together as if I could take back such impulsive words. I brace myself for worry on their part but Isabel just eyes me curiously.

"Bear what?"

"It's a very sad story," I say.

"Of course, Mimi is tragic." Isabel speaks as if I've done nothing unusual. She lifts her eyes to the ceiling. "She has never hurt anyone, never wished anyone harm. She's simply had the misfortune to be poor and sick and to have fallen in love with a poor man who cannot save her. But the important thing is that you mustn't play her like a victim." Isabel puts down her fork and leans forward, darting her gaze back and forth between Noah and me. Her slanted eyes are bright. "Mimi is an essentially happy person. She was happy before she met Rodolfo and is much happier after she meets him. She is made miserable by outside forces—by her illness and Roldolfo's jealousy—but she accepts these twists of fate as just that, not anyone's fault. She does not sit around and feel sorry for herself. In the end she lets her love bring her back to Rodolfo. She dies happy."

"Precisely," Noah says, his voice animated. "Usually it's done just the opposite—where she dies and everyone's prostrate. And that's what makes people dismiss Puccini as sentimental and easy. *Poor* Mimi, *poor* Rodolfo. But when you sing it," he blushes, which makes him look very young, "it's not sentimental at all."

He leans over his plate toward Isabel. A sudden intensity emanates from him like heat.

"Precisely," Isabel echoes Noah. "This is what coaches like that horrible little Bosco man don't understand. You don't want the audience to feel manipulated into crying for Mimi because she's so pathetic. You want them to cry for Rodolfo who is losing this wonderful creature. But we also know that he and Mimi have had something so special, so close to perfection, that even though it's been taken away from them too soon, they wouldn't have it any other way, not if it meant they couldn't have each other at all."

I drink fully from my wineglass and the room grows warmer. Then Isabel takes in a quick breath and turns to me. "You see, Eve? You see why I love this man? We are *completely* simpatico. We can practically read each other's thoughts. He is the only man who can write Catherine of Aragon for me." She picks up her fork and takes another bite of fish, still smiling her radiant smile, but now it is for the whole room—for Noah, for me, for Leo's empty chair. "You know," she continues, chewing delicately. "What Noah and I are doing is quite risqué."

Noah makes a little noise in the back of his throat.

"Well, at least a bit unheard of, isn't it Noah?" He just looks at her. "These days it's almost impossible to mount an important new opera. The money involved, the influence! Luckily, I still have a bit of *that* left. And with the way opera is going—getting more Hollywood all the time—a singer, even one of my . . . well, of my long-standing-ness . . . has to watch out for her own career. No one else will. The great parts won't get handed to me forever. You have to *make* them happen." She puts down her fork again and reaches over to pat Noah's hand. He curls his fingers around hers and they stay that way for a minute before she pries her hand away again. "Of course Noah is *everthing* I've been looking for. But it is true that he doesn't write in the typical contemporary idiom and thank god for it! He's writing me a magnificent, *singable* part. And I swear to you," she reaches for his hand again, "we are going to take the world by storm you and I."

I can see by his face that if she'd said, *You and I are going to turn into jackrabbits* he would have had complete faith in that too.

Isabel asks Noah to help with dessert and insists that I relax. I pour myself the last of the wine and listen to the distant sound of clanging dishes. At first I float nicely on the wine, taking in the lush surroundings, but soon Isabel's words about the opera, about brief but perfect love, weigh me down. I pick up my empty wineglass and head for the kitchen. I keep my hand on the hallway wall, since the floor seems suddenly slanted.

I step inside to light much brighter than the yellow candles and fire. Noah and Isabel stand close together by the sink. Isabel's face is pale and Noah's is flushed and he is breathing hard but Isabel is perfectly calm. She raises a hand to her hair and brushes a strand into place while she says my name and smiles. "I told you not to clear," she says brightly. "You're the guest."

"Oh, uh," I stutter. "I'm sorry. I was just . . ."

"It's fine, Eve, relax," she says without a trace of concern in her voice. "Have some more wine. Noah, be a dear and get a bottle from the closet, will you."

Noah doesn't move from his position by the sink and he still has the startled-deer look on his face.

"Noah." Isabel touches his arm gently and he flinches. She looks calmly at him and he finally turns and walks to the cabinet. "Eve is enjoying the wine," Isabel says pointedly as Noah fumbles with a wine opener. He stops, looks at her, then at me, then back at her. He nods. And there we are in a painful tableau, me awkwardly clutching my wineglass and averting my gaze, Noah with the wine bottle in one hand and the corkscrew in the other, the cork skewered to it like bait. His face the color of the wine, as I'm sure mine is; only Isabel seems completely unruffled. Noah looks so painfully vulnerable that suddenly I have a strong urge to protect him.

No matter how much she tries to draw us in, the rest of the evening is Isabel's performance, keeping up endless chatter while I let my head bob, which she takes to be nodding, and Noah stares darkly first at her, then at me, back and forth like a metronome. I feel an unaccountable kinship with him as we sit at Isabel's feet—both of us unhappy but fascinated; a mesmerized audience longing for something that continually eludes us.

Halfway back to the cottage I remember that I didn't ask them about going into town for supplies. When I reach the house again I look up where the living room window glows amber. From this distance and with that pale light I can only see silouhettes—one shapeless figure steps in front of the window and reaches her arms up so that her dress floats around her like angels' wings. She is unhooking the high curtains and as she does so another figure obscures most of the light behind her. The curtains fall closed and I stand there shivering, with the flashlight making a doll's spotlight at my feet and my heart beating furiously against my chest as if I've just seen something frightening.

In the morning—well, it isn't the morning, actually, it is afternoon when I finally awaken, bleary headed—I dial the number at the house but they don't answer. I write a note about needing things at the store, and after throwing water on my face and my coat on over sweats, I trudge up the hill again, squinting in the cold sunlight. Once I think I hear something behind me, like voices whispering. I turn, but there's just the graceful curve of the road back to the cottage.

Isabel's car is still in the driveway. I slip the list of my needs under the front door. As I walk back it occurs to me that I have become as certain of Isabel's eagerness to help me as I once was suspicious of her motives. While I'm not sure why she has decided I am someone whose friendship she wants to cultivate, I no longer doubt the sincerity of her urge to help me, as Mimi would help any lost creature, and I can almost imagine a time when life will have some normality to it again and I can repay her kindness.

By the time I get back to the cottage, however, my supply of goodwill has been depleted by the taste of metallic moss in my mouth and a pain like razor blades at the back of my eyes. An inadvertent glance in the bathroom mirror as I down three aspirin confirms that at my age, an excess of alcohol shows up on the face. My eyes are red-rimmed.

I flop down at the desk and glance at the next letter in the pile. *Dear Eve, I am a single mother of two and I have been following your story religiously, combing the papers for news of your progress. Since we are a fishing town, we do get our share of boating accident stories. Why, you may ask, did yours grab my eye? I, like you, am a woman of vision, of dreams. My children's father left me when I sought to better myself by going back to college. Like you, I have a boy and girl. If I had a husband like yours, I, too, would have set sail to show them the wonders of this planet of ours. How you must treasure the two years you had to accomplish this! What joy you must take in the splendors your little ones were privileged to see! In my Cross-Cultural Literature class we have been discussing . . .*

Dear Fish Lady, I write. *I have no doubt that the father of your children made a wise decision when he left you. My guess is he thought if he had to hear one more of your pretentious sentences he might do harm to you or himself or your precious children. Take my advice. Quit school, get a good job and make sure you keep your children near you at all times. Don't worry about showing them the planet. That's your selfish dream, not theirs. Sincerely, Eve Miller.*

On Monday, a week after she arrived, Isabel goes back to the city. I put on *Don Giovanni* for the first time and receive a phone call from Nigel Baker, the agent Myra saw.

"How did you get this number," I say, biting down hard on the pen I'm holding.

He gives a short laugh. "Oh, I believe your mother gave it to me. But you don't need to worry, I wouldn't be in this job very long if I couldn't keep secrets. I don't mean to intrude, and do let me extend my deepest condolences for your loss." He has a high-pitched, upper-class English accent which is so perfect it sounds fake. "I'm so keen on meeting you."

"Why?"

"Well, to discuss the book deal. The possible book deal." I go to the kitchen and pour myself a glass of red wine, taking a sip before speaking. Nigel Baker seems unfazed by the long silence. "Is there an actual book deal?" I say, unsure of what I want him to reply.

"Not yet, but as soon as you say the word, one will be in the works. There's keen interest out there in your project. But frankly, and I don't mean to sound crass, but we're most likely to get the best advance the closer to . . . the incident we move. I'm sorry to be so blunt, Ms. Miller, but this is about your future among other things."

"What other things," I say, the wine making me almost friendly.

He clears his throat. "Look. You may decide you don't want to do this. Frankly, I don't know if I could in your place. But if you think there is even the smallest possibility that this might be good for you—moneywise, catharsiswise, or . . . whatever, you should probably give me permission to act on your behalf now. Making no commitments, you understand. There could be a very big deal waiting out there for you, Ms. Miller. I would take care of everything—money, press, even housing if it came to that. Your life would be taken care of. You wouldn't have to worry about a thing except to write the book. How does that sound?"

It sounds like Isabel's life—someone else handling all my affairs, my bills and letters, my needs and wants. Even given my present circumstances, I'm not sure I'm cut out for that.

Maybe it's because I'm not really an artist. I wanted to write my whole life but instead I went to work in an advertising agency and before I married I stayed up nights paying bills and budgeting for vacations. I called repairmen and fixed broken toilet handles. I used up time I suppose I could have been writing being responsible for my life in all its mundaneness. On the other hand, I imagine Isabel young, spending every waking minute opening her throat and singing to the sky. I imagine her eating, drinking and sleeping music while the landlord sent her overdue notices and she paid full price for groceries, never clipping a single coupon. No wonder she married Leo. She needed someone to take care of her quickly. What if I had married someone like Leo? What would I have written then?

"I can't imagine what I would do with tons of money," I say to Nigel Baker when it seems the silence has gone on too long.

"I understand. Only I read the other day that the Maritime Safety Board is about to announce its findings about what exactly happened. If indeed you did want to go ahead, timing that with a book deal—"

"Timing the book deal with what?"

"The announcement?"

"What announcement?"

"Didn't you know?" He sounds confused. "The report will be out in a few days. I thought you knew."

"I don't read the paper," I say, teeth clenched. My head begins to ache.

"Are you all right?"

I make some kind of sound.

"Maybe I should ring you next week," Nigel Baker says softly.

"Good idea," I say. I hang up and turn *Don Giovanni* up very loud.

10

The weather has turned bitter cold when Noah shows up Monday morning to take me to town for supplies. When he walks in I am sitting on the couch in my coat, my hands stuffed in the pockets, staring at the television. I guess he came in of his own accord because I didn't hear the doorbell. He says, "Will you be warm enough?"

Oprah is interviewing a movie star. His life is going fantastically, he says, with his new movie, his new wife, his new production company. Nothing of interest for me. "Maybe I should go back up to the house and get you at least a scarf. Eve? Well here, come on." He steps nearer to me and takes the wool scarf from his neck and holds it out to me.

"Here," he says, sounding exasperated. He removes his leather gloves and wraps the muffler around my neck, lifting my hair with all the gentleness of the nurses at the hospital. The muffler is warm from his body, and I smell something familiar and even though I am trying to keep my mind blank I still think *Charlie*; still feel my eyes well up, think *Charlie* because they used the same aftershave it's that simple that stupid and sudden and unbidden these geysers of grief that now lift me from the couch and into the bathroom to lock the door and lean against it and bring the scarf up to my face and breathe him in.

Then Noah is knocking on the door, saying my name, panic rising in his voice "Are you all right in there" and I'm thinking if I stay very close to him all day I can smell the aftershave two hours from now and then five and then when it seems to have worn off altogether but if you press your face right into the crook of his neck and breathe deeply you can still get a whiff of cinnamon and something musky; if I breathe him all day I might be able to smell my whole past on him.

When I come out he is in the kitchen, the phone at his ear. "I'm all right now," I say, touching his arm. He looks at me, looks at the phone. "You sure?" His expression is a combination of impatience and concern. I nod and slowly he hangs up the phone. "I'm all right now," I repeat, stroking the muffler I've wrapped so tightly around my neck that it's hard to breathe.

The drive into Kent is less than ten minutes. I ride the whole way with my eyes fixed on the scenery, keeping my mind blank, breathing Charlie. Identical clapboard houses dot the hillside. The houses look compact and comfortable as if families who get along with their neighbors must live in them. The main street is less than a mile long and looks like a street in Disneyland.

The market is small with aisles so narrow the shopping carts are doll sized. Noah grabs a cart and walks in ahead of me. I follow him blindly with a cart of my own, pulling necessary items off the shelf while barely looking at them: rice, tuna, 7-Up—Jess's favorite but I got Coke last time for Nick—dried kidney beans, a few steaks, powdered milk, first brands I see, no comparison shopping today, no references to my meticulously crafted budget or shopping list because really, I don't think I could bear to see Jessie's shaky scrawl or Nick's painstaking one, because inevitably one or both of them would find the list and add in their two cents—nail polish, a *P. Worthington Oppenheimer* mystery, Post Toasties.

By the time I reach the checkout my cart is full and Noah is there unloading. When he sees me he stops, a box of echinacea tea in his braced hand.

"What," I say.

"Uh, nothing. Just . . . that's quite a load you have there."

"It's supplies."

He hoists up the sack of rice. "What will you do with all this?" he says.

"We'll cook it, what do you think we'll do?"

Silence. Noah continues to stare and now I notice the cashier is staring too. Noah lowers the rice back into my cart. "It's just that it seems like an awful lot of rice, Eve," he says gently. "I mean, ten pounds of rice will last you a very very long time, won't it? And all the rest of this stuff?"

"We need it for our . . . it's . . ." I look in the cart and see everything I would buy on a supply run for the boat bought without thinking or even checking to see if we were out because except for the steaks, which were meant to be a treat since we hadn't had meat in so long, we always used up these supplies, always needed them replenished.

"Oh," I say, fumbling in my purse, "I have the right list somewhere. . . ."

"Here." Noah puts his tea back in his cart and comes over to me. He takes the list I've dug out of my bag and puts his other arm around me, tight. "Let me take you back to the car," he says.

"I need some things," I manage to say.

"I'll get them for you." He guides me out of the store. I'm sure he's annoyed and embarrassed by me, thinking how he didn't sign on to take care of a crazy person.

When he comes back to the car I am sitting with my head back, eyes closed, my brain ricocheting between the reality of the cold car and the dream of this only being a port of call, being nowhere that I have to stay. I hear him open the car trunk and feel the car dip with the weight of the packages. Then he gets in the front seat, blowing on his red hands. "It wants to be winter out there," he says. Then, after a minute, "You all right?"

"I'm sorry," I say.

He fumbles the keys in the ignition; the engine turns over. He fiddles with the car heater, pulls his gloves from his pocket and puts them on, then grips the top of the steering wheel as if bracing himself. "I guess you felt sick."

"Something like that." I feel him look at me again. "It's just that I haven't been in a store in a while," I say, to intercept his stare. "I got confused."

He gives a little forced laugh. "Hell, it usually takes me twenty minutes to remember if I like gel or paste toothpaste. At least you knew what you wanted."

"Well," I say, "you learn to move like lightning once you start shopping with children." It just came out unbidden. The word "children" exploding like blasphemy.

"Oh," Noah says. "I'm . . . sorry, I forget this was your first trip. To town; to a store."

He looks so anguished that I have a real urge to pat his cheek. "Don't be," I say. "I never liked shopping that much. It was a pain in the ass, if you want to know the truth."

He smiles hesitantly. "There was . . . you had a boy and a girl?"

I nod. The car heater kicks in at last and the car begins to warm up. The engine thrums. Noah never takes his eyes from me. "What were their names?"

"Nicholas and Jessica." I speak their names aloud to Noah, sending the syllables out into the freezing air for the first time since I voiced them that night, screamed them into the oblivious sea.

Then he says, Do you want to go get a cup of coffee and I say, I want to go get a drink.

It is eleven o'clock in the morning. There is only one bar in town. The bar is so dark it could be midnight or dawn. There are two neon signs spelling out beer names behind the bar and a clock that sits above a mechanical walrus fishing in an ice hole, endlessly lifting and lowering his line as the seconds tick by. We sit at a sticky table. Noah orders tea and I order a martini. As soon as we sit down I worry that he doesn't want to be there, that he only suggested we go someplace because he is afraid to be stuck alone with me in the hermetic environment of the car. When we are served he asks for honey, and the bartender, a young man with huge biceps and a buzz cut, sneers at him.

Noah sips his tea with a pained expression on his face. I shudder at the first rush of vermouth—too much vermouth—burning my throat, coating my veins. I try to sip, not gulp. Noah coughs.

"Tell me about your work," I say, so that he won't make me leave.

"You don't want to hear about that."

"I do," I say, and then as an afterthought, "It will take my mind off."

He looks at me rather hopefully, I think. "What do you want to know?"

"Did you always want to be a composer?"

"For as long as I can remember."

"Why didn't you want to be a rock musician? Isn't that what most people your age want to be?"

He grins. "If that were true, there wouldn't be any classical composers at all, would there? Somebody has to prefer classical."

I smile weakly.

"Anyway," Noah continues, "my father was a bassoonist with the Boston Philharmonic. There was always classical music in the house. I got used to it the way other kids got used to Sinatra or the Beatles."

"Did you go to music school?"

"Oh, yeah," Noah says derisively. "That almost cured me of wanting to be a composer." He looks up into the dim room. "I tended bar to put myself through the conservatory. I could always go back to that."

I wait but he doesn't say anything more. His teacup is almost empty and so is my glass. I signal to the bartender, who is leaning against the corner of the bar and watching the television hanging from the ceiling across from him, his thick arms crossed. I wrack my brain for another question: "Why didn't you like music school?"

"It's a long story," Noah says. He peers knowingly at me. "You don't really want to hear about all this, do you?"

I make myself meet his eyes and say, "Yes, really I do. I'm becoming interested in classical music, at least in opera, and I'm interested in how you got started."

"You strike me as someone who really isn't interested in anything," he says. "Not that I blame you," he adds quickly. "I'd be bouncing off some padded walls if I were you, I think."

I look Noah straight in the eye. I say, "You're right. I'm not really interested in much. But I like to listen anyway."

So Noah talks about being an anachronism at the conservatory because he couldn't fall out of love with melody. He talks about his first opera, *Lincoln*, and how Isabel discovered him and changed his life. His deep voice, brightened by enthusiasm, seeps into my skin like steam and lulls me. When the bartender arrives at our table with my martini and a hot water pot, Noah looks down at his empty cup as if trying to remember what it's doing there. The bartender pours water into his cup and walks away, sniffing. "We should get back," Noah says, suddenly sobered.

I take a long drink. By this time the alcohol has worked its magic. I am floating a little above us, watching from an aerial vantage point

Noah's curls fall into his eyes. I want to prolong the feeling, the moment, want to lift my glass with heavy arms one more time. "Why do you suppose you chose opera, instead of some other classical music?" I ask.

Noah stops dipping his weak tea bag in his cup and shrugs, smiles almost conspiratorially. "Same reason we all fall for opera, I suppose. We crave the drama."

I rise a little unsteadily and Noah gets quickly to his feet and takes my elbow. I force myself to endure this gentle touch. We stop at the bar and I reach into my coat for my wallet but he has already pulled out money. I say something about starving artists but he says, "Isabel is very good to me," in such a shy, embarrassed voice, that I say nothing more.

Leo and Isabel both come the next weekend. Leo says it will be the last time for a while, since Isabel's two concerts are the next week and then she starts right in with *Madame Butterfly* rehearsals. They tell me this when they stop by on their first day back, knocking at my door at noon when I am sitting transfixed in front of the stereo, listening to the first act duet between Rigoletto and Gilda over and over, having programmed the CD player to repeat it ad infinitum.

Leo and Isabel perch on the edges of the furniture as if anxious to leave as soon as they've arrived. They are just looking in on me, they say. Leo tells me their plans while Isabel examines her fingernails. I'm still not clear what part he plays in her schedule—does he just watch her, Svengali-like, at rehearsals, or are there actual tasks that he needs to complete on her behalf? Or on behalf of the Career—which seems somehow to belong as much to him as to her, which she doesn't seem to mind. I always think that Isabel looks a little larger than life except when she's with Leo. Then she looks like exactly what she is—a small woman with a large head.

"I'm hoping you're still doing your walking, Eve," Isabel says. "I like to get more exercise right before performances. I thought we might take a couple of walks together this weekend."

Leo winks at me as if we both find her a bit silly. "Of course, you're going to be doing a lot of practicing this weekend too, aren't you, Isabel?"

"Yes, Leo, but I can still take a walk, can't I? Jesus." Isabel stands up abruptly. I have never seen her get angry at him before. I wonder if it's Noah's influence that has made her a little bolder. I expect Leo to rise to his full height and intimidate her, but he remains seated and chuckles.

"All right, darling," he says. "I'm acting the brute, aren't I, Eve?" Another wink. "I'm just concerned—it's Isabel's first full-length performance since she got sick in Sydney."

"I've made an appointment for my tonsils after *Butterfly*," Isabel says, playing with the porcelain figures on the mantle. "Then everything will be fine," she adds morosely.

I go walking with Isabel. We are both wrapped in scarves and hats and gloves and coats. There is talk of snow, and wind periodically stirs the enormous pines that line the trail. She is chatting about her upcoming recitals in a church in midtown and how much she looks forward to their being over so that she can begin work in earnest on *Butterfly*. "It may be the last time I get to do the part," she says, "and it's perhaps my favorite."

Isabel shrugs herself deeper into her coat. She stops at the next rustling of the trees and cocks her head. I turn around but all I see are the pines moving in the wind so that their layers of outstretched branches sway gracefully, like women's arms adjusting hoopskirts. We walk in silence for a while. A squirrel skitters across our path and Isabel follows it with her eyes, looking back in the direction of the house. When she turns around she says, "How is it for you here?"

"Fine," I say, automatically.

"Leo and I are so pleased that you've decided to write."

"I haven't decided," I say.

"Oh, I thought that you and Nigel had come to some arrangement."

"I haven't made up my mind."

"You don't want to talk about this, do you."

"Well," I say.

"Huh. I think in your place I would be wanting to talk all the time."

"Really," I say.

"I don't know." She starts walking again. "Maybe because I'm an actress. I just think that if I had that much emotion I wouldn't be able to keep it inside the way you do."

"What makes you think there's so much emotion in me," I say. I clench my fists, waiting for her response. This new propensity to burst out with the first thing that strikes me is worrisome.

Isabel stops again, her expression more pitying than shocked. She speaks quietly. "I can't begin to imagine what is in you and it's presumptuous of me to try." This seems to me a very kind thing to say and I bite my lip and walk on. "This is another reason why I hope you do write a book," Isabel's voice floats to me from behind. "So that you can share what this feels like with others, perhaps help those who've been through something similar."

Now I stop. "Oh, really," I say, turning back to her. "So what you're saying is that I am somehow obligated by virtue of my circumstances to do something for the world's edification." I am clenching my fists again.

Isabel moves to catch up to me. She puts a gloved hand on my arm. "Of course not, Eve, that's the last thing I mean."

"I'm sorry," I say sullenly. A crow dives close to us and lands on a branch, staring out at the sky, which has turned the color of tin.

"What do you think of Noah?" Isabel says as we resume walking.

It takes me a minute to adjust to her breathless change of subject. I pick my words carefully. "He's . . . he's different than he first appears. Friendlier. I like him."

Isabel laughs. "You sound so surprised! I think he's wonderful." She stares at the crow, who does look a bit like Noah, now that I think about it—sharp nosed and black clad. "He's immensely talented and very sensitive and . . ." her voice trails off. "Anyway." I feel her furtive glance. "You know, Leo is not an easy man. It's hard for him to love me." She blinks a few times but doesn't elaborate and keeps her gaze to the sky. "Leo forgets to be kind sometimes. Noah, now he is very kind." I'm surprised to see that there are tears in her eyes. "Noah is so very kind to me," she says. "He makes me feel young." She turns and walks on.

Each time the wind comes up I smell her sweet perfume and try to imagine what it would be like to be her. To be gifted, not just with talent, but with the opportunity to use that talent; to be beautiful and exotic even in late middle age, to be adored by so many people, almost all of them strangers, and to live daily with a man who appears not to understand the first thing about you—and to pine for the love of a boy young enough to be your son. Mostly, I wonder what it would be like to have these as your blessings, these as your problems. I marvel at the things that make people cry.

As if on cue there is a cracking of leaves and branches and Noah emerges from the woods. He tromps toward us in dark boots and a long overcoat and his hair is tangled into his eyes. He's frowning but when he catches sight of us his face lights up. "Hey," he says.

"Greetings," Isabel says gaily. He approaches us and touches her arm. She brings her hand up and covers his with her own. "Hi Eve," Noah says, looking at Isabel. I can hear his deep breaths, smell the soap he's just showered with, the whiff of freshly applied aftershave.

"I think I'll go back," I say.

"No," Noah says, "No don't," Isabel says and they take their eyes off each other long enough to look at me with alarm, so I keep walking with them, falling more and more behind so that by the time we round the next big curve of the trail I have lost sight of them completely.

We walk for twenty minutes or so. The trail circles around to the front of the house and when I near the turn just before the house becomes visible they're waiting for me, standing next to but apart from each other, their eyes bright and cheeks flushed, the air between them thick with their quick breaths. A small smile plays on the edges of Noah's mouth and Isabel has that serene countenance that makes her look even more like a work of art. We walk up the drive together.

Molly says, "I don't know how much I should tell you."

"Tell me as little as possible," I say.

"There were almost two hundred people," she says. "The rabbi who married you was there."

"That," I say, "is more than you need to tell me."

"Charlie's best friend from high school spoke," Charlie's mother, Lucy, says. "Dave. You probably never met him."

"No," I say.

"They had a kind of falling out. Some teenage boy stuff. Who remembers." Lucy laughs mirthlessly. "But he spoke so movingly of Charlie. Of their wild ways." The same laugh. A pause while Lucy clears her throat. "The girls couldn't speak."

She calls Charlie's sisters—both well past fifty—"the girls."

"I wanted Ed to, but he couldn't either. A friend from your ad agency did, though, and people from the marina, the boatyard, the yacht club, all that." Pause. She's waiting for me to ask who specifically each of these people was. People I know I should be grateful to.

"Sounds nice, Lucy," I manage.

"When are you coming home?" she says with false brightness, as if she's trying to convince herself that I'm simply away on a brief vacation, as if I have Charlie and the kids with me. Whereas Myra tends toward the melodramatic, seeing disaster in the smallest mishap, Lucy comes from the Pollyanna school of coping. Nothing is so bad that a good attitude can't make it right again. Charlie inherited this, just as I inherited much of Myra's doomsday outlook. We therefore drove each other crazy in a crisis.

I can picture Lucy holding the phone a fraction of an inch away from her lacquered hairdo. I can see the fake smile that never reaches her eyes which she trots out like an admonishment, her sagging chin trembling with the effort of her good cheer. It makes me tremble too, with the urge to wipe out her ridiculous sunniness. And so I say, "What home?"

Lucy makes a little sound and then says, "With your family, Eve."

I twist the knife. "My family?" I say. "My *family*?"

Now Lucy is crying. "You do have family left, Eve. Don't say that you don't." I am silent, listening to her try to control her sobs. "For god's sake, Eve, you're all we have left."

And I lose my breath then; I feel like I did the time we went sledding in Big Bear when the kids were little and I got on the sled first to show them it wasn't scary and I came down that baby hill on my stomach and went straight into a tree, ending up flat on my back and gasping, thinking I was dying that innocent day, thinking it was the end.

"Lucy," I say, "I'm here," I repeat until her crying subsides.

"So who exactly were these people who spoke at the service," I ask her.

"All your friends were there," Myra says when she gets on the phone. "Some I hadn't seen in years. Sheila and Jeannie and Robin from junior high, and of course Annette and . . ."

"Uh huh," I say.

"It was pretty obvious that the rabbi didn't know Charlie well. But he said nice things, heartfelt things. And then George spoke."

"George? Molly didn't tell me that."

"She was under the impression that you didn't want to hear much."

"I don't."

"Well then." Silence. "He was very eloquent."

"Okay, Myra."

"What?"

"Go ahead and tell me."

"Not if you don't want . . . if you feel you can't . . ."

"Give me the brief version," I say and close my eyes. And hear, from the things my mother tells me, how my brother-in-law loves my sister more than I realized, how he spoke for her and for our mother, how he made their loss a presence. He spoke last, Myra says, and everyone agreed that George was the one who'd said it most powerfully, articulated how every day we walk the earth we are imperiled and how the only antidote to that unshakable truth is to hold tighter to those we love. Now Myra is crying again and it occurs to me that grief spreads like an oil slick, washing up on the shores of people you never even think of, sticking to the soles of lives you merely bump up against in the most superficial of ways and lives you haven't touched in years.

"One other thing," Myra says. She's taken a long pause and dropped her voice. A sure sign that something portentous is coming. "Yesterday, right after we got home from the service, there was a letter waiting."

Before she left I'd signed a paper giving Myra power of attorney over my bank account and other official business I might be called upon to handle. She is dealing with the insurance company and the bank and interviewing lawyers for this phantom lawsuit she has in her head, in which miraculously the world is righted by the stroke of a judge's quill pen.

This letter, from the U.S. Coast Guard, Myra explains, was addressed to me. "I assumed you'd want me to open it," she says. "Shall I read it to you?"

"Just give me the gist," I say.

Myra says, "They've established definitively the ship. The ship that . . . hit you."

"Yes." My voice a croak in the back of my throat. I am not breathing.

"It was a fishing boat, just as you always said."

"Yes."

"A Russian fishing boat, bound for New Zealand. They had the Russian police involved in the investigation too. It's been . . . international."

Still not breathing.

"There may be criminal charges."

The phone is so tightly clutched in my hand that it's like a part of my body.

"Honey? Are you there?"

I clench my teeth and speak through them. "What happened," I say.

"Are you all right? Are you sure?" I can't speak again so I wait and eventually she goes on. "It's still a bit murky. There was no malfunction of their essential equipment—radar or anything. Apparently, their refrigeration system wasn't functioning well and they had a full load of fish, so they were in a hurry to get to port. They were exhausted. They were on autopilot. The officer on watch—well—they think he may have fallen asleep. They'll be looking into it further, believe me."

"Someone fell asleep."

"Well, that's one theory. It would be criminal negligence, I don't see how it couldn't be, but in Russia, who knows . . ."

"Myra Myra have you never heard of eyes a whole ship's crew and lookouts they always have lookouts as we should have as we should have Myra!"

"Honey, I—"

"Myra, tell me this one little thing. Tell me where in the letter it says this Myra and then everything will be all right. Tell me, WHY

THE FUCK THEY DIDN'T JUST SEE US TELL ME THAT MYRA, WHY DIDN'T THEY SEE US!"

"Eve—"

But I slam down the receiver and then try halfheartedly to pull the phone from the wall but when it doesn't give right away I just let the receiver dangle, stare at it for a while, then back away from it; I stumble into the wall behind me. The pain shoots up my neck. I throw myself to the corner of the small kitchen and my shoulder meets drywall, think *this is good I could do this for a while*. I head into the living room and hit the mantle with my fist; something shifts but doesn't fall from it. When the doorbell rings I'm still doing this; the door opens even though I thought I locked it and I'm thinking, *maybe, just there I might have broken a wrist*. I feel strong arms around me. I'm lifted off the ground a little, my legs are dangling, and I'm smelling soap and coffee and feeling his rough cheek when I flail my head around and he's saying my name and trying to carry me into the bedroom saying, "I'm going to call 911 if you can't calm down." I hear that clearly so I gulp in some air, try to relax, and he has me down on the bed, holding me there, his touch seeming to be light but how could it be since I can't move but he does it with such ease almost with nonchalance, disinterest in his face. I say, "How do you do that," and he looks startled. Stares down at me, says "What?" "How do you do that, hold me down like that." He grins. "You forget, I used to work in a bar. I've handled way worse than you."

A little later he calls from the bathroom, "Which ones?" and I'm tempted to say: All of them, but instead I say "The little white triangular ones—two please," and he brings me the pills and water. He sits on the bed while I take the pills, still with that disinterested green gaze, his disheveled hair over his eyes.

"My boy had green eyes," I say.

He doesn't flinch. Keeps staring at me, reaches out his hand and smoothes some damp hair off my forehead. "I'd like to see a picture of him sometime," he says. And I close my eyes against the sadness and pity in his.

11

I spend the next two days with 1) numerous bruises and a sizable bump on my head and a sore wrist, 2) a few bottles of wine, 3) *Bohème*, *Tosca*, *Rigoletto*, *La Traviata* and *Pavarotti's Greatest Hits*, 4) a growing pile of increasingly creative replies to my sympathy mail.

On the third day Noah calls and asks me to come up to the house for dinner. "It's lonely up here," he says. I give him every opportunity to get out of it. Don't you have to work—I'll work later; You may not have enough food—Isabel stocked this place like I was going to get snowed in; and finally—I'm not sure I'm up to the walk, if you want to know the truth.

"I'll come there," he says, and hangs up before I have a chance to say anything else.

He shows up twenty minutes later with two bottles of chardonnay in one hand and in the other, a picnic basket containing a package of chicken breasts, a canister of breadcrumbs, a box of rice, a head of lettuce, one green and one yellow pepper, a carafe of homemade salad dressing, and a pint of New York Chocolate Chunk ice cream, which he informs me I must not die without tasting. The tip of his long nose is red from the cold and he's frowning a little as he sets his burdens down on the small table in the kitchen and declares that he has to put on his wrist braces right away as the weight was more than he anticipated. "You'll have to open the wine." He brushes the hair out of his eyes impatiently and I think this was probably a bad idea, now he's going to blame me for some impairment of his creative powers. When I hand him a glass of wine his wrist is already wrapped up and I ask him how it feels. "Horrible." He looks at me. "Hey, it's not your fault. I played too long today. I wasn't careful. I was excited because it's going well."

"I'll cook," I say.

"No, no, I'm fine." He starts over to the stove but I hold out my hand. "Go sit down," I say. I almost say his name, but my mouth closes around the "N" and doesn't want to open again. Something happens when you say someone's name for the first time. Something intimate and irrevocable.

"I didn't invite you to dinner so that you could cook for me, especially with your injuries."

"Why don't you go sit in the living room," I say.

I turn my back and pull a heavy skillet out of the cabinet.

"Shall I put on some music?" Noah calls from the other room.

"Sure." I pour olive oil into the skillet as vigorous violins begin their concert. In the package of CDs Isabel gave me were some Mozart symphonies and I assume this is one of them. The violins swell as I shake out breadcrumbs from the canister onto a plate. I am shaking canned Parmesan cheese into the breadcrumbs when I hear Noah's voice behind me.

"I never thought of doing that before."

"What, using Parmesan? It's only the canned stuff. I can't remember the last time I saw a hunk of actual Parmesan."

"You know the deli in town actually has a respectable selection of cheese. Next time I take you you can pick some out."

Which suggestion pleases me more than it should. I dredge the chicken breasts in the breadcrumbs, then lay them in the skillet, where they sizzle in the hot oil. Immediately the summer smell of olive oil and herbs rises in the small kitchen. I breathe it in. "It seems a long time since I cooked anything," I say.

"Are you a good cook?" he asks.

"Not particularly." He gets a worried look on his face and I laugh. "Don't worry, I'm good enough. Just not a gourmet, like you."

"Well how could you be," he says a bit indignantly, "with two kids. My nephew won't eat any food that isn't orange. How the hell are you supposed to be creative with *that*?"

"Exactly. The second year of our trip my daughter told me that if she had to eat one more potato—even a french fry—she'd throw herself overboard. How weird is that for a seven year old?"

"Ketchup too?"

"Oh no. Ketchup she'd still eat."

"Well," he says with great sincerity, "it is an officially designated vegetable now."

And we are both laughing.

"When I was a kid," he says, "my best friend, Jared Conrad, used to eat dirt by the platefuls. I thought it was cool but the one time I tried it I puked." He laughs, then stops, frowns. "Hey, I hope it's okay, you know. Making jokes. Talking about Jessica."

I stop what I'm doing. "You remembered her name."

He reddens. Looks away. "Yeah, sure."

"That's nice," I say, almost a whisper. There is as much tension in the air as if we'd just kissed.

Noah sets to work tearing the lettuce into the colander I've put on the table. I watch him for a while, examining the hunch of his embarrassed shoulders, feeling oddly like I already know him.

"So you're really getting into the music, aren't you?" he says, breaking into my silly thoughts.

"I guess so," I say, and try to sound nonchalant. I prod the chicken with a fork. "It's . . ." I stop, searching for the words which will make me sound intrigued rather than obsessed. "I spent all these years thinking opera was torture—like listening to a Jim Nabors record, or something."

"Who?"

"Like the Partridge Family, say."

"Ah." He nods. "And now what do you think?"

"Well, now I think it's more like Joni Mitchell."

Noah looks skeptical.

"You know who she is?"

"Of course I know who she is. 'Woodstock.' 'Both Sides Now.' The sixties."

"Yes, but she's done a lot more than that. She was the person you listened to when, you know, when you were a teenager, when your heart was breaking, or you thought no one could feel as misfit as you; she said everything you couldn't. She got me through my adolescence relatively intact. And opera is like that. It says everything you know and feel but can't articulate. It pulls all the big emotions out into the open. It's . . . a revelation."

Noah stops making the salad and stares at me. "Wow," he says. "You've *really* gotten into it."

We sit over refilled glasses of wine and full plates. Noah found a candle in the back of a cabinet and it's burning between us, stuck in a mound of aluminum foil.

"The chicken is a little overcooked," I say.

"It's brilliant."

"I'm out of practice."

"It's nice to have company."

"When do Isabel and Leo come back?"

Noah glowers. "Not for a while."

"Why?" I say.

"Leo. The recital reviews. Leo's paranoid."

I look questioningly at him. "The reviews were . . . not great. Actually, they stunk. But she's been sick. So her voice was maybe not perfectly on, but it's like, she's all washed up according to them and Leo's freaking. Making her stay and work with this Bosco person on *Butterfly*."

"Making her?"

"Well, I guess he's got her freaked too. She doesn't exactly take bad reviews well—who does. So she does what he says. She says he knows what's best for her but I don't think she really even believes that. And I don't think he's only worried about her voice." He glances at me then looks at his plate. "I think Leo doesn't want her coming out here, regardless."

I can't tell if he wants me to ask why or not, but at any rate, I don't. "Well, the less distractions you have from your work the better, I suppose," I say.

He laughs. "I guess that's one way to look at it."

Later we wash the dishes in the cramped little kitchen; every time one of us makes a move we brush up against the other, with many awkward apologies. "Tell you what," Noah says lifting a wineglass to the light as he dries it. He is just next to me and I can smell him, can imagine his dark-clad arms closing around me and clutching me the way they did the other day, calming me, and I scrub the plate I'm washing vigorously, finding hidden stains. "Let's make a regular thing of this," he says, though it sounds more like a question than a suggestion. I keep my eyes on the sink. "Not every night, but now and then, we could eat together—cook for each other—make sure we take care of ourselves while Isabel's gone. What do you think?"

"I'm going to New York at the end of next week myself," I say. "I have all these appointments."

"Till then," he says. "When you feel like company."

"We'll see."

All Noah says about Isabel again is right before he leaves, when he's buttoning his long black overcoat and wrapping his muffler around his neck. He thanks me for cooking, for joining him for dinner, hopes we'll do it again, then, in a voice so small he sounds younger than Nick, he says, "I miss her."

The next day I am taking a long walk in which my mind is blissfully blank when I see a deer poised between two tree trunks sniffing the air and actually wagging her tail. Later, *Great Opera Overtures* on the stereo, the phone rings and I realize that part of me has been waiting for it like a schoolgirl, all day, my body poised like the deer's.

"What could we do with ground beef, do you think?" he says.

Just as I'm nearing the house I hear a rustle from somewhere in the woods and it sounds so much like whispering that it makes me turn every time, my heart pounding.

I knock but there's no answer and the door is open so I walk in. I hear Noah's tense voice. "I know," he is saying, "but I can't keep waiting like this. You're driving me crazy and I think you like it."

I start to back out again but he emerges with the phone to his ear and, seeing me, looks at first anguished and then relieved. He says "Uh huh" and waves me toward the kitchen.

I am just pouring a small can of tomato sauce into a bowl in which I've mixed the chopped meat with onions and herbs and breadcrumbs when Noah appears in the kitchen. "Isabel's going to try and come next weekend," he says, going to the closet that holds the wine. "She said to ask you if you wanted to join them for Thanksgiving." He hands me a huge goblet filled halfway with red wine. "I finished Act Two today," he says.

"Congratulations," I say. We clink our heavy glasses and Noah grins.

"I think I owe it all to you," he says. "Last night *nourished* me."

Later when we are eating meatloaf at the dining room table, he says, "You know what I like best about your conversation, Eve?"

"What."

"How little there is of it. You don't make small talk."

"Don't I?" Surely that's all anyone does, I'm thinking.

The next day we go into town again. Shopping, drinks, a routine now. This time we buy the food together, consulting on whether he likes arugula, whether I'm willing to eat veal. The array of possibilities for feeding him stir memories of the satisfaction of filling up someone else. We buy a hunk of Parmesan at the deli counter and a case of wine so we don't drink all of Leo and Isabel's and stuffed olives for martinis, using up both our funds. I offer to write him a check but he refuses.

Later, at the bar, he says, "Do you mind my asking—what you do for money?"

I snort. "Why should I mind about things like that," I say. "I have money we'd saved. And there's more coming from the insurance settlement, I suppose."

"And a lawsuit?"

"I guess so. If my mother decides to pursue it. Or my in-laws."

"You don't want to?"

I look at him. "Why would I want to, Noah?"

"I would, I think. Some kind of satisfaction."

Without thinking I put my hand over his and then quickly withdraw it. He doesn't move. "Think about it, Noah. Do you really think there would be an ounce of satisfaction in a lawsuit?"

He nods. Sips his tea. The bartender has gotten used to him by now—tolerates him mostly because I drink enough for both of us. "But what if you run out of money?" Noah says.

I shrug. Then I speak in that unbidden, spontaneous voice that has been coming out of me lately: "Remember the first time you smelled a skunk?"

He looks at me quizzically. "I guess so. I mean yes, I do actually. I was camping. It was foul."

"Do you remember how up to that moment, if you thought about it, you thought that a skunk would probably smell like all the worst smells you could imagine—excrement, garbage and body odor, maybe, all rolled into one? And how surprising it was to smell the real thing—which was entirely new, unlike any odor you'd experienced before? How completely off guard it took you?"

"Yes," he nods vigorously. "Exactly."

"That's what this life feels like to me. If I could have predicted how it would feel now, I would have drawn on all the tragedies I've ever experienced, like my father's death and my grandparents'. Our first dog getting hit by a car. I would have assumed I would feel what I felt then, only more of it. I would have thought there'd be a context, I guess. But this is like a . . . a new planet, a new universe. This is skunk smell. So I don't worry about what I'll do for money if it runs out—I do what people ask me to because it seems to matter to them. I'm trying to write because my mother and Isabel and Leo and this agent all think that's a good idea. Isabel says stuff about helping others by 'sharing my pain' and a lot of the letters I've looked at talk about God, about faith. Almost everyone has an idea of what it takes to cope. But I'll tell you something, Noah, there's only one way to get through this, at least for me, and that is to get through the second that just passed and the one we're in right now and the one coming up. Each second is another one you've survived and that's how you keep yourself walking the earth."

Noah lifts his hand to my face, blots it with his fingertips. "I'm sorry," I say.

"Seems to me you should be crying *more*." He gives a low laugh. "Jesus, I'm doing it too, huh. Telling you what would be good for you."

I wait for him now, I have to admit it. I move about the rooms feeling the air displace wherever I've passed, as if everything is held in readiness till he comes. I cooked an omelette tonight—diced peppers and onions and only a couple of drops of milk in the eggs the way Charlie taught me. Only a little cheese, just enough to give the omelette some weight, since Noah thinks he's lactose intolerant. I told him he just doesn't eat regularly enough. He said, "Maybe so." And bowed his head over his plate and finished everything on it—the omelette and the hunk of oatmeal bread and sautéed potatoes and onions. "I shouldn't have this," he said, smiling at me. "But you're such a good cook."

And I don't care if it's a line; he says it with sincerity and gentleness, reminding me what it's like to feel of use.

After we eat we sit in the living room, me with a glass of wine, Noah with herb tea or occasionally brandy. Noah picks out a CD—

usually something baroque or an opera—he doesn't try to broaden my horizons. "This time is for relaxing," he says, stretching out on the couch while I sit in the chair nearby. We turn on only the lamp over the desk so that most of the room is bathed in a greenish glow. We often sit for a long time without saying anything, just listening to the music or the voices, letting them seep into our muscles like massage.

Sometimes he talks about his work. He looks at the ceiling and describes a particularly difficult passage that he struggled with all day, his failure to bring the music up to the drama of the moment. "The scene in parliament when Catherine appeared before the peers and Cardinal Wolsey and the papal legate. And she refused to recognize their authority over her, over the legality of her marriage. I mean Eve, you should see this speech. It's absolutely brilliant—riveting." Noah, like Isabel, is in love with extravagant adjectives when it comes to talking about his work. Ordinarily this is a characteristic I would despise as too reminiscent of my own pretentious artistic days. But it seems such an integral part of Isabel's personality that I can't think of her as speaking any other way. As for Noah—sometimes the lavish words sound foreign in his mouth but it reminds me that he is still young and perhaps has not yet developed a vocabulary of his own.

". . . as dramatic as any aria I've ever heard. I mean, Robbie, the librettist, has shaved a word or a line here or there to make it fit the cadence, but otherwise, we're using the original text, Catherine's actual words as recorded." He sits up. "You should hear her. Absolutely *regal*. The most incredible courage. This one woman who was completely alone and without allies. Can't you just see Isabel in that role?"

His bandaged hands slice and punch the air. "The question is whether I can make music that's worthy of the speech, of Isabel."

"I'm sure you can," I say.

He laughs. "You have no idea if I can, actually."

"That's true. But I can see how much you want to, and that's half the battle."

"Maybe." He searches my face, for signs of dissembling, I suppose. But I only have to look at him to believe in him.

"It will be great," I declare.

He laughs again. "Yeah, well, you're prejudiced." There is something intimate in that remark—the assumption that I feel for him something that would cause me to champion him unconditionally is the first acknowledgment that we are coming to need each other.

The next night he is in a far less voluble mood. The work has not gone well and he eats his dinner morosely, then flops on the couch. We listen to Verdi and make a few comments about the predicted snow. Just when I am thinking that it is time to go to bed, he speaks to the ceiling.

"You should talk. You hardly talk, you always just listen to me."

"I like listening to you," I say.

"But you. There must be so much that you think about." He sounds plaintive, almost angry. I stand up and go over to where he lies on the couch. Without thinking I put my hand on his left shoulder, feeling his warmth through the thick sweater. Feel his breathing. He looks up at me, his eyes unreadable.

"Noah," I say, "I can't *really* talk."

And he says, "All right. But when you can." That simply.

What I might tell him! How he fills my head now, how I plan what I will make for him and what I might say to draw him out, ease the tensions of his day. How I'm fascinated by the way the black curls graze the corners of his eyes, how I wash my hair every day now and am suddenly conscious of the bags under my eyes and my still weather-toughened skin.

"I talked to Angelique today," he says.

"Who?" I say, grateful for the interruption of my thoughts.

"Angelique, you know. My . . . ex-girlfriend."

"Oh." For a moment I'm annoyed at his impatient expression. As if I'm supposed to remember something as minor as his girlfriend's name, as if I keep tabs on his personal life.

"I mentioned that I've been thinking about her as I write the character of Mary Tudor and she's thrilled. Sure it will make her immortal."

"Isn't Mary Tudor the one you said became 'Bloody Mary'?"

"Uh huh."

"The one who burned people at the stake?"

"That's Angelique for you." Noah laughs. "I'll tell you one thing, if Angelique was a queen in the 16th century she wouldn't be above burning a few heretics at the stake herself, just for yucks. She's pretty . . . strongwilled."

"As long as she's not a religious fanatic," I say, hoping this will end the conversation.

"Far from it," Noah goes on, oblivious. "Art is her religion—and me, I sometimes think. She's really helped me shape my career, given me lots of support." His face turns serious. "I'll always be grateful for that." He shoots me an anxious look.

"It's all right," I say. His love life has nothing to do with me, after all. My desire for him—if that's what it is—is for his mere presence, the way it fills the emptiness of this room.

"Well, it was great in the beginning," he's saying. "We were like each other's muses. She's eight years older than me and pretty well established in the art world. She made it possible for me to quit my day job and compose full time."

"And what did you do for her?" I ask.

"What do you mean?"

"Well, what does she get out of the relationship?"

"Oh. Well, I guess she gets . . . to feel useful or complete." Noah frowns. "But for months we've barely talked. It's like we stay together out of history, because neither of us knows what else to do . . . until now. Do you know what I mean?"

I look away, afraid the heat surging through me will show on my face. It's not dislike—how could I dislike a woman I've never met?

"I think," I say, "that sometimes love is just what you're talking about. It's not what you feel, it's what you remember feeling."

"I just know that every time I try to talk to Angelique about breaking up she sweet-talks me out of it. I'm weak. If it hadn't been for Isabel, I'd probably be in that loft forever."

"And you're sure you don't want to be?" I find myself holding my breath.

Noah hesitates, stares at his bandaged hands, then peers up at me from under his lids, suddenly shy. "I'm almost never sure of anything, if you want to know the truth. But don't tell that to Isabel."

"If you won't tell her that I keep you from your work sometimes."

We smile conspiratorially at each other.

The growing wind sounds like thunder outside the windows; the faintest ticking of the porcelain clock over the mantle is still audible. Soon Noah's even breaths indicate that he's fallen asleep. I tiptoe into the bedroom and get the extra blanket. The lighted clock in the bedroom says 1:20 A.M. I bring the blanket back into the dim living room. I move the coffee table back, shooting blades through my back in the process but barely feeling the pain. I kneel at Noah's feet and pull off his worn boat shoes. Lifting his feet by the ankles I cradle them in my arms—they are surprisingly heavy and exude a faint sweaty odor that reminds me of fevers and illness. I lower his feet onto the couch, as gently as if they were perishable. He stirs and shifts, says "I should get back," sleepily, a quick snort of air. Then he is asleep again. I spread the blanket carefully over him, just under his chin.

His head is twisted to the right at an odd angle, crushing one of the throw pillows. He'll have a stiff neck in the morning. A thick mass of hair hangs over his brow and eyes and without thinking I reach down and lace my fingers through it, combing it back against his scalp. His scalp is humid. He opens his eyes just when I am taking my hand away and I freeze. He turns his head toward me, smiles, takes hold of my paralyzed hand, drawing it back to his face, pressing it against his stubbly cheek, pressing himself into the curve of my palm as if it were a pillow. "Night," he says, closing his eyes and as soon as he nestles back in I remove my hand. I hold my hand by the wrist as I move like a sleepwalker back to my room. I stand in the dark room for twenty minutes or so, the wind rising to a howl outside, breathing in short, raspy pants, thinking I must never, ever do that again.

In the beginning Charlie made love like a starving man. He roamed my body, his mouth moving from my lips to my shoulder to the crease under my breast then back to my face, as if I were a feast laid out before him and he didn't know what to sample first. Each part of my body that he touched felt suddenly unfamiliar, as if I had never known that this particular area of my upper arm, this exact circle of nerves on my breast that now jumped alive had ever existed. We stopped using birth control after our second year of marriage—sooner than I wanted but later than Charlie did. Children, like everything else in our marriage, were to be dictated by the voyage.

Except that Charlie was thwarted. Because I didn't get pregnant. After a year we began to try in earnest. Then, predictably, our lovemaking changed. Nothing was ever the same again. We were suddenly slaves to the calendar and the clock, obsessed with my body temperature, my hormones, my bleeding. We had tests. We had passionless, practical sex. We held my legs up in the air afterward. We had me take a tablespoon full of cough syrup every day. We had Charlie switch to boxer shorts. The doctor said we were both fine and just to be patient. Charlie was a very patient man ordinarily, but this thwarting of his plan did not sit well with him. So we spent at least two years not liking each other very much as he tried to get me to take fertility pills, have procedures, get shots. It was the one place where I resisted him. I said, you get yourself shot up with hormones, you burst into tears every five minutes and gain weight and risk ovarian cancer. Me, I'm content to let nature take its course.

12

At the last minute Noah decides to accompany me to the city. I can't say that I tried hard to stop him. I think of him as a sort of curtain—heavy, soundproof and soft velvet—between me and the rest of the world. We ride the train and then the taxi in our usual silence, though I can feel his growing excitement as we near Isabel's apartment.

Isabel greets us as if we were her long lost children—hugs for both of us, sheer delight in her laughter. She and Leo comment repeatedly on how well I look.

They take us to our rooms and I sit on the familiar bed and try to summon up blankness. I'm not used to this many voices or bodies together at once. I'm not used to sharing Noah. I'm not used to caring.

Later we sit rather awkwardly in the the living room, the darkening city sparkling like a sputtering star through the glass doors to the terrace while Leo talks about their recent activities: rehearsals and coaching and therapy for Isabel's throat.

"Yes, it's been brutal," Isabel says brightly. It's the most she's said in a while. She's mostly sat quietly as Leo talks, her head swaying on her shoulders as if she were a marionette responding to his cues, her earrings flashing in the subdued light. She looks particularly beautiful to me tonight—the light catches the red in her upswept hair, her face is as smooth and pale as cream, her eyes are heavily made-up and dramatic against her opaque skin. She is sipping wine and staring alternately at Leo and Noah.

Noah has given over his usual black turtleneck for an eggplant-colored one which contrasts strikingly with his black hair. His eyes are magnetized to Isabel's face and every time she looks at him it's as if the room falls silent even though Leo is chattering away; I think, how can Leo not feel this, how can he pretend this isn't happening?

Leo is prattling happily about how *Butterfly* is already sold out when they don't open till after Thanksgiving.

"Leo," Isabel interrupts him irritably, "*Butterfly* always sells out. It sells out as soon as people hear it's playing. All the runs are sold out."

"Why yes, my darling, that's true, but your run sold out first."

"That's because I'm in the 'A' cast," Isabel says. "The 'B' and 'C' casts sold out minutes after ours did."

"And why are you in the 'A' cast?"

Isabel laughs. "Because they don't dare kick the old broad downstairs."

"Isabel, that doesn't sound like you," Leo says, his voice tense.

"I'm just trying to be realistic, Leo," she snaps.

"Your voice is magnificent," Noah says impulsively.

Isabel bestows her most beautiful smile on him. "Thank you for having faith in me, Noah." There is an almost imperceptible emphasis on the word "you." "After the operation it will definitely be more reliable."

"So, Noah, do we have you to thank for Eve's rosy cheeks?" Leo says.

Noah breathes out a little sigh. "Yes, we've been keeping each other in good health, I think."

"Well, I'm just *so* glad," Isabel says. She is wincing a little, as if her wine has suddenly fermented. "We can see the most *marvelous* improvement, Eve. And you're moving less stiffly too. Is your back better?"

"Quite a bit," I say.

"Do we have Noah to thank for that too?" Leo says.

"What do you mean, Leo?" Isabel says sharply.

Leo looks blankly at her "Well, I imagine it's easier to get exercise when someone joins you. And since—"

"I'm working all day," Noah interrupts. He looks at Isabel. "I don't have time for walks," he says to her in an earnest tone.

"I should think not," she says.

"But we are so pleased that you two have become friends, aren't we Iz?" Leo says, his face inscrutable.

"*So* glad." Isabel downs her wine.

"Noah is working very hard," I say. "I barely see him."

Leo picks up his wineglass and studies its contents as he swirls it. "I'll bet your girlfriend will be pleased, too," he says to Noah, "to hear that you're closer to the end than the beginning."

"Uh," Noah says, watching Isabel.

"I hope we're going to see her at Thanksgiving," Leo continues.

"Uh." Noah looks at Leo, then back at Isabel. "I. We're not really together anymore."

"Oh, I'm sorry. I didn't know." Leo sounds genuinely bothered. He shakes his head. "Well, now, tell us more about the opera, Noah."

I close my eyes as Noah begins to talk. The candles on the coffee table flicker and waltz, music filters through speakers hidden somewhere in the room and without much effort you could imagine a nearby crowd of beautiful young people decked out in ball gowns the colors of summer ice creams, in tuxedos and stiff collars, a small orchestra playing in the corner and much laughter mixed with the dancing, and a woman who looks like Greta Garbo, fragile and exquisite, who nurses a secret heartbreak. There is a moment in *La Traviata*'s second act (whose music I could hum right here) after Violetta has secretly agreed to give up Alfredo for good, where he comes upon her preparing to leave him. She pretends to be as happy and carefree as ever. She tells him she loves him and that she is only going away for a day. "Amami, Alfredo, quant'io t'amo!" she sings: *Love me, Alfredo, as much as I love you*. Every time I hear it I dissolve. Because Violetta knows. She leaves and she knows it's for good and she knows that Alfredo mustn't know—her greatest sacrifice is that she can't say a proper good-bye. Every time I hear that scene I am consumed by the question of whether it is better to be prepared—to know what's coming even if you can't speak—or whether to be caught unawares is the kinder fate: You are prevented from saying good-bye but up to the last minute you get to live in the illusion that you don't have to. Now, in this lovely room with the smell of comfort and ease hanging in the air along with the thick tension, I press my hands to the pain in my chest as if I could keep the new loss trapped there, as if this might save me from having to hear Noah's departing words.

Leo leaves for Chicago the next day. He will be gone two or three days, arranging more recital bookings for after Isabel has her tonsils "yanked," as she puts it. Now I understand why Noah was so eager to come to New York with me. I see almost nothing of him or Isabel for the next two days. I go to the orthopedist, who reluctantly agrees to one more refill of painkillers.

To Dr. Shepard, the therapist, I tell optimistic tales of my evenings with Noah, of my love of the city and pride that I am getting around by myself and she says she's glad I'm showing some interest in life again. As I am gathering my things to leave, however, she says she thinks I still have to deal more directly with the accident. "Noah and all these people who are being so kind to you can help you through this, but they're not a substitute for grieving," she says.

"I know that," I say, "but I have forever for that."

She has the grace to say "Good point," but then adds, "They're also not your family. You do have to go back to your family some day."

I've been buttoning my coat. I look up at her then. She is leaning forward in her leather armchair, staring intently at me. "You have no idea," I tell her, "how often I think about that. How much I want to. Go back to my family." She settles back in her chair, smiling encouragingly, waiting no doubt for me to finally begin talking about my mother, my sister, my home in California. "Not that family," I say.

When I arrive back at the apartment I hear singing from down the hall. I walk through the pristine rooms longing for the cottage where a few of Noah's dishes are still drying in the rack and the couch is curved with the shape of his body. When I get to the room at the end of the hall that Isabel uses as a music studio, the door is open. She is in front of a music stand, singing an aria unfamiliar to me, though after a while I realize it's in the exaggerated, foreign-sounding tones of opera English. Noah is across from her, playing on a large keyboard he holds in his lap. Neither of them notices me. Noah is playing like a blind man, his every nerve and muscle focused on Isabel, on the beautiful but occasionally croaking sounds that emerge from her mouth. "Here more *piano*, I think," he says suddenly. "She's dying here, right?"

Isabel stops singing. "Darling," she says. "*Please* don't interrupt while I'm singing. If you have a . . . *suggestion*, make it when I pause. Never stop me mid-phrase. Not at this early a stage."

"You mean in the process, or . . . in my career?" Noah says, scowling.

Isabel laughs. "Both, I guess. Anyway, enough of this. You said you'd listen to *Un bel di* if I'd do this bit for you."

"This is for you too, Isabel. This part is written for you."

Isabel walks over to him and strokes his hair. "I know, and I'm so excited about it. But for now, let's focus on the bird I have in the hand, not the two in your bush. On to *Butterfly*!"

The floor creaks as I shift my weight and she turns and sees me. "Eve! Come in! We were just about to do some rehearsal of *Butterfly*. Sit down."

"I'd love to hear something of Noah's opera," I say impulsively.

Isabel smiles broadly. "Would you? Well we're all very excited and when the time comes you'll hear everything. For now, I have to put bread on the table with Cio-Cio-San, so we'll all just have to suck it up and listen to *Un bel di* for the gazillionth time in our lives. Even if you don't know the opera's music, Eve, believe me, you know this."

And she's right. It's music that I've absorbed somehow through the years—probably from car commercials. It's nonetheless beautiful, and even the small quaver in Isabel's throat doesn't diminish its lure. Noah, too, is soon entranced and when she finishes Isabel claps her hands like a child who's finally pleased her difficult parents.

That night, over Chinese food, I tell them I'm leaving.

"Oh, but surely you'll stay a few more days!" Isabel says. "I wanted you to come to rehearsal tomorrow."

"I'm a bit worn out. I think I'd just like to get back to the cottage and rest." I look at Noah, who is doggedly spearing some sesame noodles with his chopsticks.

"Well, if you're sure," Isabel says.

"Yes."

Noah speaks to his plate. "I should go back with Eve."

"Oh no, not yet. We're having such a *super* time, and . . . I'm sure it's just as . . . productive for the work as your actual writing. Say you'll at least stay a few more days, Noah." She coughs. "Leo won't be back till Monday and I so hate to be alone." Noah looks sharply at her, then at me. His face is twisted into an unreadable grimace.

"What if Eve needs to go into town," he says.

"I'll be fine," I say, before either of them can pretend to be concerned.

Isabel puts both her hands flat on the table. "It's settled then. We'll be sorry to see you go, Eve, but you'll be back next week for Thanksgiving, I'm sure."

At that moment she sounds just like Myra when we'd visit with the children after my father died. No matter how long we stayed, when it was time to go, Myra was as great a diva as Isabel, injecting her pleas for us to stay with such pathos and self-deprecating need that it took superhuman effort—and Charlie's ability to joke Myra through anything—for us to get out of there. We never escaped without a commitment to the exact date of our next visit. The children always left close to tears they couldn't explain. I used to want to kill Myra for that.

As I am closing my suitcase the next morning Isabel comes to my room. She is attractively rumpled in a pair of jeans and a man's plaid flannel shirt. She keeps moving around the room, fingering the things she comes upon—the carved post of the bedframe, the silk of the lampshade. "We're doing Thanksgiving here and we want you to come back. We do it every year. Have about twenty people, including Leo's mother. You'll love everyone." Her voice lacks her usual enthusiasm and she is looking everywhere but at me. "You and Noah can come together, unless I convince him to stay until then. If so, then we can send the car for you."

"You've done enough already."

"You can't be alone on Thanksgiving. Myra would never forgive me."

"You let me worry about Myra. I'll be fine."

"But why? Why don't you want to come?" Now she peers at me with a kind of hostile curiosity.

"All those people," I say.

"But you are doing so much better," she interrupts impatiently. "My god you're practically living with Noah; you can't tell me you're not able to stand any society."

"Excuse me?"

"You know what I mean." She waves her hand at me. "You couldn't stand to have any of us around a few weeks ago and now you seem to be doing just fine in his company. So why can't you—"

"Isabel, we've had a few meals together, period. That doesn't mean that I'm ready to go to parties. I mean give me a break, Isabel. . . ."

I pause, breathless. I don't care if she throws me out right now. I knew Noah would stay with her as long as she asked. How unbelievable that after all that's happened, and all the evidence that pointed to the fact that I was no longer meant to be involved with people, I have so easily fallen into feeling needed again. Feeling need.

But Isabel is contrite. She grasps my arm, speaking in her sincerest, most earnest tones. What was she thinking and of course I don't have to come and please forgive her. "It's true, I've been a little jealous of you and Noah," she says, with a joyless laugh. "Here I am stuck in the city with Leo driving me like a workhorse. And I think of you and Noah there with your cozy dinners and your *fantastic* conversation—he's told me how *marvelous* you are—and I want to be there with you, not slaving away for Leo's peace of mind. Sometimes I just feel like . . ." She brings her hand up to her forehead and brushes away an imaginary wisp of hair. "I keep waiting till I get to do what I want, you know?"

And then I am comforting her, hugging her and patting her back, murmuring "it'll be okays," not sure how we got here.

"Well now . . . that's enough self-pity for one day, don't you think?" She pulls away from me, her laugh bright and musical, sounding like some Victorian heroine determined to keep her chin up. Then she declares us friends again and sails out of the room.

At the train station they both hug me, their huge overcoats smothering. Noah whispers to me, his breath warm against my ear, "I'll see you in a couple of days." I think, It sounds like a promise, but it's just another form of saying good-bye.

I spend the good part of the next few days wandering the three rooms of the cottage, the silence like a fog, and the realization that truly profound absence is a presence in itself. It's the weekend so there are no good talk shows on television. There's only the pile of "fan mail" on the desk.

When I lost my Harry I used to sit in the kitchen all day with his 45 lying on the table. I kept picking it up and putting it in my mouth. Then I would think of my babies, and of their babies, and I would put it down again . . .

And: *I thought I would die when Jennifer ran in front of that bus. I watched her go and it was like slow motion and I would of went after her if I'd of thought fast enough but then it was too late. Then all I wanted to do was die. If it hadn't been for my faith in our Lord Jesus Christ . . .*

And: *I want to recommend a book to you. It saved my life when my son finally passed. I was ready to check out, I can tell you. This book, it's by a rabbi believe it or not. It's about how to figure out why bad things happen and how God always has a plan and such. I'm sending you a check for twelve dollars so you can get a copy. . . .*

I want to kill Noah.

With his fucking dinners and conversations, revelations and dreams. Intimacies. Getting me involved again, seducing me into something close to feeling when he felt no more for me than he did for a servant. Of course it was easy to leave me, easy to stay away for good with no regrets and here I am, my heart hollowed out again.

Don't let me stop you, I write the suicidal widow.

Dying's harder than it looks, isn't it? I write the bereaved mother.

I don't read anymore, I write the rabbi nut. *Waste of trees.*

But Noah does come back, at the end of the week. The afternoon of his return, he picks me up to go shopping, surprised that I'm surprised to see him. He's different though, distracted, frowning a lot, as if he were trying to work out some mathematical equation. Write it down, I used to say to Nick, it's easier to see the problem on paper. Once Nick saw things in black and white he always came up with the right answer. But Noah seems to only half hear anything I say. I'm not surprised when he says he'll have to work hard for the next few days, to make up for all the work he didn't get done in the city. I'm not surprised that he avoids my eyes when he says this.

On the boat we celebrated birthdays and Charlie's and my anniversary. We celebrated the birthday of Theo, our cat, who, when we set sail, we left with Charlie's oldest sister. We threw Brenda Bride, Jess's doll, a wedding with a scantily clad wooden man, a souvenir from

Fiji. But we gave ourselves permission to skip all national and religious holidays for the duration of our trip. There'll be plenty of Thanksgivings and Passovers when we get back, we told the children; this trip will be a holiday from our holidays. At first they were suspicious. Did this mean we'd have to have school on days they would have been off at home? No way, Ma, Jessie said. But once we'd assured them that on Presidents' day and the Fourth of July and Thanksgiving and all the others, we'd take the day off lessons, they were more amenable. As long as there was still a cake with each of their names on it at the appropriate time (a harder feat than it sounds on a sailboat in the middle of the ocean with only the tiniest of refrigeration space and every inch of it hoarded like gold), as long as we sang to the distant and slightly retarded Theo, as long as there were presents of some kind, they were happy.

I haven't seen a Thanksgiving in two years. God knows I haven't eaten turkey and cranberry sauce in that long. Nor have I missed them, I tell Noah when he calls from the house the day before Thanksgiving to try to convince me to come to New York with him. "It's good to hear your voice," I say (thinking, ohmygod, was that a Myra-insidiously-guilt-inducing thing to say?).

He coughs. "I've been so busy," he says.

"I know," I say.

"I'm coming over," he says, then hangs up. My heart starts a silly pounding and I can't stop myself from checking my face in the bathroom mirror and smoothing down my hair. When I lift the lipstick to my mouth my hands are shaking.

Of course I'm not going with him. I haven't spent time with him in almost a week. No cozy dinners, no long conversations. Of course, it's for the best, acclimating me to a solitary state again. And yet I wonder if longing for his company is better than returning to indifference.

13

We sit across from one another in the living room and stare for a while. I have been seeing him in my mind's eye for almost a week—but in that imagining he looked a lot more like Nicholas than he really does. I am foolishly hoping he notices that my face has filled out a bit.

"You have to come with me," he says after a while. "All those masses of people. I won't know any of them and they'll want to know all about me."

"Isn't that a good thing?" I say. "There'll probably be people there who could be good for your career."

"I know I should do it, but without someone there I feel really comfortable with—it'll be the worst kind of torture. I know Isabel. She's been talking me up for weeks to her friends. I need someone at my side. What if I make some kind of huge blunder?"

"What about, uh, Angelique?"

"I told you," he says angrily. "That's over."

"Does she know that yet?"

"My god, now you sound like Isabel."

"Well, I'm just thinking that if you haven't actually broken up with her yet it might be a nice thing to take her with you—"

"I want you for my companion," he says flatly.

I feel a rush of pleasure. "What I'm saying is, is that if I didn't come, having Angelique there would help. It would also show Leo—well, it might ease some tension if you did."

"Don't kid yourself," Noah says. "He couldn't care less if I bring Angelique or not. It wouldn't change anything. I mean, come on Eve, you know what's going on." He looks straight at me. "I know you. You're not always in your own world, even if that's what Isabel and Leo think. You see what's going on."

Secretly pleased, I say, "You mean about you and Isabel?"

"You don't mind, do you?"

"Mind?"

"I mean, the fact that she's married. You can see that she and Leo don't exactly have a great marriage."

I sit still in my chair, hands spread over my knees. "I don't know," I say. "What constitutes a great marriage?"

"Come on." He snorts. "He sees her as a cash cow. But I appreciate the artist in her and I don't give a damn how much money she makes or doesn't make. She's afraid of what kind of alimony Leo would go for, but I tell her not to worry. I don't need much at all."

"Yes," I say quietly, "but Isabel. She needs . . ."

"Catherine of Aragon is going to be her signature role. She'll be able to sing it till she's seventy. She won't have to worry about a thing."

His face is luminous—he is seeing a shining future. I want to say, Noah, don't count on the future. But would I say that to Nicholas if I had the chance? Even if, like Violetta, I knew how things were going to turn out? Instead, I say, "Noah, be careful."

He smiles. "I know, I know. Believe me, I am not usually an optimistic person. I expect disaster all the time. But I swear, when I'm with Isabel . . . I think that only good things can happen. Leo doesn't scare me—nothing scares me as long as Isabel loves me. Leo and Angelique have to be dealt with. *Butterfly* has to finish, Isabel needs her operation, then we'll be together."

I don't know what else to say, so I say, "You sound happy."

"I am. And I'll be happier when . . . well, right now she . . ." He looks over my shoulder to the front door. "She's a, you know, a diva. A little overly dramatic. The jealous type. She says I have a thing for older women. Maybe I do." He catches my eye then looks away again. "I mean, she's what—twenty-plus years older than me, and Angelique is eight years and you're . . . what?"

"Fourteen."

"Yeah, fourteen years older. I do like older women, it's true. But Isabel doesn't exactly understand our friendship—yours and mine."

The fist in my chest tightens.

"She worries that . . . that it's something more. I mean, she gets that you're in no position. But she's no idiot. She can sense how you and I . . . have become close." I know he's looking at me but I stare at my hands. "She is jealous of my having any feelings for anyone right now. And I've done everything I can to persuade her that she has nothing to worry about. But she wants me not to eat dinner with you so much."

"So much?" I say hopefully.

"At all. For now," he adds quickly. "I plan on talking about it to her again this weekend because I don't want to give up . . . but if it causes her real distress to know that you and I are spending time together, if it impairs her ability to work, or to work things out with Leo, then, as my friend, I'm hoping you'll understand. . . ." His voice trails off, miserably. I don't know what my expression looks like, but the next thing he says is, "I'm going to speak to her again. I'm sure I can make her understand."

I walk him to the door where he leans down and kisses my cheek. It feels like a whisper against my skin. I put *La Traviata* on the CD player, walk to the bathroom and shake out two pain pills into my palm. There's only about half the prescription left. For the first time since the hospital I reconsider my options. A little relief now, or a stash of pills to do with as I like at some point in the future. If only I had even Myra's amount of faith, there would be no contest. But I cannot convince myself that there is even the most abstract of after-lives, that in death one is in any way reunited with loved ones, or granted some kind of rest or peace. To me death is still a complete blackness, not empty, but stifling, like being wrapped for all eternity in a heavy blanket, like being buried in the sea.

I put the pills back.

Noah doesn't give up on me. He calls on Thanksgiving from the Steins' apartment, his voice low and boozy. "They're right in the other room," he says, trying to whisper but not quite succeeding. "I told them I'm calling Angelique. That pissed Isabel off too, of course, but it threw her off track." He chokes back his goofy laugh. "What are you doing?"

"Watching football," I say.

"Bullshit."

"No really. There's nothing else on. It looks like it's starting to rain. Is it there?"

"You okay?"

I say yes.

"There must be fifty people here. Every time I turn around there's another person who wants to meet me. Oh, guess who's here! Schmidt—the guy from New York City Opera. He asked me about *Catherine*. Isabel told him."

"That's great," I say.

He lowers his voice again. "Yeah, it is. I mean if we debuted here! Unlikely, but who knows. At least there are contacts here who . . ."

"That's great, Noah." I hear laughter from a long distance away.

"Eve? I'd still rather be there."

"You're having a great time and you know it."

"Yeah," he chuckles, "But I wish you were here."

"You should get back."

"Okay. I'll see you when I get back. Promise."

"Okay." I hang up and stare at the bright uniforms dashing across the television set, picturing Noah in Isabel's bedroom, his braced hand cupped around the mouthpiece of the telephone, whispering excitedly to me. It begins to rain on the football field. These are the kinds of conversations I would have had with Nick when he went off to college—him off in another room so that his buddies wouldn't think he was a Mama's boy, whispering of his latest exploits, his favorite class, the new girl in the room across the hall. Nick, I'd say, are you drinking? And he'd say, It's just a beer Ma, in an affectionately irritated voice and I'd say, You're not going to be driving, Nicholas, are you? and he'd laugh—the low throaty laugh that I imagine he would have developed after his voice broke—a cross between my father's croak and Charlie's chesty chuckle, and he'd say, Ma, the dorms are all in walking distance and besides, I'm not drunk Ma, don't worry, will you? And I'd say, Remember that night you were out all night at so and so's party—that gave me a few more of these gray hairs—and we gave you hell and grounded you for a month until we found out that you'd been the designated driver and got home so late because you had to drive like twenty people home, and he'd say, Yeah, Ma, that was a long time ago, and I'd say, Just be careful Nicholas, that's all we want, your father and I—that you be happy and work hard and be very very careful, and he'd say, You worry too much Ma.

The bright uniforms turn to mud in the rain. The score flashes on the screen. Five, seven men jump into a pile of flailing limbs and flying mud, as if they were little boys, playing the way little boys do, at once serious and carefree.

Molly says, "We're thinking of you and wish you could be at our table. We are giving thanks for what's left to us."

"Yes, for your family, that's good."

"And you, Eve, we're giving thanks that we still have you."

Myra says, "Molly made a beautiful dinner. We said a prayer for Charlie and the kids. We all felt better. I miss you so much Baby, we all do."

"I love you Myra," I say faintly.

"Our lawyer contacted the fishing company. But it's all very complicated because of international law. Still, he's sure you have an excellent case."

"That's good, Ma."

"The kids want to say hi. You want to say hi to Aunt Eve?" Myra says.

I start to tell her no but Alice, the youngest, is on the phone with a chirpy hello and then dead silence. So I bite my lip and then ask her about school and how was the dinner and what did she get for her tenth birthday which I am realizing only as I speak to her was just the other day and she ends the conversation by saying "We all miss you," and I can hear Myra prompting her in the background and Molly calling to Kevin and Sarah to get on the phone and I say Myra, please, no more. So Myra yells back that Aunt Eve has to go and she'll talk to them next time and I whisper Thank you Ma. Just when we're about to hang up, an extension is picked up and I hear George's thin voice.

"Just wanted to say hello, Eve, hear your voice."

"Hi George. Thank you for your kind words at the service. I heard how moving your . . . speech was."

"You know if you ever need anything."

"Thank you," I say remembering the day that Molly brought him home for the first time. They were both seniors in college and George had stringy hair down the middle of his back and what we used to call Poindexter glasses, which would now be considered quite trendy, and unlike the few boyfriends I brought home, George was not temperamental or taciturn—he began a political discussion with my father that lasted through most of dinner and he praised my mother's cooking, thus effectively counteracting their first reaction to his hippie looks. I remember thinking he was slick. That he would make a great lawyer. I never fully revised that opinion of him but now it seems that I underestimated his capacity for deep feeling, for family loyalty, for compassion. "I'm very grateful," I say to George. He laughs. "You just get better and come home Eve. We'd like to see you at our table next Thanksgiving, okay?"

We've actually had this conversation before, in another life—Molly and me tugging at who gets to host Thanksgiving, Passover, Fourth of July barbecue. Sometimes we left it to Charlie and George to hash out so we didn't end up killing each other. My table versus your table.

On Saturday of Thanksgiving weekend I go into town alone for the first time. Noah left me the keys to the Honda, which I never thought I'd use. I've been driving since I was fifteen but it's been over two years since I've been behind a wheel and a shiver of fear runs through me as I open the door and sit down on the cold seat. I have images of losing control of the car and plowing into a line of children descending a school bus, or a mother and her five little ones crossing the street. I am clumsy getting the key in the ignition, locking the seatbelt, figuring out the heater. I let the car run a long time without moving as I have seen Noah do—warming up a car in frigid weather being somewhat foreign to a native Californian. My head begins to ache so I open the window a crack. I wonder whether you feel really sick with this method or whether, if you lock the garage up tight enough and block all the holes, you'd fall asleep before you felt any discomfort. The garage is behind the house and to the right, away from any line of sight. Something to store at the back of my mind.

The car jerks and leaps as it moves down the drive. I keep throwing my foot on the brake every time the car moves further than I meant it to and I'm sure I look like someone practicing to drive on a stick shift as I chug and cough my way into town.

I buy a case of wine and the guy at the liquor store carries it to the car. He always wears a backwards Yankees cap and a dirty white apron and he gives me a friendly smile. "Where's your friend?" he says. After a minute I realize he means Noah. "Away for Thanksgiving," I say.

"Not all alone are you?" he says, looking concerned.

"Oh no," I say, "I'm very busy." He stares too long at me so I get out of there as fast as I can.

At the grocery store I stick to my list and make it to the checkout in record time. Ahead of me, a young woman holds a large bottle of Coke and a bag of pretzels. When I approach she turns around. She is about Noah's age, very pretty, with a profusion of red hair spilling out in ringlets from under a purple beret, and pink, freckled skin. She is wearing glasses whose wire-rimmed frames are barely larger than her actual eyes. Only people who give the illusion that clothes bought in thrift stores are brilliant original designs could get away with glasses like this. She smiles, showing teeth so straight and white that they look painted on. "You have more than I do, do you want to go ahead of me?"

"Usually it's the other way around, isn't it?" I say, trying to return her friendly gaze and gesturing for her to go ahead of me.

She chuckles. "Yeah, but I'm in no hurry and I thought you might be. Thanksgiving weekend and all that. Frankly," she says, placing her two items on the conveyer belt, "I hate Thanksgiving. I'm glad to be out of the city for it."

"Not from around here?" the cashier says although she knows that perfectly well already. Her name is Rose and from what I can tell in my now regular visits to the store, she misses nothing.

"No. Visiting relatives," the girl says, fishing in her wallet.

"In town? Maybe I know them," Rose says, taking her time to pack up the groceries.

"Oh no, they actually live out of town." The redheaded girl speaks brusquely, clearly not interested in having a small-town conversation. She grabs her bag and gives Rose an insincere smile, then shoves her way quickly out the door.

"New Yorkers," Rose says disgustedly to me. I feel a moment's pleasure at her including me in her contempt for outsiders. As she is packing up my bags, she says, "Where's your friend this weekend?"

It is snowing lightly when I leave the store, really just a thick rain. Still, I'm nervous about driving in it. I've never driven in snow in my life. When Charlie and I took the kids up to Big Bear that time—one of the few non-sea vacations we took—he did all the treacherous driving. The kids got a huge kick out of Charlie huffing out of our car in the middle of a mountain road to put chains on the tires, having scoffed at the sign a few miles back that warned that chains were necessary. At the time the skies had been clear and Charlie had said "It's worth the gamble." So now there he was using language he never used in front of the children, snapping at me when I didn't put the car in gear fast enough or didn't hear what he was saying over the driving winds. The kids thought Charlie was funnier than cartoons and I encouraged the lighthearted atmosphere. But I was a little worried—not about our predicament, but about my faith in Charlie. When we'd passed that sign I'd been ready to stop and put on the chains, but when he said it wasn't necessary, I believed him. I knew him to be competent in the elements. How could I not have faith in a man who always behaved as if he knew what he was doing? But when I saw that all that he had done was take a gamble—no more informed or savvy than I myself would have been—I wondered what that meant for our impending voyage.

I put on the mittens Myra bought me and am fumbling with the lock on the car door when I hear a voice behind me.

"Hi."

I turn around. It is the young woman with the red hair. "Remember me?" she says smiling. "Listen, I wonder if I could ask just the tiniest favor of you."

I wait. She smiles wider. "I wonder if I could snag a lift from you. I'm super sorry. But I'm developing the worst cold and it's getting so nasty out. I walked here from my hotel but now . . ." She looks doubtfully up into the sky. "I'm thinking I really shouldn't walk in case it gets any worse. Would you mind? It's maybe five minutes from here. Would it be any trouble?" She has been nodding throughout this whole speech, as if confirming her own words to me, or inviting me to agree with her. There's something engaging about her brashness, her wild hair and tentative nodding head, so I say okay.

"My name's Ray," she says, sticking out a strikingly white hand. I take it by the fingertips then turn and open the car door. She flounces in, settling her paper bag of pretzels and Coke on her lap. "And yours?" she says, smiling brightly.

"My what."

"Your name?" She nods, encouraging me.

"Eve," I say automatically. But her face is blank; she doesn't appear to recognize me or my name.

"Well hi, Eve, nice to meet you. Thanks so much for bailing me out. It's the Kent Arms, you know it?"

I shake my head.

"Original name, huh? This town is not exactly happening, but then, I guess that's why locals like it, huh?" She nods away, watching me maneuver clumsily out of the parking space in front of the market. "Don't you find it a bit provincial after a while? I mean, don't you just want to cut out sometime?"

"What makes you think I'm not a local?" I say.

"Oh!" She draws back as if I'd just revealed I had a contagious disease. "Are you?"

I brace myself for sudden recognition. But maybe she isn't the type to read tabloids and watch lurid info news shows. Her combined air of sophistication and adolescent vigor make her hard to read. I keep my eyes on the road. "I guess you could say I'm transplanted," I say. "For the time being, I'm a local."

"Ah, cool." She settles in her seat. "Turn right at the next light."

The car lurches as I overshoot the turn. "You okay?" she says.

"Fine. I'm a little unfamiliar with this car."

"Tell me about it. I never drive in the city. I only got my license a few years ago. I'd be the same way. You're doing fine," she adds with an especially vigorous nod. We are driving through the main part of town, which consists of one long street and three others that feed off of it, on which stand the post office and two more banks beyond the one on Main Street.

"Why do you suppose such a small town needs so many banks?" Ray says.

"Good question."

"Yup, it's a small town all right," Ray declares, her head doing its dance. "Cute for like five minutes. You originally from the city?"

"No," I say, trying to ignore the cloud of red hair that keeps dipping into my line of vision.

"I could tell you weren't native. You don't have that Kmart Special look."

I say nothing.

"Oh don't listen to me, Eve, I'm heavily PMS'd and I'd dis Mother Theresa whenever that happens. Turn right."

"I think Kent is kind of charming," I say, though I never thought that till this minute and feel a defensiveness I can't explain.

"Oh it is, it is. I dig the bookstore, actually—it's got all kinds of stuff you'd have to scour Manhattan for."

Now we are at the outskirts of town. Ahead lies the highway. Ray has me make a few more turns until we're on a street lined with stark white beeches and Cape Cod cottages that looks like something out of a picture book. Ray points to a building at the end of the street—three stories and a colonial, rather than Cape Code design. She turns to me. "So what are you doing in Kent, Eve, shopping for a post-Thanksgiving party?"

"I'm staying with friends," I say.

"I hear there's a lot of famous people who own houses up here off in the rural parts. I hear they have some great old places. Hopefully my relatives will drive me around to see some." She looks at me wide-eyed, her glasses catching the glint of what little sun there is. It crosses my mind that she wants me to offer to take her on a tour.

"I wouldn't know," I say. I pull up in front of the building. A large wooden sign that says "Kent Arms, Est. 1879" creaks in the wind. A man wrapped in a thin jacket with a black watchman's cap is standing in front of the building, scowling and blowing onto his cupped red hands. A large leather camera bag hangs from his shoulder. Ray becomes flustered. "Oh, that's my boyfriend," she says quickly. "He's probably pissed off that I'm late. Oh shit! And I forgot to buy him mittens!" She leaps out of the car as soon as I stop and runs up to him. Something in her eagerness to get to him makes me think there is something about him she doesn't want me to see or know. I sit uncertainly for a minute. The man is talking furiously to her but I don't hear anything he says. She keeps putting her hand on his arm and he keeps brushing it away and glancing over toward me. He's married, I decide. His wife is in the city having a pathetic Thanksgiving dinner with their fatherless children while he tells her he's working in Cincinnati, couldn't get out of it, Love you babe. I begin to pull away when Ray runs back to the car.

"My stuff!" I shift into Park and lean over to open the passenger door. Ray sticks her head inside as she reaches for her bag. "Would you like to come in for a cup of tea? Meet Danny? We don't know anyone here."

"What about your relatives," I say.

"Oh. Uh, them." She coughs. "My . . . mother's cousins. They talk weather like twenty-four hours a day. Danny's about to have a cow. Come on and see the inn. It's really very charming." She smiles encouragingly at me, and I suspect that Danny is upset she brought some stranger to their doorstep and she is trying to delay a confrontation. How easily people like to suck other people into their lives. I tell her I have to go.

"Okay," she says, crestfallen. "But maybe we'll see you around? We're here for a few days. Where are you living?"

"A ways out," I say, thinking I really do sound like a local.

"Oh. Well. Okay. I didn't mean to pry or anything. Listen, thanks a billion for the lift. Take care."

"Yes," I say, "you too."

She pulls her bag out of the car and gives me one last look before turning around and heading back up the drive to the impatient Danny. A short way down the street I look in the rearview mirror and they are still standing on the porch of the Kent Arms. Ray's arm is raised in a slow farewell wave.

I eat New York cheddar cheese and crackers and listen to *Rigoletto*. The CD player is set on Repeat for the section in the first act when Rigoletto is telling his daughter that she must take care, she must never venture outside the walls of his garden, as only danger and deception await her there. In a beautiful counterpoint she replies that she will obey him and that he needn't worry, but already she knows that she has deceived him, that she has talked to a man she met in church. And so in her imperfect obedience already lie the seeds of her own destruction.

The phone rings. "I'm going to see Angelique," Noah says morosely.

"That's probably a good idea."

"And Robbie. He's got a good chunk of the Act Two libretto to show me."

"Good."

"So, I'll probably stay here for the week."

"Fine," I say.

"Leo has to go to Philadelphia. They're making noises about canceling Isabel's tour. He'll be gone a day or two."

"Uh huh," I say.

"You'll be all right, Eve?"

"Of course I will," I say, seeing the week stretching like a dirt road before me.

"I'll be back in no more than a week. Then the following week we go back together, you and I, for *Butterfly*."

"Yes," I say automatically.

"Okay. Want me to bring you back anything from the city?"

"Just yourself," I say. It is something I have said a thousand times to Charlie when he's away on business.

An awkward pause.

"Meanwhile you should go into town to that dress shop next to the market and buy yourself something. Opening night at the opera, you know." His voice is so affectionate and concerned it makes my throat hurt.

14

I tell myself I'm not listening to Isabel's recording of *Butterfly* because I want to hear it fresh, without any preconceived notions about how she or any of the other singers should sound, without knowing the story. Isabel has told me that the opera house recently installed screens for subtitles so I can go into the performance with only my decades-old memory of colorful costumes and suicide at the end. But the truth is, I don't want to hear Isabel's exquisite heartbreaking voice for a while. I don't want to be moved by this woman to whom I owe so much and yet who is presently keeping from me the only thing I want.

I call Nigel Baker. He sounds inordinately happy to talk to me. "Did you get my letter?" he says.

I confess that I have not picked up the mail since the Steins and Noah have been gone.

"We have three interesting bites. I want to go over them with you."

"All right," I say, since that's why I called. "This would be money up front, right?"

"Usually half the advance before and the rest when you turn in an acceptable manuscript."

There's a few thousand left in the bank, and there could be a long delay in getting the insurance money. At this moment it seems impossible to stay in this cottage by myself, pining after a stranger more than my own family, knowing that yards away from me is the unobtainable object of this perverse, inexplicable desire of mine.

Nigel is throwing out huge sums of money, hundreds of thousands. In my imagination I buy or rent a tiny place for a year or so. In that period I will surely have done my time—given Myra another year, finished some piece of writing, amassed a small sum to leave her, made myself walk the earth for 365 more days.

"I have nothing firm yet, but in a week or so—" Nigel says. "I think Leo said you'll be in the city soon?"

"December 16th. Can't we do it sooner?"

"Possibly."

"As soon as possible," I say.

"Sounds super. I'm so glad you're with the program on this, Eve. Talk to you soon."

We hang up and something is doing a tango in my stomach so I go for a walk.

I haven't gone very far down the path before there is a snapping and rustling noise, like someone creeping through the forest. I stop and look around but there's nothing to see except stark tree trunks. There is no breeze. I hold myself very still, a thrill of adrenaline shooting through me. It is broad daylight in this secluded area that almost no one knows about. Still, a shadowy figure could be lurking behind the fattest tree, watchman's cap and thick gloves, knife posed, visions of mayhem glittering out of steely eyes. I should turn back; I should walk on—quickly. I close my eyes and see him approach, the glint of the knife in the dull afternoon light, the mindless hatred in the snarling face. The first prick of the blade at my throat, like a spark jumping out of a fire.

The sound does not repeat itself and I open my eyes. I've been watching too many post-O.J. shows. I forget there are animals in the woods—we saw four deer on one of our walks a couple of weeks ago. I wait a little longer, see nothing, hear nothing more. Still, I turn back.

When I first met him I thought Charlie was fearless. He had two much older sisters, both of whom were out of the house by the time he was ten. His parents were close to forty by then and used to girls, so either they paid less attention to the dangerous and crazy boy things he did or else they were too tired to worry about him much. So he grew up climbing precariously sloping roofs, mixing questionable chemicals in his toy chemistry kit, jumping off high cliffs into shallow rivers, swimming in riptides. Miraculously he came through his childhood with only one broken leg and one broken fin-

ger, the wind knocked out of him so many times he was used to it, and enough cuts and bruises for three children. It's a wonder he survived at all, Ed liked to say, but you knew he was secretly pleased, after a decade thinking he was to be only the father of girls, to have been blessed with such a man's boy, such an intrepid, stalwart son to enliven his middle age.

Of course then, as an adult, Charlie was adventurous. Of course he swam too far in the ocean and crewed on boats with too little experience and took his own boat out too far in bad weather. This certainly worried me, but Charlie's unflinching confidence and resolve lulled me.

And yet when it came to my being on the boat, and later the children, Charlie was like a fussy old lady. He'd insist that the children wear their life jackets at all times, even when we were just cruising around the bay for a short jaunt before dinner at the harbor restaurant where Jessica would have her Shirley Temple and Nick his Roy Rogers and they would fight over who got the biggest cherry. Charlie might later unwind with one more Jack Daniels than he should have but on the boat with the children and me he was hyper-sober and almost annoyingly vigilant. It crossed my mind more than once that he behaved this way for my sake, to convince me how careful he'd be on our journey, how safe we'd all be, how much safer even than we were in our own home where there were break-ins and gangs and bad schools just waiting to corrupt and hurt our children.

We never talked about how I felt about the trip. He never asked me what I wanted after he asked me in the beginning, twelve years before we actually set sail.

I think he was afraid of what I might say.

At night if we heard noises he would leap out of bed, grab the policeman's flashlight he kept under his side of the bed for just such circumstances and go tumbling downstairs to defeat the intruder, who—thank goodness, I used to say—was never there.

He killed spiders and ants.

One summer day our neighbor, Mr. McKay, slapped Jessica for breaking his daughter's guitar when she was over there playing. Charlie invited Mr. McKay out of his front doorway onto his perfectly manicured dichondra lawn. "If you ever speak to my child again," he said, "let alone lay a finger on her, I will take you down," Charlie said, never touching him, never raising his voice above a low rumble, while I stood in the street trembling, imagining Mrs. McKay phoning the police, although, as Charlie said later, she was probably afraid that that was what we were going to do.

Charlie was never helpless, never without an answer to a question or problem. When I was mad at him I called him a know-it-all.

Of course it is this very quality, this intrepid doggedness, that made him go after Jessica in the ocean. So it did kill him in the end.

Maybe I should buy a typewriter. My laptop is somewhere off the coast of Australia at the bottom of the Pacific and I'd like to go low-tech this time. The pad is running low. My hand gets tired; the pens run out. I'm amazed at how quickly the words spill onto the page. There's something almost tranquil about it. When I write the stories I can believe that I am doing the very thing I meant to all along—chronicling our story for Nick and Jess to read someday, to show to their children.

I also need a dress for the opera. So I trudge up the hill to the car. Once something rustles behind me but I know before I turn around that I will see nothing. I am beginning to harbor secret desires about these noises, this sudden powerful sense of being watched. I am hoping, against all the intensity of my disbelief, that I am being haunted.

The clothes at The Gilded Cage all have a gossamer feel. There are dresses that hang like shirts, shirts that button in funny, asymmetrical places, pants with so much material they look like long skirts. Everything seems to be either black or variations on the same pale shades of gray and beige. After the bright greens and blues and yellows of the island markets we visited on the journey, it's as if the world has been de-colorized. I haven't seen a lot of women dressed up since I got back to the states. Maybe these anemic colors and loose designs are what "they" are wearing these days. Maybe this is some savvy fashion designer's answer to the culture's obsession with thinness. I should have come home sooner and taken advantage. A joke! My breath catches in my throat and I remove myself from the store, lean against the outside wall, waiting for something awful to happen. How could I how could I what was I thinking how can I be making a joke even though I never said it out loud I've been so good since Noah has been gone, at not smiling, how dare I now they'll go away if they were haunting me they'll leave me now.

I sit down heavily on the bench between The Gilded Cage and the market, listening to my breathing.

"Eve?"

I look up.

"Hi! It's Ray, remember me?"

It takes me a minute to adjust to the sight and memory of Ray, whose nodding head under her purple beret makes me dizzy.

"What a coincidence! How are you?"

I blink at her.

"Uh, Eve? You okay?" Her nodding head insists I am.

"I'm fine."

"You sure? You look a little green around the gills. D'you eat anything this morning?"

I don't answer, hoping she'll go away. "You been sick?" she says. "Let me take you for a cup of coffee."

"No, really," I say, but somehow she's urging me up, leading me to the diner down the road, a freestanding building shaped like a railroad car. Inside, the counter is filled with people and there's only one free booth at the back. Ray settles me there and then sits opposite. She pulls out menus from the holder and hands me one.

"I'm not really hungry," I say.

"At least get some tea. And maybe some juice. Get the energy and vitamins in you."

I shrug. The waitress comes over and Ray orders scrambled eggs, bacon and two orders of toast, "in case you change your mind," as well as two orange juices and two herbal teas.

"So!" she says, when the waitress is gone, "How have you been?"

She plunges on, ignoring the fact that I haven't spoken. "I'm . . . we're staying on a bit longer than we thought at first. Danny is . . . he's an amateur photographer and he got interested in the scenery so we decided to take a few more days. I have some time off so it's working out nicely."

I watch her head bob and wonder what Danny has told his wife about their extended stay.

"I'm still hoping to get that tour of the country houses. My relatives are so busy. They pretty much expect me . . . us to fend for ourselves."

The teas and juices arrive. Ray pours three sugar packets into her tea. I scald my tongue on mine. "So tell me about where you're staying," she says, lifting her cup to her lips.

Over her shoulder I see two people get up from their seats at the counter and two more move in to take their places. The four of them have to sidle around each other to maneuver their way in and out and it reminds me of the galley on the *Orlando* when more than one of us was in there at once.

"I'm out in the country," I say.

"Uh huh," says Ray, clearly expecting more.

"My friends are pretty private," I say.

"Oh." She puts down her cup and grins. "Well, what about you, then? Where are you from originally?"

I figure the quickest way to get out of here politely is to exhaust her questions. "California," I say.

"No shit? My sister lives out there. In L.A. I love it out there. You from L.A.?"

"Yes."

"So you're here on vacation then?"

"Sort of."

"You have family back there?"

"Some."

"You married?"

I drain my juice. "Yes, I'm married," I say finally.

"I guess you must miss him a lot."

I grip the juice glass. "What do you mean," I say.

She looks nonplussed. "Oh, I just meant . . . I figured he wasn't with you and that's hard, you know, around holiday time."

Her expression is guileless—maybe a little stupid. It's not her fault. She's just trying to be nice.

"Yes," I say slowly. "I miss him."

"And kids? You have kids?" Now she's smiling, waiting for me to take out pictures, ready to ooh and aah, a dull, bored young woman with too much time on her hands. I stand up abruptly, gripping the table. "I really do have to go now," I say, and maneuver may way out of the booth, not looking at her, blundering down the aisle of the railroad car, hearing her call my name or thinking I hear it, pressing against people who look at me oddly but with no curiosity, pressing forward till I'm out the door into the blast of cold air, not looking back.

Jessica was curly-haired and willful, and reminded me of what Molly had been like as a child. She was entirely a girl, loving dolls with long hair and frilly dresses and tiaras and my makeup, and jewelry and perfumes, even though we gave her Nicholas's stuffed tool kit when she was three and read her gender-neutral children's stories.

I had been more like Nick as a child: studious and a bit eccentric. He spent long hours in his room reading, playing quiet games that he made up and that required only one player. Jessica brought new girlfriends home by the second day she was at school. Nick had one good friend, Henry Havers, who used to sleep over every couple of weeks. Their favorite activity was playing in a spaceship they'd rigged out of cardboard boxes and blankets that they kept in our backyard and spent hours in, presumably flying to various planets. They were the quietest two boys I'd ever seen, their faces set in concentration when they were having the most fun. It disconcerted Charlie some, to have this solemn, bookish little boy, but he was proud of Nick's intelligence and ingenuity. Nick was the only child I knew who never complained of being bored. He did things like take apart Charlie's grandfather's old watch and put it back together so that every piece was back in place. It didn't work, of course, but then, it hadn't worked before.

And yet, despite his natural tendencies, Nick wanted desperately to be included in the group of vigorous boys who played soccer in the park behind our house. I wanted so much to spare him the pain of their rejection, but each time, I managed to hold myself back from saying anything. I thought, in my arrogance, that I understood everything I needed to know about how a mother cannot protect her offspring from all pain.

Jessica had an infectious laugh and a much more lighthearted disposition than her brother. She was quick to anger and tantrum and just as quick to recover. Even as an infant Nick never cried much or got frustrated, but when he was upset he was much harder to cheer up. They were so different they seemed to come from two different families even though they were only a year apart. Charlie used to say that one was a relief from the other.

They were both hard in coming—with Nick I had a particularly hard time—and while I was in labor both times I screamed to Charlie that I wanted to give them back. And after they were born I finally understood profoundly that whole I'd-lie-down-in-front-of-a-train-to-save-you thing.

And of course none of that matters. Loving someone doesn't save them. Loving someone, I am now convinced, is at best useless, at worst, dangerous. If I had loved Charlie a little less I might have tried to convince him to stay home.

Noah is sitting at my table again, eating a cheese sandwich I threw together for him, not expecting him tonight, not sure if I should ever expect him again. He's electric from the cold and excitement—the reception he received from the opera people, the sessions he had with

Robbie, the idyll he had with Isabel. "But mostly, I was imagining the letters you were probably writing." He smiles.

On a whim whose provenance I still can't identify, I told him recently about my rapidly growing collection of replies to my mail. Far from being appalled, he said he thought it was the smartest thing I'd done so far. Which I guess was the response I'd counted on, since I wouldn't dream of telling anyone else.

"I've added a few to the 'out' pile," I tell him.

"Can I see?"

"Yeah. Maybe you'll have some suggestions." We smile like children with secret decoder rings, keeping this ugly side of ourselves from the world, reveling in it. "First finish telling me about your trip. Did you see Angelique?"

His face falls. "It was dreadful. I tried to tell her definitively that it was over. I started to tell her and she just kind of ignored me. Changed the subject, diverted my attention to the new couch and this piece she's working on. Bulldozed me, as usual."

It sounds like something less than bulldozing to me, but all I say is, "What are you going to do?"

"Shit if I know." He seems to be waiting for advice.

"I don't know," I say. "Maybe write her a note?"

He laughs. "Of course! And you're just the person to help me."

"I didn't mean that kind of note."

"Well, I have to come up with something. I mean, it's ludicrous for me to stay with her—to sleep with her out of some kind of sense of obligation, right?" He stares at his sandwich. "I did sleep with her, you know. Do you think I'm an asshole?"

My fingers tingle like they're going numb. I clasp my hands. "You know what, Noah," I say evenly, "these kinds of questions—they seem so . . . I don't know, don't take this the wrong way, but somehow . . . irrelevant." I peruse his face, his long nose and sharp chin and the green eyes and think how dear this face has become to me, and I wonder if I meant what I just said.

Noah reaches over and takes my hand. I start to pull away but then let my palm rest in his. "I understand why you feel that way Eve. But I hope you don't always." I savor the warmth of his skin.

"What are you thinking," he says softly.

I pull my hand away and walk over to the sink as if I've forgotten something there. I stare for a while at the chipped porcelain. "I'm remembering," I say finally, "sitting on the bunk with my son and watching television. We had a game of trying to find American shows no matter where we were. We always found them."

"You had a television on the boat?"

I smile. "And a VCR and a computer and a washer and a dryer. All the comforts of home. My daughter loved to steer the boat, for some reason we could never figure out, since she was not usually interested in anything that might get her dirty. My husband used to say it was a control thing."

Noah chuckles.

"So Charlie used to take her on deck and let her steer and that's when my boy and I would sit on the bed and watch TV. We'd make a big bowl of popcorn—"

"A popper too?"

I nod. "And we'd prop up the pillows and lie side by side and after a while, after we'd finished the bowl of popcorn, I used to take his hand—it would be lying between us, right next to mine, and I'd inch mine over because if I took his too obviously he'd snatch it away. He was seven and then eight and too big to make it easy for his mother to hold his hand. But if I crept up on him and took hold he'd let me; he'd close his fingers around mine and we'd stay that way for most of the show. His hand was smooth too, in the beginning. For a little boy, you know, he wasn't very physical, not into sports and rough play and he had hands like a much younger boy's when we started our trip. But after a while they got rough, more like you'd expect, from the work he did on the boat—the sails, the ropes. I used to run my thumb over the calluses on his palms; I used to think that these were the first signs of the man he would become."

Noah squeezes my hand and when I take it up and hold it against my cheek, he lets me.

Later, in the semidarkness of the living room, with soft jazz playing on the radio and two large brandies in our hands, in our usual positions, me sitting, him lying on the couch, I say to the back of his head, "I've had the strangest feeling lately."

"What?"

“When I go outside, take a walk or go into town, I have the strangest feeling that I’m being watched.”

“Really.”

“Yeah. Sometimes I hear noises, you know, like someone walking behind me or hiding in the trees. But sometimes it’s just this sense, this feeling of other presences. I turn around as fast as I can but I never see anything.”

“It’s pretty woodsy out there. There’s all kinds of strange noises. Animals, the wind and stuff. When I first got here I couldn’t sleep for three nights straight. I was used to sirens and honking and drunks coming out of the bars at four in the morning. I thought it was too quiet here. But once I got used to it I realized it isn’t really quiet at all. It’s just a different kind of noise—country noise.”

“Yes. It’s like it is on the ocean. You expect it to be silent but in fact there’s a whole set of sounds that can keep you awake if you’re not used to them. At home we lived in a housing development. The only noise you heard late at night was dogs barking and the occasional creaking of someone’s garage door. But that’s not what I’m talking about. This is something else.”

Noah sits up. “So what do you think it is?”

I consider telling him—after all, why did I start this conversation? But then I realize how ridiculous the words would sound in my mouth, so I say, “I don’t know.”

“You think it’s them, don’t you,” he says.

I hold my breath, not sure I heard him right.

“You think they’re with you. I totally believe in that, Eve, that missing someone enough can, you know, make them make themselves known to you. I mean, it’s never happened to me, but Angelique, she felt it when her father died.”

“Of course,” I say, “You’ve said yourself Angelique is a bit loony.”

He laughs. “True, but when it came to this—she used to be so quiet about it, so *un*theatrical that I could feel it really happening to her. She’d whip around suddenly, say ‘did you feel that’ or ‘did you hear that,’ and when I said no, she’d shrug or something, didn’t try to make a big deal out of it. She missed her father so hard.”

“That’s just it. I don’t know if I’m missing them hard enough to deserve it.”

He is silent at that.

Right before he leaves I ask the one question that matters to me. "Can you come back?"

He smiles. "That's the one good thing that did come out of seeing Angelique. I figured, if I'm going to see her, then I can most certainly see you. I mean, I love Isabel, but she shouldn't control who I see. I have to cut it off with Angelique, but I don't have to give up my friends. When we're together, permanently, Isabel will be more confident. Anyway, she's not hurrying to tell Leo anything, so why should I give up my only friend here?"

And I say thank you and he says no, thank *you*, and even though we laugh, we mean it.

Myra has filed a lawsuit against the Russian fishing company. Criminal charges are pending against the captain of the boat, whose officer on watch either fell asleep or got drunk or somehow neglected to keep an eye on their radar long enough to notice a yacht with four people on board in their path. The insurance company still dithers. Myra tells me the story was on *Hard Copy* again this week when the criminal charges hit the news. "Birdie must have had more pictures to sell those bastards," she says. "I called and threatened to sue her. She said I was too sensitive. The lawyer doesn't think I have much of a case but he said he'll send her a threatening letter. She didn't have even have a decent excuse for why she did it. They paid good money, she had the nerve to tell me. Bitch."

"Myra," I say, "such language."

"Well, you sound more cheerful."

"Do I?"

Noah and I are in town buying me a dress for the opera when I see Ray and her boyfriend in the window of the diner. She's reading from a pile of papers and he's devouring a hamburger. I move Noah quickly away when I see Ray glance up. As we walk through town I keep thinking I hear her chirping greeting. For reasons I can't quite fathom, I can't get Ray and her hungry friend, whose hapless wife and kids I picture so clearly, entirely out of my mind.

At the pre-Christmas, "50% off" sale at The Gilded Cage, I find a long-sleeved, black knit dress with a drop waist and buy it without trying it on. At the shoe store on a side street I buy black pumps and a matching purse. I do all this in a flush of shame, certain I should not be dressing up, going out to be entertained.

At home I put on the dress and stand in front of the full-length mirror on the back of the bathroom door. Closing my eyes, I move into my own line of sight and open them slowly, squintingly, as if watching a scary movie, distorting the picture just enough to make it unrealistic, palatable. The black dress clings to my torso and flares out at my hips. I open my eyes wider; the fabric stretches tight against my ribs, but my breasts curve softly out and the dress falls surprisingly nicely. I lift my gaze tentatively; my once-tanned face looks as if it has been whitewashed—eggshell pale, the eyes larger than I remember, with spidery lines spreading from their corners, the creases from my nose to my mouth more pronounced. My hair falls past my shoulders in heavy waves; it has been over two years since I chopped if off for convenience. I consider wearing my hair up for the opera, but when I gather it onto the top of my head to see what it looks like my cheeks seem to sink under the cheekbones. I let my hair fall back down and my face softens, though it holds a definite expression of surprise.

It isn't that I haven't looked at my face in the last four months; in fact, since Noah has been coming over I've regularly put on lipstick and fussed with my hair. But I haven't looked at the totality of the picture in a long time. The shock is that I recognize this woman in the mirror. I expected to be completely transformed; instead, I'm a thinner, paler, version of the same old me.

How could I still be vain enough to be pleased that it's not a whole lot worse?

15

We are in the inner sanctum of the Stein house, the studio upstairs where Noah works. It is sparsely furnished—a small white room with white-painted floors and a grand piano as shiny as a new car. There is a scarred wooden desk covered with music and other papers.

I am sitting on a chair holding Robbie's libretto. I start out following it while Noah begins playing the overture and Act One of his opera, and eventually I let it rest in my lap as I close my eyes and merely listen. Noah gives me the important plot points as he goes along: "The opening is at Kenilworth Castle—Catherine's prison. She is dying and asks her jailer to get a message to the king, begging him to let her daughter see her one last time. While she's waiting she reminisces."

He plays music that is exquisitely plaintive. Parts of it raise the hairs on my arms. In many sections it reminds me of all the operas I've been listening to but there's something harsher about it, more staccato, with strange leaps between notes that I've never heard before.

"Here she's fifteen and it's the wedding procession, her marriage to Henry's brother. Think drums. A timpani." A proud march with hints of what I think of as Elizabethan music—the kind that songs in Shakespeare plays are set to.

"Here's the proposal scene. Henry is finally king, in love with Catherine and now able to claim her. He has an aria about what a great benevolent king he plans to be and how with Catherine at his side he knows he can accomplish this. He's a baritone. Imagine winds and brass under this." And I hear Henry's booming voice, his idealistic song—our future, yours and mine; I can't do it without you; I do it all for you. It's there in the notes that rise and rise and then drop suddenly. That's the seduction—the low insistence saying we share this dream.

"The final scene of the first act: Five years later, the birth of the princess Mary. After four miscarriages, Henry has his heir. First the love duet—the happy couple renew their vows of devotion. Then recitative: Henry tells Catherine that he will leave her to rest. She has made him so happy because now he knows that soon he will have his son. After he's gone Catherine has the closing aria. She sings of her love for Henry but her fear about his obsession for a son. Then she looks at the infant Mary—big crescendo here—she vows her devotion and protection for this tiny baby who may one day be queen. Against any who wish Mary harm, against even the king, if necessary, she will fight to the death for her daughter's safety and honor. Aaaand . . . curtain."

He sits for a moment, his hands still poised dramatically over the piano. Then he turns around to me, his face damp with sweat. I smile a little, remembering my first impression of him as deliberately cultivating the tortured artist demeanor. Now I don't even think he knows he does it. He smiles shyly. "That's it, that's the first act."

More than an hour has gone by since I sat down in the chair to listen to him. The room has grown dusky, the only real light coming from the small lamp over the piano music.

"I don't know what to say," I tell him. "Except that I can hear it. Just from your playing, I can hear the music, the singing. I can hear Isabel breaking everyone's heart."

His shoulders relax, His eyes grow bright. "And the story? You think the music goes with the story? You like how the story proceeds?"

"I'm not sure what you mean."

"The story. I changed it a bit. I mean, not from the facts, just the way we were presenting them. That's what I met with Robbie about. It was because of you."

My heart thuds. "What do you mean?"

He is shy again, swiping at hair that is no longer there. "In the original version we were emphasizing the events more. Catherine's aria at the end of the first act was all about how she was going to fight—it had way more foreshadowing. What am I trying to say? I guess I just realized that we were avoiding the psychological truth of the character. I mean, because we didn't really understand it. How could we? Anne Boleyn, the next wife, is easier for someone like me to understand. She was all blind ambition. She didn't care who would be destroyed by her plan to marry the king. When Catherine held out against the divorce, Anne was the one who saw to it that she was separated from her daughter. Anne had no children of her own at the time so she couldn't possibly conceive of what her vindictiveness would do. She wanted what she wanted when she wanted it, and anyone who stood in her way was asking for trouble."

"Why didn't you write an opera about Anne Boleyn then?"

Noah laughs. "Well, for one thing, it's been done. *Anna Bolena*. Donizetti. He depicts Anne as a victim of love. Believe me, she was no victim. Besides, I wanted to write a more mature woman for Isabel, someone with way more life experience. But me and Robbie, I mean, after I got to know you I thought, what do two thirty-year-old men know about survival? Now I'm thinking about Catherine like that—she had everything thrown at her—her life was nine-tenths misery to like one-tenth happiness. She was married to Henry's brother for a year before he died and then she had to sit around in obscurity and poverty until the old king died and Henry rescued her. Then after like only five or six years of marriage he becomes chronically unfaithful to her, then twenty years later he wants to divorce her, disown her daughter. She's sent off to what's essentially a prison where she's kept in more poverty and disgrace, cut off from the only two people she loves in the world, her husband and her child. And still she doesn't sink under it. She retains her faith that one day her family will be reunited. Maybe even more amazing, she retains her religious faith, her belief that God will protect her."

"Uh huh," I say dully.

"She loves the king till the day she dies. But I was just depicting it, not really understanding it. I didn't think about how she felt very much. Kind of thought that was up to the singers to bring to the music. But . . ." He shifts uncomfortably on the hard piano bench. "Knowing you, getting to know you has made me realize that I have to put her internal state into the music somehow—that I was avoiding how it *felt*, and without that, we just have hollow music. When I played the new stuff to Robbie he suddenly understood exactly what I was trying to say."

"I don't know what you mean, really, Noah. I don't know what you're saying."

"Are you upset?"

"I don't know," I say.

"Oh jeez, the last thing I wanted to do was upset you. I thought . . . I wanted you to know how much you . . . knowing you has inspired me. My work."

I press myself further back into the chair. "So you're saying you've been studying me? You're comparing me to some woman who's been dead for 400 years?"

"No, no, Eve, Christ that's not what I meant at all. God, how could you think that?" He gets up from the bench and comes over to my chair, kneels down in front of me, grabs my hands and won't let them go when I try to wriggle from his grasp. "Listen to me. *Listen to me*." He grips my hands tighter. "What I've been trying to tell you is that you have . . . I care for you. I . . ."

"Okay," I say, trying to get up. "Okay."

He moves his hands to my arms, holding me down. His weak little hands suddenly so strong; like everything else, a lie. "I am trying to tell you that you have made me think about pain and loss . . . you've made me want to portray it—make it mean something. I see you struggling to find one good reason to stick around the planet and I realize that I don't know the first thing about suffering. But I do know that I've come to value you in this short time and there must be so many other people who need you to stick it out."

His fingers dig into my wrists. The pain helps me fight the rising panic. Then he pulls me forward and holds me against him; he's shaking against my chest and the unbearable images recede and instead of kelp and salt and decay I smell his sweat and the stuff he uses in his hair. He kisses my neck and then my cheek and then my mouth. I have not been kissed on the mouth in so long, I think, but it hasn't been that long, it's been four months or so, a little more if you don't count Charlie kissing me goodnight that night, a small peck on the last night because he was peeved with me, with my lack of enthusiasm and my exhaustion and my selfishness, but two nights before when we made love—a little angrily, as if we were daring each other to back away—his mouth was against mine for real. And this kiss, on the mouth, close-lipped and desperate, is too long to be innocuous but the impulse is already over before his lips touch mine. I don't pull away and I am instantly ashamed. He lets me go suddenly so that I sink back into the chair, as if his precious hands have gone weak again. He shakes his head, repeating "I'm sorry, I'm sorry," like a litany. So then I touch him, lift his chin, smooth his hair back and say, "It's all right it's all right," because it is, because if he did it again, kissed me, passionately this time instead of almost passionately, I would open myself to it as surely as I could not open myself to the rising water.

The next day, a long black car stops in front of the cottage. Noah is waiting inside in his dark overcoat. His hair is slick with some kind of gel and still a tendril or two is hanging in his eyes. Deliberately, I think. He smells of aftershave. The driver is different from the one who drove us here from the airport back in September. It seems like a very long time ago that I rode down here, sandwiched between Myra and Isabel, blank and stunned. If they had been driving me to the edge of a canyon to push me off, I think I would have gone along with that too.

"You look beautiful," Noah says.

I am wearing one of Isabel's coats, maroon cashmere with a mink collar, which would be elegant if my wrists didn't protrude from the too-short sleeves. I clutch it around me and nod awkwardly. "You too."

I stare out the window at the darkening roads but I am as aware of him next to me as I am of my own body. My hands are in my lap, clutching my purse, and all I can think is *take my hand take my hand* as if I were a schoolgirl on a date, as if I imagined some kind of future. The urge to be touched by him is so strong that I have to hold my breath and dig my fingernails into my palms for minutes at a time to keep from reaching for him.

"Before you know it we'll be on our way like this to the opening of *Catherine*."

I have been seeing him so hard in my imagination that his actual voice, low and cheerful, startles me.

"I don't suppose I'll be with you," I say.

"What do you mean? Why not?"

"Oh," I say, not looking at him. "I expect to be long gone."

"Gone where?"

"I don't know yet."

He's trying to get me to look at him but I keep staring out. A light snow has begun to fall. The cold radiates from the window glass. "I'm going to leave as soon as possible," I say.

"Huh." Noah shifts in his seat. "Of course I knew it wasn't going to be like this forever. I guess I wasn't thinking about how it would be though. You know," he turns back to me. "When Isabel and I are together we'll probably spend more time in the city. I mean, when I write I'll probably want to go back to the house but otherwise, I'm not a weekend-in-the-country kind of guy. So, you know, you could possibly take over the house. I mean, be the caretaker, kind of. You have work to do, too, right? You don't want to have all the hassle of pulling up stakes until you finish your book."

"You are so goddamn sure everything is going to work out," I say.

His eyes widen. "What does that mean?"

"Jesus, Noah, you have so much faith in yourself. And in Isabel. It's so . . . so naïve. You're not *that* young, for god's sake. You just assume that you and Isabel are going to end up together, end up with the house, the apartment, that Leo and Angelique are just going to disappear when you want them to. Like everything is guaranteed to go according to plan."

It's unclear which of us is more shocked by my venom. "I know things may go wrong," he says, sullen now and shifting away from me. "I'm just trying to help. To work out a way for us . . . for our friendship to be maintained."

I feel again his dry lingering kiss in the darkness of his studio and then I think of being around him and Isabel for the next few days—she hanging on his arm, his words, his looking down at her like she invented language.

"I wouldn't count on our friendship lasting," I say flatly.

"Jeez, Eve, it seems like everything I say to you lately you misinterpret. What's wrong anyway?" He's frowning at me and his lips are pursed and wet. I can almost taste them.

"Are you still upset about the other night? Is that why you're talking about leaving? I don't know what else to do Eve, I've apologized, I didn't mean anything by it and I feel as if everything is falling apart because I said the wrong thing just once. And did the wrong thing. What can I say or do to make it better? To make up for it?"

Kiss me again.

"Did you say something?"

"Kiss me again."

And he does.

What sex is like. I was going to write it down, a kind of manual for my children—mostly for Jessica because frankly, you could put into a thimble how much I know about men's experience of sex. This I could tell Nick: That in my observation (which I'd be the first to admit can be wildly faulty) men can have good sex and great sex and they can even have crummy sex, but that if they come, they've never really had horrible sex. Also, in my limited observation, men often resist coming, as if it were something painful or unpleasant. They seem to think that longevity is the most important weapon in their sexual arsenal—armed with the ability to stay hard for extended periods of time they can vanquish any woman's resistant orgasm. Which is not to say that they don't like quickies. But when they're really concentrating, when they are, say, making love rather than fucking, then this idea that the longer they last the more they impress you takes hold. Personally, I might have told Nick, I get tired after a certain point. I get sore. (I might not actually say that.) I wouldn't mind a little less longevity and a little more fore-play. Or post-cuddling. Or sleeping. But then I'm your old fuddy duddy mother, I might add, to make him laugh.

What else I would tell them: The best quality you can look for in your first lover is kindness. My first lover was Jack Gowan, a painter I met in college. I was embarrassed that I'd reached the advanced age of nineteen with my virginity still intact. In my day, that was tantamount to having a disease. Jack was the perfect lover.

He said it was an honor that I'd chosen him to deflower me. And Jack was so gentle. He instructed me—the way I'd hoped to be instructed—specifically, playfully. And when it was over, although it clearly had been nothing of the sort, he avowed that the whole thing had been great for him. Find someone like Jack, I wanted to tell Jessica.

I would tell them both that the cliché really is true, though for years I myself didn't believe it. That sex is better with someone you love. I would probably not tell them how much experience I actually had, but I would at least hint at the idea that Charlie was by no means technically the best lover I ever had.

How could I avoid clichés in telling them? Maybe I would say that when I made love with Charlie something happened that should have been happening between us without our having sex. The closest I can come to describing it is a feeling like the one you have when you're really tired and you finally get to sink into your bed, pull your covers up and close your eyes. That moment just before you fall asleep, when all the nerves and bones and muscles of your body are aligned toward the same blissful, almost primeval end. A sort of dropping away, dropping into something you won't even be able to describe later, like sleep.

You have no idea how little this has to do with orgasm, I would tell them.

When Noah kisses me again the feeling is like that muscle spasm thing that happens when you sleep that causes you to dream you've fallen. My stomach drops away and I grab onto him for support. My thoughts are crazy and jumbled: *yes* and *don't* and *what am I doing* and *Isabel* and *what does Noah think he's doing* and *I should be adding up the number of people we're betraying now* and *what can the driver see behind that smoky glass* and *don't stop please kiss me like this forever.*

And then we are crossing the bridge and entering the city—we both sense it at once and pull away. And we are embarrassed again, turning away from each other, discreetly wiping our mouths and straightening our hair. "Oh man," Noah says, "Oh man."

He reaches over and takes my hand and holds it between us on the car seat. We drive across town in silence, the driver weaving expertly in and out of the seemingly unmoving traffic. We arrive at six o'clock almost to the second at the restaurant across from Lincoln Center where we are to meet Leo and Angelique. Noah drops my hand abruptly and reaches for his door handle while the driver comes around to my side to let me out. I stand on the curb huddling in Isabel's coat while Noah talks to the driver. When he's done I turn toward the restaurant before he can speak to me.

It is cavernous inside—one huge room with white-clothed tables crowded together. My coat is lifted from my shoulders. A riot of flashbulbs goes off and I turn back toward the door, my heart thudding. But to the left is a large table of partyers who sway together, arms linked, in front of several people holding cameras. Noah takes my arm and more flashbulbs go off. The din is unbelievable. "I don't know if I can take this," I yell to Noah, but he doesn't hear me. He's scanning the room, though how he can see in all this noise is beyond me.

"There!" he shouts. I follow him through a maze of tables. We arrive at one set for eight people behind which sits a lone woman with a halo of blonde ringlets and cat's-eye glasses with pale blue frames. She smiles broadly at Noah, who inches his way around the table to her side, bends down and kisses her freckled cheek while she looks at me. "This is Eve," Noah says, waving a hand at me. "Have you been waiting long?"

"Not long," Angelique says in a chirpy voice. "You're almost on time. You should ride around in limousines more often." As she says this she grabs my hand and pumps it athletically. She has the kind of sunny good looks that were so popular when I was in high school. Her eyes are a sort of milky blue and look enormous behind her glasses. Her nose turns up perfectly at the tip. When we were walking toward her I thought she looked about twenty years old, but up close I can see the finely etched lines that run from her nose to her chin on either side of her mouth and the deeper ones that slash her forehead. Her dress scoops low across her neck, revealing the same thin white skin stretched across two protruding collarbones. I can't believe this, but I'm actually finding some satisfaction in the fact that with her vintage glasses and girlish outfit she looks like a woman hanging on a bit frantically to her youth. She continues to study me as she says, "I've heard so much about you. It's such a treat to finally meet you."

I smile lamely back and sit down. Noah takes the seat on her other side. "Why the big table," he says. "We're not expecting more people, are we?"

"Not that I know of," Angelique replies, still looking at me. "I told them I was with the Stein party and this is the table they showed me to. Maybe the diva is going to arrive with an entourage?" She gives me a knowing look. I just keep smiling like an idiot.

"I told you, she's not coming," Noah says petulantly.

Angelique turns to me. "Fabulous dress, Eve! It goes perfectly with your lovely hair."

I mumble a reluctant thanks, convinced now that I have bought the un-hippest dress to be had in the State of New York. "So I hear you've become quite the opera fan," she says to me. "Personally, I still can barely sit through it. All that bellowing. But, since Noah's writing one, I guess I have to get used to it." She puts her hand on Noah's shoulder without turning toward him. Her hand is blunt, with stubby fingers and thick, raised veins along the top. A worker's hands.

"Of course, I'm thrilled that he has this opportunity. To work with someone as . . . great as Isabel Stein! And so lucky, since who knows how much longer she would have gone on?"

Noah reddens. "Shall we order a drink?"

"Oh yes." Angelique claps her hands. "Something colorful—with fruit, don't you think? Something summery?"

"Sure, that sounds good," Noah says.

"To celebrate all our new friendships!" She kisses him on the cheek and he pats her shoulder.

"What do you suppose would be the drink that comes with the most paraphernalia? Umbrellas, the works!" Angelique seems so genuinely enthusiastic that it's hard to dislike her simply on principle.

A waiter arrives at our table, puffing with exertion. Noah orders tea, and without asking, orders me a martini. Angelique lifts one almost nonexistent eyebrow, but continues to chatter to me, as if determined to make me her best friend by the end of the evening.

"You should come to our loft, Eve, I bet you've never been to one before. It's fantastic, isn't it, Noah? Huge and light. You could see some of my work if you're interested." Angelique leans closer to me. "I'm so excited about the latest stuff. It's on the way to being good at last, isn't it Noah?" She turns to him, eyes shining.

"Yes," Noah says gravely, looking straight at her. I can tell he means it.

"Oh, Sweetie, I can't wait for you to see how much it's progressed—you'll be so proud of me!" She leans her head against his shoulder. "What an exciting time it is for both of us. Don't you think, Eve? And Noah tells me you're writing a book?"

"Well, yes," I begin.

"Did Robbie call by any chance?" Noah interrupts.

"Oh gosh." She puts her hand to her cheek, looking crestfallen. "I'm *so* sorry. Yes, he did, and how could I forget to tell you?" She looks and sounds distraught.

"It's okay, honey, I just wondered." Noah says gently, squeezing her arm.

"No, the least I could do is get your messages right. When you're at such a critical point in the work."

"Really, don't sweat it. I'll call him later."

"Oh, but he left a different number and I completely . . . well, I don't have it with me. It's back at the loft. You'll have to wait till we get home tonight. That won't be too much trouble, will it?"

"Of course not," he says, hugging her. Over her head he shoots me a hopeless look.

But I heard that "honey."

By the time Leo arrives I'm on my second drink. Angelique has been talking nonstop, mostly about friends of hers and Noah's, the various things she needs him to do around the loft, travel plans for some nebulous time in the future. Periodically she turns to me as if for approval—with a "right Eve?" or "don't you think?" in that friendly, encouraging voice that makes me want to join in the conversation in spite of myself.

Then Leo is there, bringing with him the smell of cigar smoke and cold air. He's at his most charming, standing above us in an impeccable tuxedo, black on black on black that sets off his silver hair to greatest advantage, sweeping his gaze over Angelique as if she were a model he planned to paint, holding her hand for a while after he's shaken it, smiling his seductive smile. He has barely to flick an eyebrow and the waiter is there and he is ordering another round and a martini for himself, checking the watch that gleams gold against his black cuff. "I've only got about a half hour," he says, twinkling his eyes at Angelique. "Isabel likes me to be backstage before she goes on." He takes a deep breath and lets it out in an elaborate sigh. "She's been at this for over thirty years and she still gets stage fright like it's her first time."

"God, so do I," Angelique says. "Before an opening I'm a basket case. I have a surefire cure though. The night before an opening, I make a huge pot of my mother's coq au vin. All that simmering relaxes me."

Noah shakes his head. "Yeah, she makes so much she ends up feeding the whole building."

"How generous," Leo says.

"Not really," Angelique leans toward him and drops her voice. "I'm kind of a lousy cook. It's really not very good coq au vin."

And they are all laughing, lifting their glasses simultaneously and moving into a spontaneous toast, which they refuse to end until I raise my glass and join them.

"So, you are every bit as charming as we imagined you would be," Leo says. "I don't know why Noah has been hiding you away for so long."

"Neither do I," she says, grabbing Noah's hand.

I stand up. "I'm going to the ladies' room," I say.

I elbow my way to the front of the restaurant and push against the door, stepping into the night air. I take a few gulps, and hug myself against the frigid air.

Somewhere someone is leaning on his car horn and cabs and other cars are rushing past in a nonstop stream of roaring engines and squeaking brakes. Across the street Lincoln Center is aflame with lights. For the first time I notice the Christmas decorations strung across Columbus Avenue in front of Lincoln Center.

What was I thinking? I have been so successful at blotting Christmas from my mind that I haven't really let it register that it's five days away. I hardly watch TV anymore; I keep the radio on the classical station that doesn't play Christmas music; and although certainly the Steins and Noah have mentioned Christmas, they always refer to it in terms of scheduling rather than festivities. *Butterfly* happens right before Christmas, Isabel's operation is two months after Christmas, etc. Nobody has talked about trees or presents or anything else that would really make it sink in that the holiday is approaching.

Now, shivering in the subzero air of the city, there's no getting away from it. Almost every one of the many pedestrians (so many pedestrians!) rushing by have shopping bags of various sizes and shades of red or green or a combination of both. I hug myself closer, my fingers going numb, and I begin to cry.

When I duck back inside, Leo is approaching, shrugging into his long overcoat. "Walk with me, Eve," he says. His hand goes to my back and he steers me again toward the entrance. I think he is speaking to me as we walk but I can't hear him.

"What?" I say, "What?" until we are at the bar.

He maneuvers me against the one empty place at the bar. The bartender appears as if summoned. "You want something?" Leo asks me. I shake my head. The bartender peers around at me, his tired eyes searching my face. I bow my head. "Listen, Eve," Leo says, leaning toward me, "a quick word of advice. Be careful."

"Excuse me?" I say. The edge of the bar digs into the bones of my back.

"People recognize you here, are you aware of that? If no one's approached you it's because they're too drunk or self-involved. You won't be able to escape entirely, though, as long as you're around Isabel."

As if on cue, a flashbulb from an indeterminate direction goes off in my face. Red sparks dance in front of my eyes.

"You want to know the first lesson you learn when you're involved with someone famous? Discretion. You may not realize it, but if you are anywhere near someone who is in the limelight, a little of its reflection hits you. You have a bit of a spotlight of your own, now, so you need to be doubly careful. I learned this the hard way, Eve, I'm just trying to spare you some heartache."

"Leo," I say, "I have no idea what you're talking about."

He leans closer to me. I can see the pores on his smooth shaven face. "Maybe not. But you will. Listen, I don't begrudge you anything you want, anything you take right now. In fact, you might even be doing me a favor if you go after what you want. Just be discreet, is all I'm saying. For your own sake."

My heart pounds in my ears, drowning out the restaurant noise. How can he know? There have been no witnesses. Then I look more closely at him and see in the twitching at the corners of his mouth and blinking of his icy blue eyes that he's speaking to me not about what he knows but about what he suspects—or hopes for.

16

On the plaza in front of the Met, beautiful people parade in beautiful clothes and smell of beautiful flowers and spices. Tuxedos and billowing gowns, wealthy laughter and air kisses. But there is a smaller group whose dress is much more eclectic: blue jeans and velvet muumuus, cowboy boots and rhinestone tiaras. They give the impression of a kind of genteel shabbiness, but what's most remarkable about them is their faces. They all have the same avid, blazing look—they clutch souvenir programs to their chests as if hugging the singers themselves, or they fiddle with bird-watching-sized binoculars, as if intending to worship every pore on Isabel's face. Where the first group is relaxed and chatty, this group is silent and coiled, huddling near the entrance of the theater, counting, one imagines, the seconds until they are seated—most likely not in anything close to the orchestra section. This can be none other than the group that Isabel once described as "high-end Deadheads."

The three of us stand uncomfortably by the geysering central fountain. Noah has been trying to pull me aside to say something, but Angelique has a firm grip on his arm. She shivers in her gauzy dress and fringed green shawl, but she is unwilling to go into the theater yet. Her head swivels madly and she seems to find what she's looking for as she waves to some people across the plaza. Noah and I turn to see a couple waving back. "It's Tony and Anne, Noah," she says, and pulls him away to go meet their friends. She looks over her shoulder and waves me to join them, but I shake my head. Angelique shrugs and grins. "We'll be right back!" she calls.

I stand by the fountain, near two men from the Deadhead crowd who are talking excitedly about Thomas Jacoby, the conductor of tonight's performance, and apparently a rising star.

"He's never worked with her before," one man says. He is startling in blue faux-fur earmuffs.

"That could be good," says the other man, who is wrapped in an overcoat that brushes the ground.

"Not likely. Her talent . . . it's not something any hack can just walk in and do justice to. Think of the EMI *Bohème*. That was Von Karajan, for Chrissakes. And still he overpowered her. Obviously favors the tenor."

"True," the other man nods. "The RCA is the only Stein *Bohème* worth listening to."

"Is that with Domingo?"

"Salvador."

"Of course." They are silent for a moment, rapt.

"You read what Opera Dot Com said about her, of course," the overcoat man says.

"Typical bitchiness," earmuffs says. "I barely read that rag anymore. They're always jealous of any diva over thirty. Look what they did to Callas."

"Oh, well, Callas . . ."

"There's no difference! Isabel is every bit the diva Maria was. All these critics care about are the money notes."

"But still, there has been quite a lot of press about Stein's voice problems—" says his companion.

"*All* singers have voice problems now and then." Earmuffs seems genuinely furious. "She's timeless." And he crosses his arms as if that puts an end to it.

"I agree, of course," overcoat rushes to say. "Oh look, they're opening the doors." They hurry away, heads down, hopes high.

Noah and Angelique are heading back in my direction, arm in arm.

Inside, the opera house is tastefully opulent. Red carpet, spiky gold chandeliers. I feel a thrill of excitement as we move with the crowd into the theater. Gilt boxes rise on either side. We sink into our plush orchestra seats. It's as if I'm in some European turn-of-the-century movie; glittering women smooth their gowns beneath them and smile beatifically at the dark, silk-clad men at their sides. I expect them all to pull out fans. Angelique has manipulated the seating arrangement so that she is between Noah and me and Leo's seat is to my left. I am actually grateful for the distance. Whatever it is that Noah wants to say, I can't imagine one thing it would please me to hear.

"Ooh, what's this?" Angelique says. She leans forward to look at the translation screen on the seat in front of her. As soon as she does, Noah leans behind her and catches my eye. I need to talk to you, he mouths, and then she is touching his arm, looking at him, pulling him forward to show her how the screen on the back of the seat works.

"Subtitles, how clever," Angelique says, clapping her hands. She startles me by turning in my direction. "You're so quiet, Eve." She is smiling but scrutinizing me. "Of course, it's amazing that you're here at all, isn't it. It's just wonderful how you're bouncing back from your ordeal."

"Angelique," Noah says darkly.

"You know, if there's anything I can do . . . if you ever want to talk or anything. . . ."

"Enough, Angelique," Noah says. Her head jerks as if he had slapped her. They glare at each other and Angelique opens her mouth to speak.

"Here we are, ready to go!" Leo arrives at his seat at that moment, all suave heartiness. He settles beside me, unaware of the tension coating the air. "Curtain in five minutes. Isabel is her usual wreck. She asked me to tell you all how happy she is that you are here." Angelique turns her furious face to him and Leo flinches. Then Angelique glances up at the ceiling and her face goes from enraged to enchanted with no stop in between. "Oh look!" she says. We follow her gaze and see that the gold chandeliers are rising into the ceiling. I have never been so happy for things to go dark.

The curtain rises on a Japanese house with tatami screens nestled next to an actual babbling brook, shaded by cherry trees. Then the tenor is onstage—John Barr, the man Isabel has been complaining about for the last month—playing Pinkerton, American Naval Officer. He is followed by Goro, the Japanese marriage broker. I press the button on the screen in front of me. Goro is showing Pinkerton around his new home, which is being prepared for his Japanese bride. "Where is the bridal chamber?" Pinkerton asks, arrogant and dismissive of his host—just the way Isabel has described John Barr as a person. I try to follow the story but cannot concentrate. I am aware of Angelique's every quiver. Most of all, I can feel Noah two seats away. He is no doubt filled with his tortured artist version of confusion and angst. He wants to murder—or embrace Angelique. Or both. He wants to grab Isabel off the stage the minute she arrives and run away with her. He wants to kiss me again.

Then Isabel is onstage and everything falls away. Cio-Cio-San arrives with her bridal retinue, carrying a parasol and wearing a creamy white kimono. She was singing before she appeared and is still singing as she climbs the path at the back of the stage. This is not the younger, healthier voice I'm used to from the recordings. It's slightly gravelly and the vibrato quavers. If I notice this, I wonder what experts notice. Still, when she arrives onstage her presence is so strong that despite her diminutive size, you can see and hear no one but her. Her head is bowed in an uncharacteristically shy way, and the tight wrapping of her costume causes her to walk in mincing, hesitant steps that suggest modesty and youth.

But Leo is clicking his teeth as if he's dissatisfied with something. When the American Consul asks Cio-Cio-San her age and she says fifteen, Angelique whispers in my ear, "she wishes." Then I want to throttle her myself.

The mock wedding takes place. Already I can predict what will happen. It's clear that Cio-Cio-San is taking this all a lot more seriously than her dallying American lover. She has even defied her ancestors and converted to Christianity for him. Then she is left alone with John Barr. He wants to go bed. She wants to exclaim about the glories of love, the beauty of the night. Barr's clear, pealing tenor is bright with barely suppressed longing and suddenly I believe him myself—I believe that he loves Cio-Cio-San, that he worships her and wants only to show her how much even though I know in my gut that he's going to destroy her. The music builds and finally, at the end of the act, he has her down on a tatami mat, he has unhooked her waist sash and exposed one shoulder, on his way to exposing much more, as the curtain comes down. There is applause. Then Isabel and

Barr and all the other soloists come out in front of the curtain and the applause swells slightly. The performers smile and bow—holding hands, except for Isabel and Barr, who stand side by side without touching. Everyone waits while Isabel exits first, then they follow. Then Barr comes out alone. The applause grows; is close to thunderous. Then Isabel comes out alone. Almost imperceptibly the applause fades; is now more polite than thunderous. Her smile wavers then sticks. Leo clicks his teeth again. The lights come up. Leo is frowning.

People are rising and heading out of the theater for intermission. Leo doesn't seem to be able to make up his mind what he wants to do. "I guess I won't go backstage," he says finally, as if this is a very important decision. So we all head to the lobby.

Leo goes for champagne while the three of us are buffeted by audience members who seem much surer of where they're going than we do. "Goodness," Angelique says, giggling a little, "such energy in this room."

"How do you like it?" Noah says.

Angelique flutters her fingers at her throat and laughs some more. "Oh, Sweetie, it's fine. Very pretty. Of course your Isabel isn't exactly what I expected."

"Uh huh," Noah says, moving toward me.

"She's so *tiny*, for one thing—she looks so huge in her pictures. But obviously that's just her head. It's, like, enormous, isn't it? She's actually prettier than her pictures, I think. Wouldn't you think she'd update her head shots? Oh my god, Noah, I just had the most brilliant thought!"

She grabs Noah's arm. "Why don't you ask your Isabel if I could do new head shots for her? I've been doing the most awesome things with the camera lately, wait'll you see it. Collages. Well, you saw the beginnings of it last time you were here but now—oh they've grown so much. And I could do some amazing pictures of her. That head! I could capture her mature quality so she doesn't look like she's trying to hide her age. Oh say you'll ask her!"

Noah covers her hand with his. "I don't really think she'd be interested, Angelique," he says.

"Why not?" She blinks rapidly, eyes wide.

Noah sighs. "*Because*, she has a very busy schedule, for one thing, and for another, she has someone she hires to do all that for her. No offense, but I really don't think your work would be Isabel's cup of tea."

Angelique looks nonplussed. Then she laughs brightly. "You are so in love with her, aren't you," she says.

Noah goes pale. My heart seems to be taking a pause. I find myself moving a step closer to him, as if to shield him from a blow. "That is the most ridiculous thing I ever heard," he says vehemently.

"What's the most ridiculous thing you ever heard?" Leo says. He is carrying a small tray with four champagne glasses balanced on it.

"That Noah is in love with your wife," Angelique says, gaily.

Leo lifts one graceful eyebrow. Without missing a beat he says, "Well, of course he is. Everyone falls a little in love with Isabel, especially musicians. She'd be disappointed if they didn't." He hands each of us a drink. It takes Angelique a moment to lift her hand to accept hers. "It's nothing to worry about," Leo says. "It's not *that* kind of love. It's infatuation you know. Like you would feel about a rock star. It doesn't really mean anything."

Act Two and it's all bearable until Isabel brings out the child. I don't remember a child from when I saw the opera so many years ago. Cio-Cio-San is going to give her son up to her husband, who has married an American woman and wants to take his son back to America. Cio-Cio-San says she will give him up only if Pinkerton comes for him himself. Her maid suspects she plans to kill herself and sends the little boy to her. She could not look at him and then commit suicide, surely. She sees her little boy, three years old. She blindfolds him with the sash from her white wedding dress and goes behind the screen. He sits obediently, patiently, waiting for her. She gropes her way from behind the screen, a red slash across her midriff, and collapses at the feet of her little boy as Pinkerton comes running onstage. The curtain comes down.

She saved him, her little boy. She gave him a life. She abandoned him. He lived. Survived. She didn't have to watch him die.

She took the easy way out.

Wild applause; the lights flicker and people come and go from the stage. Isabel alive and smiling, hugging the little boy. It's just a play;

it's all over. They are calling my name, plaintive, soft, louder, and softer again, like waves. Eve. I feel people rising, sudden light, I am being pushed forward down the aisle and seeing wavering glitter—it could be jewels or light or the sun dappling the tips of waves. When I try to stop, to focus, I'm pushed forward again and I hear my name again, insistent this time. The whisper touch I feel at my side and back is strangers brushing up against me. Eve. Then an arm is at my back. "Come over here," the voice says. *Charlie*? "Sit here." I am lowered to a velvet bench, the arm still grasping me tight. "You're all right," the voice says and I can't help it, he sounds so caring I think *Charlie*. "Why didn't you do this earlier?" I ask him. "Do what?" "Love me like this," I say. "Shh," he says, "don't cry. It's all right. Don't cry."

And then the rushing sound stops. "Is she all right?" I hear the voice from behind where my face is pressed into his chest. Then another one saying "Should I get something? A glass of water?" And then his voice again, "Eve, do you have any pills with you?" I smell smoke and dry cleaning fluid and my face is scratching against a black lapel: Leo's. We're back where we were before, the theater, after the opera. It comes into focus like an old home movie, grainy and slashed with black lines at first and gradually clarifying itself into the dark walls and red carpet and brass handrails on the stairs. "Breathe," Leo whispers to me, like I used to whisper to Charlie right after he'd come—collapsed on top of me as if he'd returned from a long, arduous journey. "Breathe."

Slowly I disengage from his embrace. It was Leo who was holding me. Angelique and Noah are standing above us. Angelique's thin hands flutter. "Give her air," Angelique insists, "Give her air."

"Yes, I think we need some air," Leo says, standing up. "Noah, why don't you take Eve outside and I'll take Angelique backstage. You join us there when . . . when you're ready."

"Let me help—" Angelique says but Leo has his hand firmly on her back and is steering her away.

"Can you stand up?" Noah says, his voice like feathers across my face. A couple walks by and stares at us. Then another. My eyes sweep the emptying lobby. Back near the doors to the theater a couple is standing, watching us intently. The woman has a mass of red curls piled on her head and tumbling down again. The man is holding something small and shiny up to his face. “I know those people,” I say to Noah.

“Don’t try to talk yet.”

“No, really, over there.” I point before I think and they see me. They turn away quickly. She leads the man off to the left, toward the water fountain. “It’s Ray,” I say. “The woman I met in Kent. I think she was at the restaurant before, too.”

“You’re having a little anxiety attack is all. Just try to be quiet and take deep breaths.”

I clutch the lapels of his jacket. “I’m telling you, it’s Ray.”

“Okay. It’s Ray. Now do you think you can go outside with me?”

“What is she doing here?”

“I don’t know. Maybe she likes the opera. What difference does it make?”

“They were staring at us. Why didn’t they come say hello?”

Noah laughs under his breath. “Well maybe they were uncomfortable. You . . . we’ve made a little scene here. Come on.”

He helps me up and the room tilts, the floor slanting away from me. “Whoa,” Noah says, holding me tighter. “I’m going to take you home.”

“Where?”

“Back to the apartment.”

“But there’s the party. Isabel will be upset.”

“I’ll come back if you’re all right.”

“No, I’m fine, really. I can get back by myself.”

“I’m not going to leave you alone, Eve.”

I sag a little and he’s there, holding my arms. “We’ll just go backstage for a minute, find Leo, get the key to the apartment.”

He is walking me as he says this, holding me against him and moving me in a seemingly random pattern around the plaza. We pass in front of Avery Fisher Hall. Through the glass walls I see a restaurant and notice two little girls sitting with their backs to us. Each is wearing a black velvet ribbon in her blonde hair and the same velvet dress with white lace collar, though one is black and the other green. The mother looks like a larger version of them—short blonde hair held back by a velvet headband. Her husband has a graying goatee. The parents are smiling and nodding their heads, as if their children are giving them an insightful critique of the evening's performance. I imagine that the little girls are old hands at this scene by now, taking for granted the plush theater and glorious music, the expensive food and late hour. The worst tragedy they will know may be the death of a grandparent at an appropriately advanced age, the untimely running over of their German shepherd. Otherwise, they look inviolable. Part of me believes they are, by virtue of their handsomeness, their privilege, by virtue of the fact that I've probably used up a number of families' tragedy quota. The other part of me imagines a poisonous spider leaping out of one of the Christmas boxes of the little girl on the left and fastening itself to her leg, the one on the right falling victim to a pedophiliac Latin instructor at her exclusive school. Part of me wants to warn them; the other part of me wants to be them. I hear again Isabel's tortured voice as she kneels in front of her stage child and tells him to tell the American Consul that his name is *Trouble* but when his father comes back his name will change to *Joy*. I say to Noah, "This is a hard time."

"I know," he says.

"Holidays."

"Oh," he says. "Yes. We'll just get the keys." And he steers me back into the opera house, down the staircase in front of the box office, through glass doors and into a parking garage. There he stops, clears his throat. "Listen, this may be one of the few chances we have. Can you talk to me for a minute?"

I start to say no but he will dog me until I listen to him so I might as well get it over with. He leads me over to another set of doors that say Stage Entrance and I lean against the wall. He paces a short distance either way in front of me as he speaks, ignoring the gas fumes and the steady stream of people passing by on the way to their cars. "I just think we should straighten out the . . . what's happened. With us."

"I know what it was, Noah. I know how you feel about Isabel and that kissing me doesn't change that. I had no intention . . . I guess it's like a cut when it's bleeding a lot, you know?"

"Eve—"

"You know how you apply pressure to a cut and it stops the bleeding and it also lessens the pain for a while? But then if you keep the pressure up the pain comes back—even gets worse. That's what this is like. People are afraid to touch me. I think they think bad luck is catching or something. No one has held me except for my mother. And you. And being held by you helped. But it would only be for a while. Really, Noah, you don't have to worry, I do know that."

He's been pacing this whole time but now he stops in front of me, his brooding face close to mine. "You and your metaphors. Skunks; cuts. You think that's all this is?" he says. "Are you sure? Then how do you explain my . . . response? You have yourself all figured out, but I don't know *what* I'm feeling." He grimaces. Impulsively I reach forward and take one of his hands. He covers my hand in both of his and moves beside me, his coat touching mine. "Eve," he says miserably, "what if I'm in love with both of you? Shit, sometimes I think I'm even still a little in love with Angelique."

"Now you're being melodramatic," I say.

He glares at me. Then suddenly breaks into a grin. "Maybe I am. I'm an artist, aren't I?"

I smile back. "I hope you're not going to use that excuse your whole life."

"Why not? Everyone else does. Isabel does."

"It's one of her less attractive qualities."

"What are we going to do?" he says.

"Well nothing, I would think. You have enough on your hands just with Isabel."

"But you know, I *like* you so much more than her."

I disentangle our fingers, pulling my hand, warm from his, away.

We elbow our way through a crowd of people to the door of Isabel's dressing room, through which more people are spilling. The comingled odors of perfume and sweat. Leo's figure towering above the crowd. The clink of glasses, the occasional shout of greeting over a generalized cacophony of conversation and laughter. I see Angelique now, off to one side in a kind of bubble of space. She's holding up a full champagne glass and staring at its pale contents. Behind me someone asks someone else what they thought of the ending of the opera. I hear "A bit of a liberty with the direction . . ." before I move away. I hear other snippets of comments: "Barr magnificent," "Jacoby at the peak of his powers," "sets old hat," but nothing specific about Isabel.

"There he is! Noah, Eve, where have you been!" Isabel's voice is slightly hoarse and theatrically shrill. A wide-sleeved arm waving just behind us. Angelique's face opens at the sight of Noah and she moves to speak to him but he has already turned to Isabel. A space magically clears around Isabel, who is standing regally still in a long, kimono-like robe, her arms outstretched, awaiting us. Noah pauses at the edge of the circle, looks over his shoulder at Angelique, then steps into Isabel's embrace. She holds him fiercely, but she gestures to me over his shoulder. "Eve!" I allow myself to be swept into her embrace as well. Flashes of light and cameras clicking. Isabel edges us around a little bit as if to get us into frame. She places us one on either side of her, an arm barely reaching around each of us. "Isabel, there are cameras," I hiss. I wriggle out from her arm and she looks startled at first, as if she can't imagine who would refuse to have their picture taken with her, but then she really sees me and her hand goes to her mouth. "Oh, I wasn't thinking. Yes of course." She pushes me slightly to the side and then turns an adoring smile to Noah. "Everyone, everyone!" She never takes her eyes off him but has commanded a hush in the room. Two men with elaborate cameras move into a better position. "I want you all to meet my brilliant friend, Noah Stewart. He is *the* most talented composer working today. Bar none." She puts a hand to her mouth and giggles. "Ooh, I think I made a pun! Someone run to Barr's dressing room and tell him he's finally the topic of conversation!" The crowd laughs appreciatively. "Anyway," Isabel continues, "I know that many of you know Noah already from his *Lincoln*. Dallas a couple of years ago."

"Houston," Noah says, under his breath.

"Yes of course, Houston! Magnificent! I said, right then and there, that boy will go far. Now I want you all to remember his face and his name. You especially." She waves her hand at a woman with a notepad standing near the photographers. "You will want to record that you were here on the evening I announced the fact that he is writing an opera for me." A low murmur fills the room. More than one eyebrow lifts, and quick whispering erupts. "Noah is working on a piece based on the life of Henry the Eighth's first wife," Isabel says.

"Who commissioned the opera, Isabel?" the woman with the notebook asks, pen poised.

Isabel laughs her musical public laugh. "Why no one, darling, that's the beauty of it. We're up for grabs, so to speak. We've already had much interest shown from a number of quarters. We're just thrilled to be working together."

Leo eyes Angelique speculatively. She's smiling and bouncing on the balls of her feet. I can just imagine what she'd do if a pair of pom-poms were nearby. "You will be hearing from this man, mark my words," Isabel is saying. She reaches up on her tiptoes and pulls Noah's face down to hers. As the cameras flash she kisses him briefly but hard on the lips. Both Leo and Angelique look like people who have taken bad drugs that have just kicked in.

Isabel maneuvers Noah into the crowd and in seconds he's smiling and shaking hands and brushing away the errant shock of hair like a seasoned politician. Once or twice he throws me a helpless glance, but I've had enough. Some time after Isabel's speech, Angelique whispered in my ear that she was going to the bathroom, and she hasn't yet resurfaced. I have it in my head to take her with me—whether to spare her or Noah embarrassment, I'm not sure.

Leo's back is to me; he's talking earnestly to a man and woman dressed so simply that I suspect they are among the wealthiest people here. After the initial surprise of Isabel's display with Noah, Leo seems to have become indifferent. I tap his back.

"Excuse me, Leo? I'm sorry to disturb you."

Leo turns around. A flashbulb goes off behind us. I cringe. "Oh, Eve. Yes?" He is impatient, peeved that I interrupted what I now think was a bid for funds.

"I'm sorry. It's just that . . . Noah was going to get the keys and take me back to your apartment. But now he's—"

"Yes, well. Isabel's got him on the circuit already." He says this for the benefit of the elderly couple who chuckle politely. "You can have my keys, but you better wait for Noah. Let him take you."

"I'll be all right."

"I don't think you should be alone."

"Actually, I was thinking of giving a ride to Angelique."

He smiles at me, not unkindly. "The car is at the stage door. If you're going you should go now because we need the car to get to the party."

"I can take a cab. . . ."

"No no. You don't even know where you're going. Our driver will look after you." He drops his voice. "Go on, Eve. It's a good idea, actually." He glances over in Isabel's direction then closes my hand over the keys.

"Thanks, Leo," I say, unable to decode his sudden kindness now and back in the theater, his mysterious concern in the restaurant.

I edge toward the bathroom. Uncertain what to do, I stand there for a few minutes during which a man in a red blazer offers me champagne, flashbulbs go off in my face, and two other women arrive to use the bathroom. I take two of the champagne glasses, down one and start in on the other. Finally, I call Angelique's name. At first she doesn't answer but after I repeat myself a few times she opens the door a crack.

"Angelique," I say, "I'm leaving now. I thought I'd give you a ride home."

"Leave? Is Noah coming?" Her voice is rough and she coughs.

"Uh, no. He's staying a while. But you looked ready to leave and I know I am."

She moves her head away from the door and for a minute I think she's going to shut me out. Then I feel a steel grip on my arm as she pulls me into the bathroom, sloshing my remaining champagne, and slams the door.

We stare at each other. Then Angelique smiles that yearbook smile. "So, we're leaving him here, are we? In the diva's clutches?" Her voice drips with amused disdain, as if she's suddenly found Noah to be beneath her devotion.

"Maybe it's best," I say.

"You think so?" She curls her lip. "Really? And, of course, you are in a good position to judge, aren't you."

My face goes fiery. I gulp the rest of my champagne.

"Well, it gets boring after a while," she continues. Her voice is light but I don't like the way she's looking at me, with narrowed, rapidly blinking eyes, as if she can't quite make me out. She reminds me of nothing so much as Theo, our cat, when we were coaxing him out of some hiding place for something he knew he wasn't going to like. Theo knew when something unpleasant was in store. Every time we had to take him to the vet we'd all put on falsely hearty voices and talk loudly about going to the "supermarket" or the "park," but Theo wasn't buying it. We'd discover him under a bed and the look on his face was uncannily human—an admixture of terror, fury, and the wounded glare of one who had been cruelly betrayed.

And Angelique, too, despite her lighthearted manner, seems coiled to me—as Theo used to be at his most threatened—as if afraid I'm going to take her someplace she doesn't want to go or tell her something she doesn't want to hear. "Well," I say, "I'm leaving. You can stay if you want." I turn to the door.

"Do you know what artists need money for?" Angelique says suddenly.

I turn back. "Excuse me?"

"I mean, aside from the basics? Time. Probably one percent of the people who are producing art, I mean art that gets seen, get to work full time at it. Most of us still have to take second jobs to make ends meet. To real artists, success is measured in terms of time they get to do their art. I gave that to Noah." She smoothes away a few ringlets sticking to her face. "He wasn't much of a bartender, you know. He used to give too much liquor or make the drinks too sweet. The only thing he's ever been any good at is music and women."

There is a loud knock on the bathroom door. "Hellooo!" someone calls out. "Sometime tonight do you think?"

"We should go," I say.

Angelique keeps up a steady stream of pleasant chatter as the limousine navigates the glittering streets. How lovely it all was, how happy she is for Noah, how excited about her own work, her plans for the loft.

As I'm getting out of the car, she grabs hold of my overnight bag. "Is he coming home tonight?" she asks.

"I really don't know, Angelique."

She shrugs. "Either way. This is his big night, too, in a way, I guess. No big deal. Goodnight, Eve, nice to meet you finally." We do her hearty handshake and the limo drives away.

I set my bag down in the foyer of the apartment and head straight for the sliding glass door to the terrace. I fumble with the locks and pull the door open to a blast of wind. Buildings taller than this one glow to the right and left, shorter ones directly in front. And further in the distance, water, benign and beautiful, shimmering in the city lights. The night is as clear as glass.

I envisioned giving this kind of view to Jess and Nick one day. I could imagine their gasps, see the city reflected in their eyes. Actually, all Nick would have had to experience was one subway train hurtling through the flip side of the city, and one evening's worth of ambulance sirens; all Jess would have had to see was one horse-drawn carriage in the park, one elevator with an actual operator, and they'd both have been enamored forever. I envisioned standing with them on some great city height, leaning back against Charlie's solid chest, holding a shoulder of each of my children.

I lean far over the railing. Things on the ground look bigger than you'd think—I can see the faces of people walking by on the night-active street. This doesn't seem that high up at all. It seems possible to survive a fall.

I've heard that when human beings are in high places some primal urge draws them to the precipice, urges them to come down the fast way. I've heard this is why some people are afraid of heights—they don't feel strong enough to resist the lure of the fall. I've always liked heights: high-rises, roller coasters, airplanes, and am fascinated by how far you can go and still see the world. You'd think you could see it from the ocean too, but it's not the same thing. On the sea what you see is the vastness of emptiness; what's impressive is how much space the world contains that contains nothing. This was Charlie's kind of view—he'd look out at the waves and see something transcendent: the immensity of it all, the life teeming below the surface, the speck we made on the seascape.

The thin railing digs into my stomach; I lean farther over, stare down, wait for the urge, imagining headlines the next day: Diva's Death House. But the urge will not accommodate me.

Before finding my way to my room, I sneak a look at the master bedroom on the other side of the apartment. Taking up most of its substantial space is a four-poster mahogany bed with ruffled chintz pillows and a thick flowered duvet. It seems entirely Isabel's. I wonder if Noah slept there or if she came into his room. Or if, as seems most likely, she sent him away after they made love. It's not hard to stand in her doorway and imagine them together on that bed. The images fill me with a kind of furious nostalgia, as if I'm an ex-lover with unbearable memories.

My room is a smaller version of Isabel's. The posters on the bed are shorter, the duvet less plush. By the time I've taken off the rumpled dress and climbed under the covers, I'm already dreaming.

When Jessica first rescued Theo the cat, Charlie and I made a half-hearted attempt to get rid of him. We told Jessica that Theo would distrust and fear us because of the neglect and deprivation he'd undergone. Only until he meets us, Jessica said. She was four years old then. What could we say? We fed and cleaned Theo and held him shivering in our arms through a number of miserable nights and before long we had all come to adore him, despite his obvious deficits of intelligence—he's the baby we'll always have, Charlie said. For a while he was seriously considering taking Theo along on the voyage but I convinced him that poor Theo would probably kamikaze overboard in no time. He couldn't stand the vibrations of the dishwasher; what would he do on a rough sea?

The good-byes were difficult. We had dinner with Charlie's older sister Pam and her husband. They had two cats already and two indifferent dogs, and their kids were grown and married. They were happy to add to their brood. Nick and Jessie sat morosely at dinner and barely touched their food.

Both children cried on the drive home. Charlie was sullen too that night, I remember, partly because Pam's husband, who rarely opened his mouth except to pontificate on the human condition, had lectured Charlie about the foolhardiness of our adventure. "I know you're experienced, Chuck, you're prepared in one way. But have you ever actually confined yourself to a small space with two young children and nowhere to escape to? Two young children, Chuck, that's a big undertaking." No one else ever called Charlie "Chuck."

"As if I haven't thought of all that," Charlie hissed. "If that guy isn't the most pompous ass ever placed on this planet. Shit, he talked to me like he used to talk to me when I was ten. He was a pompous ass then and he's one now."

Which prompted the children to clamor for a story about Charlie as a little boy, hiding behind the couch when his sisters brought home dates, then bribing the couple to make him disappear, amassing quite a fortune.

I sat silent. I was thinking about what Pam's husband had said. I, too, thought he was a pompous ass, but he was articulating the same concerns I'd been voicing to Charlie for some time.

Coming home, the ride up the hill out of Simi Valley felt like a revelation to me. Our valley, the San Fernando Valley, emerged suddenly in the dark, a carpet of glittering lights. Somewhere in there was our home, our school, our friends. I had the ridiculous feeling that it all wouldn't be there when we got back and I started to shiver. I stared hard out the window, my teeth chattering, filled with a kind of dreadful certainty that we wouldn't be back.

Then Jessica screamed the way she does when Charlie has completely cracked her up. "Oh Daaaady!" and Nick was rolling over the backseat in mirth and Jessica said, "Mommy, Daddy's making it up, isn't he?" and I turned in my seat and smiled at the now gleeful children and the feeling passed, replaced by a more diffused melancholy that I told myself was just nerves, cold feet, nothing that wouldn't pass the moment we stepped onto the deck of the Orlando for good.

17

I wake up at 10:30 and the apartment is silent, the rooms as still as paintings. I stumble my way to the kitchen, find coffee beans in the freezer and gingerly approach the elaborate coffee machine, the kind that grinds beans right into the permanent gold filter. In the couple of years I've been gone, coffee seems to have become even more of a gourmet conceit than when we left.

I pour the recommended amount of coffee beans into what I hope is the correct receptacle, turn the dial, hold my breath. The grinder makes an enormous din and I rush around looking for a dishtowel but I can't find one so I quickly take off my robe and throw it over the machine to muffle the sound. The coffee-making part seems easy enough—swing the filter around to the other side, fill the receptacle with water, press another button. Only now there are granules of coffee everywhere—the sides of the machine, the counter, the flannel of my robe. I rip some paper towels off the roll over the sink and wet them, creating a thick brown slush on the counter. I step back, fighting the urge to throw the soggy towels against the custard-colored wall and smash the gurgling coffee decanter to let the liquid run muddy onto the tiled floor.

"Need any help?" Isabel is standing at the entrance to the kitchen in a pink silk bathrobe that sweeps the floor. Her hair is in beautiful disarray and her head sways as if it's a bit too heavy a burden for her this morning.

I catch my breath and say, "I'm sorry, did I wake you? I was trying to make coffee."

"Jesus, we never use that thing. It sprays coffee grounds everywhere." She moves into the kitchen and retrieves a large green sponge and Liquid Comet from under the sink. I step out of the way and she proceeds to expertly wipe up the counter and the floor with the sponge and the cleaning liquid, rinsing it clean with some fresh paper towels. She hasn't entirely removed her after-show makeup from last night. There are patches of pink on her cheeks that look like dried powder, and black smudges under her eyes. She is squinting like a person dangling a cigarette from the corner of her mouth as she straightens up, eyes my spotty bathrobe. "My suggestion would be to stand in the bathtub with the lint brush."

I nod. "Sorry for the mess."

"No problem. Well, since you've made coffee, we might as well have some. Leo usually picks up *lattes* at the Starbucks on the corner, but this'll do for now." She gets cups and spoons and opens the refrigerator for milk. It contains a carton of orange juice and a few to-go containers.

I hold my robe in my lap and we sit down together at the table. Isabel lets her head hang forward a little, as if that eases its weight. I study the jagged part her uncombed hair has made falling around her face. I can just make out the incipient quarter-inch of gray roots against her scalp and am surprised, then surprised that I'm surprised. She's fifty-six years old.

"So!" Isabel says. "Tell me what you thought of the opera." Her voice is heavy and hoarse.

"Well," I say. The images flood my head: Isabel on stage in her white kimono, blissfully happy, thinking she always will be; holding her little boy as she demands that her husband return to her; giving up her boy, then giving up herself.

"God, did you think it was that bad?" She lifts her head, squinting at me.

"Bad? No, I didn't think it was bad."

She peers at me. "Are you crying?"

"No," I say, bringing my hands up to my face. "Yes," I say. "I do this a lot when I hear opera," I add quickly.

"*Fantastic.*" She reaches over to touch my hand. "It moved you? Of course, everyone always cries at *Butterfly*. You'd have to be made of stone, right? But it wasn't my brightest hour. I'm so glad you still liked it."

I don't answer. I'm not sure "like" is the right word. The music was exquisite, the sets and costumes impressive, but the story hurts to think about.

"I can't believe how Barr behaved last night. I swear, if I don't kill him by the end of this run it'll be a miracle. That high C trick he pulled! Gave him two ovations, left me looking like a schmuck." She shoves back her hair with all the force as if it were the hated tenor himself. When she catches me watching her she laughs. "You have no idea what I'm talking about, do you? It sounds stupid, but these things matter. They matter *a lot*. You know how we both hold the note at the end of Act One? All the applause and oohs and aahs? That's a high C—a kind of famous moment in the opera, you know? And experience has taught me—especially with megalomaniacs like Barr—that you should work it out beforehand how long you will hold the note, you don't leave it to chance or the professionalism of the tenor. So we agree to do the count exactly as written, right? No special embellishments or tricks to show off—I figured this would be the best way to keep the peace, since the bastard has been trying to outdo me from day one. Anyway, so we agree on the count—two and a half beats for the first measure, one and a half for the second, then immediate cutoff, in unison, beautiful, right? And there we are, hitting this note the audience has been waiting for, which is no mean feat at my . . . with my throat, I can tell you, and at the end of the count I stop, and that asshole not only holds till the end of the goddamn measure, he starts bleeding into the next measure for two beats where the orchestra is playing a D minor, which I need hardly tell you completely clashes with a C!"

She glares into her coffee cup, stirring it, even though she's drunk most of its contents. "I will never, *ever* work with that man again. I don't care *what* I'm offered. You know we've made two recordings together. You probably have them in the pile I gave you."

"I think I do," I say. "The truth is, I don't pay much attention to the names of the singers except for you."

"Aha, a true fan." She laughs; her spoon clinks against her cup. "Anyway, I guess I did all right last night."

"You sounded beautiful."

"Leo wouldn't agree with you, I'm afraid. He practically said 'I told you so' last night. I tried to make him see that Barr was cutting me off, but he keeps insisting it's about doing more what the coach says, about taking care of my voice. Frankly, Eve, I'm so tired of taking care of my voice that I feel like . . . I don't know . . . *smoking*." She leans her head on her hand. "Do you know how much of my life I've put into singing? Since I was thirteen. Thirteen! My mother got me a singing teacher when I was twelve thinking I would be the next Judy Garland. But by college it was clear that my voice was more suited to opera. I had this one teacher—he took over my career. I trained with him all through college and he helped me get into Juilliard. I did my first Met competition when I was nineteen. But singing's like professional sports—you have to practice, every day, for hours and hours. You can't go out if it's too cold or too hot; you can't go anyplace where people might be sick; you can't stay up too late. You have to learn a zillion other languages. You are *always* studying. If not voice then movement or acting or language. I had almost no adolescence, you know? I was a virgin till I was 21. I only had two other lovers before Leo. I've been at this forty-three years, Eve, pretty much nonstop. If Leo had his way, it would never be over. But I deserve a break."

"Does this have something to do with Noah?" I say.

She lifts her head from her hand and looks directly at me. "Does what have to do with Noah?"

"Why you're telling me this?"

"Huh." She sits up. "Well, I don't know, Eve, maybe it does. I thought I was confiding in a friend, but maybe it's just a way to talk about Noah."

"No, I . . . I'm glad to talk to you, Isabel. It's just that I hardly feel in a position to counsel anyone about how to live their life."

She pats my hand again. "I'm certainly not asking you for advice. I'm more trying to . . . I want you to understand about me."

"Okay," I say.

She grips my hand. "I've worked too hard and too long to let it all slip through my fingers now," she says. "I'm a selfish bitch, I know that. But my career is really all I've got. It's all Leo's got. I will do anything to keep it going. Even if people I care about get hurt." Her long nails graze the flesh of my wrist. "Understand me?"

"Sure," I say, even though she seems to be contradicting herself with every new sentence.

"Good. Because I really like you, Eve. I want us to stay friends, no matter what happens." She pushes back her unruly hair. "Speaking of Noah, I'm supposed to meet him later. Provided, of course, that the ever-present Angelique lets him out of her sight. I couldn't convince him to stay last night—it's like he's fifteen years old when he's around her and he's afraid of getting in trouble with his mother." She laughs. "By the way, what did you think of her?"

"Well, she—"

"Of course she's young—not an old hag like me. She's even younger than *you*, Eve."

We're both silent for a moment, thinking, perhaps, of Angelique's fashionable ringlets and schoolgirl grin.

"Leo would only say that she was charming," Isabel says suddenly. "Intense, but charming. Hell, I'm intense."

"It can be a very attractive quality, you know." Leo enters the kitchen, dressed in a burgundy sweater and corduroy pants. He eyes us with amusement.

"Charming my ass," Isabel snorts. "I wouldn't trust her as far as I could throw her."

"You sound positively jealous," Leo says, taking a seat at the table.

"Give it a rest, Leo, will you?" She pushes her chair back roughly and takes her coffee cup to the sink. "I'm getting the paper and getting back into bed. I'll see *you* all later."

After she's gone, Leo says to me, "She's going to look for a review even though she knows it probably won't be in the paper till tomorrow. The later the better, if you ask me." He pours himself a cup of coffee.

"Do you think it was a failure?" I whisper.

"You were there, what did you think?"

"I thought it was . . . fine."

Leo shakes his head in mock disappointment. "Eve, Eve, you've been listening to opera for months now. You must be able to tell when someone's 'on voice' and when they're not. You heard her sing last night. Did she sound like she does on her recordings?"

"Well no, but—"

"There are no 'buts' at this level. Her opening night, the 'A' cast, and she was just adequate. She might as well have been horrendous. The papers will skewer her. There've been too many rumors about her health, about her exceeding her reach. They're just waiting for her to fail."

He speaks dispassionately, like a critic himself.

The next morning, there is a cup of Starbucks coffee waiting for me on the kitchen counter. I can hear Leo and Isabel's voices from behind their closed bedroom door. They seem to be fighting. At least, Isabel seems to be yelling at Leo. Every once in a while I hear his softer, calmer baritone under her rapid-fire monologue.

I try to ignore them. The newspaper is spread out over the kitchen table. It is open to the review of *Madame Butterfly*. "A Mixed Bag of Butterflies," says the headline. I quickly scan the article. The reviewer sings Barr's praises, using phrases like "come into his own." Then Isabel's paragraph: "At fifty-six Isabel Stein is certainly not the oldest working soprano—Tebaldi sang into her sixties; Freni is still singing. But Stein, whose celestial lyric soprano catapulted her to an early spot in the stratosphere, may have overstayed her welcome. Her Cio-Cio-San last night was certainly sincere, but that's about all that can be said about it. Gone are the pure and heady upper notes, the rich middle and low registers La Stein is famous for. The word *pianissimo* seems to have disappeared from her vocabulary. For dramatic acting there are still few divas who can rival Stein and despite the problematic vocals, her rendition of *Tu, tu, piccolo Iddio!* still wrenched sniffles from many audience members. But Stein evoked the hopeless dignity of the tragic geisha through sheer willpower, not with her singing."

I sit at the table and listen to muffled voices in the other room, imagining Isabel's pain, testing it against my own.

Leo and I sit across a large glass desk from Nigel Baker, Leo perusing the contract I'm about to sign. "A hundred thousand now, a hundred when the first five chapters are submitted, the other three hundred when the manuscript is accepted for publication. You can't do better than that Leo, not when they haven't seen word one yet," Nigel is saying while I stare at the studio portrait of his wife and children on the desk corner. "This is a great deal."

Leo holds up a hand and continues to read. I spoke to Myra before we left and she convinced me to let Leo accompany me. "They'll eat you alive, Eve," she said. "Leo knows what he's doing. He's a lawyer, a manager. You let him look over that contract before you so much as dot an 'i'." I told her that I couldn't see how anyone giving me a half a million dollars for something they'd never seen could possibly be ripping me off, but she would have none of it. She talked about movie rights, paperback rights and I wondered where she learned all this stuff. But it's easier to go along. And I do have something like eighty pages written by now. I have no idea if it's what everyone's expecting, but it's not that hard, telling myself stories.

Nigel has a perpetually worried look on his face. A bottle of Perrier sits on his desk and he compulsively pours refills into his glass every time he takes a sip.

In the photograph, the wife has big hair. I'd estimate the two boys to be about four and seven. The younger one's mouth is wide open, displaying a multitude of teeth. The older one looks as if he's about to break away from his mother's embrace. We took some pictures like this. They were always our least favorites but the relatives loved them. We all looked airbrushed and two-dimensional. Charlie and I preferred photographs taken when we were all caught a bit unawares—sloppy or sleepy or not smiling. I sent all the copies of the studio pictures to Charlie's and my family. I suppose that's how Cousin Birdie ended up with the pictures she sold to the papers. Now I wish I had kept at least a wallet-sized version of those posed pictures. I have the feeling that the only bearable way to remember their faces is with the sheen of artificiality.

Leo has a few legal quibbles to which I don't pay much attention. Then I sign and date the contract. Nigel shakes both our hands vigorously, looking relieved. "I've been waiting a long time for this." He beams. "How does it feel to be rich, Eve?"

I look at him. He clears his throat and says. "How about a drink to celebrate."

"Good idea," I say.

We go to a bar down the street, jostling through hordes of people. When we reach the curb I look ahead and see a swarm of human bodies so dense it looks like an anthill. The image wavers and Leo's hand tightens on my arm, another spontaneous act of protection that startles me.

An hour later I am struggling into my coat, a bit unsteady on my feet, Leo making a phone call in the back of the bar. Nigel Baker downs the rest of his bourbon and turns to me. "If there's ever anything you need, you must be sure to ring me. Our relationship goes beyond this book, you know. I'm here to make things as smooth as possible for you. When you start touring, I want to be sure that you are always comfortable."

"Touring?" I say.

"Well, yes. You'll probably do six to ten cities on the East Coast. I don't think they've quite worked out the West Coast yet. This is a *good* thing, Eve. It means they're putting a lot of push behind this book. It's the only way to sell books these days."

"Uh huh," I say.

"You seem surprised."

I laugh to make it seem like I'm joking. "I forgot about selling books—I forgot they weren't just giving me the money to keep me occupied." Nigel chuckles. "Actually," I say, "there is something you can do to help me."

"Name it."

"How would I go about looking for my own place in the city?" I speak quickly, expecting Leo back any minute.

Nigel cocks his head. "You're thinking of leaving the Steins?"

"I have to go some time."

"Yes, I suppose so. Naturally, I can set you up with some real estate agents whenever you want. Are you thinking of buying or renting?"

"I have no idea." I try to imagine owning a home again. "Rent, I guess."

Nigel starts to ask me more questions, but Leo emerges from the back of the bar and I put my hand on Nigel's arm. "For now, I'd like to keep this just between us," I say.

The orthopedist says I'm healing nicely and the shrink asks if I want to cut out the antidepressants. "You're kidding, right?" I say.

"It's up to you," she says in that quiet voice of hers. "You're still grieving, obviously, but antidepressants aren't for that. Your actual depression seems to have lifted." I consider forcing myself to weep just to prove her wrong. But she makes it clear that it's my call, and she renews the prescription, reminding me yet again not to exceed the dosage. I nod like an obedient dog.

When I first get back to the apartment I think no one's there. The hallway is dim. But then I hear voices from Isabel's bedroom: Noah and Isabel, trying to whisper but regularly erupting. I creep down the hall and stand just outside Isabel's door. It sounds as if Noah is talking through clenched teeth. "This has to stop. I feel crazy."

"I don't know what you're so worked up about all of a sudden," Isabel says soothingly.

"I've told you what. You won't commit yourself and meanwhile I'm totally confused about what you feel."

"What *I* feel? Darling, I think it's your own feelings you're confused about."

There is a pause. I step closer to the door.

"Shit, Isabel, I've been begging you for months to finally do it and you always have an excuse. Timing, or Leo's stress, or . . ."

"Or Eve."

Another pause. I wonder at the coolness of Isabel's voice. She sounds like someone *practicing* being upset.

"Nothing happened, really," Noah says. "Hardly anything to speak of. I've just—I've been waiting a long time, Isabel, and Eve . . . she's so . . ."

"Victimized?" Isabel says contemptuously. "You're such a pushover, Noah. It's the same thing with Angelique. Her I'm-your-best-buddy-no-matter-what routine that drowns you in guilt."

There is a rustling sound, then a clinking, like glassware.

"What do you want me to do then?" Noah says, sounding defeated.

"I? I want you to do what you want, of course. If you want Angelique—"

"You know I don't."

"—or Eve, then fine. Otherwise, if it's me you want, I'd say first you should break it off once and for all with Angelique. Then I suggest you explain how things are to Eve. She's much stronger than you think; and she's a pragmatist, for all her seeming fragility. She'll understand."

There is dismissal in her voice and so I quickly move away from the door and flee to my room. Once there, I sit down on the bed and try to decipher the coolness, the almost scripted way that Isabel spoke. I know it's something I should take note of, be wary of, but I can't say why.

That night, a faint tapping on my door awakens me. I struggle up from the bed. Noah is standing in the hall looking sleepy and disheveled, his shirt untucked and his hair going in a dozen different directions. "Can I come in for a minute?" he whispers.

I let him in, running my hands through my hair.

"Can I talk to you?"

"Are they asleep?"

He nods. He tromps over to the bed and sits down, hanging his head slightly. "I had a long talk with Isabel today," he says, looking at his stockinged feet. The toe of his right sock is threadbare.

"We talked about how nothing is going to go anywhere until I make a final break with Angelique, you know." He looks up at me, as if pleading with me to agree.

I want to smooth back his hair, touch his arm.

"So I'm going to do it. Tomorrow. I need to, don't you think?" Again, the pleading look. "I wanted to ask you a favor," he says, ignoring my silence. "I want to know if you'll come with me."

"To talk to Angelique?"

"Yes."

"What for?" I say.

"I don't know. She seemed to really like you. She has a kind of block about my leaving her."

"And you think she'll somehow believe it if I'm there? Do you want her to think you're leaving her for me?"

"No, I—"

"Jesus, Noah, could you pull your head out of your ass for a minute? Do you really think that your little drama is the only thing that matters? Have you given one thought to how Angelique might feel?"

"That's like all I'm thinking about!"

"Well how about me, then? Have you given any thought to how I might feel?"

Noah grimaces. "I'm sorry, Eve. I'm just . . . confused."

"You can say that again." And as suddenly as it rose, my fury disappears. I flop down onto the bed next to him. "So I'm not the most important thing in your life; you shouldn't be in mine. I think, though, that this is something you have to take care of on your own."

He hasn't taken his eyes off me and now his expression flickers, as if he's seen something in my face that discomfits him. He takes my hand. "When I'm talking to Isabel everything seems clear and straightforward. Then I come in here and . . ."

"It's late," I say quickly.

"Eve," he says.

"Go on now," I say.

"Yeah, okay." He continues to sit there, to look at me. My body is doing this strange nerve dance; every inch of my skin prickles with that anticipatory pain of a limb that's fallen asleep starting to wake up. I press up against him as much to make the sensation go away as to kiss him, which I also do. He kisses me back. Puts his arms around me. At one point it occurs to me that he needs to shave, that my face will be red and flaming tomorrow, just like in high school. His right hand moves to my breast and then away, quickly, as if stung. I pick it up and put it back there. Noah makes a small sound in the back of his throat—a moan of desire or disgust, I'm not sure and I don't care. I urge him on. It's not that I don't try to think all the right thoughts. I try to anticipate how much more miserable I'll be tomorrow than tonight. But none of the ideas will form. Under the sweep of Noah's hands over my flesh, the obliteration of my mouth under his, not a single concept will form itself to stop us.

18

Noah goes alone to Angelique's. And I spend the morning wandering the city, telling myself it's to scope out neighborhoods, look for "To Rent" signs on local apartment buildings. But really it's to get out of Isabel's house and to try to quell this ridiculous elation I feel. The one image I can't erase from my mind is one I didn't actually see: Isabel and Leo sleeping down the hall from us last night, oblivious.

There is no snow but the air is frigid and I bury my nose in the woolen muffler Leo's loaned me. Fresh from the cleaners, it smells like nothing, for which I'm grateful. I walk with my eyes straight ahead, my hands buried in my coat pockets.

For a while I try to concentrate on the buildings I pass to size up their relative safety, convenience and cost. It feels like a game, though—I can't really imagine living in New York any more than I can imagine living anywhere else. It's like the dream of last night, this whole illusion that a new life can begin. But I'm actually enjoying the illusion. I'm having fun, I tell myself, knowing I should feel guilt but feeling only wonder. I buy an oversized pretzel from a sidewalk vendor on the Steins' street, York Avenue, its doughy tastelessness satisfying in my mouth. I head west.

At Lexington I pass a large newsstand and remind myself to stop there later to pick up something called *Manhattan Rents*, a magazine Nigel told me about that lists available apartments. At Fifth Avenue I walk along the park with its bare branches until I find myself at the Metropolitan Museum. Despite the weather, the steps are packed with people bundled like arctic explorers, smoking, laughing, speaking in a dozen different languages, eating hotdogs from the cart at the base of the steps emitting an odor of mustard. As I climb the stairs, people part good-naturedly to make way for me; some smile, some say hello in heavily accented English. Perhaps I'm smiling? I enter the cavernous hall where the voices of hundreds of visitors bounce off the high ceiling. I get in the line to check my coat and even when the couple in front of me turns and gives me frank, searching stares, I don't shrink. What are the chances that they know who I am, anyway? They are both wearing backpacks and down jackets; they don't look like people who read gossip magazines or watch much TV. When they start speaking to each other in German, I am reassured. Besides, I feel somehow unrecognizable today, rendered incognito by my transformed mental state.

Feeling lofty and generous, I pay twenty dollars—twice the recommended admission price—at one of the entrance booths and receive a metal button to pin to my sweater. I'm rich now, money that I can do who knows what with after I give a good chunk to Myra and Molly—maybe commission an opera of my own, or at least a concerto or something that will give Noah work after Isabel is finished with him.

Following the crowd, I walk past medieval paintings and tapestries. This crowd seems to know exactly where it's headed and that's good enough for me. And then we are passing into a darkened room. Boys' voices sing Christmas carols from unseen loudspeakers and dominating the space is the largest Christmas tree I've ever seen, lit as artfully and lovingly as any priceless work of art in this whole place.

I go through a door into galleries that are airy and lightfilled, newer and less reverent. I am drawn by a shimmer of turquoise gown so brilliant you can almost hear the silk rustle. "Princesse de Broglie," by Ingres. I move closer to the painting and stare into the woman's dark, calm eyes. Now here is an expression I can understand. A small smile plays about her lips, as if she were sharing a private joke with the viewer, as if she knew that confidence didn't ensure happiness, but she intended to enjoy as much of life as possible. One arm is folded around her waist, ivory white, like her face, hugging her own warm body, savoring a private moment. It hits me suddenly that for all her elaborate costume, her expertly coifed hair and lavish dress, she is not that long away from someone's bed.

There's a sudden weakness in my legs thinking about last night, about urging Noah beyond where he wanted to go, savoring both the hunger and the power I felt over him, and, it must be admitted, over Isabel.

It's not that making love with Noah wiped out memory or pain. But something happened that had not happened till then, something transforming that had nothing to do with Noah or our little drama. Halfway through, when Noah was stroking me so gently and murmuring endearments, my name, apologies, I started crying. The tears came out like an orgasm, hard and cathartic. Noah stopped for a moment, said my name in a questioning, tentative voice. Go on, I said, just go on, and every stroke, every caress after that was like salve on a wound, like what pills and alcohol do but without my losing consciousness. I felt lighter when I got up. It wasn't happiness. It was ease.

When Noah was moving in me last night I thought of Charlie, of how much slower he used to go, how he used to try to wait for me—which I sometimes thought was out of love and sometimes thought was out of duty—and Noah's abandon was actually refreshing. I wasn't suppressing thoughts of my family, shoving away guilt. They are there in my mind even now, as I look into the blue lady's serene countenance, and they make me sad, but something is alongside those thoughts now, some glimmer of how it might be if I were to go on. How it could be bearable to go on.

On the way home I stop at the newsstand. A man with a dirty change apron around his waist moves up and down the line of customers thumbing through his wares. I scan the magazine racks for the rental guide.

I don't avoid looking at certain titles, don't even give gossip magazines and tabloids a second thought. I am yesterday's news, and besides, all day I have been feeling some "in" word—invincible, invulnerable, invisible?

The headline doesn't really register at first. It could be about anyone really; its prurient innuendo is generic: EXCLUSIVE: MISSING ACCIDENT VICTIM FOUND IN LOVE NEST. This is plastered across a tabloid whose name I don't see. Even the line below the headline stirs only a vague unease: LOVE TRYST UNMASKED: SINGER'S GENEROSITY BACKFIRES. It says "singer." I am thinking Madonna, Michael Jackson, Frank Sinatra. But something registers in me, because I pull the newspaper from the rack and read the lines under the headline, avoiding the photograph that fills the rest of the page: *A missing victim found, an innocence lost. After almost six months, the whereabouts of a boating accident victim are revealed and she may not be all that grief stricken.*

The picture is of Isabel, Noah and me in Isabel's dressing room. Isabel is between us, her arms around our shoulders. She is smiling glamorously, her wide mouth showing her perfect teeth. She looks dazzlingly happy. Noah looks stiff and startled; I look weary, blank-eyed.

I yank one of my heavy gloves off with my teeth and rifle through the pages with remarkably steady, if damp hands. The article is near the front, unmistakable. More pictures. Grainy, washed out, they look like they've been smeared with Vaseline. But it is unmistakably the cottage, the surrounding naked trees. And although our features are blurred to the point of unrecognizability, there are Noah and me, just leaving or just entering, I can't tell. In one shot we are both standing with our backs to the cottage and he has his arm around my back, his hand protruding under my opposite arm, next to my breast. It is clearly one of the times when my back was bad and he was helping me to the car. He might still have disliked me at this point, but of course the picture gives a very different impression.

My heart is smashing against my ribs. I lean against the newsstand. I don't read anything yet, just turn the page to see the next set of pictures. These are a lot clearer, obviously taken from closer range. There are five smaller shots on this page, all of Noah and me or me alone in Kent. One was taken in the market: we are standing over the meat bin; Noah is holding up a package of some red meat but he's looking at me and I'm smiling, almost laughing back at him, the look of affection in my eyes unmistakable. Other shots are of us going into the bar in Kent, Noah taking my coat in the restaurant across from Lincoln Center, Noah holding me outside the opera house in what surely looks like an embrace. Then there is one of me alone, coming out of the dress shop in Kent with a package. I can't imagine what is scandalous about this so I force myself to look down at the caption and read: "Less than six months since her entire family was wiped out, Miller finds herself a pretty dress at a fashionable boutique. 'She has definitely shown more interest in her appearance lately,' her hostess says."

I read another caption, seeing my breath coming out in short smoky bursts in front of me. "Everything changed once she and Noah became 'close,' says Stein." Underneath that: "By Ralene Williams. Photos by Daniel Matthews." So it is Daniel Matthews, whoever he may be, who has been circling me like a panther, silent and stalking, rustling the occasional twig. . . .

Oh. Ralene. As in Ray. Ray of the nodding head and funny glasses. Ray and Danny. The illicit couple at the Kent Arms. Ray and Danny weren't looking for seclusion; they were looking for me.

I scan the pages, absorbing enough to get the gist of the article. Eve Miller couldn't have been that miserable to begin with, since she began a torrid affair with a composer practically young enough to be her son within a few months of the loss of her family. She imposed on the kindness of a famous opera star and repaid that kindness by taking the composer away from his work, carrying on under her hosts' nose. All the cards and letters and money she received, it is implied, have clearly been wasted on this ungrateful Jezebel. Even the book deal is mentioned, as is Isabel's performance in *Madame Butterfly* and upcoming recital tour. At the end of the article is our family portrait again; I don't read the caption there.

Someone touches my arm and my stomach flips. "Excuse me." It is a woman clutching a copy of *People* magazine. "Are you—"

I don't know what kind of look I give her, but she steps back as if horrified. I make a run for it.

I've half run down to Third Avenue before it strikes me that I am blindly returning to Isabel and Leo's apartment on York. I was thinking, wait till they see this, how outraged they will be. I even imagined Leo calling the publisher of the paper for me, or confiscating all the copies in the entire city. I imagined Isabel weeping for my distress, putting her arms around me. At Third and 79th I wait, panting, at the corner, pressed in by crowding, hurrying pedestrians. As they swell behind me to cross the street, it hits me with a pressure many times that of those anxious human bodies. I elbow my way back up onto the curb and realize that I am still clutching the newspaper that I haven't paid for. The sidewalk is bright from the lights of the shops and restaurants on the avenue, but it is still hard to read the text. I can make out again the numerous quotes from Isabel dotted throughout the article and under most of the pictures. She was not just approached for comment on an already-written article, she was interviewed for it—she who had been the most understanding of my need for privacy, the most outraged at the omnivorous press.

Leo. It has to be that he forced her into it somehow, threatened or badgered her until she finally gave in. Isabel would never just sell me out to get her name back in the tabloids.

And the pictures. How did they get those "exclusive" pictures? Someone had to tell the photographer and Ray where I was, details of my schedule. Well, Leo again, of course.

A strong breeze comes up. I am standing in the middle of the sidewalk shivering, my feet and hands gone numb, the newspaper crackling in the air. People sidle around me, avoiding my eyes. I duck into a coffee shop. Clutching my coat to my chest I ask for a booth near the front and sit in a seat facing the window. I order coffee and whatever soup they serve and keep my eyes trained on the window. But why should Ray appear? She's already done her job.

I drink the coffee, but the smell of the soup makes me nauseous and I ask the waitress to take it away. I can't imagine going back to Isabel and Leo's, and yet, where else could I go? It is completely dark now and I have about forty dollars cash, no credit cards, no friends in this city. I could try to check into a hotel, but with no suitcase and no credit cards I'd probably have a hard time. I could go to Noah and Angelique's loft, but somehow that seems worse than going back to the Steins'. The thought of Noah makes my whole body blush. I practically forced him, thrust myself upon him, and now he has to contend with . . . all this. If he hated me now, I would deserve it. On the other hand, maybe he hasn't seen the papers. Maybe I could be the one to tell him what happened. Maybe we could face the Steins together.

At that moment I am seized with a longing for Myra. Myra would know what to do next. I can envision her marching up to Leo and skewering him with her rage at his betrayal, reducing him to a blithering babble of apology. And sweeping me up, wrapping me in the protective blanket of her wrath, carrying me off to safety and blessed anonymity.

I grope my way to the phone in the back of the restaurant. I dial my phone card number and then Myra's. She picks up on the second ring and doesn't seem at all surprised to hear from me.

"How are you," she says, sounding almost disinterested.

I barely trust my voice. "Myra," I say, "the papers."

"What?"

"There's a newspaper article," I begin, and then choke out the story. Myra simply says, "Really," as if she already knows. Then she asks me rather coldly if I am all right.

I plug my right ear with my finger, thinking that the reason I don't hear the customary sympathy and worry in her voice is because the outside noise is distracting me. "No," I say.

"What?"

"Myra," I say, "I don't know what to do."

There is a long silence. Then she says, "I told you to come home with me, but you wouldn't listen."

I swallow, then speak again. "You know it's not true, don't you? You don't believe all that crap they're saying?"

"Frankly, Eve," she says, in her best out-of-my-childhood authoritarian tones, "I don't know what to believe. I don't expect that you would act exactly rationally after all that's happened. I mean, I never understood why you wouldn't come home with me and I don't understand what's happening now. In your fragile state, anything could have happened between you and Noah and . . . the Steins."

"But. But even if everything they said were true, why are you mad at me, Myra?" I am crying softly now, dripping tears onto the phone receiver.

"I'm not mad. Don't cry, Eve, I'm not mad." Her voice softens a little, but I know it is just because I am crying—she never handled my tears well.

"You are," I say.

"I'm disappointed. Not mad."

I hold the phone away from my face to sniffle and wipe my eyes with the back of my hand. When I put the receiver back to my ear she is in the middle of a sentence.

". . . their kindness this way. I mean, from the beginning you've been less than grateful, you've been suspicious of their motives. What exactly did you expect? I warned you that not everyone would be looking out for your best interests, didn't I? Now you're upset about exactly what you feared might happen. I'm not entirely surprised about all this. I saw a commercial for *Hard Copy* tonight. Apparently Isabel's going to be on next week. I mean, Isabel on *Hard Copy!* That's like . . . like Picasso appearing on *Hard Copy.*"

"Nobody's above it," I say softly.

"Oh, and suddenly you're the expert on fame?"

"It's the learn-by-doing method."

Myra clears her throat and changes her tack. "I'm not going to judge your actions, Eve, that's between you and . . . well, God. I won't presume to know what you were going through to make you embark on something like this thing with Noah . . . so quickly. When I lost your father, the last thing I thought about or wanted was . . . I don't doubt for a minute how much you loved the kids and I thought you loved Charlie—"

"I did love Charlie," I say with empty desperation.

"But whatever happened, you can't say you had no part in it. You chose to be there instead of here, didn't you?"

I catch my breath. She's right. When I was a child and got into trouble at school or had a fight with a friend and told Myra about it, the first thing out of her mouth was always, "What did *you* do?" She would refuse to believe that anything that happened to me could be out of my control. But at least I can see what she meant. Everything that's happened up to this moment has been a chain of events traceable to my decision to agree to the voyage.

"I have to go now," I say, no longer crying.

"Wait, Eve? Darling, don't hang up. I'm sorry. I don't mean to sound so harsh. I believe you. If you say you weren't . . . if you and Noah are just friends."

"Thank you," I say.

"I think this whole thing is just so unfortunate. The TV ad made it sound like . . . well, like Isabel was a little in love with Noah and that you were . . . well, never mind. I'm sure it's all blown out of proportion."

"I have to go."

I hold onto the receiver for a while after hanging up, leaning my head on my hand. When I look up, the clock on the coffee shop wall says 5:00. Isabel has a performance tonight.

The check is waiting at my table The waitress is seating a middle-aged woman with two teenaged girls at the table across from mine. One of the girls has a face as narrow as a paper clip, cheekbones sticking out. Her neck disappears inside a thick turtleneck sweater and it seems as if her clothes sit there without her. One bony wrist protrudes from her sleeve as she reaches for a glass of water and sips it stingily. The mother and sister study the menu nonchalantly.

"Roast chicken sounds good," says the mother brightly. "What do you think, Taylor?"

The normal-looking girl beside her says, "I was kinda hoping for a hamburger. Could I, Mom?"

"A hamburger it is!" cries the mother. "How about you, Steph?" she says. The emaciated girl blinks in slow motion, as if it's painful. "I'm still looking." The mother and Taylor order and the waitress waits for Steph, looking at the ceiling, the far wall, anywhere but at this child who is disappearing.

"A green salad with lemon wedges on the side, please," says Steph.

The waitress scribbles. "Anything else?"

"That's it," says Steph.

"How about eggs, Steph, it says they can do egg whites only, if you like," the mother says with a kind of suppressed panic.

"Salad is all I want."

"Or fish? You could broil fish with no fat, couldn't you?" the mother pleads with the waitress.

"Sure."

"No thanks."

"Steph, honey. It's dinner."

"I had a huge lunch today. I'm still stuffed."

The mother's face slowly melts into despair. She hands the waitress her menu. Then she sets about rearranging the salt and pepper shakers and the sugar holder, as if their precise and correct location on the table could prevent her from attempting to sweep her child into her arms and carry her off to safety. Except there is no safety, this mother knows that as few mothers do. I catch one more look at Steph before leaving the restaurant. She has an expression of such joyous triumph on her face that it strikes me with full force—maybe for the first time—the immense power inherent in the word *no*.

An excruciating crawl in a cab to the opera. The face of that starving child in the restaurant—her exultant, if misguided control of her universe burned into my brain. How many times in my marriage could I have put my foot down: The day that Charlie pronounced the shakedown cruises a success, that we had sufficiently practiced our reefing and anchoring skills, that we were ready to leave? The day he first told me about the *Orlando* and said it was time we made the purchase? The day he asked me to marry him?

I have a sudden image of Charlie standing on deck, hair wild in the wind, beard overgrown. I say, Charlie, I want to go home. Simply, without anger. And just as simply, he turns the boat around and takes us home.

He would have. All I had to do was say what I wanted. All I had to do was say, No. Unlike that mother in the restaurant, I could have saved them after all.

At which thought I clutch my stomach, letting the pain ride over me like a labor contraction. Now that I see the enormity of my culpability, maybe I'm going to die right here, in this cab in the middle of a traffic jam. Maybe this supposed God will pluck me from earth, doing the hard part for me. I wait, but all that happens is that I am honked at as I struggle out of the cab at Lincoln Center, apparently for taking too long to get the hell out of the way.

At the backstage entrance I give my name to the guard. He peers at me. I glance down at the newspaper on his chair, but it is the *New York Times*. He is probably just wondering if he knows me, if I deserve to be announced to the diva so close to performance time. "She'll want to see me," I say in my most self-assured voice. After a final once-over, he disappears down the hall.

Her dressing room door is closed. I hesitate, wondering if knocking lessens the impact of my entrance. Muffled voices from inside. I turn the handle of the door silently. Isabel is sitting at her dressing table, looking down at Leo, who kneels beside her. They are entirely transfixed with each other, and though they are silent, they don't seem to have heard me enter. Then Leo turns. He smiles.

"Ah, Eve."

Isabel twists around in her seat. She is wearing her black geisha wig that makes her head look even larger, and a white silk dressing gown. Her face is pale. "Eve!" she cries, as if I've been away for years. "Come in! We wondered where you'd gotten to all day."

"You look frozen stiff," Leo says, standing up. He comes toward me, reaching, I suppose, for my coat. I clutch it tighter and he stops halfway across the room. "Can I get you something hot to drink? Tea? We might have some instant soup here."

"No."

"Well sit down, at least," Isabel says, ignoring my tone. She waves to a chair near the door. I take a few steps toward it, then stop. I can see her dressing table now. It is littered with the usual makeup wands and jars and brushes, but there is also a pile of newspapers.

"Eve, what is it? Let me get you some tea." Leo moves to the other corner of the room and pours some hot water from an electric kettle there.

"You seem upset," Isabel says, looking perplexed.

"Don't," I say.

She raises her brows. "Don't? Don't what?"

"Pretend."

Leo brings over a mug of tea. I take it automatically and sip. As soon as the hot liquid hits my chest I begin to shiver. Leo rushes toward me and takes the cup away, then guides me to the chair I had refused to sit on. "You're frozen through. What have you been doing, standing outside all day?"

"I want to know why you did it," I say. The words come out wobbly because my teeth are chattering.

Isabel lets her jaw drop. She looks over at Leo, who is standing near my chair. Some silent communication passes between them. Then Isabel speaks again, in the voice she uses to eager fans. "And we would be talking about . . .?"

"Did you think I wouldn't see the paper? Or that I wouldn't care?"

Leo clears his throat. Isabel maintains her confused look. "Are we talking about the article that came out today? Surely you understand about that?"

"What is there to understand?"

Isabel laughs. Leo shoots her an annoyed look. "Well," she says, as if she were explaining basic mathematics to me, "I would think that after all this time with me, with us—" She waves toward Leo but he takes a step back. "—that you would understand my position. How it's important at . . . this stage of my career to keep my name in the public eye. And yours too. Surely Leo's explained that to you. There's no way a first-time author is going to earn back a huge advance if she's not willing to get out there and be recognized. That's all these articles are, Eve, some harmless gossip to keep up all our profiles. You shouldn't take them any more seriously than that."

"Articles?" I say, emphasizing the plural.

"Well, yes." She smiles. "If we're lucky, the other tabloids will pick up the story and by next week we'll be all over the newsstand."

"I think perhaps Eve is a bit . . . disturbed by the means by which you're getting this publicity, Iz. I told you—"

"You told me what, Leo?" Isabel fixes her gaze on him like a laser beam. He is unable to meet her eyes.

"It's just that Eve isn't part of this . . . of our world. She didn't go looking for this."

Isabel cocks her head, as if considering. "Well, no, that's true, but . . . well, Eve, you must have gotten used to all the curiosity by now? And of course there'll be even more interest once your book comes out." She leans toward me, speaking with soft encouragement. "You do want the book to do well, don't you?"

"I didn't even want to write the damn book," I say.

"Forgive me, Eve, but I don't quite believe you. I mean, some things, some aspects of the process are more unpleasant than others, but you've had good reason to write this book and I don't think you should be ashamed of it." She sits back and chuckles. "We're so alike; I've always felt that. We think in terms of *outcomes*, you and I, we think ahead."

"I'm not like you," I say, but even as the words come out I know she's not entirely wrong. Haven't I spent all these months feeling our connection, marveling at how much I relate to this woman who moves in such different, headier circles than I? Haven't I compared our marriages, how trapped we both were because of husbands who were in their separate, deceptively kind and loving ways, dictatorial? Haven't I felt over and over that because she can wrench feeling from me with her beautiful voice that she is the only one who in the least understands what I'm going through?

Isabel shrugs. "I suppose it's not for me to say. I haven't gone through anything remotely like what you have." She pauses, raises her pinky finger to her mouth, absently gnawing on it. "And yet, I've felt our connection from the first day I met you. After we first talked . . . it almost *was* like it happened to me, I felt so deeply. I sensed a kindred spirit in you." She glances at Leo across the room and drops her voice. "Hell, we even have the same taste in men."

"I don't know what you're talking about," I say under my breath.

"Really?"

I can feel her trying to get me to meet her eyes. I keep mine resolutely focused on my clenched fingers.

"Oh, who knows," she says, throwing up her hands. "Maybe I've been off base from the beginning. But I still think I've done you a favor, ultimately. Really, Eve, I do." She stretches her hand toward me, drops it halfway there. She sighs. "Leo, will you be a dear and go find Frances? It's after six and we haven't begun my makeup. And I need to warm up."

Leo glances from Isabel to me, a lost expression on his face. "Are you sure?" he says, looking at me.

"Of course I'm sure, Leo, I go on in less than two hours. Eve and I will be just fine."

Leo sidles over to my chair and does something that shocks me. He leans over and kisses my cheek, his hand resting on my shoulder. Isabel coughs. Then Leo whispers in my ear, "I'm sorry. I tried to warn you." And then he is gone.

"So!" Isabel says. "I'm afraid I'm going to have to kick you out in a minute too, Eve, since I need a good two hours alone before performance." She turns back to her mirror and fiddles with a round tin of white makeup. "You're welcome to stay, of course; I can have Leo go find you a house seat. I know how much this opera means to you. But I want to be sure we're *completely* square before you go. It would be *dreadful* to think there were hard feelings between us. I really do think you'll thank me for what I did, in the end. It will help all three of us. God, you think Noah isn't going to be grateful to get his name and his face into print?"

"No," I say definitively.

She stops mixing her makeup and looks at me in the mirror. She narrows her eyes. "Oh, yes," she says, "I forgot. You imagine you know Noah better than I do. I think you imagine you know him better than he knows himself. But I guarantee you, Eve, you're wrong about him. He talks the line that every undiscovered artist has ever talked. How his art is all that matters and publicity and self-promotion are beneath him. Let me tell you something, Eve." She turns to me with a soft expression that resembles pity. "There is no serious artist alive whose goal is not to get his work out to be seen by the public. You think when the offers start flooding in for commissions, when the coverage of *Catherine of Aragon* is huger than a first-time composer usually gets, that he'll remember how all the interest in him got started? Or if he did remember, that he'd care?"

"You really don't care about him at all, do you," I say.

"Care about him?" Her voice goes up almost an octave. "Of course I care about him. I *adore* him. I'll confess that a very small part of me did the interview to let you know I knew, to let you see how jealous I am that he cares for you. If you were . . . if you hadn't gone through what you've gone through, I would have confronted you."

"So this self-serving . . . betrayal was the *kindest* thing you could do."

"But don't you see, it was, in fact. Not just for me, but for all of us. For our careers: mine, Noah's and yours."

"I don't have a career."

"But of course you do, Eve. You're an author now, a professional victim."

Her words leave me momentarily breathless. Then I straighten my back and speak with all the self-righteousness I can muster. "Here's what you don't get, Isabel," I say, "I don't 'want' Noah the way you think. I am not your rival. I'm Noah's friend."

She lifts her eyebrows, laughs. "Eve, I think you are being less than honest with yourself. I may be stretching my career to its limits, I may be imagining I can keep a lover young enough to be my son, or that Leo will stand for it forever, but I don't delude myself as to my desires. I know what I want and what I'm willing to do to get it. You feel guilty for every emotion you have except grief, and so you pretend not to feel anything. And that's why Noah will choose me over you. Because whatever exalted idea you may have of him, he's ambitious. I let Noah know that our strongest asset together is our shining future. You let him know that you think of yourself as having no future. Which do you think is ultimately going to appeal to him?"

Every word she's spoken hangs in the air like suspended text. It's like I'm reading it more than hearing it, trying to pretend none of it makes sense. The only thing that comes out of my mouth sounds like the whining of a child who's just lost a game: "I don't care what you say, I know this whole thing is going to upset Noah a lot."

"Well of *course*," Isabel says. She turns back to her dressing table. "All I'm telling you is don't think he won't get over it. And now, I'm so sorry, but I really do have to ask you to go." She looks up at the mirror again. "You'll be all right? Do you want to stay for the performance?"

"No, thank you," I say woodenly.

"All right. I suppose we'll see you later tonight then? Or maybe you'll want an early night. I want you to know that you're welcome to remain with us for as long as you like. Nothing that has happened has to change that. Certainly not Noah. He'll work things out for himself; I'm not worried. Though I wouldn't be very happy if he kept sleeping with you." She narrows her eyes. Is she making an accusation or asking me a question? Keeping my lips clamped together, I stand up and pull my coat around me. I've apparently been sweating inside of it as I'm suddenly limp and humid.

"Will you answer one more question?" I say, fumbling with the buttons.

Isabel has begun dabbing white makeup on her face with a sponge. She lifts her eyebrows in the mirror.

"Did you plan this from the beginning? Is this why you asked me to come stay with you? To somehow use my story to . . . help yours?"

She frowns. "You know," she says, "to be honest, I'm not sure. I certainly felt nothing at the time except real compassion for you. It was Leo who thought of the publicity possibilities, but it was all as a joke, at first, his way of . . . well, he didn't like that I was always taking in 'strays.' Then later he grew to actually like you, and he wasn't keen on blowing your cover. He didn't know I was doing the interview, by the way."

"Or that I was being followed? That someone was snapping pictures of me without my permission?"

She lowers her eyes. "Yes, well, the writer told me they couldn't do a story without pictures and I knew you and Noah wouldn't exactly *pose*, so . . . but that was sneaky, and I am sorry for that." She turns toward me. The left half of her face is ghostly white and greasy looking. The right side, the naked side, looks pale and haggard. It is the first time she's ever looked her age to me. This gives me a jolt of satisfaction. "But to answer your question, Eve, I wanted sincerely to help. I still do. It's just that I began to see the possibilities of how we could help each *other*. I hope you will some day too, and won't stay mad at me."

The coat is buttoned, the muffler wrapped. I walk to the dressing room door. "Eve," she says, just as I am stepping outside. I turn back. "You will too, you know, just like Noah."

"Will what?"

"Get over it."

I leave the door swinging open.

The red light on the phone machine flashes on and off in the gloom of the Steins' apartment. I tell myself I am done with worldly concerns like telephones, but it is likely that one of the calls is from Noah. I go over to the machine. The readout shows there are eight messages. The first three are from Myra, asking in increasingly distressed tones for me to call back. The next three are from Molly with the same message and tone. The seventh is longer.

"Eve," Molly says, with that urgency that always signals disaster, but which Molly uses for disasters as trivial as not being able to get me on the phone easily. "I'm sorry to leave this message—I wanted to talk to you, but I've been calling all day. I just wanted to tell you that . . . not to worry about Ma. About what she said. She called me after she talked to you, pretty frantic to reach you. She felt terrible about your conversation and thinks that . . . well, that you think she's mad at you. It's been a tough week for her, is all. Did you remember that yesterday was the anniversary of Daddy's death?"

(Oh my god, how could I have forgotten?)

"You know how she gets around this time of year. She's out of it for weeks. And this year it was . . . particularly hard. She's been really emotional. You know: Myra but more so." Molly lets go a small laugh. "I took her to the cemetery yesterday and when we got back to my place she immediately radars onto a vase with dirty water in it from some flowers that had died. And Myra, who hasn't stopped crying since we left the cemetery, starts scrubbing this vase, lecturing me on the damage to good glass that old water can do. Says stuff like—" and now she breaks into the Myra impression she has perfected over the years. "'You know, Molly, you really should get the kids to do some of the cleaning up around here. If you made a list of chores and posted it on the fridge then they'd be more likely to do it and this place would look halfway decent.' You know the stuff. Stuff I thought I'd trained her not to say anymore. But during this time, it's like she reverts to some old version of herself—or she imagines that we are some old version of *our* selves. Like I'm ten years old again and a hopeless case.

"Anyway," Molly pauses, breathes heavily, "is this machine still going? I hope so. Anyway, if you'd just give Ma a call, give her a chance to apologize, I think you'd both feel better. We all love you, Eve, and I'm planning my trip out there now, as a matter of fact, just trying to get the time off work. I'll call you when . . ."

The machine cuts her off. I stop the tape before listening to the last message. I don't think Molly and I have ever talked as adults about our difficulties with our mother. I assumed, since she was constantly held up to me as a shining example of daughterly behavior, that she had few difficulties of her own with our parents. I thought she and I had nothing in common.

Finally, I run the last message. Noah. He sounds angry and tearful at the same time, his voice coming out in breathless pants. "I'll be over in a little while," he says. "It's four now. I'm going back to the loft to pick up some things and then I'll be there. Wait for me." No indication as to whom he is addressing his words.

I leave the living room in semidarkness and go to my room. I pull out all my bottles of pills from the drawer of the night table, but even as I do so, I know it's a melodramatic gesture designed for an audience I have constructed in my head, composed of the Steins and Noah and I guess Molly and Myra and the ghosts of my dead family. See, I address them silently, as I line the bottles up and stare at the shadowy piles of pills in each, See how serious I am about the turn my life has taken. But this is nothing like the time two months ago when Myra first left, back in the cottage. I am perfectly lucid this time, playing a part no less dramatic than one of Isabel's. Cio-Cio-San with her samurai sword.

I sweep the bottles into the suitcase and go to the closet for the rest of my clothes.

19

I guess I'll check into a hotel and call Myra for money. I'll stay in the hotel room till I figure out what to do next. It no longer seems feasible to move permanently to the city. I am utterly exposed here now; every person on the street is a potential predator. Isabel was right about that too: I am a celebrity of sorts, whether I like it or not.

Myra would be scandalized at the unfolded heap of clothing on which I close the suitcase's worn lid. By the time I snap the latches, I am breathless, my fingers tingling. I don't think I have moved this quickly, with this much purpose, in a long time. My back feels fine; my nerves on edge, but not unpleasantly. I forgot how invigorating anger could be.

The only hotel whose name I can think of is the Plaza. Well, why not? I have all this money even if I don't have any cash, and I'm in need of some pampering. Just as I have made this decision, the phone rings. I lift it without hesitation. If Isabel can invade my private life then I can invade hers.

"Eve?" Noah says.

I lose my breath for a minute. I've been lumping him in with the world I am about to march righteously out of. But when I hear his deep, anxious voice I am instantly reminded of how his voice matches his skin—milky smooth and tempting as ice cream.

"Something terrible's happened," Noah says. I am still picturing his naked body and fighting the heat in my own.

"I know," I say.

"You know? Oh, no, not that," he says impatiently. "I mean that, but more. It's Angelique. She's done something . . . really really stupid. Listen, can you come meet me?"

"Where are you?" I say. Angelique has probably thrown him out and he's at a friend's house.

"At St. Vincent's Hospital."

"What?"

"That's what I've been . . . Angelique is here." I shake myself out of my stupor and focus on what he's saying. "She's fine. She's going to be just fine. She made this half-hearted attempt at cutting her wrists."

"Oh my god, Noah—"

"Really," he says impatiently, "it's not as bad as it sounds. She didn't even need stitches, it turns out. But I brought her in anyway. I think she just wanted some attention."

The harshness in his voice chills me. "What happened?"

"She sure knows how to stop traffic, I'll give her that. Will you come over here? I have to stay until the doctor comes again. I—" and here his voice cracks, "—could use some company."

I should be repelled— I am repelled, but I'm also not yet immune to the need in his voice, to the place it stirs in me. I ask him the name of the hospital again. He says the cabby will know where it is. I hang up and put on my coat and muffler, flip off the lights and lug my suitcase to the door. I can't imagine staying with Noah but I know I won't come back here. Until this moment, I have never felt the full weight of my homelessness. Leaving the keys on the foyer table, I walk out of the Steins' apartment, closing the door behind me so gently that it doesn't make a sound.

By the time I've lugged the suitcase from the cab to the elevator to the pysch ward on the third floor of the hospital, my back is aching. Before me is a long corridor. Somewhere a television or radio blares. I set my suitcase down to catch my breath. At once the smell is apparent. Hospitals everywhere must smell the same way—that acidic, disinfectant-like odor somewhere between lemons and alcohol. I remember it from my father's illness, from Sydney, even from all those years ago when Molly's friend Maria died.

About halfway down the hall is the waiting room, the source of the blaring television. A thin black woman sits on a fraying couch, hands clenched in her lap, eyes riveted to the television set, above which is an oversized crucifix, the Christ gazing sadly down like a disappointed audience member. Some news show is on, but from the way the woman is staring at it I know my face could be in full close-up on the television screen and she wouldn't recognize me. She tears her gaze from the set to me, her eyes pleading. As soon as she sees me she turns right back to the show. I'm not what she's looking for.

I ask the nurse at the station at the end of the hall where Angelique's room is. She looks bored enough to take an interest in me, especially with my suitcase. But her eyes show no recognition and she disinterestedly tells me the number. At the door to the room I peek into the tiny window and can just make out the curve of Noah's forehead leaning over the foot of the bed. I knock softly, then open the door. Noah springs up from the chair and grabs me by the arms.

"Thanks for coming."

"Will you get my suitcase? It's just outside the door."

He looks puzzled, but complies. I step further into the room and bring my gaze slowly around to the figure in the bed. Angelique lies under a light blanket, only her head and neck showing, her skin as white as the sheet folded so neatly across her collarbones. Her eyes are closed and the blue veins that snake across her lids pulse. She looks as if she's lost twenty pounds since I saw her the other night. The only thing that proves she's alive is the even lifting and lowering of the blanket.

"She's sedated," Noah says behind me.

"She looks terrible," I say.

"Yeah." He comes up beside me. "She bled a lot." He stares down at her through narrowed eyes. I can't read if his expression is angry or worried. "They're keeping her for twenty-four hours, then they're going to re-evaluate."

I nod. We watch her silently for a while, both of us concentrating on the rising and falling blanket. She looks so tiny and light in that tightly made bed that she could be a child.

"What happened," I say, finally.

Noah coughs. "She saw the paper at the newsstand. She bought every copy. Then she came back home and threw them at my feet. Pretty melodramatic, huh?" He grips the rail at the side of the bed and keeps his eyes on Angelique's mummified face.

"Jesus, Noah, she was upset. Can't you understand that?"

"But the thing is, she never seemed that upset," he says plaintively. "Last night I told her I was leaving. I didn't let her change the subject this time. I swore it had nothing to do with Isabel. And she was nodding and smiling and everything, and talked about us growing apart and two artists not being good together and all that. She didn't seem at all surprised—hardly even fazed. She even laughed a little."

He brings his hand to his face and rubs his eyes with his thumb and first finger. Then he turns and makes for the chair at the other side of the bed where he slumps down. "That's why I don't get this. She's always been so . . . I don't know, so relentlessly optimistic about things. It's not like I didn't think she'd be hurt, I just didn't think she was this . . . *into* it all." He sighs. "And then it also turns out that her work has taken a turn for the worse lately. She just found out yesterday—her gallery dropped her. I swear, Eve, I didn't know that." He looks up at me with pleading eyes. "I never would have . . ."

"It's okay," I say.

"I thought everything was fine. I thought I'd even misjudged how much she cared for me in the first place. So I grabbed one of the papers and went down the street to Starbucks. I sat with my . . . with my *caffè latte*," he nearly spits out the words, "and when I came back to the loft the bathroom door was closed, locked." Here his voice breaks and he looks down at his hands. He seems not to recognize them.

"Of course," he snorts, "the key to the bathroom is above the doorframe. It's not like I had to break down the door or anything, though maybe that's what she wanted." He glances over at Angelique, then back down at his hands. "Anyway." He takes a ragged breath. "Anyway, there she was in the bathtub—just like something she's probably seen on some cheesy TV show. Her arms over the sides, bleeding onto the tiles. She opened her eyes when I came in and smiled. She actually *smiled,* Eve. She said, 'I'm glad you're here.' I mean, if that isn't crazy, what is?" He looks at me, his eyes bloodshot and puffy, searching my face for sympathy. I stay by the bed, feeling the bedrail grow hot under my grip.

"It's not anyone's fault, it's just . . ." he trails off and puts his head in his hands. The posture pulls loose something in me and I go over and bend over him, stroking smooth the dark curls. He breathes hard against my collarbone.

"Damn," he says, into my chest.

"Shh," I say.

Angelique groans and we pull apart, stare at the bed. She moves her mouth like a baby rooting, making little sucking noises, then lies still again. I pull up the other chair next to Noah's and we sit together in silence for a while, our hands on the edge of our knees, fingers touching.

After a while he goes downstairs to get us coffees. The silent clock across from the bed reads 9:00. Right about now Isabel is probably on stage sitting in silent vigil as the music surges and the chorus hums, her hand on the head of her tiny son, her face to the sea.

Angelique grunts. Porcelain white and child-like, her fragile features contort and relax rhythmically, as if she's having a bad dream. I reach down and stroke a limp ringlet from her clammy forehead. "I'm here," I whisper over and over, as if it would mean something to her, as if she were Jessica, half-awakened from a nightmare, terrified and alone. I'm exquisitely aware that loneliness is not inevitably removed by the presence of others. But then again, you never know.

Noah returns with coffee that tastes metallic and weak. Still, I sip it greedily for its warmth and familiarity.

"Listen," Noah says. "About all this stuff. The article. I hope you know I didn't have anything to do with it."

"I know," I say.

"I can't believe how awful it must be for you."

"Just me? What about you?"

"Well, yeah, of course. But. It's not the same. It's silly and awkward for me. But it's just stupid gossip. I'm not as bothered by—" His gaze lights on Angelique and he lowers his head. "Of course," he stammers, "it's horrible for the people I care about. . . ."

"Isabel predicted you wouldn't be too upset."

"Isabel." He speaks harshly. "I guess you figured out that she must have . . . I mean, maybe it was Leo who arranged it but she's the one—"

"Leo was almost as surprised as we are. Not so much that something happened like this, but at this particular thing. I think he thought she'd do something a little less . . . lurid."

"So you're saying it was all her idea? Do you really believe that?"

He wants me to say no, to let Isabel off the hook. I say nothing.

He sighs. "I guess you're right. She's not above exploiting . . . even you. But Eve," he takes my hand, "don't be too mad at her. You should feel sorry for her. I mean, look how desperate she is. She really thinks that stunts like this are the only way to get interest in her going again. She should have faith in her voice, in her *gift*, but she doesn't. This last batch of reviews must have sent her over the edge."

"But of course she would have had to have planned all this well before the reviews came out," I say. "And I don't even know how long ago someone started following me. For all I know this has been going on since right after I came."

He's silent. No further defense. He drinks his coffee and concentrates on Angelique's pale face.

"I better go now," I say.

"No, wait, please." He puts his coffee cup on the floor and grabs my hand as I start to rise. "Don't go yet. I want to tell you—" He stops, stares at my hand, brings it to his face, pressing it against his cheek. The stubble there tickles my palm. "Nothing has really changed, you know. I mean, Angelique . . . well, she'll be all right. I'm staying at the loft till she—or the doctor—decides when she's coming home. Then I'll move out."

"Back to Isabel's?"

"I don't know." He loosens his grip and sits back, taking in my suitcase and then me. "Where are you going?"

I look down at his face, swollen, unshaven, confused. My hand in his grows hot. "I'm not sure."

"Come back to the loft with me tonight. Stay there till you figure out what you want to do next."

Thankfully, this is the moment the doctor comes into the room. "How is everything?" he says in a lilting Island accent that I find very soothing.

"She hasn't moved," Noah says. "Oh, this is my friend, Eve Miller. Eve, this is Dr . . ."

"Jones." He shakes my hand perfunctorily, then walks over to the end of the bed. "Let's take a look, shall we?" He reads the chart. There are no machines here, no monitors or IV drips. The lack of apparatus makes the whole thing feel a little surreal, like a dream of being in a hospital. Dr. Jones lifts one of Angelique's bandaged wrists from under the blanket and unwraps it. Noah and I look at each other to avoid seeing the wound.

"Well," Dr. Jones says as he rewraps Angelique's wrist, "physically everything looks fine. But we take these gestures seriously. . . ." He pauses, looks meaningfully at us. "I think it's a good idea to admit her for twenty-four hours of observation. I'll have a good talk with her tomorrow. After that, assuming nothing untoward happens, she'll be free to go. Unless she voluntarily decides to check into a facility. You understand that?" Noah nods "For now, the best thing Angelique can do is rest, and then we'll see, yes?" He smiles insincerely at us and is gone.

"Well," Noah says. "I guess we should go. I can come back tomorrow. Will you come with me?" Noah leans over and kisses me lightly on the cheek. I close my eyes.

I look over at the heavy suitcase. I can't imagine carrying it one step further. "Okay," I say.

The loft is in an industrial building downtown from the hospital. We take a service elevator with an old-fashioned sliding metal gate to get there. The room is as huge as I imagined it to be, divided by contents rather than walls. A kitchen area, a big bed on a wooden frame painted the palest shade of turquoise, an overstuffed couch strewn with multicolored pillows. In the far corner, a beautiful old grand piano. Next to that a rolltop desk painted with broad streaks of blue and yellow. To one side are canvasses and easels, half-finished paintings, drop cloths, a huge paint-spattered table. From what I can see, Angelique's work is abstract, splashes of incredibly vivid colors: cobalt blue, custard yellow, blood red. I'm too tired to explore further. By the time we are actually in the loft Noah is holding my arm by the elbow, guiding me toward the bed. I let him support me, seating me gently on the mattress, taking off my shoes, pulling down my pants, unbuttoning my sweater. I vaguely try to brush his hands away but don't put up too much of a struggle. When I'm shivering in my tights and long-sleeved tee shirt he goes over to my suitcase and rummages around in it, finally finding my nightgown. He takes off the rest of my clothes so gently I can barely feel it. At one point his hand brushes the side of my right breast. I open my eyes. He is looking at me, his face red, his eyes intense. He seems to be waiting for me to say something but when I don't, he says, "Sorry," and continues dressing me. My teeth are chattering. As he guides me under the sheets I say, "Don't you have any heat in this place?"

He laughs. "Yes, of course, sorry. I guess I'm so used to it. I'll get it going right away. You get some sleep now."

"You know, I've figured something out," I mumble as he fusses with the radiator.

"Shh, just rest now."

"No, it's important. It's about who will look after Angelique."

"I will."

"No. Not you. She needs someone better."

Noah stops what he's doing. "What the hell does that mean?"

"She needs to be with someone closer. With a stake in what happens to her. Someone who'll be there later."

"If you mean family, Angelique doesn't have any."

"Oh," I say. "How awful." Out of nowhere, I am crying.

He rushes back to the bed and touches my head. "She'll be all right, Eve, don't worry. Everything will be all right."

That's the last thing I remember him saying. Then I am dreaming.

I dream that the four of us are washed up on the sand like beached whales, flopping and barely alive. Myra comes along. Tanned and unfazed in a flowery sundress, she was just taking a walk on the beach, she says, when she saw us. She peers down at us lying there, arms spread at odd angles, mouths gasping, and she shakes her head, frowning. "You all look just terrible," she says. I know she is glad to see us anyway.

When I awaken it is just after midnight by the clock radio on the multicolored stool next to the bed. Noah sleeps beside me, curled into a fetal position, his bare left arm flung across me. He is snoring lightly. It's a pleasant sound, like a child whispering. The loft is toasty. The radiator knocks. Noah doesn't move. The weight of his arm is comforting. I slip out from under his touch. There are blinds over the huge windows that cover three of the walls of the loft, but enough light filters in from the street for me to gradually make out the objects in the room. I see a chest of drawers that I hadn't noticed before. I tiptoe over there and open drawers surreptitiously until I find a pair of heavy sports socks to put on. Then I tiptoe to the kitchen area where the phone sits on a counter. I take it with me into the bathroom. Squinting in the harsh bathroom light, I take in the claw-footed tub and the tiles painted various bright shades of blue and yellow. Angelique has made it a beautiful room. I sit on the toilet lid and dial Myra's number. She answers on the second ring.

"Eve, is that you?"

I have a hard time catching my breath.

"Eve, darling? Are you there? Is that you?

"Yes," I say at last.

"Thank god, thank god. I've been trying to reach you all evening."

"I figured."

"What? Why are you whispering? What time is it there?"

"After midnight."

"Where are you?"

"Staying with a friend."

"With a friend? You mean you left Isabel's?"

"Yes." She waits, but I don't say anything more.

"Listen, I feel so . . . so terrible about earlier. The things I said. I don't know what made me say them. I don't even believe them, not for a minute. I can't believe I would even for a moment make you feel like, like . . ."

I let her struggle for a minute, than I say, "It's all right, Myra. Don't cry."

"But to think. I know you called me because you were looking for . . . you needed me and I didn't come through for you. It's unforgivable."

A fist clenches in my chest. "Don't *say* that." I speak more harshly than I intended. "Of course it's forgivable. Jesus, Myra, you had a lot on your mind today. I forgot . . . I wasn't thinking about Daddy."

"But," she pauses and I hear her fumbling, then blowing her nose, "but you needed me. I want you to know that I'm always there when you need me. That's my job, even when . . ."

"You can't always be there when I need you, Myra. Nobody can."

"Of course not," she says quickly. "You figured out better than I did that you need to find . . . your own comfort."

"Yes, well. I don't think I've been doing a very good job of that."

"Oh darling." She breaks into fresh tears. "I wish I was there right now, holding you." I press the phone closer to my ear, imagining her in her living room sitting on the old couch that she's had my whole life, re-stuffed and re-covered but never discarded. I imagine the mantle above the fireplace crowded with family pictures, the finger painting I did in nursery school, the pillows Molly needlepointed for some long-ago Mother's Day still adorning the couch. I imagine snuggling close to Myra and smelling Chanel and the waxy perfume on her lipstick.

"Me too," I say very softly.

I don't think she heard me. "Not because I think you can't take care of yourself. You can. I always knew that, or I never would have left you."

"But—"

"But I know that I could help. We all could. Maybe I've been a little mad that you haven't seen that. Maybe that's why I was so hard on you when you called before. I really am sorry, darling."

"It's okay, Myra." The sound of her voice, so soft and pliant now, is hard to hear.

"So what are you going to do?"

Just when you expect Myra to start telling you what to do, she turns around and asks you. It's annoying. "I don't know," I say, "I'm thinking. But listen, I want you to do me a favor."

"Of course."

"Apparently Molly is planning a trip out here?"

"Yes, she's arranging things now. Why? Don't tell me you don't want her to come, Eve, she'll be devastated."

"But now's not a good time, Myra. I may not stay here. So there's no sense in her coming till I know where I'm going to end up, right?"

"Are you thinking of coming home?" She says this in a near whisper, her voice halfway between excitement and trepidation.

"Maybe. I don't know. Give me some time."

"Of course," she says breathlessly. "Of course. You take all the time you need, darling. We'll be here. I'll talk to Molly tomorrow. She'll

. . . if she knows you're coming home she won't mind at all waiting a little, I'm sure."

"I didn't say I was coming."

"I know, but if there's even a chance. Oh Eve, I know being there has been good for you, but now, now after what's happened . . . I still can't believe that Isabel and Leo would have allowed it. But they're not family, are they?"

"No," I say. "They're not family."

"I love you, Eve."

"I love you too, Myra." It's the first time I've said that more than mechanically since the accident.

After we hang up I sit for a while on the toilet lid. I keep seeing that moment in my dream where Myra walks up to us spread-eagled on the sand and says, "You look just terrible." I know Myra is speaking only to me, because Jessica and Nicholas could run around naked with straws up their noses and peanut butter in their hair and they would still look perfect to her—and she never criticized Charlie, at least not to his face. It's only my disheveled and battered appearance that she is commenting on. But it's also me she's going to gather into her embrace. Even now, my bottom growing cold from the toilet lid, my eyes crusty with lack of sleep, my aloneness palpable in the chilly room, I see Myra standing on the hot beach frowning, arms akimbo, the flowered dress swirling in the sea breeze, and I feel something close to certainty that we are saved. That I am saved.

Back in the main room I creep over to the desk and turn on the lamp there. Noah snorts, but doesn't wake. After some rummaging I find a small sketch pad, half its pages gone. I take the pad and one of the chairs over to the window furthest from the bed. A strong floodlight shines almost directly into the loft from the roof of the building across the street. I uncap a pen and prepare to write down the dream. But that's not what comes out.

The truth, the real truth, is this: That very night I was thinking of leaving. I was imagining a completely independent life again—how different it would be now, all these years later, how much more I would appreciate solitude. The picture was simple this time: no bohemian salon or artist's garret, just a small place of my own in a big city, a modest income from writing, maybe Theo for company. Younger men for lovers. Plays and concerts. Museums. Good reviews and modest sales of my books. The ocean nowhere in sight.

It was raining on and off. The seas were choppy. There'd been a big storm the previous night, one that had kept us all up. We're all overtired, I thought, explaining my own heretical thoughts to myself. I never considered how I would tell Charlie and the kids I was leaving, how they'd take it. In my fevered imaginings my children would be unscathed by the desertion of their mother. Frankly, in those imaginings my children barely existed.

I was cold even though I wore my jacket. It helped me stay awake to shiver as I sporadically checked the instruments and the autopilot. Mostly I sat in the cockpit, staring into the inky emptiness, the hazy light from the three-quarter moon flickering as clouds raced over it. The canvas dodger sagged from rain. I remember thinking at one point—and in my mind, this point occurred seconds before the accident, as if the very thought brought the boat into our starboard hull—something that caused me to sit up straight and find it hard to breathe. It wasn't a new thought. It had been germinating since before we began our journey, and had been growing the whole time we were on the boat, even when I was happiest, when I looked at my children sweating and laughing in the sun, or when Charlie lay beside me at night and pulled me so close he left me breathless, even when a breeze would magically transform the ocean's texture from that of a polished stone to rough wood, or when we were visiting some exotic place, like that ruined temple on the Marquesas Islands whose fierce tiki heads made both kids dash into our arms, or the time a whale followed alongside the boat off the coast of Fiji. Even then, the other feeling was there, festering. What I finally said to myself that night was that I was here not out of choice but out of circumstance. I had let my need for peace and stability overwhelm my real desires. I had let Charlie trap me.

I was on watch, supposed to be protecting my family. Instead I was thinking of myself as some fairy-tale princess imprisoned by the prince, of how cheated I was. The accident may have happened too fast for me to have done anything—that's what they tell me—but how could I not conclude that by thinking those thoughts instead of standing vigil for my family, I might as well have been praying for disaster?

It was after midnight. The boat lurched through increasingly angry waves. The wind roared like an oncoming train though the rain had stopped. We were sailing on a port tack so the starboard rail of the boat was almost at water level. I must have thought briefly about going to the bow to look out, or calling Charlie to do it. I must have at least considered it. But we were so tired, and the visibility so bad. The sails were reefed for the storm, everything battened down. I must have told myself it wasn't necessary. But I have no memory of thinking any of this. Maybe things happened too fast for me to consider all the ways that we had failed, all the mistakes I was making.

I tell myself now that I wouldn't have seen anything had I gone to check. My view of the starboard side was blocked by the sails. And still it wouldn't have mattered—I could no more have taken us out of the fishing boat's path than I could have brought the storm to a halt.

At first I thought the noise was a thunderclap. It was earsplitting and the boat trembled with the blast, then spun on an axis. It happened so fast I barely had time to register that this couldn't be thunder, let alone call "All hands on deck." It felt like hours before I heard Charlie calling my name and somewhere further off, Jessica screaming. I moved toward the cabin, but Charlie emerged before I got there, struggling up the cabin gangway with Jessica in his arms. She clung to his neck, her nightgown flapping in the wind, Brenda Bride, dressed in a soaked wedding gown, dangling from her free hand. Charlie must have put Jess's furry red slippers on her; I remember standing there on the deck of the dying Orlando and thinking, At least her feet won't be cold. Jess's mouth hung open in dreamy awe, as if she were trying to figure out if she was really awake.

Charlie was shouting something I couldn't hear in the roar of the storm; his face spun as we did and I fell over on the deck, retching.

Then we were sliding rather than spinning, the Orlando being pulled along on a current like the suction of a huge vacuum cleaner. Charlie's hand was on my back and he was still screaming and now I made out the words: "Life raft." But the boat was pitching something awful. The three of us crawled toward the foredeck and the life raft, Jessica still clinging to Charlie's neck and crying out that she'd lost Brenda, where was Brenda? And only when we got to the secured metal canister containing the life raft, when the Orlando's cant was suddenly more precipitous and I held my breath but we didn't go down, not yet, only then did I wonder where Nicholas was.

Charlie thrust Jessica into my arms and I held her almost absent-mindedly, saying "There, there" into the wind while she sobbed, while Charlie struggled with the cord that was supposed to release the steel straps holding the canister closed. The straps were not springing free the way they were supposed to, the way I'd seen them do in a hundred rehearsals. I worked my way to him to help pull the cord just as the boat slipped sickeningly further into the water. I held Jessica tight with one hand and with the other managed to grab the cord just under Charlie's hand and we both pulled with our whole bodies, trying to unlock the life raft, so secure that we couldn't get it free, while another wave came and almost knocked us down. And Charlie's voice was in my ear now saying, "We can't get it, corroded . . . the boat's going down, get to the dinghy, leave it, leave it Eve." Jessica almost fell out of my arms as we crawled to the dinghy attached at the stern. I said, "Where is he, where's Nicholas?"

Charlie's hands were on the dinghy rope and he turned to me, his face stricken, unrecognizable. "We were hit," he said. "Starboard side." "Yes," I said. Then I pushed Jessica at him and he grabbed her instinctively, but he reached for me too when I stumbled toward the cabin. Somewhere in the back of my mind was the knowledge of what the next wave would do to us, but that information was irrelevant to me at that moment. I shook Charlie off and started across the deck, heading to my boy, concentrating on how his face would light up when I got to him, how he might even say, "Where were you Ma, you didn't forget me, did you?" And how he might be sitting up because he'd been reading in his bunk, not sleeping as he should have been at this ungodly hour of the morning; I was thinking so hard about his face that it's all I saw, not the tilting deck, as the boat eased her way into the ocean, not the knowledge that Nick had been sleeping in the convertible mid-berth that put him right in the path of whatever hit us, that he had only moved there a few weeks ago when he decided he was too much a boy to share the same berth with his sister anymore.

Later I thought, Please let him not have been reading in bed, under the covers with his flashlight like all the little bookish boys in the world. Let him have been fast asleep, dreaming, feeling nothing.

But the water burying Nicholas was rising up the cabin gangway toward me and the Orlando was so tilted now that the next wave knocked me back toward the stern. Through the din I thought I heard Jessica crying and so I went back to her, as simply as that. I let Nicholas go.

At the stern Charlie had just gotten the dinghy loose from its davits and lowered it into the water, where it flew away and then jerked back when it reached the end of the painter rope attaching it to the Orlando. Charlie pushed me over the side after it, then set Jessica down on the deck. I saw this from where I was dog-paddling in the churning, frigid water below. He took her hand and turned to her and said something which caused her to nod and set her jaw and, I imagine, to grip his hand tighter as they stepped to the rail and jumped in together. And then the three of us swam to the tethered dinghy that was riding the waves. We climbed in and Charlie released the bowline hitch and the painter sprang free and followed the Orlando like a wild tail as she made her final journey, rising up into the sky and then sliding down like a torpedo, smooth and swift, her lights winking out, sinking so quickly it made you wonder if the boat had ever been there in the first place.

There was no time for asking ourselves what happened to Nicholas. When the Orlando went under, we were suddenly in darkness and it took some time to adjust our eyes to the wavering moonlight. The seas were so rough that we had all we could do to keep the dinghy upright, a losing battle. We were pitched over three, maybe four times, till finally Charlie said that by constantly righting it, we risked damaging the dinghy and sapping our own strength, so together we heaved Jess onto the top of the capsized dinghy and yelled out that she should lie low while Charlie swam around to the other side and we both dug our fingers into the strakes on the hull and pulled ourselves up, so we could grasp each other's arms around Jess. "Hold on to our arms, Jess," Charlie roared and, mute with terror now, she grabbed our embraced arms and lay on her stomach, her face turned toward me so that I could see the wildness in her eyes, the pleading downturn of her mouth, begging me to make it stop, and for a moment my grip on Charlie slipped, so natural did it seem to take her in my arms and promise it would all be over soon, but Charlie said "Eve," and I grabbed him tight again.

All I could do was talk to her through the night, trying to shout over the roaring winds, "Hold on Jess, just hold on," trying, believe it or not, to sound cheery, as if this were all just a great adventure and we'd left Nicholas at home with a cold and boy was he missing out.

The waters off Sydney in July are described as medium cool. After about an hour, medium cool felt like dipping into a liquid iceberg. With our grips locked it was hard to tell who was shivering more; even when he surely must have lost most feeling, Charlie's fingers still dug fiercely into my forearms, our frantic embrace quivering with cold and pain and terror. I soon found that there was no room in my survival arsenal to cry, to think, to ponder. Every inch of me, physical and mental, was concentrated on holding on to Charlie in the face of the waves that seemed designed for the sole purpose of pulling us apart. Jessica lay there shivering, nightgown plastered to her body, eyes struggling to stay open. Charlie was still able to weep. Occasionally, when the moon wasn't obscured by clouds, I saw flashes of his sweatshirt floating balloon-like around his chin, his hair and beard glued to his skull; but what I remember most is the sound of him calling out for Nicholas, his voice unrecognizable to me, animal.

There's a stretch of Highway 5 between L.A. and San Francisco that is so flat and straight that it's been known to put drivers into a trance. They find themselves having gone twenty miles or more with no memory of the drive itself, the landscape, time passing. It's a terrifying experience because you think you have been something like asleep, that you weren't concentrating and that you escaped terrible destruction only by sheer luck. But this experience is almost never the cause of accidents. The truth is that you are in a kind of altered consciousness during these zoned-out drives, and your senses are as keen, if not keener, then ever. Your brain registers every sight, sound, smell—it simply doesn't communicate the information to your conscious mind. You are, in effect, hypnotized. That's what the next few hours were like. I don't know what happened exactly, though I do know that at some point during this time Charlie said "Eve?" like a question and then he said, "I'm sorry," so humbly that I knew he meant I'm sorry for everything, and I tried to see his face but it was too dark right then so I forced my numb hands to grip him tighter. I know that there were moments when Jessica relaxed her hold on our locked arms. I talked to her constantly, saying, "Don't let go, Jess, just a bit longer." Gradually, she had only the strength left to say that she wanted to go to sleep, so we began to yell at her to keep her awake—once Charlie even let go to slap her. I was not thinking about anything except the next second and the second after that; I was only waiting for the sea to subside.

When they asked me afterwards, I estimated it was about four hours. Four hours of hypnotized survival, doomed optimism that these winds, these ten, maybe fifteen-foot waves, this cold and exhaustion couldn't go on forever, that we'd right the dinghy and sail to shore like the Swiss Family Robinson, that Nick would perhaps be waiting there for us.

I remember Jessica saying one last time, "Mommy, I'm so tired." I remember saying one more encouraging insipid thing to her like "It won't be long now," as another wave hit us. She was still there after that one; it was the next wave that took her. Perhaps it was the biggest wave yet. Perhaps I only want to think that. How could I have saved her from the hundreds of waves that had been hitting *her all night and not have saved her from this one? Was this the one that Myra's God was hoarding for us, just when we were imagining an end in sight, just when we were thinking it couldn't get worse?*

Jessica just got too tired—too tired to respond to my cajoling, pleading, encouraging, Charlie's loving, urgent voice. Her fatigue was stronger than all three of us. She slipped away while the wave was upon us. Our arms long-since numbed, we didn't know she was gone till the water was momentarily calm again and the moon emerged from the clouds. I said her name, harshly, unbelievingly. I got one good look at Charlie's face before he went after her. All night Jessica had been blocking my view of him but now she was gone and I saw his frantic eyes, the grimace of physical pain on his face and I screamed, "Charlie, don't," but he did, he called her name and plunged in after her, without even acknowledging that he'd heard me.

A stupid, foolish, selfish thing to do. A mindless act of instinct; an animal will.

It should have been me. I'm the mother, after all.

Once Charlie let me go, I slipped into the water. But I made my numb fingers once again find purchase on the hull's strakes.

The hours of waiting for Charlie to come back, refusing to imagine him not coming back. The sky gradually clearing, stars pinpricking the dissipating clouds, the moon bright in the night sky. I was shivering with a cold that seemed to emanate from inside me, fighting with myself as to whether I should take off my sopping clothes to avoid hypothermia, eventually gambling that the danger of overexposure was higher, assuming that the clearing sky indicated a sunny morning. The sea calmed soon after the sun got hottest—maybe it was noon by now. I righted the dinghy and climbed in, finding out only then that I'd done something to my back, welcoming the pain that wasn't excruciating enough. The next day, when I washed ashore on the rocks, the dinghy was battered to shreds. I lay on the rocky beach floating in and out of consciousness as day turned to night and then to day again. Sometime during those hours I heard a helicopter and still had the ridiculous will to raise my arms and feebly wave, to feel my heart quicken at the prospect of rescue.

Noises and helicopter rotors and voices and strong arms lifting me gently and whispers and needle pricks and blessed unconsciousness and waking up in the hospital and all the rest. The terrible knowledge.

Tonight it seems less of a punishment and more . . . something like a mandate: I survived.

By the time I finish writing, a tinny daylight has begun to illuminate the street. The sketch pad is damp in my hands. I've filled ten pages with frantic, heavy handwriting. I hear a rasping, choking sound and realize it is my own breathing. I've been crying quietly for some time, which accounts for the blurred text in front of me. It doesn't matter. I don't think this will go into the book. I'm not even sure there will be a book, come to that. I'll talk it over with Myra, see what she thinks. With Charlie's folks. It seems to me now that the three of them have a kind of wisdom of suffering I don't have, being too close to the events themselves. I've been relying on the wrong people to help me find my way.

An image of Isabel arises unbidden in my mind's eye, white faced and suffering on the stage, clutching her child to her one last time. How much I wanted to believe in the genuineness of her anguish, which made me feel we could be of use to each other. But now I see that it is the music that is real and pure and healing; Isabel is simply its conduit. Myra has been trying to tell me this for some time, I believe. She was glad that I was listening to so much opera, never worried that it was obsessing me. She wanted me to see Isabel as a generous host and perhaps a friend, not as my salvation. That's one of the reasons she wanted me to pack up my CDs and come home—to all the genuine torment, but also to communion.

Noah stirs. I quickly wipe my eyes and stretch. I've been in the same position for hours. I remember how back at the cottage, I marveled at the fact that I hadn't owned a real bed for so long. Closing my eyes, I see with such vividness that it seems to already exist, a queen-sized bed all to myself, thick and downy, tucked in the corner of a light-filled room far enough from the Pacific not to see it, but close enough to know it is available. I have this feeling that I could walk down a street in Los Angeles somewhere and the room would be there, beckoning to me. And I would be home.

I walk over to Noah's bed and look down at his face, so slack and vulnerable. I reach down and touch his stubbly cheek. He sighs and turns away from me. I creep over to my side of the bed and take off my nightgown before slipping in beside him again. His eyes flutter open and focus on me for a minute. Then he is asleep again. I push my naked body as tightly against his as I can, letting the heat from his skin warm my icy limbs, taking my last bit of comfort from the sight of his face. I can see under the exhaustion and dishevelment exactly the face I want to memorize—the one I will take with me along with the other faces that are lost.

epilogue

Dear Noah,

I received your letter a while ago; of course I was happy to hear from you, don't worry about that. Nigel, the agent, has been keeping me up-to-date. He sent me the clipping from the Times *about the* Catherine *showcase. Congratulations. It seems to have received an enormous amount of attention for what was essentially a rehearsal. Nigel said it was hard to keep Isabel's operation low-key after all the attention she was getting right after I left last year, but that it made the good reviews for the showcase that much sweeter, since the critics were just waiting for her to falter. Whether they loved her more for her performance onstage or off is, I suppose, a matter of debate.*

Isabel also wrote to me a couple of months ago. She was redecorating the cottage, she said, and had come across a few of my things. She casually mentioned that you had moved out of her house. She said that you and she had had more "artistic differences" than she anticipated. I suspected even before I got your letter that the circumstances were a bit more fraught than that, but I'm not surprised that Isabel would be reluctant to admit that you two had come apart for more personal reasons. She said she was pleased that you didn't go back to Angelique's—for your career's sake. Overall, it was a self-obsessed, charming letter—just like Isabel.

After much teeth gnashing, I decided to write her back. These days I find it soothing to practice the social niceties as often as possible. I wrote a brief note saying I had been out of touch with everyone. I told her that whatever I had left behind she could get rid of.

Of course it's you to whom I really should have written. No, I didn't go out for the world's longest cup of coffee the morning I left, as you suggested. It's nice of you to say that no explanation is needed, because I don't have much of one. It's just that the night when we came back to your place from the hospital, I knew I was done in New York; I had to come home.

I know you were going through your own difficulties and I'm sorry for disappearing without a word, but I just couldn't say one more good-bye, especially not face to face.

I'm glad to hear you still keep in touch with Angelique. I spotted her name in a New Yorker *gallery listing. It's always good to learn that people have come back from disaster.*

Of course my life is not nearly as interesting as all of yours. My period of infamy is over, thank God. It's all very simple now. When I first came back I stayed with my mother a couple of months, at first out of lack of alternatives, and then because I really wanted to. This one night, a week or so after I got back, I woke up to find my mother sitting on my bed stroking my forehead, the way she used to when I was sick. She had the same look on her face too, a kind of loving frown, a hint of impatience. I was thinking it was going to get awfully maudlin around Myra's house and that I should probably think about moving on, but then she almost scowled at me and said, "You really should do something with all that hair," and I thought, yep, this is home, all right, and that's when I decided to stay a while.

Now that I've moved on to my own place, I still have dinner with Myra once a week, and my sister Molly and her family often join us. At these dinners I find myself watching Molly's children in wonder; not because they are so much bigger and older-looking than I remember, but because they remind me so much of us—of Molly and me, of our family. We eat Myra's huge meals and Molly's kids run around the kitchen and her husband tries to get them to sit down, and Myra tries to get me to eat twice what everyone else does and Molly chimes in that I'm far too thin which is not at all attractive in a woman my age, then waxes rhapsodic about teaching and tries to convince me to join the "family business"; and I remind her that just last week she told me teaching made her understand nervous breakdown, and we eat till we're loosening belts. It's as if Molly and I were little girls again, sitting at our mother's table, sniping and complaining with abandon, because we knew, with that certainty exclusive to childhood, that we were safe, that we were where we belonged.

I bought a little house on a crowded street on the west side of L.A. about twenty minutes from Myra's house and ten from Molly's. It has burnt orange tiles on the roof and white walls. The rooms are cozy and quiet. I moved in with little more than some books and Theo, our cat. His long stay at my sister-in-law's seems to have further confused him; he now mis-

takes himself for a dog and refuses to leave my side. I have tried to start a vegetable garden in the tiny backyard, an urge that struck me one day like a bizarre craving, since I've never successfully grown so much as a weed before. I planted radishes and carrots because my next-door neighbor, a woman with two jobs and a three-year-old daughter, who also manages to grow all her own vegetables, has assured me that even the most inept of gardeners can't fail to raise these. Carrots and radishes are two of my least favorite vegetables, but I enjoy going out to the plot every day and looking for the first sign of green.

Thanks to the insurance settlement, I don't have to think about earning money for a while. As a favor to Molly, I've been picking up my eleven-year-old niece, Alice, from school a few times a week and bringing her back to my place till Molly comes home from an afternoon class she's taking. Of all Molly's children, Alice is the one most like her mother. She has many opinions about my garden and what will make the vegetables grow, and she likes nothing better than to go into my bathroom and experiment with the makeup I hardly ever wear. Apparently this is forbidden fruit in her house, so I am quite the favored relative at the moment. Alice also adores Theo and has actually managed to seduce him into coming to her for a limited number of caresses. I've tried putting on opera for her a couple of times, but she tends to clamp her hands over her ears and make faces, so now I let her listen to KPPR, Power FM.

Contrary to what I feared, most of the time being with Alice evokes no memories at all and I simply enjoy the present. And on those few days when I fall silent or can't look directly at her, Alice putters in the garden for a while with the back door open. Like Theo, she always keeps me in her line of sight.

Every morning I write at a scarred oak desk next to my bed. There's a window over the desk which cranks open and closed. I don't know exactly what I'm writing. I sent back the book advance. That's really why Nigel first wrote me, trying to talk me out of quitting.

I write a lot of letters. I'm afraid these wouldn't interest you as the old batch did: When I write to the people who still manage to find their way to me, I now send back bland, comforting aphorisms about the power of time, of faith, of appreciation for what's left. I am not as cynical about platitudes as I once was—who am I to say what's a platitude and what's the truth?

In one drawer of my desk is a pile of photographs my mother gave me when I got back home. They're from the shoe boxes of pictures that we left with her when we started the trip. There's a couple of me in the hospital holding my son, Nicholas, newborn, in my arms. I look tired, a little stunned. But Nick—in the picture Nick is fixing his eyes on the camera as if it promised a fantastic new adventure.

There's some Polaroids from the day before we left, the four of us squinting into the morning sun in front of my mother's house, all anxious grins. I don't keep any of the photographs out, but every once in a while I open the desk drawer. Sometimes I'll look at the pictures a long time and realize I haven't swallowed in all that time. But that doesn't make me put them away for good.

Mostly, if I'm sitting at the desk and not writing, I listen to opera. I have expanded my repertoire somewhat, but I still go back to the old favorites, the operas you helped me understand. I will always be grateful for that. While the opera plays I settle in my chair and stroke Theo's head until he's vibrating under my fingers. I stare out at the little yellow house across the street that has sunflowers growing on the lawn. I watch the women passing on the sidewalk, jogging with strollers, or girls roller blading, hanging onto skinny boys. If I'm at the desk early enough, I watch the men and women in their expensive suits pull their cars out of their garages and begin their busy days. I envy their innocent lives, but not so much that it hurts. I listen to Isabel—and now quite a few others—singing of sorrow and loss and I am also happy for my neighbors' innocence, glad that there is music that can stand in for real suffering.

Oh, and when I open the window first thing in the morning, I can smell the ocean, did I mention that?